ZEROED OUT

JACOB MARKROF

To request permissions, contact the publisher at www.jacobjmarkrof.com/contact/

Paperback: ISBN 9798422130979

First paperback edition March 2022

All artwork, editing, and layout by Jacob Markrof

Printed in the USA

JM Publishing
Portland, OR

www.jacobjmarkrof.com

Dedicated to Dannielle,
For always listening to my absurd story ideas

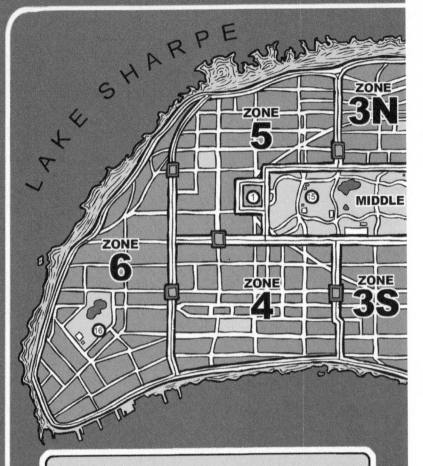

OMEGA CITY 6

1. OMEGA TOWER
2. NAKAMOTO TOWER
3. NATIVE SOCIETY
4. DEADFALL DISTRICT
5. RED LIGHT DISTRICT
6. SYNTH ROW
7. REFUGEE ALLEY
8. EXILE LANE
9. PLEASURE PEIR
10. OUTER GATE
11. QUARENTINE ZONE
12. HOPE CITY GATE
13. LEGEND'S TABLE HOUSE
14. THE POND
15. COCERT GROUNDS
16. ZITKALA-SA PARK
17. WAR OF 2084 MEMORIAL
18. THE WAR TRAINING GROUND
19. THE FARM MUSEUM
20. DASHWOOD TAVERN

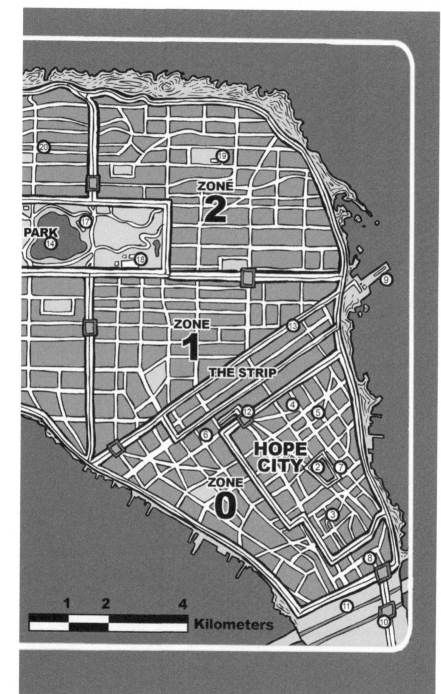

TWENTY-FIVE

"Just my luck," Zed sighed as he watched the final score of the ultra ball game roll across his retinal heads-up display. The loss was going to put him back more credits than he had available. He finished off his vodka rocks to wash the painful loss away while his internal system gave him a strong audio-visual reminder that he was now broke.

"You go bust again?" A rough voice asked from his side. It was Rodriquez, a thick-necked enforcer who liked to think he had more authority than he actually did. "You have to stop with those stupid bets, Takeda. The Burners will never beat the Bandits. City Five is just too damned good."

Zed brought up the bar's drink menu on his HUD and punched in another order of vodka. "I just like to root for the home team."

"The home team?" Rodriquez laughed. "City 6 has a dozen ultra ball teams, and eleven of them are better than the Burners. You just like throwing your credits away."

"You know what they say about gambling? High risks equal high rewards."

"I think you mean big losses." A synthetically intelligent robot was about to set Zed's drink down when Rodriquez swiped a few credits at the automated bartender. "Here. Let me buy you a drink."

"I won't turn it down if it's free," Zed said, sliding the glass his way and punching the menu one more time, "but I will double down."

"There he is. Big bad Zed Takeda. Always the tough guy. War hero, star enforcer, gambling addict, and a lousy alcoholic."

"I think you forgot part-time asshole," Zed mused, and slid the second shot over to the big man. He raised his glass and said, "I wouldn't want to fly alone."

"You son of a bitch," Rodriquez laughed, picking the glass up and taking a long sip. "You're alright sometimes."

The highlight reels were still playing on his retinal display, but they were too painful to watch. Ultra ball was an advanced version of American football, but with all the players jacked into synthetic bodies. They used the Level 3 virtual protocol, which meant the player's avatars were based on their physical attributes. Since they wouldn't be seriously hurt when their avatars were slamming into each other, ultra ball became known as a type of no-holds-barred kind of sport. As he watched one of the Burner's arms get snapped back in half, he swiped his fingers through the air to turn off the feed.

The Daily Double wasn't the type of place Zed usually hung out at. It was small, cold, and uninviting. He wasn't particularly fond of the synthetic bartenders or the digital pop music they kept pumping out from the sound system 24/7. But he didn't have to tip the bot, and it was the first bar outside of Hope City. Because most of the patrons were enforcers waiting for gigs, the owner allowed a duty board to be placed above the bar, so people didn't have to sit and stare at their displays while they waited. That was a big plus. Today Zed wished the board wasn't even there, because every time he looked up there weren't any new gigs and the bar was filling up fast.

"A lot of people from the force here lately," Zed said, as he scratched a bit of grime off from the bar top.

"This dry spell has been hard. I'm not asking for more crime in No Hope, but if work doesn't pick up soon, I know quite a few people who are going to have to move down a zone."

"Yeah, there are only so many patrols you can go on before the credits just aren't worth the time. I'm sure things will even out," Zed ignored thoughts of the rent that was due in a few days and the credits he didn't have to pay for it, "and when it does, I'm sure we will be knee-deep in scum bags and autodoc visits."

"I hear that, brother," Rodriquez said, taking another long sip. "You're doing alright then? Still living large off that big-time bust?" He made a motion to the duty board, where Zed's name was shown next to one of the top three collars in recent history.

"Come on, that was ages ago," Zed sighed, shifting in his seat uncomfortably. "The credits are long gone. I wish someone would knock my name off that board already. I got lucky. Right place, right time. Plain and simple."

"Well, at least you're lucky at something," Rodriquez slapped Zed on the back while he chuckled.

An advertisement for the upcoming Ishi concert started blasting through the bar's sound system. A large holoscreen projected a 3D image of the young pop star into the room as she danced around. Her concert was the kickoff for this year's presentation of The War, one of the most anticipated events for any Omega City citizen. A two-week-long event that placed average citizens in a level 4 hardcore virtual battle simulation. If you survived the conflict, you could come out rich. But if you didn't survive, then you were dead and it wouldn't matter.

"Could we turn this crap off?" Rodriquez complained, "It's giving me a headache."

The synthetic bartender looked over blankly with its vacant, unblinking eyes. With a digitally modified voice that was permanently monotone, it said, "You know I can't do that. It's house policy. This feed stays on all the time. I don't like it any more than you do."

"Right. You have musical preferences. That's just great. Would you at least turn it down?" Rodriquez griped. He turned to Zed while pointing at the dancing hologram and said, "You know she's not even real—or like him, one of them SI's. It's like watching a damned cartoon."

The bartender didn't break from pouring out a continuous stream of drink orders while it looked at Rodriquez and said in a different voice, that sounded prerecorded, "Adjusting the volume or changing the feed goes against the rules of the Daily Double."

"Oh, shut up, you freaking robot," Rodriquez cursed, taking a chip of ice and tossing it at the bartender, who ignored the minor assault.

"Give it a rest," Zed said, rubbing his right shoulder as a pain suddenly shot through it.

"You doing alright? You've been rubbing at that shoulder all day."

"No. I'm fine. I just think it's time for my meds."

"You're still getting augment aches, aren't you? When are you going that thing replaced? I know you're partial to that piece of junk, but you can't even tell the new ones are there anymore. And they look like the real thing."

Zed moved his metallic fingers back and forth in a ball-like motion and said, "I don't want a new one. I didn't want this one in the first place. Besides, it's too many credits."

"Too many credits he says. That's rich." Rodriquez threw his hands in the air and shrugged his shoulders while chuckling to himself. "You must love the constant pain. But okay, go ahead and do your business. I'll watch the board and let you know if anything pops up."

Zed stood up and walked away without responding to Rodriquez's jabs. It would be a waste of his time to get into a back-and-forth argument with someone so stubborn. Making his way through a group of enforcers who were crowding around the opposite end of the bar looking for a round of drinks, he heard his name called out a few times in celebration. He only put his hand up and waved them off. Like he said, he just got lucky. He never asked to be a hero.

He slammed through the door of the unisex bathroom and was happy to find it empty. The light above the sink was blinking in and out as if it had a short in its connection. In a cracked mirror he saw an aging face looking back at him through the strobing light. His salt-and-peppered hair was slicked back and noticeably long past due for a trim. A five-day-old beard covered his square jawline that matched his broad shoulders. His scowling brow cast a shadow over his deep-set eyes and shrouded them in the darkness of his contours. An ancient scar ran across his right cheek, causing parts of his beard to not grow and bits of his skin to be off color. Even though he was what most people would call ruggedly handsome, he wasn't big on looking at himself in the mirror more than necessary. It was just another constant reminder that time was running out. There were countless augmentations, operations, and DNA modifications that he could have done to extend his life, maybe even live forever. But living forever seemed worse than death.

Pulling an EZ-Injector out of his black leather jacket, he held it up to the blinking light to make sure it was the correct drug at the correct dose. When he was confident it was the right one, he set the needle down and took off his jacket. Underneath he wore only a dark-grey tank top and a thin gold chain over a muscular littered with small tattoos that were reminders of moments in time rather than attempts at vanity. He moved his body so his right arm was facing the mirror, revealing the extent of his metallic augmentation.

Electric-blue lights ran vertically along the synthetic arm inside notches on the black-on-grey graphene, with the soft glow humming in and out like it was breathing. The surgical arm replacement ran from his fingers to his shoulder, stopping just short of his deltoid. There was a small circle above his metallic bicep, with a hole for injections. He inserted the EZ-Injector and fed half of the fluid in. That was easy. The hard part was next. Taking the needle out and resting it on his deltoid, he took a deep breath. Then as quickly as he could, injected he himself with the drug.

Holding back a painful scream, he hit his left fist on the aluminum sink and grunted. It felt like fire running through the right side of his chest and down his phantom limb. It was this inconvenient pain two times a month for the rest of his life. Failing to take the injections would be terminal. The drugs helped his body accept the augmentations. This was extremely important, because if they were rejected, then his body would grow painful calluses around the connections and the augment itself. Like a tumor, the calluses could grow too large and cut off proper blood flow in his body.

As he walked back to the bar, he searched his other pockets for a different dose. The pain in his chest was excruciating, and it would take hours for it to recede. Thankfully, there was a drug for that. There was a drug for everything in Omega City 6.

"I miss anything?" Zed asked, standing next to his seat at the bar.

"Board is still blank," Rodriquez replied. "Can you believe they are doing the War of 2084 this year? And I thought we had it bad."

"Brutal. I need to visit a script box. Watch my seat?"

"Sure thing."

The air chilled his neck the second he walked outside, causing him to turn up his collar. Under the dome, the seasons were only an atmospheric simulation. The OS attempted to mimic what normal seasons would have been like in the time before, but it was running off data that was centuries old. The old saying, 'you can't predict the weather,' didn't really apply anymore. If the OS said it was going to rain on Tuesday at five, then it would rain on Tuesday at five.

The prescription dispenser—or script box—was only a half-block away, so Zed didn't worry too much about the cold. The streets of Zone Zero were quiet as usual. Autocars quietly raced back and forth in their endless duty of transporting passengers and/or goods. Hundreds of delivery drones zigzagged through the air in a dance of synchronicity, like a swarm of insects over a hive. Countless lights flashed from advertisements and street signs, reflecting on the damp pavement in zigzagging madness. With all the electronic life filling the cold night, the streets were nearly empty of human beings. The ones that were out wore dark colors and blank expressions, walking around like phantoms in the misty street light.

The Daily Double was between an autodoc and memory clinic on Synth Row—a two-block stretch of synthetically intelligent operated businesses. It wasn't a place that people congregated, as they went there to get whatever a human couldn't do done, and then get back to Hope City. The lack of the general public hanging out in the vicinity was the main reason enforcers hung out at the only bar on the row. Zed kicked a pile of trash out of the way and approached the script box. A few inputs later and the painkiller that he wanted popped up on the screen. He swiped the credits over and a small plastic bottle dropped out of the dispenser. Easy as that. He chewed on the chalky tablets while looking across the street at the massive tower that occupied almost all of Zone Zero.

Hope City, or more commonly referred to as No Hope City by people from the numbers, was a sixty-story superstructure at its highest point and had a footprint of over two hundred blocks. It was once a collection of identical, block-sized buildings for low-income families or those in need if assisted living. The OS originally designed it as a place of rehabilitation, for those who had messed up and zeroed out, or those who had just come from the outer lands beyond the dome. The idea was for people to have a safe place until they earned their way back on the Living Supplemental Income, and back on the Grid. But that plan didn't pan out. There were just too many people in the Omega City System, and not all of them could qualify for the LSI. The Minimal Supplemental Income didn't give them more than a pot to piss in. So, eventually, it became a place for people stuck under the dome who didn't want to live under the constant surveillance of the OS without the benefits of the LSI.

Hope City started as a place of peaceful rehabilitation but ended up a lawless claimed territory by thugs and gangsters. The more people that moved there, the more stories were added, until it became a massive amoebalike structure. The startling statistic was that more than a third of the entire population of Omega City 6 lived in roughly the same amount of space that was used for a public park in Zone Six.

Zed tossed the empty drug container in a recycler and started walking back to The Daily Double when an alert flashed on his HUD. A message popped up by an unlisted identification number, which he thought odd because his own number was unlisted. He had paid a lot of credits for that too because it was a pain in the ass getting ads sent to you all day. He swiped his thumb over the control pad on his index finger and brought up his messages. It was the only one there, so he hit the link and it opened on his display. It read:

> Enforcer Takeda, I am in need of your services. My daughter is currently missing. I am willing to pay handsomely for returning her to me. Please use an OS counsel booth to contact me as soon as possible. I'd prefer to talk face to face while we go over the details. My number is in the attachment. I cannot stress the urgency of the situation enough.
>
> Signed, Priscilla Banks

Zed sighed. It was a fetch job. And he knew a job was a job, and credits were credits, but fetch jobs were for rookies. As if he didn't already know, his system gave him another reminder of his lack of funds. He cursed a few times under his breath before he pulled up the local area map on his display. It had been a long time since he needed to use a counsel booth for a gig, so long that he had forgotten where the closest one was. Seeing that his tab was closed and his drink was empty, he didn't feel the need to go back into the bar. The booth was only a few blocks away, so he took a deep breath of the cold air and made his way down the gloomy streets.

"Welcome, Enforcer Zed Takeda," the synthetic voice of the OS subroutine, often referred to as SuR, came through the booth as he sat down. The booths had many purposes for Omega citizens, from simply talking about your problems to someone—or something—that would listen, to voicing your concerns about civic-related things to the Council of Seven, or transferring data over a secure server. The screens inside started flashing red before the voice spoke again. "Warning. Warning. Mixing alcohol and narcotics is not safe."

"Thanks for the advice," Zed said, reaching into his pocket for his virtual reality connectors and punching away at the touchscreen.

"Is there anything troubling you today? I see you have upped your dosage of pain medication again. Would you like to talk about that?"

"No. I'm just here for a data transfer."

"Acknowledged. The OS is always with you," the voice said as the lights in the booth dimmed to a soft-violet color for his virtual link.

"Don't remind me."

The booth was a small, rectangular glass box with a single chair and a touchscreen. When the booth was unoccupied, the glass was clear, but when someone locked the door and engaged the system, the shatterproof glass was blacked out to prying eyes. Once engaged, the inside glass turned into a seamless holoscreen that could project any image the user desired. Some people were prone to panic attacks when leaving their living quarters after long periods of VR and not in an avatar. The booths were a safe place to regroup, and a lot of people actually did turn to the OS for soothing words of consultation. There were thousands of them scattered around the city in all kinds of locations, with some being bigger or nicer. This particular one smelled like a portable bathroom.

"ID number 9671-29 to connect with one Priscilla Banks at—"

"Connecting," a different synthetic voice cut in before he could give her identification number. He also found that odd, but it was turning out to be an odd day. "Connected. Please engage the virtual simulation now."

He applied the two virtual pads on each of his temples, pressing them down firmly so they wouldn't fall off because they were old and due for replacement. Leaning back in the chair, he closed his eyes, causing flashes of light to shoot through his consciousness. He could see the booth around him dissolve into thousands of little dots, each representing a chip that was connected to the net. With trillions of chipped data points in the city, it looked as if he was shooting through a star field at warp speed. He began to shake from the intensity, causing the nanobots in his bloodstream to activate. They held his body motionless as the lights unified into one giant blast that instantly brought him through to the virtual world. He was now inside his digital avatar body in an empty black void. Just a simple exchange room, Zed thought, as he calmly looked into the darkness.

"Enforcer Takeda, I presume," a firm female voice asked from behind him.

"Call me Zed," he said, turning to see a gorgeous middle-aged woman in an elegant gown lavished with dazzling jewelry. This was more than your average street skin. This was a top-of-the-line, premium-grade, deluxe-package digital avatar. Probably a replica of one of her favorite avatar models she wore in real life, maybe a Satoshi 5000, or an Ulbricht 6X. His eye twitched a little, thinking about the price tag one of the beauties held. "Pricilla Banks?"

"Yes," her voice projected from the synthetic head, with the lips moving only a fraction of a second behind her voice. "Forgive me for messaging you directly, but I needed someone I could trust with this job and not some random enforcer who saw the posting. You came highly recommended by some friends of mine."

"So that's how you got my number."

"I can assure you they were reluctant to share it with me, citing your private nature. I respect that. Nothing digital is safe anymore. Anything can be acquired for the right price. That's why I insisted on using the protected counsel booth. I'm well aware that I could have sent the information over a text-based message, but I can't trust there isn't a data thief in your vicinity. Wherever you may be." She paused and looked him up and down as if she were admiring a wild animal. "I'll get right down to it. My daughter Juna is suffering a momentary lapse of reason and has traveled into Zone Zero."

"I see," Zed tried to put some sort of empathy in his voice, "that can be troubling. Do you know when she left, exactly?"

"She left earlier to have a spa day with her girlfriends. But instead of checking into our building's spa, she got on the maglev to Dakota Park. I messaged you once she transferred over at the Z train terminal."

"You have a tracker on her, then?"

"Of course," she huffed, "but I don't need it or an enforcer to tell me what her intentions are with the way she is leaving a trail of transactions. The OS watches over us all, I know that, but not in Hope City. That's why I need you to check in on her. Watch over her personally and make sure she doesn't do something too foolish."

"I think you might be confused. I'm not a babysitter."

"I don't mean to insult you, or to question your integrity." Priscilla's lips made a slight snarl when she said the word integrity. Zed didn't react outwardly. His face remained expressionless and as hard as stone. He was used to the wealthy expressing their distaste for people less fortunate than them on a regular basis. He simply made a mental note as to the type of person he was dealing with. "My Daughter Juna means the world to me, and I am looking for a paid bodyguard to ensure her safety. I was told you were the best. Think of it as hired security, if that works for you."

"Right," Zed said, while searching for the timestamp from the job posting on his HUD as they talked. "She is already in Hope City. Let's say thirty minutes and counting. Time is essential in these cases. I'll need to move fast."

"A man of action, as I was promised," Priscilla smiled with firm lips and a deep sense of satisfaction in her eyes. Zed made another mental note. "I read your credentials, Enforcer Takeda. You're not one for the second life, you don't own a synthetic avatar, and your VR bed hasn't been registered in years. You're the type of man who prefers the hands-on approach," she said while eyeing up his physique. A notification of a completed file transfer popped up on his display while she continued to talk in an almost sultry manner. "I appreciate that. It's hard to judge a person's character from an avatar alone. You never know who really is behind that silicone facade. I insist on personally meeting anyone who comes in contact with my Juna, but in this case, I'll have to make an exception."

"Hope City isn't a safe place."

"You have some synthetic augmentations, don't you?" she asked curiously, changing the subject. Her eyes looked directly at his right arm, causing Zed to put it casually behind his back. That information wasn't on his basic profile. She had done a deep dig on him, something that would require not only a skilled net diver but also a lot of time and a lot of credits.

"A half-hour is plenty of time for a whole lot of wrong."

"Oh please," she hissed, "We've all had our days slipping out to Dakota Park or Hope City for a little adventure. Kids need a little real-life excitement to shake up all that time they spend in virtual. I was somewhat of a fixture at the Gato Loco back in the day myself."

"Whatever you think of as an adventure in your days—slumming with the lower classes or fraternizing with the help—is far from the reality of the present."

"What are you implying?"

"I'm telling you that in the century since you probably last left the Six in person, Hope City changed from the romantically scandalous place that you remember into a place for zeroed out pimps, sex traffickers, thieves, and murderers. It's full of drugs, gangs, and prostitution. The moment your daughter goes through the front gates, her tracker can be digitally wiped, and the OS surveillance will end. Where she will end up, and what will happen to her then will be anyone's guess."

"Don't be silly," she laughed nervously. "This is an Omega City, there isn't any of that. The OS protects us all. None of what you say is true."

"Look, lady, I wouldn't have a job if it wasn't true." Zed looked into those empty, synthetic eyes. He knew right then why she chose this over-the-top glamorous avatar for a business meeting. Because it was like the model she went out in when she was young, and everyone wanted to feel young again. "Like I said, thirty minutes is plenty of time for any one of those people to get to your daughter."

"Well, what are you waiting for, then?" she asked, raising her hands in the air.

"Half up front," Zed replied, while taking a step closer.

"My terms of service were payment upon the return of my daughter."

"And my terms are half upfront."

"There are plenty of other enforcers looking for work tonight."

"Yeah, well..." Zed sighed, knowing that it was the truth. "Twenty percent. I've got expenses." He gritted his teeth. "I'll need to take an autocar there and back, and if I run into any trouble—"

"I'm sure you're capable of handling anything Hope City can dish out. Five thousand credits. That should be more than enough for travel expenses and any inconveniences you should have along the way."

"Five will suffice."

"Good. You have her information on the file I've sent you, and you have your expenses covered. Anything else?" She stood there adjusting her synthetic hair and smiling like she knew something devious. At the same time, his system chimed to notify him of a deposit made to his account. Five thousand flat.

"That should about do it. Good evening, Mrs. Banks."

"I'll see you soon, Enforcer Takeda."

The VR link suddenly cut, and he was shot back to reality. He immediately punched the wall of the counsel booth with his right fist, causing the glass to crack a little. The OS instantly fined him for the damage, credits were pulled from his account, and his morality rating dropped a single point.

Fuck!

He hated dealing with people from Zone Six. Pompous, first born, DNA-enhanced meat sacks with 3D printed organs, dozens of avatar bodies, and millions of hours in virtual. They had more credits than they knew what to do with, but their moral ratings were so far in the gutter they would never ascend. They take their LSI like every other citizen, but they might as well flush it down the toilet because it meant that little to them. Five thousand credits? That didn't even cover his loss on ultra ball. He knew full well he wouldn't be taking any goddamned autocar in any direction. When he found this Juna Banks, the little brat could take a train home like everyone else.

TWENTY-FOUR

He used his enforcer privileges and punched up Priscilla Banks' profile, which came up with a big fat RESTRICTED notice. Son of a bitch. It took a lot of credits to have a profile blocked from an enforcer. He could take the time and perform a lengthy workaround, but the general information that was there was enough for now. Name, sex, and age. The basics. At two hundred and twenty-four, Priscilla was definitely old enough to be a first born, maybe even a first citizen.

He swiped the air and a photograph of a young woman was shown on his display. She had just turned sixteen, with a thin frame, high cheekbones, and a naïve expression. Juna Banks. She had the usual golden-brown pseudo-Polynesian skin type that had been in fashion at the DNA clinics for some time, but with modified bright green eyes, silky blonde hair, and accentuated cheekbones. The profile Priscilla had sent him noted she preferred to be called Jewels. Yes, like a precious stone. There was nothing about this girl that didn't say money from one glance. She was a perfect mark for a street thug. If she turned the wrong corner in Hope City, she'd be shaken down for all her credits. But if she took a really wrong corner, it would be a lot worse. He wouldn't let that happen. Rent was due.

He exited the counsel booth calmly. Looking around, he caught sight of something familiar out of the corner of his eye. It was just a simple, non-descript cement bench; nothing special. But the memories that specific bench were connected to suddenly flooded out and struck him motionless. A name whispered in the air—*Natalia*—and his nervous system shook. A ghost of her appearance was conjured. A pale face hidden behind streaks of long black hair, piercing eyes that seemed to see through him, and a smile that made his heartache.

He realized then that it had been ages since he had walked down this block, maybe even avoiding it unconsciously. He strolled over to the bench and looked across the street at the entrance to Hope City, remembering all the times he and Natalia would sit there and share their complete disdain for the place. Their hatred for those grimy streets brought them together, but their dreams of a day they could finally escape its clutches and never come back intertwined their destinies forever. He hung his head in shame, knowing she would be disappointed in how things had turned out. Even though he got out, he now spent most of his days patrolling the streets he once so wished to put behind him. But maybe it wasn't the criminals that he was searching those twisted streets for. Maybe it was the ghost of her memory. He shook the feeling off and adjusted his jacket. Clearing his mind, he focused on the job. That was the only thing that mattered anymore. Find the bad guys, and make them pay.

He climbed a set of stairs that led to a grouping of pedestrian bridges, all headed to the entrance of Hope City. As he came closer to the front gate, he thought the exterior walls were growing. One layer of concrete, a layer of lead, a layer of steel, then another of concrete as if in preparation for war. Beyond the wall, there was an ever-growing pile of surveillance equipment and decommissioned synthetic bodies. The pile of electronic junk was more than a monument of hatred towards the technology that had embedded itself into society like an unwanted virus, it was a message to the Omega Systems and any other synthetic that wanted into the Hope City. Simple enough, STAY OUT. It had been there so long though that no one paid any attention to it anymore, and no synthetic would dare approach the gate.

Guards were visible in protected perches, ready to pull the trigger on their massive EMP rifles as they digitally scanned the crowds for non-humans. A big semi-circle steel sign that read Hope City reached across an expanse between two giant concrete pillars. It was originally placed during the construction of OC6, but after the wall went up, someone had spray painted the world No in front of Hope as if to reference Dante by saying, "Abandon hope, all ye who enter here." The name stuck with the people, so no one washed it off.

He had to go up a few more flights of stairs until he reached the entryway platform. It was one of two ways to get in and out of the city, the other being the subway terminal a half-dozen flights below. The gateway was four streets wide and six stories tall. Two lanes were dedicated to autocar traffic and the other two to pedestrian, and all were subject to scans by both the OS and HC gate security. Two monolithic concrete buildings framed this picture of a city within a city with haunting silence. As he came out of the darkness of Zone Zero, streaks of blue and pink neon assaulted his night accustomed eyes. Bright white light strobed from advertising holoscreens and LED signs from hundreds of shops and eateries, flashing in and out manically. The inside of the city was a canyon of buildings with a webwork of crisscrossing walkways. What little could be seen of the sky was heavily dotted by delivery drones that zipped through the air ceaseless day and night. The air was noticeably different as he crossed the threshold of electronic scanning machines, not only in temperature but in smell. Over ninety percent of the people on the streets of the Grid were in a synthetic body. No matter how hard they tried, a synth would always smell like a synth; silicon, hot copper, and plastic. Hope City had a humid stench to it, and that wasn't necessarily a bad thing. It was real, and the people inside it were real.

Over the sounds of heavy autocar traffic and thousands of people moving about the busy gateway, he could hear the thumping of The Deadfall district not far off. That was where he was sure he would find Juna. Because Hope City didn't have the constant OS surveillance that the rest of the city did, there were plenty of rules and laws that could easily be broken. Drug use was high on that list, and that's why the biggest and most popular nightclubs were found in Hope City's Deadfall district. A floating oasis just beyond the gate that called to Omega citizens of all types with its flashing lights and endless, pounding, electronic music. A twenty-four-hour, never-ending party that was the commercial backbone for Hope City. There was a constant flow of people coming from the grid, with their LSI credits ready to spend. Almost every person who Zed had to track down was found at one of the nightclubs that populated the brightly lit adult playground, with the exceptions being idiots who took wrong turns. But navigating Hope City was difficult, even for the people who were born there. There was no rhyme or reason as to how the streets, alleyways, and aerial walkways were laid out. A wrong turn could have you stuck with a knife in your back.

Having patrolled the streets for years, he wasn't even paying attention as he made his way through the twisting labyrinth of pathways that pulsed with light from the long holographic advertising panels. Pink-neon light strips ran along the white and black tiled walls that formed tunnels through buildings, as people bustled about in shadowy masses. A half dozen blocks later, he came to a large moving stairwell with a bright digital screen over it. The words *The Deadfall* illuminated in a shimmering gold design over the stairwell packed with people taking one step at a time in an unbelievably leisurely manner. Eventually, he came to the top, and the district opened up in all its glory. Dominating the right side was a large, open, elevated platform that looked over the rest of Hope City, with island bars serving up any kind of cocktail you could want. A DJ was on a lit-up platform surrounded by massive speakers blasting music for a modest-sized crowd.

Opening up the tracking system on Juna showed that she had come this way. Not surprisingly, the tracker cut out shortly after. OS trackers didn't work in Hope City, because they were blocked along with all other forms of surveillance. There were a lot of low-level street thugs whose only job was to walk around and run a device over any pretty girl or boy they came across. The device would short out any outside trackers that were still operational, in case the marks were picked up later by someone else higher up. Even though the OS didn't have its eyes watching over the people of Hope City, that didn't mean there weren't other types of surveillance systems in place, especially in a high-profile area such as this. Zed cut his way through the crowds to an enforcer security station.

"You there, Richie?" Zed asked, as he tapped on a laminate counter in front of a young woman who was intently staring at dozens of monitor screens. "Anything interesting?"

"Oh, hey Takeda," she said, looking up from her screens and adjusting her vision. Zed could see that she was watching something else on her HUD by the way her pupils were illuminated. "No man. It's been super quiet for weeks now. A couple Royals on the eastside scouting the area, and you can probably see the Bruiser thugs over there," she motioned to a group of young adults with half-shaved heads, red leather jackets, and ripped-up black jeans. They each had small tattoos above their right thumbs—a symbol of their gang affiliation. "No colors though, thankfully. Just some petty drug dealing, but I'm not gonna bother with that. I have the system tracking their movements if more show up, or if anything big goes down. Not to complain, but these quiet stretches are boring. Thank the OS for ultra ball, right? You come out on top today?"

"I don't really want to talk about it."

"Hope you didn't deal with any of the local bookies. Chip to credit conversion rate is out-of-control right now. People from the Six holding onto chips like they're gold or something. You can't spend chips in the numbers, and they never come down here, so I don't get why they would even want them."

"That's why I only place my bets with bookies on The Strip these days."

"Probably a better way to go about it, especially with your luck," she chuckled and smiled at Zed. He did not find her jest humorous, and looked at her with a murderous stare. Richie adjusted her posture and said, "So, you come down here to just shoot the shit, or do you need something from me?"

"I think you know the answer," Zed said, slipping over the file on Juna Banks. "I got a lost girl from the Six on my hands. Need to keep her safe. Her private tracker went dead a few minutes ago. Hopefully, it's just the congestion from the clubs."

"A scout probably got her, fucking scumbags. I'll plug it in and hopefully we can find her," Richie said, grabbing the file out of the air and feeding it into the surveillance system. "A lot of guys on the force hungry for credits right now. That can only mean the bad guys are just as hungry. We have to stay vigilant."

"Sharks never sleep," Zed mused, as he watched her go to work. She patched the OS profile in on Juna and ran it against all the surveillance and enforcer feeds currently in the district. It was similar to the system the OS used, but at a fraction of accuracy and power.

"I think I have something, but I'm not sure."

"Does this help?" Zed asked, as he transferred over a thousand credits to her account.

"Oh, there she is," Richie announced sarcastically. "Security camera got her just outside of Club Dead End. Looks like she was with someone. Trying to get a different angle for you."

"Goddamnit. That place is a shithole," Zed cursed, leaning over the counter to see Richie's holoscreen.

The timestamp was from about five minutes ago, and he could clearly see a man run his hand over the back of her neck with a small device. Richie caught the man's face from a different angle and sent a screen capture over to Zed's system. Without wasting time, he plugged the image into his enforcer database. Even though he wasn't connected to the OS, a file of known criminals, open jobs, and bounties were stored on each enforcers' system, and automatically updated when on the Grid. Shit, Zed thought, as he watched the list of crimes scroll past his eyes.

"You better get moving," Richie said, as she watched the same list on her display. "This little prick deserves an ass-whooping."

He made his way past the bigger clubs with clever names like Inferno and Euphoria and hustled to the far end of the strip where Club Dead End was. The club was known for not checking identity at the door, patting people down, or having strict drug enforcement rules. This led it to be very popular with the younger crowds and local undesirables. He was stopped at the front gate, which was composed of a crude chain-link fence with big cannon lights behind it, by a bouncer that seemed to be three times his size.

"Entry is ten chips," the bouncer said, his extremely large hand holding Zed back by his chest. Zed protested that he was on enforcer business, but the bouncer only said, "I don't give a shit. Ten chips."

"All I've got are credits."

"Exchange," the man grunted and pointed towards a digital reader. Zed cursed, seeing the new price of three hundred and fifty credits flash before his eyes. He confirmed the transaction, and the ogre-like man let him pass.

The club was dark inside, with a thick fog filling in the spaces that the strobing lights pulsed through. Silhouettes of people moved back and forth to a digital rhythm that was coming out of mounted speakers all over the room. Shirtless and sweaty people moved rhythmically together with multicolored drinks in their hands and a cocktail of drugs in their bodies. The perp would want someplace quiet to talk to the girl so she would let her guard down, possibly near the back. It was not uncommon for a place like this to have false walls that people and other goods could be smuggled through—especially if the club was in on the take. It was getting harder to tell what gang controlled what club. Through shooting streams of laser lights over the heads of patrons, he saw a hallway in the back that seemed to head further down. Pushing his way through people that did not want to move, they repaid him with slurs and elbows.

Down a purple-colored hallway that was littered with people chewing on their tongues and spun out on junk, he found a second bar that was less populated, with less intense music, and a variety of furniture for people to occupy. They had to be here. Turning up the brightness through an enhancement in his system, he could see the faces of the people at the bar. It only took a second to find what he was looking for. Juna stood out easily enough. Even though she attempted to dress down, her clothes still looked like they cost a year's worth of rent for most people in Hope City. And there was no way to hide her DNA-enhanced genes that made her perfect skin and hair seem to radiate light in the dark room.

The young man sitting next to her had his back to Zed, but one quick look and it was plain to see the kid was bad news. Red laces in the boots, ripped jeans, leather vest with gang insignia patches, and a spikey hairstyle that was intentionally self-induced. He was a poster boy for Deadfall scum. On approach, Zed could clearly see that the kid had his hand on a small stun gun attached by a strap on his left thigh. A few more minutes and the girl would probably be unconscious and shuffled down a damp tunnel.

"I just got this one done," the kid bragged, raising his right arm and showing off his new tattoo that glistened and moved in the dim light. It was obvious he was distracting her attention away from his other hand that was now gripping the stunner. "I had a killer tiger design here before, but my guy convinced me to strip it for this one. It's cool and all, but I can always go back if I want."

"Juna Banks?" Zed asked for procedure, as his system already made visual confirmation of her identity. The girl gave him a quick frightened look, probably not expecting anyone to know her.

"Get lost, creep," the kid said, not turning around. "We're talking here."

"Juna, it's time to go," Zed commanded, keeping his eye on the dirtbag with his back turned. "I am here to escort you home."

"My name isn't Juna," she pouted.

"Jewels," Zed corrected, "Please, if you would come with me."

"Look asshole," the kid bawled, pulling the stun gun up to his side, but not revealing it, "she said she's with me, now fuck off."

The kid seemed to be moving in slow motion, and a smile came across

Zed's face. It was time for the part of the job he actually enjoyed. Before the kid could get the gun up to firing level, Zed had his hand twisted behind his back. Catching the stun gun with his free hand, he smashed the barrel straight into the kid's spine. The bruising it caused would last a few weeks.

"You're mine now, punk," Zed whispered into the kid's ear. Jewels made a slight and jumped at the sudden violence. "Hold on, Jewels, don't run away. Share screen." Zed said, connecting with Jewels' HUD.

Her vision filled with a list of crimes committed by the creature before her, with a 3D portrait of his face rotating back and forth in an exact likeness—face tattoos and all. The list kept scrolling on and on, one known offense after the other. It was mostly petty crimes like theft, drugs, and assault, but such an extensive list meant the kid was on a fast track to harder stuff. The crimes had him so far in debt to the system that he was destined for a lifetime of being zeroed out—what was left of it, anyway. Jewels just sat there shaking, with the sudden realization that coming to Hope City might not have been the best idea.

"Are you alone?" Zed barked, watching the reflection of crimes scrolling in her bright green eyes. "Did you come here with anyone?"

"No," she whispered, turning off the connection. "No, I was supposed to meet my friend here, but she bailed."

"Something wrong here Jimmy?" The man at the bar asked, finally noticing the visible pain the kid must have been in.

"This guy is a fucking synth snitch!" The kid screamed, trying desperately to rip his arm away. "Get him off me!"

"It's Takeda!" the bartender yelled while making a move for a blunt weapon hidden under the bar. Zed reacted by letting a quick blast off from the stun gun. The bartender flailed backward into a pile of glassware. Zed palmed the kid's head and slammed it onto the bar, causing him to go limp instantly. Jewels made a move to run, but her elbow was caught in Zed's grip. He gave her a quick smile. Two unconscious criminals, and the package unharmed and in custody in less than a minute. He still had it.

"You're a maniac!" Jewels shouted.

"Calm down, you'll be fine."

"Look what you did to those guys!"

"They'll be fine too."

"Did my mother hire you?" the girl shrieked, as Zed tugged at her to follow him while pocketing the stun gun. He didn't answer right away, so she said, "I'll take that as a yes. God! This is so typical of her. You know, she hasn't come out of her VR bed in years. I'm not lying. Years!"

"Not my problem," Zed said, looking around the room in case the kid had accomplices.

"Come on. She doesn't give a shit about me, so why should you? Why don't you let me go?" She pleaded with Zed, but he just kept his face forward and kept moving. "She only had me because she couldn't afford to keep her eggs frozen forever. She told me that. Do you know what that's like? Do you? I don't even know how she knew I was gone. I only left an hour ago!"

The girl continued to give Zed her life story as he tugged her back down the hallway full of rolling partiers and through the crowded club. Jewels shouted her complaints over the music, but Zed really wasn't listening. It was always the same story with runaways from the Six.

He navigated her back through the fenced-off entrance, where he found the gigantic bouncer standing in the exit. "You got a lot of nerve, Takeda," The bouncer grumbled.

"So I've been told," Zed laughed, shouldering his way past.

"Look," Jewels continued, as they rode the escalator out of the Deadfall, "I'm grateful that you saved me from that guy back there, but you can't take me home. It's like I live with a bunch of corpses and robots."

"Keep moving," Zed said, pushing her on. His system suddenly chimed multiple alerts at once. With his free hand, he thumbed the first message open, which was sent out to all the enforcers requesting their services for a gang raid in Hope City. "Jesus Christ," he said, not knowing that he had said it out loud.

"What is it?" The girl asked, looking back at him. "You get another call? See, you have better things to be doing than dragging me around. I'm sure there are real criminals—"

"Look, kid. You're what? Sixteen?" Zed growled, to which Jewels nodded affirmatively. "Then you're old enough to know better. You're also not old enough to be out on your own."

"That's just it," she pleaded. "I am on my own. Both my parents live in their virtual worlds. If I want to see them, I have to go there. I hate it. I haven't seen the real them in so long I can't remember what they actually look like. We don't even have any pets. It's just me and the stupid SI caretaker—who spends most of their time on them. Can't you let me go with a warning? I promise I'll be more careful."

"I don't think you understand how good you've got it. People are starving down here. They are sleeping three to a bed, ten to a room, and fighting over spare change. They are desperate. They are dangerous. You got lucky that kid was small time. The next one won't be." More alerts were popping up on his system, something big was going down and he was missing out on it by babysitting a princess.

"I can't go back home. It's driving me crazy."

"A word of advice. You have less than two years until you're eighteen, and then you can get your LSI and move out on your own. I suggest you suck it up and deal with it. If you need a night out, there are plenty of places in Three South off Second Ave that don't ID people as long as they pay the cover. The area is safe, and you can tell your mom that you're going shopping."

"Nothing but people in synths down there."

"Yeah, well, you're going to have to get used to it. It's the world we live in now."

"Where the hell are you Takeda?" a direct message from Enforcer Boyd shown across his retinal display in bold script.

"Look," Zed said, pointing to his right, "The train station is just down that stairwell. You can take it all the way back home safely, or get off on The Strip and take an autocar. I don't care. I need to be somewhere else right now."

"Alright, I'll go home," she said, in such a way that really didn't convince him. "Did she give you any expense money? I don't have enough for the ride."

"She didn't," Zed lied, because he knew she had more credits than he did at the moment, "but here are three hundred credits. It's all I've got. That should be enough for the train." She smiled softly at him, and then turned to head down the stairwell.

Finally, he thought, as he headed back into Hope City. A gang raid had the potential for a big payout, depending on who they were raiding and what kind of things they could confiscate. He really needed the credits. The credits! He forgot to have Priscilla Banks transfer the credits over before he released Juna from his custody. Goddammit. He immediately turned around to chase after her when he bumped right into a massive, muscular body.

"Watch where the fuck you're going," the gigantic man said, pushing Zed in the chest and knocking him to the ground like tipping over an empty can.

The man had been wearing a black hooded cape to cover his face and body, but the hood had fallen down when they bumped into each other to reveal a bald head with an augmented, glowing red eye. The two men that were with him pulled their jackets back to reveal dueling daggers as if to scare him off. But Zed had his own knife hidden in a sheath under his left armpit, and he knew how to use it. A half-second later Zed's system started flashing more notifications. A new list of crimes started rolling past his eyes, these being much more serious. Then the biggest bounty he had seen in a long time scrolled across in bold red numbers.

Tony Two Toes had been in hiding for years and was wanted for so many terrible things that the only punishment would be exile. He was a white whale of bounties. An opportunity Zed couldn't pass up. Without even thinking, he used an enforcer privilege and tried to activate a tracker on Tony's implanted chip. Instantly, his display told him that the tracker had failed. He should have known Tony would have an advanced security system. As Tony was walking away, Zed fired off a nano tracker from his synthetic arm, but it struck a crate that Tony had just moved past.

Zed cursed to himself, thinking how expensive each tracker was. He quickly fired off another one, and thankfully it hit the target and connected a link. He knew there wouldn't be that much time before Tony's system found him out. Time was short. He had to choose between the payment from Priscilla or the bounty that would be nearly impossible to catch with almost all the other enforcers on the other side of the city. It seemed oddly strange that he would just bump into one of the most wanted people in all of Omega City 6, right at a busy subway entrance. It was a little too easy, and he really wasn't that lucky. Then his system alerted him that the tracker had been detected, and he could visibly see Tony barreling away. If Tony was going to go down, now was the time. He may never surface again.

The tracker was still active even though it had been detected, so he had to act quick. His first instinct was to follow the wanted man directly, but he would have to deal with the two bodyguards that stayed behind first. That would mean he would always be two steps behind, no matter how fast he ran. The tracker put a red beacon in his line of sight where Tony was moving, with a number going up quickly that indicated distance. It looked like he had disappeared into an alley that was heading south along a wall a few hundred feet beyond, leaving behind the hired thugs as a distraction.

Not wanting to waste any time, Zed moved first and stomped on the closest guard's kneecap with the heel of his boot. He then socked him in the face with his metal fist. It was a sucker punch, and he never liked sucker punches, but time was of the essence. The other guard made a move for his dagger, but Zed kicked the man's hand right as it gripped the hilt. The guard was quick to block the next blow from Zed's fist, and countered with a different blade that was cleverly concealed. Zed stepped back to dodge the first swipe and lunged in with his metal arm to deflect the next blade attack. This left the guard wide open to a left-handed strike that stunned the man long enough for Zed to rebalance and strike with his right, knocking the second guard out cold. The fight had taken less than a minute, but that gave Tony an enormous head start.

People gave Zed space as he looked around for the tracker beacon. He found the blinking red light quickly, appearing to already be on a lower level. After waiting a second longer, Tony did what Zed wanted to by taking a sharp right. He could cut him off, but it would be risky. Taking a diagonal path, he jumped over a railing and fell down a full flight, hitting the pavement below with a bone-shaking slap. Racing through the crowds of people, he focused on the tracker beacon and nothing else. Making another course alteration, he leapt into traffic and rolled over a hood of an autocar that couldn't stop in time. The tracker was now heading in his direction, just a few feet below and fifty feet beyond.

At a club called Demon's Whip, he didn't even bother to be told there was a cover and just rammed through the entryway like a runaway train. Naked breasts under red lights filled his vision, and he realized he was in a strip club. The name should have given it away. With a shouting bouncer hot on his heels, he kept moving. He scanned the room for a second bouncer while he moved, knowing there was at least one more out there. A long bar that was nowhere near as close to the beacon as he needed it to be occupied the back wall. Out of the corner of his eye, he saw the second bouncer emerge from a dark hallway, and Zed guessed that's where the private rooms were. A dancer on stage preoccupied a wealthy-looking man at the rack, whispering naughty words into his ear. Zed took the opportunity and grabbed at a pile of chips that the man had in front of him, and tossed them into the center of the crowded room. Dancers and patrons alike scrambled desperately for the free currency. The bouncers got caught up in the commotion as Zed hurried past towards the private rooms. Down a small ramp, he went barreling through what he thought was a door but turned out to be just a black curtain. He found himself on top of a bare-chested woman, who was on top of a drunken man with a solid erection. The beacon was blinking directly in front of him, reading a distance of only a few meters.

"Get down!" Zed yelled, taking a step back and raising his metallic arm.

Leaping over the lap-dance-in-progress, Zed hit the wall and was happy to find that it wasn't made of cinder blocks. The thin wooden wall gave way easily. Suddenly he was hurtling through the air into a small alley, right at a surprised Tony Two Toes. The man was built like a tank, and he barely lost his footing as all of Zed's weight rammed into him. Not missing a beat, Tony swung his gigantic arm around and clocked Zed right in the face, sending him flying back and dripping blood. Anticipating the next move of a known killer, Zed pulled the knife out from under his left arm. Catching Tony's oncoming blade with his own was more than pure luck, these were the scenarios Zed trained for day after day. A step back, and Tony thrust forward again with a stabbing motion. A quick dodge and Zed grabbed Tony's wrist with his left hand, twisting it to cause the blade to drop. He punched the inside of Tony's arm with his right and followed up with an elbow to the gut.

But Tony could take a hit like a pro player on Sunday night. Not even flinching after Zed's attacks, he struck hard with his knee. He followed that up with a left-handed hook. Zed fell into a brick wall as Tony's fist came fast at his face. He ducked just in time, and the punch smashed into the wall. Zed lunged at Tony's gut and they both tumbled to the floor. Tony reached up and grabbed a piece of wood that had come loose from the wall that Zed had flown through. Pulling it free, he immediately smacked Zed in the face with it. The dancer was still on the other side of the wall, half-naked and screaming away when Tony changed directions and headed into the strip club.

For a moment Zed wondered if he could actually take the guy down. Tony was extremely strong and probably had a dozen augmentations that gave him a rather large edge. All Zed had to do was call in for backup. There was a swarm of enforcers not far off at the other crime scene. But that might take too long, and he'd also have to split the bounty.

Picking himself up, he darted into the club, hungry for justice. The two bouncers were already on the floor with broken noses. A topless girl carrying a tray of drinks was pushed violently out of the way. Booze spilled and glasses crashed as Tony charged out the front door. Zed quickly grabbed a chair from the Demon's Whip on his way out. On the walkway, he swung the chair around and tossed it at the back of Tony's head. People started screaming from all directions as Tony fell forward and crashed through the storefront window of a tattoo parlor next door.

Zed leaped through the window on top of the dazed Tony, but he still didn't have enough power or weight to keep him down. Tony turned and picked Zed up with one arm, carrying him through the air like a small puppy. He set Zed down in one of the tattoo chairs and held him in place by his neck while he fumbled around with some equipment. Grabbing one of the automated ink machines, he clamped it down over Zed's left arm so it pinned him firmly.

"Hope you like unicorns," Tony laughed, as he hit the engage button. The machine jumped to life and started puncturing Zed's forearm with hundreds of tiny needles working in unison. "Now stay down," Tony ordered, and punched Zed several times in the face before running off.

Zed was unconscious for a few quick seconds before the pain from the tattoo machine brought him back to life. That son of a bitch, he thought, as he removed the clamps from the machine to reveal bloody skin mixed with neon-sparkled ink. Staggering as he stood, he was thankful that he still had a large dose of painkillers running through his body, but not so thankful for all the vodka he had downed them with. The beacon wasn't that far off, because as big as Tony was, he wasn't that fast. Zed rushed out of the building towards the Red-Light district.

Half-naked men and women stood on display in glass cylinders outside of a row of buildings that were lit up with giant red lights. The gawking crowd parted as Tony chugged his way through, shouting for people to move as he ran. He jumped onto a passing autocar, leaving a giant dent in the hood, and then pulled himself up onto an overhanging roof. Thumping across the metal roofing, he made his way to a spot where he could climb even higher to an elevated walkway. Now he was a full story above Zed and moving fast. Zed tried to follow in his footsteps, but the overhanging roof gave away when Zed landed on it. He went crashing down to the ground once again.

As he lay in a dirty puddle on the pavement, looking up at the soot-covered buildings, he thought that it was over. There was no way he could catch Tony now. But as he watched the distance next to the tracker beacon, it suddenly stopped going up. To Zed's amazement, the numbers started going back down. Tony had gone down a dead end. Zed scrambled to his feet and found an alternate way to the higher level by the way of a small storage container next to a grated window.

Once he was up, Tony was charging full steam back towards him. Zed reached inside a recycler for a glass bottle and chucked it in Tony's direction. It slammed right into Tony's head and shattered into pieces. With blood dripping down his face Tony changed directions and burst right through an emergency exit for a virtual sex parlor. The people inside were jacked in and didn't even notice as the man busted up the room. He raced across the room through a door that led to a utility corridor between buildings. When Zed was entered through the first broken door two men in VR beds moaned and panted as they engaged in their sexual pleasures, still unaware of the intruders.

Down the service corridor Zed saw a door that had been pried open. He turned inside and found himself in the back of a large commercial prep kitchen. Several people were yelling at him as he pushed his way through stacks of dishes, pots, and pans. When he entered the dining room, it turned out to be a Benihana-style chain restaurant that never seemed to go out of fashion. Zed could see Tony just across a room full of flat top grills. A chef at the grill next to him had just ignited a flaming onion volcano. Seeing an opportunity, Zed caught the spatula that the chef was juggling out of the air, slipped it under the flaming onion sculpture, and flung it in Tony's direction. Another direct hit to the face. The scalding hot vegetables stunned Tony again and allowed Zed to tackle him.

Putting his entire body into the attack, both he and Tony fell into a cinderblock wall that buckled slightly under their weight. Tony immediately grabbed Zed with both hands and tossed him onto one of the flat top grills. Zed screamed and jumped, trying to keep his flesh off the cooking surface, but to his relief, it was off and cold. Tony pulled out a butcher's knife from a magnetic rack and made a huge chopping motion. Zed barely dodged the attack by rolling to one side as the knife came down so hard that it indented the thick steel. Tony quickly had the knife back up and ready to chop. Zed dodged once again, but this time the blade took a piece of his jacket. Not waiting for the third time to be the charm, Zed kicked Tony in the gut with his boot. Then, swinging his legs in a circular motion, he flung his body up and landed a haymaker with his right fist. The titanium-coated, graphene fist-to-the-forehead finally had Tony seriously dazed. Zed hit him in the face a few more times for good measure.

"I'm taking you in Tony," Zed growled, pulling out a hand restraint from his coat pocket that he hoped would be strong enough to hold the beast of a man. "The OS is going to exile your ass. ASAP."

"Bullshit," Tony exclaimed, coming back to life and lunging at Zed, causing both of them to fall into a sturdy wooden pillar that was holding up the fire extinguishing equipment.

A previous injury—separate from the one that took his arm—had caused Zed to get parts of his left leg replaced with synthetics. Even though he hated having electronics mixed in with his organics, he was grateful for the power the added augmentations were about to give him. Using the last of his strength, he placed his right arm under Tony's chin, and with his left leg pushed off hard from the pillar. They both went flying across the room, knocking over tables and chairs. When they hit the same cinderblock wall as before, it gave way under the pressure. They fell onto the city street once again, with people screaming at the sight of violence and destruction.

Tony socked Zed in the face a few more times. He felt that he was already at the threshold of a concussion. When Tony's fist matched with the back of Zed's head on the concrete, the world turned black. But he could hear Tony's heavy boots running away, so he wasn't completely knocked out. Staggering to his feet, people were standing around and gasping. He held his hand up and said it was all right, it was just part of the job. The tracker was now down a side alley that had a plume of exhaust smoke concealing it. Zed rushed through without fear and caught sight of Tony just as he was passing a DNA scan on a security door. Zed thought this must be a secret escape route. He stuck his metal hand in the door just as Tony was shutting it. The pain sensors started freaking out as Tony started kicking the door on Zed's hand. Counting the beats in Tony's kicks, Zed was able to time it just right. While Tony was rebalancing for another strike, Zed lunged through the door with his metallic arm outstretched. He caught Tony with an elbow to the chin, and they both fell back onto a rusted-out metal railing over a gigantic open pit. With a clean metallic crunch, the railing snapped under their combined weight.

They began to free fall.

Time stopped while Zed looked Tony in that glowing red eye, realizing the trouble they were both in. His mind instantly took in every detail of the surroundings and concluded rather quickly that they were both fucked. It took less than a second for them to make the fifteen-meter drop into that black hole, but it seemed like an eternity of them falling in an everlasting struggle. They were both reaching out to grab the other in a vain attempt to shift their fall. When they finally hit the dirt, neither of them moved for some time. Sounds of screams echoed off the buildings from above, with people peaking their heads out of windows that overlooked the dark pit. When Zed finally came around and moved, there was a pool of blood coming out of Tony's skull. A visual notification on his display notified him that Tony was deceased and the bounty reward was cut in half.

"Just my fucking luck," Zed cursed as he lay back down, exhausted.

THE REALITY NOW

SWAN: Good evening Omega citizens, I am Swansong McNigh, and this is The Reality Now. Tonight, I want to address the situation that has been on everyone's mind for as long as we can remember. It's been well over one hundred years since our dome at OC6 passed the recommended capacity. Despite that, every day a new batch of wasteland refugees flood into our cities ready to eat our food, occupy our living quarters, and take what precious job opportunities we have left. It's more than just jobs and housing. At what point— if ever—will the OS say enough is enough? How many more people can we push into our system before it breaks? Or, can the OS provide for us all, as the slogan states? Don't just take my opinion on the subject. Joining us tonight is Jaime Morales and Jillian Westwood. As always, I'll be asking them to pick a side!

SWAN: Let's start with Jaime. He's a Zone Three pastry chef at Chez Luv in the park, and he believes no one should be rejected from life under the dome. In his words, 'turning them away is a death sentence.'

JAIME: That's right, Swan. My mother came to the city when New Chicago collapsed. It was a rough transition, but without the Omega City I wouldn't be here today. I know there are camps of people outside the dome still waiting for entry, and that makes a lot of people worried, but having lived under the dome my whole life, I can tell you there is still plenty of space and resources here to accommodate them all.

SWAN: Right. Let's turn to Jillian now. She is a Zone Six VR film producer, and she stands firm on the idea that more people will only cause the system to collapse.

JILLIAN: We let them in today, and tomorrow we'll be hungry. I am a third-generation citizen, my parents were first born, and I can tell you that there has been a steady decline in the quality of life each and every year the gates stay open. The Council of Seven set the parameters for the city to function optimally, and we surpassed that mark long ago. So far, we have survived, but any day now it will all come crashing down and we will all be living in the dust. We need to shut the gates and we need to do it now. Take back our city!

JAIME: Your viewpoint from the Six is skewed. None of the people coming in even affect the life in your zone. Most of these refugees never even make it out of Hope City, where living situations are the real crisis we should be talking about. Have you even been there?

JILLIAN: I would never go down there. You would never catch me down there.

JAIME: Of course not. There is nothing for you. Meanwhile, in the next two zones, people do absolutely nothing for the community, and live comfortably off their LSI.

SWAN: We are straying from the subject here. What does this have to do with the refugees?

JAIME: I think we should keep letting them in as long as we can. And I think we shouldn't treat the refugees like zeroed out criminals. Do you know that only one in five hundred refugees makes it to the numbers? That's unacceptable. We should be offering them the same LSI that any other Omega citizen is given freely. The OS will provide. Do we want our legacy to be a monument of corpses outside our walls because we are too selfish to share?

JILLIAN: So, his answer is to give them more. I'll be living in the gutter by the end of the week. Sir, my family has worked for generations to build our community and you want to give it away to some beggar at the door. Their family had their choice to live here in the beginning, or any other Omega City, and they chose to stay out there. So, let them stay! That was their choice, and they should live with the consequences.

SWAN: Well, there you have it, citizens. Should we let the refugees stay in the outer lands and possibly starve, or let them in and suffocate our economy? It sounds like a tough choice to me. Maybe we should just pick a side, because this is the Reality Now.

TWENTY-THREE

On the other side of the city, Ash Starbrooke was trying to remember the last time she physically left her building or even her living quarters. Not that she was some kind of recluse, she actually loved the outdoors. It was that the outside world just wasn't for her anymore, at least not in her own body. But tonight, she threw caution to the wind and took a leisurely stroll through Middle Park. Even though it was chilly earlier, it had somehow warmed to a point that she didn't need a jacket. It felt good being out in the warm night air. The sensation of goosebumps on her skin from a drifting breeze was something that virtual reality and synthetic avatars never got right. It was a refreshing reminder she was still, in fact, alive.

The streets of Zone Six were all but empty as she made her way eastward in an unconscious manner. She only noticed a few people as blurred shapes and blotches of color many blocks away, passing under street lamps. Other lone souls in the dead of the night. Her footsteps echoed through a canyon of darkened buildings. Their dark windows looked like glossy granite tombstones towering over a concrete lawn that was devoid of pedestrians and autocar traffic. Never in her life had she witnessed such a still and quiet night in Omega City 6. Maybe the absence of other humans is what drew her out of her cozy penthouse dwellings.

Suddenly, her bare foot landed in a patch of cool damp grass. The feeling came as a slight shock, unaware that she had forgotten to put shoes on. She ignored the odd oversite, as the grass felt good sliding through her toes, and caused an overwhelming sensation of happiness. Memories of playing with her brother in the park when she was a child came over her as if her mind had connected to something long lost. Laughter, scraped knees, blue skies, strawberry ice cream, secret hiding places, ladybugs, and fields of green grass. They had known every inch of every park that was near their living quarters. Even with all the virtual gadgets, their parents had bought them, their love of the outside world made it impossible to keep both of them inside. At any hour of any day, they would be off somewhere getting into mischief.

Missing her brother, she glanced up at the night sky through the dome. It was its usual dark, empty abyss. The light pollution made it impossible for even a single star to shine through. Then, to her surprise, a few stars came into focus. One by one more shone until the sky was littered with little sparkling dots. She whispered her brother's name to herself, Anton, as if casting some kind of magical spell. It made her chest fill with a warming sensation. She knew he was still out there somewhere, no matter what anyone would ever tell her. A sharp, warm breeze blew from the west, and it seemed as if the trees were speaking to her as the leaves rustled in the swaying branches. It truly was a mystical evening.

That uplifting feeling came crashing down suddenly as sounds of heavy feet could be heard moving through the grass behind her. At such a late hour, without a single person in sight, and not even on a walking path, why would someone be so close? She immediately feared the worst. Visions flashed through her mind of a swift, cold blade slicing her throat. Blood violently spitting out and rushing down her white-lace blouse, making a red pool, thick like paint, over the soft green grass. Clenching her fists, she damned herself for letting her imagination run away again. It was disturbing. Taking a deep breath, she urged herself to turn around and face the oncoming person, knowing deep down there was nothing to fear. The OS was watching.

"Where did you come from?" she exclaimed, seeing a beautiful ebony-colored horse before her eyes. It was saddled and everything. The horse neighed cheerfully, as if to say hello. "I didn't even know there were horses in the city. But where is your owner?"

Glancing around, the streets and the park were still empty. She looked questioningly at the direction the horse had come from, but there was no one there. It was just her and the stallion, and a wonderful new feeling of excitement. She had dreamt of riding a horse ever since she first saw one. It was a rainy day when it happened. They couldn't go outside, so Anton had put on a virtual experience about wild west cowboys, and she was instantly captivated. The freedom they exhibited. They were so majestic. Gentle and powerful at the same time. She reached her hand up slowly, and the horse nudged its nose to it. The cool dampness that she felt on her palm was a pleasant counterpoint to the warm air exhaling from the nostrils. Her heart was melting. She ran her other hand through the mane, finding it soft and warm. The horse nudged her hand again and then turned its head towards the saddle.

"You want me to get on?" she gasped, thinking of all the time she had spent in a virtual horseback riding trainer, just in case one day she would find herself outside the dome and in the saddle. The dream had come to her today in the strangest of ways. There was no way she could resist the temptation. "I don't think I can pass up this chance. I'll do it! But only if you promise to be gentle." The horse neighed and nodded its head reassuringly.

Placing her bare foot in the stirrup and gripping the horn, she kicked up with a swift motion and swung her leg over with ease. It felt so natural. Picking up the reins gently, she gave a soft tug with her right hand. The horse responded by turning, so they were facing the long and open stretch of the park. What could it hurt to take a quick ride? The horse trotted forward without even being told to do so, and the small amount of movement inspired her. Before she realized it, she was nudging the horse with her heel. The horse responded by changing the trot to a full-on gallop. They darted towards the tree line with haste, with the wind rushing through her hair and causing more goosebumps to pop up all over her arms. It was exhilarating.

Once in the trees, the horse picked a line and raced on. The passing trees amplified the speed they moved, without an ounce of worry entering her mind. They zipped through the scenery like birds in flight. Ducking under neck-breaking branches and jumping over fallen trees. She had no idea that OC6 even had such a lush forest.

As they passed an outcropping of boulders, a deep, terrifying roar came from behind. Looking back, a pair of glowing green eyes illuminated the night, sending shivers down her spine. A massive shadowy figure suddenly lunged onto the path, bowling through the underbrush and chasing after them. Just as before, her mood changed dramatically. Snapping the reins forcefully, she hoped the horse wasn't already moving at its top speed. They quickly maneuvered through trees and bushes, dodging boulders and hillside drop-offs. She felt assured the horse knew the full extent of the sudden danger that was pursuing them. Glancing back, the beast had cut the previous distance between them in half. It was still a mass of empty blackness, but the green eyes were now paired with glints of long claws kicking up dirt as it ran, and pointed teeth that seemed to glimmer under the starry sky.

The horse jumped over a small cliff, with Ash holding on as hard as she could. The beast wasn't slowed a bit by the abrupt fall. Instead, it seemed to gain speed. Another large boulder outcropping was ahead on the right, and the horse steered in that direction. She could feel the heat from the beast's breath on the back of her neck. The sounds of it huffing and panting filled her ears, causing her to be overcome with terror. Again, she pictured her neck being sliced open and blood spewing out. A peek behind her shoulder revealed razor-sharp teeth chomping at the air only a few inches from her face.

The boulders were dead ahead. The horse took to the air, dodging a deadly bite. It was more than a jump—they seemed to be flying. The ground was continuously slipping away. Up and up they went until their flight reached a gentle pinnacle. Then gravity shifted, and she watched as the earth came back slowly. She was sure they were gliding down instead of falling, as the descent was gradual and easy. But as the ground came closer, she could see that the beast was still not far behind. She urged the horse to jump again immediately. Once the hooves were on the dirt, it kicked back up to leap. The beast was quicker though, and it caught one of the horse's hind legs in its massive jaws. Now there was blood gushing out for real. She cried out in agony, but her voice was lost in the whipping wind. Instead of letting her go down with the struggle, the horse launched Ash into the night air.

She was flying away as if weightless. It felt like some force was pushing her up and outwards. As she looked back through her fluttering hair, she could see the beast tearing the horse apart with murderous brutality.

Now above the trees, she could see all of Middle Park and the rest of OC6 silently sleeping. Something wasn't right. Even with all the madness going on, from one glance she instantly knew that the skyline was different. Everything was out of place. None of the buildings were recognizable at all. Her flight had once again hit its peak. But this time she suddenly found herself falling down rapidly. Trying to fight the fall was hopeless, as her arms and legs felt paralyzed. Thousands of virtual simulations in thousands of scenarios, and she had never experienced such levels of desperation and fear. The ground was coming quick, and oncoming buildings filled her vision in a mad collage of passing colors. Bracing for eventual doom, she squeezed her eye shut. But it never came. Her descent quickly slowed until it ended with a very gentle landing.

Panting heavily, she looked around at her new surroundings. Nothing seemed familiar. There were half-destroyed buildings everywhere, piles of concrete rubble, and dozens of burnt-out autocars. Words were painted on doors, *DEAD INSIDE*, and all the leaves and grass were brittle and brown. It was a corpse of a city.

Concrete steps were before her, leading up to a large brick church with immense stained-glass windows that were glowing a bright magenta from within. The light poked out from a crack in the massive wooden doors at the top of the steps. The strangeness of the situation numbed her with fear. Before she knew it, she was getting to her feet and walking towards the church. The light grew more intense as she opened the door slowly and slipped through. Only by squinting could she make out the source. A huge open book on a wooden altar below a large hanging cross. Not hesitating, she made her way down the aisle between rows of heavy oak pews. The light was blinding. The closer she got, the more it felt as if it was pushing against her. Taking the first of three steps upwards, her heart started pounding as the light seemed to emanate a low, humming, digital noise. Putting her hand in front of her eyes, she crept forward, determined to see what the source was. Once at the altar, she could see a book that looked like a bible. On the dusty pages, a strange symbol was radiating the odd magenta light. What did it mean?

A jolt came over her as something abruptly clasped onto her bare ankle. She looked down and was shocked to see a skeletal hand covered with gray bits of rotten flesh clenching her leg. Pulling away from it made it worse, as it pulled back with an equal force. She fell to the ground as more hands burst out through the brittle floorboards. They grabbed onto different parts of her body and clawed at her flesh. One leaped onto her face and dug its nails into her eyeballs. She tried to scream out in agony, but found she had no voice.

Wake up.

Ash leaped up and screamed out loud. She was alone in her penthouse, sitting upright on her couch, with a half-finished sandwich on her lap. Sweat dotted her forehead, her hair was a mess, and her vision was blurred in the nightmare's wake. Still disoriented from the dream, she looked around her living quarters absentmindedly. The sun had gone down, and the penthouse was only lit by the faint glow of the holographic screen that was still playing the feed she was watching before she dozed off. An alert started flashing abruptly on her display.

"Shit. Shit. Shit," she cursed, making a swiping gesture with her hand that turned her HUD's night mode off. Her bank account zoomed into view. She had it set to alert her when any sizeable amount was added. She suddenly had a significantly higher amount than the last time she had checked, and it was quickly ticking upwards. She immediately opened the menu to the twenty-four-hour wine store that was conveniently located on the ground floor of her building and looked for the most expensive case of wine the store had in stock. The second it was in her virtual cart, the purchase button was smashed.

"This wine better be good," she laughed sadly, as she watched her bank account fall back down to a more comfortable number.

Switching the stream on her wall-sized holoscreen to her own channel, her recent nightmare was already uploaded as a dreamcast. It was being experienced by thousands of people, exactly the way she just had, complete with the horse, the beast, and the fear-induced panic attack. With each tick of the number that indicated the virtual views, her bank account increased. Don't these people sleep? It was yet another day she regretted letting herself get neural chipped so many years ago.

A snapshot of her horrified face was the thumbnail of the video clip. Very unflattering. But her dark brown hair was silky and wavy as it rested on her soft-pink, form-fitting blouse. She was grateful that even in an unconscious state she could make herself look pretty. Waking up on the couch meant that she was still in the same food-stained pajamas she had been wearing all week, with greasy matted hair that hadn't been washed in the same amount of time. There really was a golden-brown, well-toned body underneath all that mess, she had paid a lot at the DNA clinic for the gene alterations. But in the end, it didn't really matter what she looked like. She rarely went outside, especially in her own body. And after that nightmare, she didn't know if she ever would again.

A bottle of pill-shaped supplements was on the table before her. She was trying out a new dream deterrent that her naturopath program had suggested.

After six weeks of several fistfuls of pills a day, it seemed they weren't going to work. That last dreamcast might break some personal view count record. Without getting off the couch, she picked the bottle up and tossed it towards the wastebin in the kitchen. It missed, and the crashing sound sent her white Persian cat skating across the floor. Deflating into the couch, she let out a long sigh, knowing that a sweaty, shaky panic attack with lingering anxiety was right around the corner. A thud at her balcony door signaled the arrival of her old-fashioned anti-anxiety medication. Nothing a few glasses of wine couldn't fix. Through her floor-to-ceiling windows, she could see the drone zipping away. The outside lights illuminated slowly on her huge patio, thirty-five stories in the air. Rain was coming down as she got up to retrieve the package.

"Back to the old routine," she said, popping open the box and gripping a fresh bottle.

Fifteen minutes and a hot shower later, she knew the wine wouldn't cut it. It was late, she should actually be sleeping now. But knowing herself well enough, there wouldn't be a wink of sleep until the sun filled the sky. No matter how hard she tried, she couldn't keep anything other than vampire hours. Most of her neighbors were important people, who lived very active and stressful lives. She thought they must think of her as the phantom lady of Zone Six, a stranger in their paradise. Catch a glimpse if you can. Thank the OS for Cody. If it wasn't for her, living in the Six would be hell. She was the only person Ash knew who also kept unusual hours. Maybe she was awake.

"You up? Can't sleep." Ash messaged Cody, before she started twisting away at the corkscrew, and wishing she had taken the time to order a case of screw-top bottles.

"Hey!" the reply came almost instantly. "In a tournament."

"Oh shoot. Don't let me bother you." She poured a glass and took a sip, not caring to wait for it to breathe. Mmm, she thought, tastes like wine.

"Almost done." Cody messaged back. "Tune in if you want to. Down to hang after."

● ● ●

Cody never understood why Omega City 4 always insisted on fighting at dawn. As the golden light of the morning sun sent shadows over the apocalyptic terrain, she checked her ammo clip—still half full. Level 3 virtual had a drastically different formula than normal games. The hardest part was re-training herself to not just reload after every round fired. The ammunition and guns she carried had an actual weight. If she swapped out a clip that was still had bullets in it, she would lose those bullets, and she needed them to win.

It had been more than a year since she was actually on the Paris battlefield. It had changed slightly. Explosions had knocked some buildings down, lea-ving a tangled mesh of wire and concrete. New platforms and walkways had been added to some buildings to make up for the destruction, but the cover they provided was for shit. She stayed to the older buildings even if they were structurally risky. Some of the ammo drops seemed to be in different loca-tions, but if she remembered correctly there was only one spawning point for the legendary drop she needed.

"Cool." Ash's reply came across her HUD, "I'll switch to your feed. I bought a crate of expensive wine to celebrate your victory. So hurry up!"

"Yes, mam!" exclaimed, as her voice translated to text and sent it to Ash.

The left arm of her avatar was slightly damaged, with sparks flying out of the busted silicone shell. Thankfully, it was affecting the hardware more than it was causing her actual pain. Her left hand wasn't responding correctly either. With a character build that relied on dual-wielding, her skills were seriously compromised. At least she was still in the game. The blast that damaged her arm had taken out five of her squad. KO'd. In Level 3 there was no respawning. When your avatar goes down, you go down—and it hurts like hell. The OC4 and OC3 teams were completely out of the battle. OC2 and OC5 only had scouts left. Her last squad mate, Billy_2_six, was off playing cowboy somewhere. He was an idiot, but at least he would provide a perfect distraction for sniper fire while she covered the last bit of ground needed to reach the drop. She hoped it was still there.

"You still out there, Billy?" she yelled into her mic.

"You know it, sweetheart," he hooted back.

"I'm in position."

"What's the plan?"

"Blaze of glory time."

"Alright Cody. You're the boss. Callin' the rocket now."

Looking through her binoculars at Billy's location, she could see his rocket bike zipping across the dusty Parisian streets. Zooming in further, she could see him swapping out his plasma rifle for his massive laser cannon. The plan was for him to kamikaze the position that they thought OC1 was holding in a derelict building, giving her a window of opportunity while he inevitably got shot up in the process. From her position in a fifth-story window, she looked across the daunting rooftop that needed to be crossed. There would be no cover for her run. She would be left wide open to a volley of fire from the OC1 team. That is, unless they were distracted.

"Oorah mother fucker!" Billy_2_Six yelled over his headset, metaphorically squealing out on his rocket bike while shooting off gigantic laser blasts.

The OC1 squad was known for running a defender on their team. In fact, he was one of the highest-ranking defenders in the league. A crucial part of the plan relied on him deploying a protective shield to counter the oncoming laser volley. After that, the defender would need several minutes for his skills to reload. In that time, she hoped to be within striking distance. Billy's hot-pink laser fire was ripping through buildings and striking the general area they thought OC1 would be in. Suddenly an electric blue bubble popped up on a building to her left. Perfect. Billy's laser fire had forced them into giving away their position. It was time for her to move.

The second that return fire started shooting out of broken windows, she sprinted off as fast as she could. This was the moment that made her an A-list player above the rest. She wasn't the best at shooting a gun or riding a rocket bike, but in real life she could sprint a quarter-mile in under a minute, practiced yoga and parkour daily, and held black belts in multiple martial arts. That's why she preferred Level 3 virtual as opposed to all others. Except for special skill abilities, all player avatars movements and actions were based on their user's real-life physical and mental abilities. Because she was fast in real-life, her agility was off the charts in the game.

Flying on the tips of her toes, she focused on the destination and tried not to worry if she had been spotted or not. The edge of the rooftop was coming on quick. Without hesitating, she leapt into the air across a five-story drop. Catching a window ledge with her fingertips, she flipped her momentum and bounced back towards the building she just jumped from. In mid-air, she grabbed onto the bottom rail of a blasted-out balcony. It enabled her to swing into a parallel type of jump. On the wall before her there was a three-by-two-foot window. She darted through feet first. Her acrobatic performance was the only way anyone could get inside the small indestructible room that contained the "Cloak and Shield" drop.

"They got me, Cody. I'm going down!" Billy yelled over a barrage of gunfire.

An explosion outside told the rest of the story.

She had to stay focused. It was up to her to win it for the OC6 squad. A light-purple orb glowed in nuclear-green flames, hovered in the center of the room she had flown into. Wasting no time, she placed her hand on the orb and absorbed the highly prized bonus power. Energy coursed through her body as the power engulfed her. Her avatar would be invisible to other players until she used a weapon or a skill—that was the cloaking part. At that moment, her avatar's appearance would return to normal, but she would be immune to a certain amount of damage afterward—that was the shield part. The shield wasn't enough to stop a barrage of plasma fire, but she could take a few quick shots while executing a risky maneuver. Some players called the Cloak and Shield overpowered, but getting in and out of the location of the spawning point was a challenge on any battlefield. Only a few people could actually accomplish it.

Now to get back out.

As she turned her back towards the only window or door in the concrete room, she hoped she had the strength to complete the task. Running full steam at the opposing wall, she leapt at it like a cat, pushing off with all her might and rotating her body in the air. Grabbing a ceiling-mounted light fixture, she kicked up her legs and sprang through the tiny window once again. She was still several stories up, so once through the window she had to reverse once again and grab an intact metal balcony one story below. Now it was only a two-story drop. That was something her added leg compensators could handle. A rain of laser fire rained down on her position as she let go of the balcony. Even though they couldn't see her, they had guessed her tactic and were firing blind. They were too late. Even with the shots being fired at the ground below the CnS spawn room, she was already crossing the blast-ridden street and aiming a grappling gun at a rear point of entry. Thankfully, the rulebook didn't consider the grappling gun a weapon, and her cloak remained active. The hook sunk itself deep into the plaster-coated wall. She zipped up the line, shooting right past the hook point. She landed as softly as she could through a blast hole in the building's side.

Five members of OC1 were right in front of her. Unfortunately, Billy's laser cannon wasn't able to get a clean shot on any of them before their shield went up. The defender was indeed strong. But with his skills still on cooldown, he would be a sitting duck. Checking her timer that she started when the now expired shield had first gone up, a quick calculation told her she had precious time to spare. She was gambling that their squad didn't have a second defender. Because the defender's "spotting" ability was the only thing that could counter her cloak. If they had one, she was burnt. At five to one, it didn't matter how fast she was when gunfire was concerned.

Two soldiers were still firing away at the street-side window, one facing each flank, and the defender in the back. Time for her to shine. She pulled a high-level corrosive blade out from its sheath and moved silently towards the one in the back. A quick swipe across his neck and his health bar reduced to zero. Brutality. Her cloak faded away as the first body hit the ground with a thud. Activating her double gun skill, two pistols popped out of wrist harnesses and she was ready to blast. With arms extended in opposite directions, she took out the two flanking guards with burst charges. The front two turned to her with weapons firing. The shield worked like a charm, saving her from a lethal barrage as she swiftly took aim at their heads. Two pops and the OC1 squad was history.

A metal box was on the floor in a pile of sizzling synthetic bodies, glowing red with the bold Big Gun logo in white. She kicked it open to reveal a hyper cube inside. To win the game a team needed to escort the cube off the field to their starting quadrant. OC1 had gained the box early in the match but had failed to make their escape. They were a brute force squad, not known for playing runners. Today, it was their downfall. Agility had won over strength once again. There were still some stragglers out there, holding out for the chance to get a cheap shot in and pull out a victory, but Cody wouldn't let that happen. Looking out the window at Billy's busted-up bike, she could see the bike's dedicated repair drone hard at work getting it back to operational. In a minute, she would be on the rocket bike and speeding her way to victory.

"Still up to your dirty tricks?" a message came across her vision, causing Cody to sigh. The user's name was "Vlad_The_Inhaler," who was someone she'd rather not waste time with.

"Buzz off," she said, lowering herself out the window and preparing to fall.

"Finals are coming," Vlad replied, with Cody adding a bad Russian accent to his words in her head. "I will show you no mercy."

"Bring it, loser."

"Victory will be mine."

"Yeah. Okay. Say hi to your mom for me," Cody laughed, muting Vlad's account.

The repair bots were done with the rocket bike. The sun was now high in the sky over what was left of beautiful Paris. She took a moment to enjoy being out in the real world, even if it was in a generic avatar on a blown-out battlefield. She knew she needed to move. Only a newb gets shot taking in the scenery.

Ten minutes later, she was logging off the server. Her digital avatar could finish the victory ceremony for her. She didn't feel like hanging out in virtual any longer. But she did take the time and thank all her new subs and the people who gave her digital currency as a gift. The victory purse wasn't that big after the split with the rest of her squad, but she had gained numerous followers on her channel. That would net her a lot of credits in the long run. It was still about advertising money in the end.

Taking off the virtual pads from her temples, her eyes adjusted to her apartment back in reality. A dark, empty room surrounded her as she sat up in her glowing virtual pod. The morning sun of Paris was replaced with the night sky of Omega City 6. The excitement of battle, and the glory of victory, was replaced with a dull, quiet room filled with workout equipment instead of furniture. An old t-shirt and a dirty pair of shorts replaced her legendary battle armor that she had earned through years and years of fighting. But the twinkling lights of the cityscape blinked on and off at her, reminding her that real life was still something to marvel over.

A glass of wine did sound nice.

"Hey," she messaged Ash. "I'm out. Victory is mine! HAHA. Let me shower and freshen up. I feel like a dirty sock."

"Don't waste your time. Get your butt over here before I drink it all."

TWENTY-TWO

"Where the hell are you, Takeda?" Enforcer Karl Boyd yelled into his system's internal mic, as he stood outside the Daily Double in the cold night air.

He had messaged Zed several times already because he never knew him to ignore duty when it was calling. There was no time to worry about it now. Over half of all the city's enforcers were lined up on Synth Row outside the weapons storage center, ready to move out once orders were given. He'd been pulling double patrol shifts in Hope City lately, trying to earn extra credits, and he had only been asleep a few hours when the call came through. He wiped the sleep out of his dark-brown eyes while he did his best to straighten up his thick, black, tight-curled hair and beard. Not having time to dress properly, he hoped the clothes that he picked up off the floor from yesterday weren't too wrinkly. He stretched his large arms out, trying to loosen the muscles in his extremely broad shoulders, as his stomach growled at him. Too many beers before bed.

A synthetic enforcer finally showed up and cleared the storage unit to be unlocked. Seconds after the metal roller gate was flung open, the line started moving. All gunpowder-based weapons were outlawed in the Omega System, so enforcers weren't issued any kind of weapon for their regular duties or patrols. That's not to say that they couldn't provide their own line of self-defense. While Zed was partial to combat knives and trained in multiple martial arts, Boyd was more of a brawler who wore fingerless leather gloves with padded knuckles at all times. He wasn't much of a fighter in actuality, relying on technology to keep him out of harm's way whenever he could. But being as big as he was, he found that fist-to-cuffs worked to his advantage when the situation called for it. Today wasn't a regular patrol, and they weren't on an ordinary duty call. Each enforcer was being issued a stun rifle and an identification armband. When Boyd got to the front of the line, the synthetic enforcer put his hand up abruptly for Boyd to wait.

"Boyd!" Rodriquez shouted, pushing his way through the unorganized group of enforcers. "You're on tech ops today, so grab whatever you need for close quarters and leave the guns for the rest. I have a crate of drones and other gear already on the truck."

"Roger that," Boyd said with a feeling of relief. Behind a screen and off the front line was the place he preferred to be. He had been in enough scrapes to know that eventually, he was going to get injured so badly that an autodoc wouldn't be able to patch him up. He brought the weapon menu up on his display and selected a stun baton from the inventory before pulling it out of the corresponding locker.

"You heard from Zed?" Boyd asked, as he caught up with Rodriquez.

"Takeda? Last I saw him, he was headed out to a script box. Probably at home and passed out by now. Lousy drunk."

"Zed's not one to miss out on work, especially when it's a priority call."

"Takeda's probably already in there," a different enforcer proclaimed, who had overheard their conversation, "puttin' the bad guys to bed so we don't have to."

"Alright, listen up!" Rodriquez boomed, causing all the enforcers to cut their chatter and pay attention. "Not fifteen minutes ago we received an anonymous tip from a counsel booth that members of the Roland Royals have been running a child prostitution ring at one of their known properties in Hope City. Graphic images and videos were sent over a secure data transfer to the OS, who authenticated the files before sending out the work order. I don't need to remind any of you of the severity of these claims, or the punishment that is justifiably due. This falls under the big five of crime, people. You all know what that means. They can't pay their way out of this one. If we find evidence that the claims are true, then exile for all participants will be carried out in a swift and efficient manner.

"We are heading into gang territory, so I want everyone to proceed with extreme caution. We will split up into two squads and approach from opposite ends of Roland Street. Enforcer Boyd will run tech ops, so we will wait for his intel before we strike. This is what we signed up for folks. Let's go get these assholes."

Two large, self-driven container trucks rolled up after Rodriquez finished his speech. As usual, the trucks were rentals with advertisements for a produce company strewn across the outer sides. Enforcers weren't a police force, because the Omega Cities didn't have police or jails, and they weren't a private militia because armies no longer existed. They were a cross between private security and organized vigilante bounty hunters. No one answered to anyone—except the OS—and they only made credits by catching criminals in the act, and usually only in Hope City. The OS had complete surveillance over the rest of the city and doled out automatic fines to anyone, anywhere who was dumb or rich enough to commit a petty crime.

The plainclothes group of men and women piled into the trucks, grabbing the handrails that ran across the ceiling. Small blue armbands were the only thing that identified them as a collective group. Once they were all in, the truck moved out with dozens of people swaying back and forth like on a rickety subway car. Boyd tapped into the truck's computer system and set the walls of the cargo area so it was transparent from the inside, like a one-way mirror. A sigh of relief was expressed from several people. Being able to see outside helped the sensation of claustrophobia that was thick in the air. They silently watched as the truck turned up the ramp to the entrance of Hope City.

They were stopped at the gate like everyone else. The scan of the trucks must have immediately set off dozens of alerts with the guards on duty, because they suddenly bombarded Boyd with a ton of demands and questions. As the operating host to their party, he was prepared, and promptly provided all the proper identifications, permits, and work orders from the OS. He eyed up the names of the people on duty to see if any of them were known snitches for the gangs, a few thousand credits would go a long way to keep someone's mouth shut. In this case, it wouldn't matter. They were rolling so deep that as soon as they set foot on Roland or Buxton Street, they would tip both gangs off to their presence. The guard gave them the clearance they needed and ordered the truck down a cargo service ramp.

In order for Hope City to be its own self-sustaining city, it relied heavily on buying goods from the automated factories and farms run by the Omega Systems outside of the dome. Space was needed to store all those goods, and that was the primary reason the street level of Hope City was raised three stories above ground. The commandeered space was gutted and transformed into one massive communal warehouse. Boyd looked through the see-through walls of the truck and marveled at the hundreds of people that were moving about and keeping the city alive. Hundreds of trucks lined both sides of the road with people unloading goods or packing up containers for the delivery drones that were flying around just as abundantly underground as anywhere else in OC6.

"That could be you out there, Cable," someone said in jest to the young rookie. "There's still time left to put this life behind you and work a civilian job."

"It's not for me," the kid, who looked barely a day over eighteen, said proudly. "I signed up because I actually want to help people out, unlike some of you meat sacks."

"You can start by helping me out," a female Enforcer said, crudely grabbing at her crotch.

"Better keep your head down, kid," someone else laughed. "We wouldn't want that pretty face of yours damaged. You might make some easy credits with it as an avatar model when you can't cut it in No Hope anymore."

"I'll be here long after you retire," Cable said, keeping a confident smile on his face.

The enforcer next to Boyd leaned in and asked quietly, "Hey Boyd. What's up with Cable? Is he really a rookie?"

Boyd opened up the duty roster on his display and gave it a look over before replying. "Afraid so. Looks like this is his first real gig, other than some easy patrols."

"No way he is from No Hope," the enforcer said, almost spitting on the ground as he spoke. "I bet he didn't even do a tour of duty."

"Everyone has to do a stint. You know that. He might be from the numbers, but I'm sure he spent time in the mud like the rest of us."

"Probably worked the canteen, the little prick."

"Cut him some slack, will you?" Boyd protested, adjusting his stance. "So what? He wasn't zeroed out like the rest of us before signing up. It takes a better person to work this job just because they want to." The other enforcer rolled his eyes at Boyd's comments. "Hey. Do me a favor? Keep him off the front today?"

"Sorry, KB. I watch out for no one but myself," the man said, and as if to prove a point, he turned around so his back was facing Boyd.

"Yeah. I'll remember that."

The trucks rolled to a stop under Nakamoto square. It was about as close as they could get to the target area. Dozens of brand-new luxury autotrucks with Nakamoto logos adorning their exteriors lined up along a security glass wall that blocked off a massive area to Nakamoto industries. Nakamoto was hands down the richest person in Hope City. Coming in from the outer lands as a first citizen, he played a crucial part in the break from the rest of OC6. He helped to develop the closed currency chip system that was used by everyone who lived or visited Hope City, but that's not why he was rich. Starting as a simple merchant, he made big moves early on. He understood the concept of supply and demand. His office on the sixtieth floor of the building he owned, over the massive warehouse that took up half of the underground storage center, was a testament to his business sense.

As the enforcers unloaded from the cargo trucks, a group of uniformed Nakamoto security officers moved to positions along the wall and took up aggressive stances. Boyd raised a hand to them and waited a moment for them to acknowledge or say something. He knew they wouldn't, though. Corporate security might as well be synthetics the way they were so obtuse. He swiped his hand through the air and transferred all the same credentials he had at the front gate over to their systems. By the time they got through checking everything, Boyd would be gone. Rodriquez got the enforcers into an orderly fashion as Boyd led the way to the nearest elevator station.

A dozen unique symbols glowed on Boyd's display in an electric-blue font. He sifted through them quickly until he found the one that he wanted and plugged it into his navigational system. Hope City didn't have a traditional map on purpose, because they didn't want outsiders roaming around the city anywhere further than the tourist designated areas by the front gate. Boyd only wanted the pathway to Crowbar Alley, even though he knew the way already. He linked his nav system with the rest of the squads in case anyone— in particular the rookies—might not understand where they were going. When they came to the elevator station, they divided up into small units and held the doors of the cars open until they had enough room for all of them to fit and ascend at the same time. Hope City prided itself on its verticality, having multiple different pedestrian levels on walkways throughout the entire area. A person could live and die and never set foot on the actual ground. In such an environment, elevators were crucial. The stations that dotted the city were almost as busy as the subway stations were in the numbers.

They took the ride up to the street level in unison, and when they exited the elevator cars, their sight was intimidating and impressive. They were going up against a major street gang, so they needed to be a gang themselves. Boyd balled his hands into fists to feel his leather gloves crackle over his knuckles. He felt safe thinking that the other enforcers were checking in on their own concealed weapons at the same time. If things took a turn for worse, the stun weapons wouldn't be much help.

The Roland Royals dominated half a busy commercial and entertainment district. The opposing gang, the Buxton Bruisers, controlled the other half. Running between the two major streets—Roland and Buxton respectively— there was Crowbar Alley, a neutral territory and home to the black market of Omega City 6. The Alley got its name from the twists and turns it had that it made it look like a crowbar when viewing it from above. While Nakamoto Tower was the largest building in Hope City, and only a half dozen blocks away, most of the buildings in the gang district were all under twenty stories with no aerial walkways. Having never added floors after the split, and always been under control by one gang or another, the strength of the properties was that only their people occupied the buildings and their people alone. The Royal's headquarters was at 107 Roland, almost near the eastern end of the street. The building that they had been tipped off about was at 117 Roland. Into the heart of darkness.

As they approached the western edge of Roland, Boyd launched one of his surveillance drones that was disguised to look like it was used for food delivery with takeout food and all. He made a pass of the crowded street, full of people headed to one of the gang-operated clubs that had cheap drink prices, offered plenty of flesh for sale, and usually ran illegal gambling operations out of the back. There were plenty of crimes being committed at any of these clubs at any given time, but busting up one of them for a bunch of petty fines would be like starting a war that the enforcers wouldn't win. Once the drone was clear of the street, Boyd had it run a random automated route that would eventually circle around to the rendezvous point. He had plenty of drones to use and didn't want to risk exposing them just yet by having one revealed as a probe. Once the drone was on autopilot, he shared the footage with the rest of the enforcers, highlighting the target and any potential problems they might be up against.

"Looks like we've got two sentries standing guard by the front entrance," he said over the comms system to the entire squad. "Expect them to be armed with knives and melee weapons. Surveillance systems are all over the street. I can't jam them all, and an EMP blast large enough to take them out would cause too much damage to the surrounding area. What I can do is detonate a drone flash bomb that will temporarily blind the system, giving us enough time to take out the guards and breach the perimeter.

"Thermal scans show that there are about thirty people on the main floor in the first room. Looks like some gambling tables. There's about another two-dozen people scattered on the rest of the ground and second floors. I can't identify their ages from the scans, but if this is about child prostitution, then these would be the areas to investigate. The rest of the floors seem to be residential, with over half the occupants likely to be jacked into their VR beds. I'll work on getting a drone on the inside to gather more intel before the breach."

"Excellent work, Enforcer Boyd," Rodriquez complimented him over the comms. "I want you to go with Delta group. Cut through Crowbar to Buxton and circle around to the east side of Roland. Alpha group will remain concealed on this end and stop the flow of pedestrian traffic. When you're ready, give the signal and we will start the assault. This is a no mercy mission. That means stun anyone who is in your path."

Everyone gave a verbal confirmation before moving to their assigned positions. Boyd hustled down Crowbar Alley while he launched several small drones that were basically a camera, a propeller, and a transmitter. They were hard to detect with the naked eye, but any kind of digital scan would give them away in a second. But he wouldn't need that much time to find what he was looking for. Once the drones were at the top of the surrounding buildings, he had them hold position, while he continued on foot.

The alley was another multi-level commercial area, and it was just as crowded as the surrounding streets. Hanging lanterns and street vendors selling all kinds of handheld foods gave the alley an innocent look, but behind the innocuous storefronts and trendy eateries, there were gang-fueled operations that were completely off the radar for the average citizen. As they passed the faces in the crowds, Boyd made a mental count of all the people he had busted over the years and was happy to note that most of them were now making a living that didn't involve breaking the law. In the middle of the block, there was a large brick building that once served as the heart of Hope City. The Native Society's front door was easy to miss between a decommissioned counsel booth and a busted script box, and directly under a holoscreen advertisement that was pumping out sultry visuals for a club in the red light district. It was now more of a homeless shelter than an organized community center, but it still served a similar purpose of getting people who had hit rock-bottom back on their feet. A silver-haired woman with an athletic build and faded clothes leaned on the steel doors and shook her head at Boyd as marched by.

"What the hell is going on?" she asked, as he kept moving with his group.

"Can't talk now, Val. Kind of busy."

"You can't expect me to take that as an answer," she protested, hustling up beside him. "I've got people here I need to protect. If something is going down, I need to know about it."

"Hopefully it's nothing," Boyd said, checking the drones on his display, "but it might be in your best interest to lock up in the old bunker for the night. Can't promise things won't get hairy. I'm sure we'll have triple patrols running all night."

"Are you going to be on duty? I haven't seen you or Zed around in a long time."

"I'm running on fumes as it is Val," he protested, as his body shook at the thought of pulling another double. He couldn't remember the last day he wasn't completely exhausted. "If I see Zed, I'll tell him he needs to make an appearance. That work?"

"You should be around more too. Both of you are the examples that people at the Society need to see. Times are rough, and they are only getting worse."

"You know, I ran in different circles back then," Boyd whined, as he stopped to look Val in the eye. "Zed was the one who was always hanging around with the Natives."

"That's right, he did. And maybe you could remind him of it because he seems to forget that we even exist." She glanced over at the end of the block and said, "You're marching right onto Buxton. You're not dumb enough to go in head first, so it's not the Bruisers you're after."

"I just follow orders," Boyd laughed. "Now, really, I can't talk right now."

As Delta group turned onto Buxton Street, their presence was immediately noticed. All the way down, lookouts were talking into their comms and alerting the door guards. Those same guards stood tall and slung baseball bats or machetes over their shoulders and smiled at the enforcers as they passed by. Delta group kept right on walking and ignored the comments and slurs that were being flung in their direction by a multitude of Bruisers from the streets and windows above. Part of being an enforcer was having thick skin and not letting things like insults get to you, because they were a constant occurrence in some places in Hope City. Up ahead Boyd saw an ornate building at the end of the street, with red and black banners flowing from the tenth-story windows of the Buxton Bruisers headquarters. Boyd looked a little further and could catch the gold and blue banner of the Royals flowing around the corner. He lifted a hand to signal the squad to hold up and radioed Rodriquez that they were in position.

"Building is sealed up tight," Boyd said, looking at the video feeds on his display. "I couldn't slip a piece of paper through any of the exterior cracks, let alone one of the drones. Also, further scans are telling me they have a data killer room on the basement level. Whatever is down there, they don't want us to know about it."

"Understood," Rodriquez confirmed. "A DKR sighting is enough to confirm suspicion. Give us a countdown for the flashbang, and we will infiltrate. I want everyone to watch each other's back. If things get hot, the Royals might send in an assault team from behind us. Johnson and Ziznewski, I want you watching our rear. Alert us if you see anything."

"Engaging flash bang in five," Boyd said, as he started the countdown.

When the flash went off, the squads were already rushing in and firing stun rounds as they went. The two guards at the door hit the ground like a couple sacks of potatoes. The enforcers assumed the door was locked and bolted, so a two-man team with a 'knock-knock' battering ram was the first at the door. It only took one well-placed hit to bust the lock. Boyd had his drones already flying as the door collapsed. He barked out the positions of hostiles from the drone feed, and the front-line enforcers dropped them quick. Stun blasters were going off so fast that from the outside it looked like a strobe light in a dance club. People at the gambling tables were frantically grabbing their chips. They tried to escape only to get a stun blast in the back, sending chips flying across the hardwood floors. A topless cocktail server dropped a tray of drinks and started screaming from all the stun gunfire erupting all around her. An enforcer quickly put her in a chair with restraints applied. Royals started rushing out of the back rooms with their pants still undone. Their chests exploded in light as they flew backward into the wall and slid down to the floor. Boyd navigated the drones into the rooms the Royals were coming from.

"Negative visual on the children," he said, standing in a pile of unconscious bodies. "I've got plenty of unarmed adult sex workers back there though. Some signs of heavy narcotic abuse. No signs of hostiles."

"Diggs, Fredricks, Carmello, sweep the back rooms. Delta group, upstairs with Boyd. Alpha group will remain here and hold position."

Boyd flew half of his drones upstairs. He set the ones downstairs to do a more detailed search, in case someone was hiding with a lethal weapon. Delta squad stayed a short distance behind the drones, letting the flying robots take the risk of breaching a room with an armed criminal. Boyd had multiple streams on his HUD now, but it didn't faze him at all. This was where he shined. As the drones split up into different rooms, he took notice of who and what was where. But everywhere the drones went it was more of the same, nothing but prostitutes and drug addicts. There was no one that was going to put up a fight, and no sign of children. He was about to notify Rodriquez when a real gunshot blast—from a real gun—rang out from the lower level.

"Enforcer down," came the call over the comms. Almost every heart on the assault team skipped a beat. "It's Cable!" the voice cried.

"Mother fucker!" Rodriquez yelled, probably not knowing he was still connected to the entire system. "Fall back. Someone get an autodoc on Cable. Boyd, I need you down here now. Door team, check in."

Boyd made a motion for the rest of Delta squad to continue their sweep as he raced down the stairs. When he reached the bottom, Cable was lying on the floor with his guts falling out of his chest. He was breathing short and his hands were shaking wildly.

"What happened?" Boyd asked, calling the ground floor drones back while keeping the upstairs one in search mode. He grabbed the portable autodoc from another enforcer and started punching in the programming to bring it to life.

"Cable found the door to the basement, and some asshole down there had a homemade shotgun. Blasted him at point-blank range before he retreated."

"Where did he get a gun? How many are down there?"

"How the fuck should I know?"

"Okay, applying autodoc now," Boyd said, placing a large mechanical device over Cable that buzzed to life with a multitude of small lights and moving appendages. The first thing it did was pump the kid full of drugs, then it immediately started going to work removing the shots. Blood was everywhere.

Boyd had to look away so he could focus on the situation. He needed to neutralize the data killer field that surrounded the room the person with the shotgun was in. An EMP grenade would temporarily short out the field and let them transmit drone footage. It would only be a minute or two, but hopefully it would give them enough time to locate the shooter and take him out. As soon as the EMP blast dissipated, Boyd had a drone flying down the stairwell.

"Drone is in the well. Moving around left corner," he said over the comms. The drone passed through a small corridor and into a small room. Boyd noticed several raised wooden planting beds filled with straw and rancid water. He knew exactly what it meant. "Son of a bitch. It's a saltpeter factory. That's what they didn't want us to see."

Another gunshot rang out, and one of Boyd's drone's feed cut. He immediately had a follow-up one down the pipe. This one was bigger and came with some added features. He fell back to the spot where his last drone was. Spinning around one hundred and eighty degrees, he saw the shooter running away. Boyd immediately launched a tracking bot that barely caught the gunman before he disappeared.

"I've made contact. Patching location through now. Data killer is almost rebooted. We need to move people."

Boyd shared the tracking beacon with the rest of the squad, and they could instantly see the blinking red dot on their displays through the floorboards. An enforcer pulled out a short spear-shaped device with a drill on the tip. It could burrow through almost any surface and deploy and small stun shock. It would only work if the target was directly near the device, and the stun wouldn't last long, but it would be enough for someone to close in. When the gunman seemed to have stopped moving, the enforcer slammed the spear on the floor, piercing the wood. A flash of light squeaked through the hole and the red beacon dropped a few inches. A dozen enforcers fell in directly afterwards, and a series of curses came over the comms.

"Alright, that's enough. I said that's enough!" Rodriquez shouted, pulling enforcers off of the gunman whose face was already beaten to a pulp. "Ortega, secure the prisoner and prep him for exile. Let's see how this piece of shit likes life outside the dome."

A half0-hour later, there was no evidence that led to a child pornography ring happening in the building. Some Enforcers started pulling panels off the walls, convinced they were there, but they only found support studs and insulation. Cable was in critical condition but was expected to pull through. Boyd and Rodriquez stood over the shotgun in worn-out disbelief.

"It has to be 3D printed," Boyd said, picking the gun up and looking at it. "You can still find schematics on the black market. It's a good thing he didn't have that many rounds. Kind of ironic, as he was guarding a gunpowder making factory."

"This must be what they wanted us to find," Rodriquez said, looking at long beds of animal excrement, wood ash, and straw. He covered his nose with his hand as the smell wasn't the greatest.

"What's that? I don't follow."

"The anonymous call. It must have come from a Bruiser. They wanted us to come in here and bust up the Royal's operation."

"They could have just told us this was going on."

"No, that would have taken too long. We would have planned more. Taken our time. They wanted us to come in here with stun guns blazing, today. Look, it's almost ready for harvest. See the white efflorescence?"

"This could lead to a gang war," Boyd said, shaking his head. "The Royals will have to strike back. Pride is on the line."

"We will limit the exiles to the minimum and let the Royals know we were tipped off, hopefully that will soften the blow."

"You said the call came in from a counsel booth? I could try to find out who made the call. If we could finger the snitch, that might help."

"They're called anonymous calls for a reason. The OS will never give us the details."

"There's always another way." Boyd said and then paused as if someone had hit him in the gut. A worried look came over his face as he turned back to Rodriquez, who asked what was wrong. "I have to go. It's Zed. He's issued an Enforcer distress beacon."

TWENTY-ONE

"So, how was the date?" Ash asked Cody, who was standing out in the hall-way with a bag of popcorn. Her short, black, pixie-cut hair was pulled back into a small knot and tucked underneath bright-green hoodie.

"With who? Pierre?" Cody asked nonchalantly, walking through the door and kicking off her slip-on shoes. She was all cleaned up and in fresh clothes for the first time in days. It felt amazing. She squeezed her synthetic toes into little balls on a small shag rug to ease the muscle pains in the rest of her feet, and the internal motors made little buzzing noises as the parts moved. "Oh, you look nice. I love your top, and your hair. You're back to brunette? It really is your color."

"Yeah, red just attracted too much attention. So, you've had multiple dates then?"

"No," Cody replied, grabbing a delicate piece of stemware from the rack and pouring herself a healthy glass of wine. "You know, I could never deal with that polyamorous lifestyle. Pierre was fun. No, he was actually really amazing. The scary part is I could see myself really falling for him."

"So, what's the problem?" Ash asked eagerly, leaning on the back of a barstool by her kitchen counter, intently watching the happiness that was written all over Cody's face.

"I don't think I can do an entire relationship in virtual," Cody whined, slamming the bottle down on the kitchen counter in frustration. "I know there have been some big advancements in VR sexual encounters. It is very real and all, but the translator apps are still for shit at understanding sarcasm."

"You could always learn French."

"I, on the other hand, have no problem understanding sarcasm. Besides, it's more than just that. I spend most of my days jacked in to make the credits to pay for this ridiculous penthouse. The last thing I want to do is spend the time I have with my special someone in a synthetic body. I know people are making it work these days, but it's just not for me."

"If only we could transfer cities," Ash said lazily, walking her glass to the living room couch, still looking at Cody.

"You know that's not allowed. Once you're in an Omega City, you're in for life."

"I need no reminder."

"I'll keep in touch with him," Cody said, following Ash's example and heading for the extraordinarily lavish couch. "It'll be nice to have someone I could call on if I need to get away for a while. Pierre isn't dumb. He'll understand. He probably already does."

"How is OC4? I've never been," Ash asked, adjusting the lighting in the kitchen and the living room to match their new location with a swipe of her hand.

"The change of scenery was nice, even if their Grid is almost identical to ours. But you know how it is under the dome, it's always pleasant. The food we ate was astoundingly better than anything I've ever had here, but Pierre is a chef and I think we got special treatment." Cody paused and smiled internally, biting her lower lip. "I will say their rentable avatars are amazing. They felt brand new, if you know what I mean. And their autocars. So nice. Very clean. But I guess that's because they don't let the cars from the Zero onto the Grid. You have to transfer. Might as well take the train. Also, they even have their own version of No Hope City. I think they call it New Tomorrows, or No Tomorrows. Something like that."

"Yeah, everyone has a non-surveillance district now. I'd move there if I could."

"Yeah right! There's no way you're finding this kind of vintage down there," Cody said, taking a sip of wine. "Oh, that's nice. Boy, am I beat. I'm going to need a few days off of training to recover from that one."

"I don't get why you put yourself through it," Ash said, pouring more into the glass she had just finished. The highlight reel from the tournament was still up on her holoscreen. "What's the real advantage of an L3 tournament over all the rest, anyway?"

"Nothing really," Cody laughed sardonically, "and the winner's purse is significantly less because of all the extra expenses the promoters have to pay. At least I didn't get shot this time. The pain from getting KO'd can last for weeks depending on how you went out. Which reminds me, I need to send Billy something as a thank you."

"Sounds horrible."

"The pain is beside the point, and it's about more than just the credits. It's the prestige and honor. L3 tournaments don't just happen every day, you know. I am thee reigning Big Gun champ for the entire world for the next few months, and there isn't anything anyone can do about it. I've already got tons of advertising offers. My face on a holoscreen over Middle Park. My avatar's likeness as a downloadable skin. Shred's Gym wants me as their spokesperson. I'm set for a while. Might even take some time off."

"So, it is all about the credits," Ash said while giving a smirk and rolling her eyes.

"Yeah, I guess it might be." Cody laughed. "But also, it really is the only way for me to be prominent in the gaming world. I could never be the champ in a league that wasn't based on personal physique. Level 3 is the only way. I'm sure as hell not signing up for The War."

"You're great at all games," Ash protested. "What are you talking about?"

"Oh please. You kick my ass on standard format all the time. That isn't really saying much, I guess, seeing that you're good enough to go pro yourself."

Ash took the compliment well, as she watched the last drop of the bottle trickle out into her glass. It wasn't enough, so she hopped to her feet again and headed to the kitchen to grab another bottle. The case wasn't going to drink itself. She started peeling off the seal with the tip of the corkscrew, while she said, "When I was a teenager, all I wanted was to play sports—in the real leagues that is—but my mom said they were too dangerous. Brain damage really shortens your life span. So the only way I could play was in the virtual leagues. It just wasn't the same. You know? There was something missing. So, I tried my hand at video games."

"What's stopping you from going pro in either? And don't say you're too old because you can afford all the age adjusting procedures."

"I can, and more," Ash laughed, walking back to the couch, "and that's the problem. One of these nights I'm going to go to sleep and I'll wake up in an ascension ceremony. The OS will clean my quarters out and it'll be bye-bye Ash. You won't even know I'm gone."

"Please don't go! Oh my god, I don't know what I'd do without you. Everyone else in the Six has a stick up their ass." They both laughed at that, with a tinge of sad irony as they both were shut-ins who made paltry attempts in getting to know their neighbors. Lights on at odd hours in penthouses across from each other was the only reason they met at all. "You know, you have to be the only person in the six cities who doesn't want to ascend."

"So I've been told," Ash said, swirling her wine around in her glass, watching the legs trickle down the sides.

"If you don't want to be a dreamer anymore, why don't you just stop?"

"I wish it were that easy. You know I didn't want to be chipped in the first place." Ash whined, as she furrowed her brow and threw her hands up in the air. Cody just nodded, as she had heard that complaint dozens of times before—usually in heated anger. "It's in my terms of service agreement. All of my dreams for the rest of my life are the property of Omega Systems. All of them. Anyway, it isn't possible to remove the neuro recorder without causing brain death."

"Terms of service? Sounds like terms of abuse to me," Cody said, rolling her eyes. "Stupid contracts. If you don't read the dozens of pages they throw at you, the next thing you'll know is when they own you. I can't order a pizza anymore without signing a ToS."

"I guess it could be worse. Dreaming isn't the hardest job, and the perks are great!" Ash chuckled, twirling around an empty bottle. "I'm an international star that never leaves home."

"So, what's the new dream about, anyway? You seemed kind of shook up earlier. Did you see more of those symbols?"

"Well, I was doing some research on my couch and I just kind of dozed off. I totally forgot to take my medication earlier, which would have kept me from napping. It's frustrating because naps are the worst for visual dreams. And of course, there was a new symbol. I seem to be plagued with them right now."

"Any new insight where they are coming from? You said that you had seen nothing like it before."

"Nothing yet, but I feel like I'm getting closer. I haven't reviewed the footage because I'm still too anxious, but I can punch it up for you if you want to watch."

"Sure, but just on the flatscreen, please. I'm done with holoscreens and VR for the day."

"No problem," Ash said, hitting at the air in front of her to turn off the holoscreen. The light faded slowly and the 3D video she had on slipped away. She pushed at the air again and her massive windows flickered to life as the new display screen. "I prefer it this way, anyway."

Ash started up her most recent dream sequence that began with the usual blurry images floating around in a dark atmosphere. The sounds were muffled, like they were coming from a few rooms over. If someone were viewing it in virtual, there would be a warm, soft sensation over their body as if they were in a deep sleep. Slowly things came into focus, and they saw the world through Ash's eyes as she was walking down the street outside of her penthouse. The virtual viewer would then feel as if they were walking down the street as her and feel anything that she felt. The dreamcast experience was incredibly realistic.

"You should have known it was a dream," Cody joked. "You're outside!"

"It's not funny, Cody," Ash whined, even though Cody's remark was spot on.

It was always odd reliving a dream experience because nothing looked the way she remembered it. The horse wasn't black—it was tan. The jumping sequence wasn't anywhere near as long as it seemed, and the lights in the church at the end were more of a red than pink. Small things like that she was used to, but something new caught her eye that made her think twice about the entire sequence. The beast that was chasing her had originally appeared to her as a kind of blackish blob with no defining features other than the green eyes and sharp claws. Now she could clearly make out the rippling muscles, the coarse fur, the wet, dog-like nose, and blood-coated fanged teeth that had several rows like a shark. She kept it to herself, as she didn't quite know what that meant yet.

"That was heavy," Cody said, releasing her grip she had on a couch cushion as the stream finished.

"Let's back up," Ash said, reversing the footage to when the symbol was shown. She zoomed the image in so only the symbol was taking up the screen, which was remarkably clear considering how far she had zoomed. "Something interesting I've noticed. This is my personal recording of the dream. The symbols all appear clear, like this. But I was looking through an old dream on a public server while I was out, and the symbols on them were either blurred or not visible at all. It's strange. I've had them scanned and no errors in the digital file can be found. Anyway, here is the current one. Copy screen and share." The clip transferred to both of their displays.

"That is strange. How many is this now?" Cody asked, immediately searching the internet for the symbol's likeness.

"Over a dozen, and none of them relating to anything I've ever seen in OC6."

"Yeah, I'm coming up short on this one too," Cody sighed.

"I think someone is trying to tell me something."

"How can that be possible? You can't hack a dream."

"The device the OS put in my head. Maybe it can receive images instead of just sending them. How else can I account for all these things and places showing up that I don't even know? Over a dozen similar-looking symbols can't be a coincidence."

"People dream all the time about people and places they don't know," Cody protested, "but the symbols really are strange. I would say it's a reoccurring dream, but there isn't actually anything that reoccurs. If someone is tampering with your dreams, who would you think it is?"

"I don't know, but I have a feeling it's about my brother, maybe even from him."

"Didn't he ascend? There's no communication between the cities and the seventh."

"I know, I know," Ash said, holding her hands up and shaking them as if she were holding onto something. "I can't explain it just yet. But something about all the videos we've been collecting seems personal. I just don't know how or why yet."

"Well, something sure as hell is familiar to me," Cody said, taking control of the stream by reaching into the air and pulling the virtual remote to her internal system, and displaying it holographically. She backed up the footage to where the church could first be seen and stopped. "I know where that is."

"You do?" Ash exclaimed.

"Yep, and we can go there if you want."

• • •

Ten minutes later, they were jacked in and being loaded into a pair of blank synthetic avatars on the Big Gun battlefield in the remains of the city of Denver. Ash rubbed the tips of her fingers together and she could feel every bit of her thumb gliding across each finger. It felt so real, even if her body was now made of titanium, graphene, and silicone. She was in a long, dark room that had rows and rows of wooden stalls. Inside of each, there was a blank, gender-neutral avatar hanging underneath a small LED light. She felt the harness on her back and wondered how she was supposed to get out. She had never been in an L3 environment, and she was suddenly worried she would hurt herself. Very irrational.

"You have to tell it to disconnect," Cody's voice sounded from an identical blank avatar that was walking into her field of vision.

"What does that mean?"

"It needs to know the neuro link is successful. To do that, you need to tell the suit that you're ready to command it. There are no HUD controls in L3, so you just have to tell it. In your mind, that is."

"I just think it then," Ash said, trying to sound confident. She closed her eyes and tried to think.

"You don't need to close your eyes, dummy."

"Right," Ash said, and before she knew it, the harness was releasing.

Her synthetic host hit the ground with a heavy thud. A prompt came up to let her know the system was calibrated to her physical body. While the size of the robot didn't change at all, it felt lighter in certain areas and heavier in others. She waved her hand around a bit and the response was perfect.

"You really haven't done this before, huh?" Cody laughed, watching her friend move around clumsily, like a baby taking its first step. "Really? Not even to take a trip to a different city?"

"I try to stay out of virtual reality as much as I can. The real world is weird enough. But maybe this experience will help me come to terms with it."

"Look," Cody said as her avatar was covered in digital static. It flickered for a few seconds until it came into focus and now looked like her digital gamer persona. "You can apply any skin that you want to."

"But I don't have any," Ash sighed.

"That's okay," Cody removed the image program and her synth returned to the blank slate. "At this time of night, no one will be out here besides us night owls."

"What do you think you're doing?" A raspy voice shouted, as another robotic avatar could be seen moving about the stable-like room. "Jackin' in at any odd hour you like. Messin' up the whole damned town. You can't just come down here and joyride whenever you want to, you know."

"Hey Franco," Cody greeted the grumpy groundskeeper with a small wave. "Don't worry. We'll be super safe. Take all the precautions."

"Yeah, well, you fall and bust your bike, or your bot, and I gotta hustle ass all over the zone and clean up your mess." The bot looked out to the busted cityscape and started to shake its head slightly. "The wild dogs are back. They're everywhere. They can't eat me or anything, but they sure do annoy me. Cause me a whole lot of trouble. Damned mutts."

"Don't worry," Cody said to Franco, and turned to Ash and somehow conveyed an eye-roll. "We're just going to go slow and steady. It's my friends Ash's first time."

"Oh, a newcomer?" Franco said, excitedly. He scooted over to eye up Ash even though her avatar was still blank. "It's a pleasure to meet you. Now, that's my area over there. Right over there. You touch anything of mine and I'll bust your avatar in two and send you the bill. You follow?"

"Thanks, Franco." Cody pushed Ash in the back to get her moving. "We'll just grab the first bikes off the rack."

"I'll fire up the repair drones," Franco muttered, hobbling away.

"He's a synthetic intelligence?" Ash asked once they were what she thought was far enough away.

"Yep, programmed to be ornery and everything. Probably one of the most unique one I've come across, even though all the battlefields have a similar SI running the grounds. He gives me shit every time I come here, no matter what time of day it is. Must be in his script."

They came to a long rack of numbered rocket bikes attached at the top by a thin metal arm. They were on a small dusty hillside, east of the ruins of Denver. What remained of the skyline was in the distance, with massive floodlights shining upon the carcasses of buildings that looked like burnt-out skeletons. There were scattered lights along the roads that led into the center of town, but the landscape was mostly dark with silhouettes of half-destroyed buildings creating even darker tones in the night. Cody reassured Ash that there was nothing to worry about. They were as safe as they were under the dome. The OS had autocannons around the entire perimeter that would obliterate anyone or anything that tried to get in. But that did little to make Ash feel safe. Maybe they shouldn't have popped the second bottle of wine. They certainly had gained a burst of ambition that she was now regretting.

"We're up here by the old military base," Cody said, displaying a holographic map in the air before them. A dull-orange light made a 3D composite of the city in real-time. It was handy if a building should be blasted out during combat. "I've seen that church from your dreams down here, past the golf course. I only remember it because there is a killer ramp you can take if you want to catch some air right in that location."

"Killer," Ash said flatly, accepting the bike that Cody floated in her direction with nervously shaking hands.

"Just take it slow." Cody took the grips of her own bike firmly in her hands.

Take it slow they did, which gave Ash time to take in the scenery while they cruised. At first, it was almost like life had never stopped for Denver. Houses still stood intact, with cars still parked in the driveways, ready to hit the road. As they moved along, more and more houses and buildings had walls toppled over, and cars were only burnt-out remains.

Passing a big shopping center, there was a small crater in the middle of the parking lot with a ring of burnt-out cars around it. It looked like the blast had pushed the cars outwards circularly. The shopping center itself was riddled with bullet holes and laser blasts. Bit by bit, the signs of chaos and destruction began to grow. It started with a few parts of avatars and rocket bikes strewn about the road that were damaged beyond repair and left for scrap. They were obviously the result of Big Gun battles. But eventually, the bodies in the streets began to be overwhelmingly human. Carcasses still sitting in their cars or lying flat on the pavement. Nothing but skeletal remains decaying in the wind. A street light caught the insides of a residential building, and there she saw the remains of two bodies holding each other on a rotting mattress.

She knew about the wars. She knew about the Sickness. But seeing the aftermath firsthand conveyed more than any history program or electronic book ever could. Life in Omega City was literally like living in a bubble. Maybe this was what she was intended to see. Something to shake up her reality.

They passed a pile of busted robot parts. The skull of one unit was split in half, with the electronic guts spilling out over the pavement. She thought of Cody feeling that kind of pain, and it made her wince.

"Does it hurt?" She asked, through the comms system. "When you die in combat."

"Like I said, it hurts like hell. Level 3 isn't intended to be fun, but the injuries really aren't that serious. The initial pain is mostly mental, with the VR booth sending signals through your brain to tell you you're injured. The nanobots do the rest. They put stress on your muscles and body, making them really sore for a while. But it's more like you worked out really hard and not like getting your limbs torn off. The comedown from the adrenaline that is released might actually be the worst. No pill to help you with that. Going hardcore pays out a lot more, but I'm not dumb enough to do that."

"What does that mean? Going hardcore?"

"It's what they call level 4. You break your leg in a nasty spill, your leg gets broken in real life. If you split your head open and die in VR, then you're dead forever. Only adrenaline junkies like it. You need a special VR bed for it though, and they are really expensive. I'm not trying to pay money to die. But if you sign up for The War you get to experience it all for free."

"No thank you."

"Funny thing. All these advancements in virtual reality we take for granted in our lives, because they are ingrained in our society, were developed by the people who ultimately destroyed it. Well, half anyway. The military did the groundwork and the pornography business did the rest. The military really didn't care that you could feel everything."

"Well, next time I'm at the old porno parlor," Ash said, rolling her eyes, "I'll thank granddaddy inventor for making all the sensations of the experience so wonderful."

"Okay, hold up," Cody said, hitting the brakes. "We're coming up on the church, but to get there, we are going to have to take a huge jump. You can do this. Just don't let up on the throttle. Okay?"

"Okay," Ash confirmed nervously, feeling her hands shake on the grips. "This is exciting."

"Are you sure you're up to this? Your heart rate is off the charts."

"You're monitoring me?"

"Look, I can just go up ahead and check it out. I'll share my screen with you once I'm there."

"No," Ash said, unconsciously revving the bike. "I need to see this in person. Are you sure there is no way to change the settings? Isn't there a standard version?"

"Big Gun Corp doesn't program their synths for anything but L3. Sorry. You can handle it, right? It's just one jump. It'll be fun."

"Yeah, fun," Ash said, thinking about her dream when she was flying. Maybe this was part of it. Maybe the horse had jumped in her dream to show that she needed to make this jump to hopefully find an answer. "I need to do this. Let's go before I change my mind."

"Hell yeah!" Cody shouted as she punched her rocket bike into gear.

As the bikes gained speed, the gloomy graveyard of a city turned into a blur. The grisly details of the history of destruction disappeared as her focus was only on the ten feet of pavement in front of her. Street lights went zooming by one by one. Up ahead she could see the ramp that Cody had mentioned. She had expected maybe a half-fallen bridge, or a turned-over building. Apparently, the Big Gun Corp just liked the big jumps because they had placed actual ramps at different locations around the city.

They must have passed a sensor, because when they were about a hundred meters away, running lights on the ramp illuminated along the upward curve. Cody hit the ramp first. Being the show off that she was, she did a flip with her legs extended behind the bike and only one hand on the grip. Ash, on the other hand, clenched her thighs against the bike so it wouldn't slip away. It felt like her fingers were about to break from holding on so tight. It's not real, she told herself as her rocket bike took to the air.

Time slowed down. They were only in the air for a few seconds, but it felt like minutes. She was flying and it wasn't a dream or some cheap virtual experience. If she fell, it would hurt. That terrified and exhilarated her at the same time. The air was rushing past her face. It was cold and slightly painful. She forced her eyes to stay open so she could take in the surroundings better. She recognized the church not far up ahead and braced for the ground that was rushing up to meet her. She felt it in her gut and groin as the bike's hover sensors reacted to the road below, pushing the bike upwards. Hitting the brake immediately, the bike spun sideways, and she had to put her foot down to stop from falling over.

"Now that's how it's done!" Cody shouted, raising her hands in the air and cheering.

"We don't have to do that again, right?" Ash asked, panting heavily with her fingers still tightly gripping the handlebars.

They parked the bikes in the road and walked the rest of the way to the church. Cody reassured Ash that they could just log out when they were done and the synths would take the bikes back automatically. Rounding a corner, the church rose before them. Even though it was physically identical to the one in her dream, it was nowhere near as intimidating. There were no eerie lights emanating from the interior, and no skeleton hands leaping out of the ground to pull her down. Still, her skin crawled a little, even in VR.

They approached the gigantic wooden doors directly. After a few valiant efforts, it was clear that the door would not open. Cody motioned for them to check around the side of the building. Sure enough, a portion of the sidewall had collapsed, giving them plenty of room to enter. Inside it was very dark and still. Cody activated a light on her synth, and it flooded the room with an electric glare. White light flashed through Ash's brain as she registered several rotting corpses sitting in pews, with a few still in a praying position.

"Sorry," Cody said, "I didn't realize it would be like this."

"No, it's okay. Let's just check the altar and get out of here."

They walked down the center aisle just as she did in her dream. The bare cross still hung above the altar, that was exactly three steps up. She had never been here. So how was it almost exactly the same as in her dream? At the altar they found a dusty old bible laying open. They cautiously circled it, as if to make sure there wasn't someone there who would jump out at them.

Ash slowly reached out her hand to grab the book but stopped suddenly. She was nervous and unsure. Cody nodded her head and motioned for Ash to continue. Ash moved to place her hands on the open book, but when she did, her fingers slipped right through the pages. The book suddenly disintegrated into a pile of dust.

"Son of a bitch," Cody cursed, shining her light on their hope for answers.

"Wait," Ash said, turning her own light on. "What's this?"

She brushed away some of the dust that had spilled over the altar. Underneath the soot, someone had clearly carved the symbol she had seen in her dreams into the wood. It was jagged and fresh as if it was recently made with a small knife.

"Okay," Cody said, putting her hands on her head. "What the fuck is going on?"

TWENTY

Tony Two Toes' one red digital eye looked at Zed with a kind of vacant hatred. It still had the electronic LED glow, but the light was slowly fading. Even though Tony was deceased, Zed wondered if whatever part of digital life that was still left inside of Tony's brain could see him through that synthetic eye. If so, was there any emotion attached to the images it saw? Or was it nothing more than a digital file on a dead hard drive? Existence simply boiled down to static data represented by ones and zeros.

His existential thought process broke when he reminded himself that he could be in an autocar quietly and comfortably riding to a payday in the Six right now. Instead, he was in a trash pit that smelt like old cabbage.

He should have stuck with the kid.

Even though he could see through the grating above on the street level, the light did not reach down to the bottom of the pit. Pulling out his hand terminal, he activated the most useful tool humans had ever created—a flashlight. The cold white light shone on the dirty concrete walls of the pit. He was about fifteen meters down in a space about ten square meters. No ladders, walkways, or elevators. There was no way out. All kinds of trash and refuse surrounded him. It was most likely dumped there through the upper grates by someone who was too lazy to make it to the recycler. His hand felt slimy. Shining the light on it revealed that it was covered in fresh blood.

SEVERE DAMAGE, his system notified him. REPAIR IMMEDIATELY.

He tried moving his right arm, but it lagged in response time and sent out a few sparks and hisses. It had broken his fall but had become broken itself. A vision flashed from his memory of Tony's face under his elbow when the ground had caught up with them. The metal arm had pushed Tony's skull into a large thrown-out kitchen appliance. The pressure-on-impact caused the connections from the eye socket to go through the brain tissue and skull bone. A cracking sound resonated in his ears when he looked at the mess of broken bones, flesh, and neural connections. Zed's expression was blank as he felt neither remorse nor guilt for what had happened to Tony, and that bothered him more than anything else. When did he become so cold?

"This is enforcer Takeda," he said over the comms, turning away from the gore. "Reporting an enforcer-involved incident. Requesting emergency evac. Suspect is deceased. Enforcer is injured. Over."

There was no immediate answer to his call, so he repeated his request. Again, there was no reply, just the emptiness of a dead communications line. He took a moment to think things through. It had been a real long time since he had checked an internet connection status on his system, so long that he had forgotten how to do it. After a bit of menu diving, he found the connection to be null. But that was impossible. There really wasn't anywhere in an Omega City where you weren't connected somehow. This pit seemed to be an unusual dead space. A black hole for internet connectivity. He suddenly felt naked without it, and afraid he might never get out. Thank the OS he was an enforcer. Lifting his broken right painfully, he aimed it near the doorway at the top of the pit. There was a hiss of air and a flash of light as the distress beacon launched and zipped through the air. He was relieved when connected with the outer wall and stuck. He just hoped it was far enough to get a connection to the troops.

Tony was a man made out of muscles, and he liked to show them off. His lack of conventional clothing made it easy for Zed to search through the pockets because there weren't many to go through. Over a bare chest, he wore an open maroon leather jacket that had its sleeves ripped off. He reached into the inner pocket and found a bag of shitty street drugs, a lighter, and a packet of gum. There was an empty sheath attached to his olive drab pants. Zed recalled how he had disarmed that knife earlier, and smiled. The left pocket of the pants had a few loose credit chips and a beer bottle cap. The right one only had a crumbled-up piece of paper that looked like it was torn from a larger pamphlet. Flattening the paper out, the words read The Children in a weird digital font. That brought nothing to mind. He flipped it over and there was a series of numbers scribbled on the back. It might be something. Nothing was safe on any digital format when hackers were involved. A man like Tony might find it safer to keep important things on a hard copy. Without being connected, he couldn't search a database, so he pocketed the piece of paper and moved on. But there were no more pockets to search, and he didn't feel like trying to get Tony's boots off with only one work arm.

Tony being dead was a shame. There now was no way to know who had ordered him to commit the plethora of hits that he had done on opposing gangs over the years. Organized crime all over the city was rising, even on the Grid. The crews and gangs were so well off that the hefty fines the OS doled out didn't mean a thing anymore. It was just another part of the game. Things like prohibited weapons, illegal drugs, and assault charges were one thing, but murder and rape were something else. That never went unpunished or passed off with a payable fine. Tony's hands were covered is so much of his victim's blood it was a mystery how he was able to stay at large for so long. Who had ordered the kills, and how did he escape the OS surveillance? They were questions everyone wanted answers to. With his cerebral cortex splattered all over a convection oven, no one would ever know. Zed sighed and looked around at the surroundings. A shitty place to die, he thought.

Out of the corner of his eye, he saw a rat sifting through the trash. If it had gotten down there, it must have been through a tunnel or pathway. He picked up an empty food container and lobbed it in the rat's direction. It scurried away quickly, squeaking wildly as it went. Zed watched as it went through a small crack in a far wall. He didn't need the OS to tell him there was some kind of door there.

There were no hinges or a handle of any kind, but a thin line running vertically up the wall showed that there was a movable panel. He gave it a solid tug, but it didn't budge. It was thick steel, maybe six inches, with rusted hinges and a warped frame. He shined his light through the crack, but only saw blackness. He would have given up, thinking that opening the door was impossible in his current state, but something he saw said the opposite. There were scratch marks on the cement floor that revealed the door had opened at one point in time. The way the rubbish had been pushed out of the way at a certain angle led him to believe that it had been recently.

Searching around, he found a long metal pole just thin enough to fit through the crack, but strong enough that it wouldn't break. He slid it into place and pushed against it but the door still wouldn't move. He tried putting all of his whole body weight against it and slowly the door scraped against the floor, opening bit by bit. On the last heave, the door suddenly flung open causing him to lose his footing and fall headlong into the dark room. His hand terminal skated across the rough ground. He had to fumble through the darkness after it, feeling around blindly. Taking a breath when he found it, he lifted the hand terminal so the light could show him his new surroundings. He nearly dropped it again when he laid eyes on a horrific sight.

"Zed," a young woman called out in a blood-curdling voice, while raising her hands towards him. Lying in a pool of her own blood, with guts spilling out of her chest and legs, a mess of meat and broken bones. There was a hole through the side of her face that has festered and black. "Zed! Help me Zed!"

He was so terrified that he rushed out of the room and began to dry heave in a pile of trash. Natalia? He thought, No, it couldn't be. Putting his head between his knees to focus, he came back to reality. Must be hallucinating. Standing up straight, he mustered the strength to take another look. There was nothing to be afraid of. Positioned outside of the door, his light passed over the mutilated corpse of a young woman. This time he held strong and took a hard look. No, it wasn't her. That was a small relief. But then who the hell was it?

"Enforcer Takeda," a voice came from above. "You down there?"

"Affirmative," he said, snapping back to reality. "There's no connection down here."

"What's that?"

Taking a deep breath, he yelled as loud as he could, "There's no connection down here."

"No connection? That's not possible."

"Look," Zed started, then stopped. Thinking his words through. "Just get some people down here. We've got a crime scene. Looks like murder."

"Roger that."

"And hey," he shouted after the recruit who has already running away, "get a network relay!"

• • •

The body was lying silently on the ground, eyes open to the underground emptiness. The simple garments that had adorned the young woman had been sliced off, most likely post-execution. Her neck had been cut rather deep all the way across, and the chest was split open from sternum to pelvis. The intestines were pulled out and placed on the cold cement at her side. Zed pushed his flashlight into the cavity and thought it looked as if the organs had been removed. A quick pass around the area illuminated their resting place. On a small stone ridge not far off he saw what looked like a heart, a pair of lungs, a kidney, a stomach, a liver, and some other various items that he couldn't name by sight. Zed swallowed hard. The day was taking a toll on his constitution.

He buried his nose and mouth into the side of his arm to block the stench of decay while he looked around. The room was free of debris and rather clean, considering its location. He thought the murderer could have possibly cleaned it ahead of time—or after. An interesting thought either way. He wouldn't know more until there was a proper lighting rig and a network connection. Shit, he forgot they were still technically in Hope City. He started the recording function on his system. A full analysis would have to wait until they got back on the Grid. Sounds from outside the room alerted him to the arrival of other enforcers.

"You sure left a war zone up there," Boyd said, as he jumped off the rope ladder lowered into the pit. "It's going to take a week just to sift through that mess."

"Save it for a rookie. We've got bigger problems."

"Would you look that," Boyd said, looking at Tony's lifeless body and the splatter of brains and circuitry coming out of his head. "I didn't think we would ever catch this guy. Good job Z."

"Yeah, well, I didn't either. Just got lucky. But that is all beside the point. We've got another corpse in the adjacent room."

"What? A victim? Someone Tony offed?"

"No. It doesn't appear to be, but I don't know exactly what it is yet." Zed said, searching for what kind of protocol he should be following. "Just keep the rookies and recruits out of the pit for now. Only seasoned enforcers on the scene. Preferably ones you know and trust."

Not being one to question orders, Boyd turned and started barking commands to the enforcers up the line. "Protocol Alpha 6 folks. Make a perimeter up top. Only enforcers with experience down the line. No press, no recordings. Keep it tight."

"We need lighting drones, a network relay, field analysis kit, cryo containment. You know, the works."

"That serious?"

"Just order the gear and meet me over there."

"Network relay coming down now, but we're only going to be able to access the NHC network and the OS profile database."

"That's fine. Right now, I need us all to be in communication with each other. First, we get the crime scene sealed and the base set up, then I want an armored search team in the tunnels. Night vision, stun batons, shield emitters, and body restraints. I want them ready for anything."

"Jesus," Boyd said, seeing the tension in Zed's face for the first time. "You are serious."

"As serious as brain death. Now get on it."

While Boyd was off relaying the information up the line, Zed took the network relay and found a level place where he could set it up. Not being able to communicate through the comms was like being crippled. In no way did he enjoy being constantly connected and monitored, but during the time he was offline he felt very alone and vulnerable. When his system chimed that it was on a network again, he let out a loud sigh of relief and immediately went to work.

They were only just above street level when they fell into the pit. At fifteen meters, they probably fell through the storage levels and into a sublevel of the city's structure. Possibly an existing subway access room or tunnel. He brought up a map of Zone Zero from the archives that showed the area as it was before they built Hope City. A holographic skeleton of subway tunnels and connecting rooms hovered before him in a dull neon-green. His red location beacon wasn't there. He zoomed out and his location was shown below the level of the map, just blinking in the darkness.

He queried the system to show him what the land looked like before the city was built. It gave him an authorization prompt that he passed easily. A new map appeared showing a large flat piece of land covered in farm fields. The only structures were from a solitary farmhouse that still stood where it was then—now as a museum. There were no tunnels before the city was built beyond the usual service tunnels, and there were no new tunnels on record.

"So, what have we got?" Boyd asked, returning from assigning duties to other enforcers.

"A lot of questions and no answers."

"We'd be out of a job if it were easy."

Zed looked Boyd in the eye and said, "We're going to earn our pay today. Hope you had a light lunch. It's not a pretty sight through that door."

"Nothing I haven't seen before. Launching lighting drones now," Boyd said, swiping his hand up in the air as he turned the system on. Four baseball-sized metallic drones rose off the ground and hovered in the air. "In there?" He asked, looking at the blackened abyss beyond the heavy steel door. Zed nodded, and the drones zipped into the darkness, with the two men following.

When Zed's flashlight had shone upon the grisly scene earlier, it induced a terrible hallucination—or was it a memory? Illuminated now, the room and the victim didn't seem as disturbing. Boyd still had to take a few minutes to compose himself. The chamber was the size of a large bedroom, with only a small opening in a far wall that alluded to more rooms or tunnels. Zed made a motion with his hand, and two of the lighting drones zipped through the opening. The drones would search through the surrounding area and collect data until they reached the limit of the network range. In a corner there was a small, rusted metal chair next to a broken wooden table that had several repairs made to it. Resting on top there was an old battery-powered lamp, but the battery had expired and the lamp was lifeless. In the opposite corner there was a long plank of wood resting on some cinderblocks. It was the size of a single bed, but it would be the most uncomfortable bed anyone could ever sleep on.

"It almost looks like someone was living down here," Zed remarked, thinking of prison cell pictures he'd seen in history programs.

"Do you think it was an animal?" Boyd asked, as he stood over the body with his hand over his nose. "Maybe a coyote got in through one of the exterior access pipes."

"I don't think so. Those are precise cuts made with machine-made objects. Animal claws would tear the flesh, leaving jagged marks. Look here. The skin is cut neatly."

"It's pretty gruesome. Who would do a thing like this?"

"Someone deeply disturbed." Zed breathed in, trying to disconnect from the thought process of the killer. "Tell me something. Why do you think she is on the floor when there is a platform right here? They took the care to remove each organ carefully. That would take an extremely steady hand. Why do it on the ground, and under poor lighting?"

"I don't think it's gang-related," Boyd said with his dark eyes fixated on his display, trying to avoid looking at the corpse. "She has a profile on the database. Jessie Parker. Came in from the wastes a few years back. She was denied LSI each month she applied but didn't take jobs with the gangs or on the Strip. Looks like she did hard work here in No Hope. Odd jobs, long hours. Metadata gathered from the local network says she is into heavy metal music, autocar repair, pit bulls, and vintage movies. She spends most of her spare time at local bars. Drinks a lot. No signs of hard drugs or criminal records. She's not jacked for virtual and doesn't spend a lot of time on the internet other than social sites or information pages. Her subgroup subscriptions are Nordic Thrash, Friends of Ishi, Pit Bull Lovers Only, and Anti-synth Association. Medical says she is on a mild antidepressant that you can get from any script box. Her credit account hasn't been touched in a few days, so we can rule out robbery."

"She's deaf," Zed said, noticing thin lines of off tone, flesh-colored silicon running under the girl's left earlobe.

"What's that?"

"You said she belonged to the Anti-Synth group. She's deaf. Probably born that way. But she has augmentations on her ears. Invasive surgery too."

"So what? You have augments and have expressed your dislike of any SI many times."

"Not enough to join a cult," Zed snapped. "Just take a note of it. Where is the analysis kit, by the way?"

"Coming down now."

"Christ. Get to the door and block it. We can't let anyone set eyes on this."

Boyd hustled to the door just as another enforcer was coming down the ladder with a large device strapped to his back. Boyd put his hands up to stop the enforcer's advancement. The man didn't protest and handed the device over easily as he tried to peek over Boyd's massive body to get a look through the door.

"I thought someone called for a medic?" the man said.

"I have a problem here." Zed came back to the pit, covered in dried blood and bruises.

"You need a repair shop, not a medic," the medical enforcer scoffed, only noticing Zed's severely damaged right arm. "I don't deal with hybrid freaks."

"What'd you say?" Zed asked, taking a step forward. Boyd had to put both his hand up to stop him.

"No offense or anything," the man said, putting his hands up. He then glanced up at Zed's face and a sudden look of realization came over him. "Hey you're Takeda, aren't you? You're the one who took down Ruthless Richter. Oh man, that was crazy! I bet the gang bosses didn't like that much, huh?"

"No. They did not." Zed grunted.

"Well, hate to break it to you, but you've got problems again," The man laughed as he shared his screen with Zed and Boyd. A holographic portrait of Zed rotated on their screens, and a bounty that was equal to a year of earnings floated next to it. "Hope your augments can save you again, you perverted prick."

"Alright. Time to go." Boyd said, pushing the chuckling man back towards the ladder. When he was over the top, Boyd picked up the analysis kit and said, "What an asshole."

"That's a big bounty," Zed breathed, watching the image of his face rotate back and forth.

"Don't let it get to you. That guy doesn't know shit. He's one of those dickheads who never spent time on the front." Boyd walked over to Zed and gave him a pat on the back. "Come on. You're Zed Takeda, The War hero. You took down Ol' Ruthless when no one would dare go after him. And now you just took down the next biggest low-life piece of shit scum in the city. Tony Two Toes, was wanted for rape, murder, extortion, drugs, guns, credit theft—you name it. People should be thanking you. Don't worry about the bounty. It's just a way for the gangs to save face. They know Tony's time was up."

"Yeah, well, it doesn't feel great knowing anyone could put a knife through my side just to earn some chips," Zed sighed, looking over at Tony's body being looked over by a different group of enforcers, trying to salvage the internal system. Zed rubbed his eyes with the palm of his hands before grabbing the analysis kit from Boyd. "Give me that thing. We've got work to do."

They went back through the steel doorway and Zed set the analysis kit on the ground, unlatching its restraints. Two probes hovered in the air next to it waiting for a command. He removed a digital tablet from the pack and held it up, ordering the probes to do their work. They emitted soft-blue lights in all directions as they went over the room microscopically. While they were analyzing the data, Zed went back to the body.

"From what I know of knife wounds, it looks like they sliced her neck while she was lying on the ground," Zed said as he knelt down.

"How can you tell?" Boyd asked, crouching next to him.

"The blood splatter doesn't go out into the room. Instead, it remains here around the neck. I think she was either knocked out with a blunt weapon, or a drug was used to cause her to go unconscious. Now look here. The blood pools around the cut made at the neck, but not around the abdomen where the other cuts were made."

"So, they drained most of the blood from the neck first before making the next cut?"

"I think so. I've read about the practice in a history of animal butchery. They would drain the blood so the meat wouldn't spoil in transit before the meat could be harvested. But it also makes the job of gutting that animal a bit easier."

"When is the last time anyone had to butcher an animal?"

"Way before our time. Even in virtual, they don't get that specific. And look here, the way the cuts on the neck are made. It is designed so the blood spray goes away from the killer."

"Are you saying he's experienced?"

"He—or she—must have known what they were doing. I don't see any signs of other victims unless the drones come back with something. The only explanation I can offer is an odd one. The signs to me say that this person has surgical skills."

"What do you mean? A doctor? I guess any synthetic autodoc could perform these surgeries. I got a new kidney last month," Boyd said proudly, lifting up his shirt. "No stitches or scars."

"Synthetics can't harm humans, though. It's part of the limiter code. So that rules that out. It's possible that a first citizen from the time before the dome had surgical skills."

"There aren't that many left. And doctors at that? Most of them probably ascended."

"The list of the people we should interrogate will be short then. I'll have the OS run a report once we're back on the Grid." Zed paused and looked at his tablet that had just chimed. "Analysis is finished. No signs of forced entry, so it wasn't rape. The only fingerprints in the room, other than the ones I made upon entering, are from the deceased. Same with footprints. Fiber sweep will have to be analyzed further in a lab, but from what I can see, it doesn't look promising."

"No network connection and no surveillance equipment," Boyd said, looking around the room. "It sure is a convenient place to commit a crime."

"A place that shouldn't exist," Zed said, pausing a moment to reflect on the fact, and then went back to the report. "Toxicology on the victim doesn't show sign of any significant drug abuse. Blood alcohol content is high, but not outstanding if you say she was something of a lush. High blood pressure, cholesterol, etcetera, etcetera. Ah, here we go. There is a sizeable amount of hyoscine in her system, otherwise known as scopolamine. Or on the streets as—"

"Devil's Breath," Boyd finished. "A powder that is blown into a victim's face to induce a zombie-like state. We haven't seen that on the streets in a long time."

"I'd hope it would remain that way. The OS removed hyoscine from script boxes and replicators, but you can still get it from an autodoc if you can prove that you need it because some people experience motion sickness at certain levels of virtual. Also, the seeds of the boracherro shrub can be used to make the drug. It might still be found on the black market if you look hard enough."

"The killer does seem very dedicated."

"A prescription would be much easier to come by, and it fits the surgeon MO." Zed said, looking back down at the digital tablet. "Onto the organ analysis, then. What confuses me is why they didn't take them when they were finished. It seems to me that they were removed as a kind of trophy or a memento. I mean, they are displayed as much. Look, they are propped up with care and placed with an exact distance between each like they are in a gallery. But they were just left here. The time of death is days ago, so it's not like the killer was scared away."

"We should take some pictures and give them to a net diver. See if they can image match them to something on someone's storage."

"Good thought. There is a chance the killer simply took a screen capture to remember this by. I don't think someone this meticulous would be so technologically sloppy, but it's worth a shot." Zed scratched at his stubble, while returning to the report. "Okay. The report says that the state of decay on each organ is less than a minute apart."

"They would have to have been removed in rapid succession to get that sort of timing."

"Like I said, the killer knew what they were doing." Zed said, looking over the data. "This analysis doesn't give us any answers. Hopefully, the OS will have some more input once we're topside."

"Area scan is complete," Boyd said, sharing his screen with Zed. "The pit you fell into was once some sort of industrial elevator shaft. For what though? Maybe the construction of the subway? It looks like there are a few more chambers further on and a few other tunnels that all dead end. Nothing of consequence in any of them. Drones stopped when they came to this."

An image of a digital security door shown on both their displays and something inside of Zed made his spine tense up. The tunnels were nothing but concrete and dirt. A tomb for rats to scurry through. Yet in all the low-tech surroundings, there was an extremely high-tech security door. A door that required a ten-digit pin, triple security network protocols, and made with tungsten reinforcements and steel so dense that no laser or blast would penetrate it. Zed couldn't explain why, but it felt like someone was holding a knife over his throat.

"Pack our things up. Get the body and the organs in cryo. We're done here."

"There's still a lot we could look at," Boyd protested. "We haven't even searched the tunnels on foot."

"We followed protocol and did all the scans. Nothing more to do. Let's take the data back to the OS and let it decide what to do next. Until then, I don't want a bunch of loose-lipped private dicks down here. Seal it up and move out."

THE REALITY NOW

SWAN: Good evening, Omega citizens. I am Swansong McNigh. And this is The Reality Now. Last year's presentation of The War concluded with a major victory for a few lucky citizens in Omega City 3. But at what cost? The two-week long conflict concluded with a rough estimate of over 50,000 casualties worldwide. Half of that number flatlining in their VR beds, and the other half requiring major surgery and augmentations. For some that chance at the free augments is the reason for signing up, while for others it's the lucrative reward for surviving and winning. We all know that the executives behind The War foot the bill for the surgeries and body disposal, but who is going to pay for the mental trauma that these mostly onetime soldiers have to deal with when they return to reality and to our cities? To many citizens The War is a brutal reflection of a past we should leave in the past, but to others it is both a tradition and a major form of entertainment. Don't just take my opinion on the subject. Joining us tonight is Dr. Johnathon Webber and Enforcer Rosie Hart. As always, I'll be asking them to pick a side.

SWAN: Let's start with Doctor Johnathon Webber, who is a social servant from Zone Five who specializes in trauma therapy. He thinks they should discontinue The War as soon as possible.

JOHN: Immediately would be ideal. One of the reasons we are under this dome because of war. Why would we want to glorify that fact with these horrific contests of brutality? The men and woman who return from it infect our society with the things they have learned and experienced, continuing the problem of never-ending violence.

SWAN: And never-ending it seems to be. But let's hear from a different voice. Enforcer Rosie Hart did not one, but two tours of duty in The War before taking on her current position. Most people don't return from one tour. What made you choose to go back?

ROSIE: I honestly couldn't tell you a specific reason why. Everyone called me crazy. But when I got back the first time the streets of Hope City felt more like a warzone than the actual front lines did—and they still do. At least there was a code of honor out there on the battlefield and a sense of duty. As know, to be an enforcer it is mandatory to do a tour. I signed up the first time for the chance at making some credits. I think I went back for the honor, and the understanding that I was doing it for the force.

JOHN: The prerequisite for our privatized peace keepers to be military is just one of the many problems with The War. The only training needed is how to use a gun, and how to kill. How are you supposed to sympathize with other people when that is your mindset? Where is the peace in that? And not to mention there is no help provided for the mental trauma that you endure.

ROSIE: Anyone who is dealing with severe PTSD can get a brain wipe at any clinic. It's cheap, painless, and fast. That's not an issue. The people who I work with hold on to their experiences so they know what they are fighting for. The OS can watch over you all it wants, but if a killer or sexual deviant wants to hurt you, a synthetic can't help. That's what we're for. It takes a killer to catch a killer.

SWAN: Something to remember here. The OS didn't create The War, or Hope City, the class separation, the chip currency, or the Enforcers. We did. We Demanded it.

JOHN: And that says a lot about humanity, and the Omega System. But we can't let that cloud the issue. Yes, we did take a step back in asking for these primitive things, but we have a chance to change the way we think and live now. The possibilities are endless if we accept the fact that it takes work to evolve. It doesn't start by perpetuating archaic brutalism.

ROSIE: Easy to say coming from someone in the high numbers, living off your LSI, and not seeing what happens to people day in and day out in the Zero. Come take a walk down Refugee Alley and witness all the sick and homeless there digging through recyclers for food scraps. There is no LSI or MSI for them. There are too many people in this broken system. It wasn't part of the plan. This city—all the Omega Cities—are overcrowded. The War lightens the load. Some might die, and that is awful, but the ones that make it out have an actual fighting chance. The crime against humanity is letting all of this continue. Not just The War. You want humanity to evolve? Start with economic equality. Start by lessening the gap between the have and the have-nots.

JOHN: And I agree with what you have to say about the economical divide. But I still don't see the connection between the gap of the wealthy and the poor, or what overcrowding has to do with mindless violence and bloodshed. I am here saying that we need to end the broadcast of The War as entertainment. End the necessity for enforcers to do a tour of duty. Plain as that.

ROSIE: Next time I'm in a knife fight with a gang member in Hope City, I'll remember to ask them to play nice, because that's what your logic says to me.

SWAN: Well, there you have it, citizens. Should The War be allowed to continue a system of perpetual violence in order to train our peace keepers and influence population control, or should we discontinue it all together and focus our efforts on ending classism? It sounds like a tough choice to me. Maybe we should just pick a side, because this is the Reality Now.

NINETEEN

Ash knew that memories fade over time. It was an inevitable fact. Even the ones we want to hold on to forever degrade in clarity the longer we live. The neurons in our brain die off as we age if we don't actively access the memories stored in them. With all the advances in DNA modification, the understanding of the human genome, brain mapping, digital jacking, and even dream recording, we still cannot download memories from a brain to save for a future time—or as some wish—to load them into a new brain. That's one of the many ways humans and synthetics differ. A computer can forget about a file or an image for decades or centuries. All it takes is for a user to access it and the file can be brought up with crystal clarity. No net losses. So, we keep mementos to remind us of things we want to remember, even if that might mean we keep them on a digital file.

She lugged an old box that had been buried deep in the back of her closet out into her living room. The sun was setting over the west hills and her apartment was painted in a soft amber glow. She wasn't in a sentimental mood, so she turned the lights up in the room without even thinking about it. She needed to see clearly. The dreams had to be connected. After seeing the symbol carved into the pulpit last night in that decaying church, it was obvious that something bigger was going on. The symbols were more than just her subconscious dealing with past trauma. It wasn't a coping mechanism, a reoccurring dream, or some kind of nightmare induced by eating cold pizza before bed. No, these were deliberately shown to her. She knew it was a hard sell. The word crazy had been on the tip of her tongue for weeks now. The previous night only made things worse.

The box she lugged across the floor was all that was left of her brother Anton. She didn't know why, but the dreams were making her think of him. It wasn't like he was in them, or that there were hidden messages sent by him in the imagery. It was just a feeling that came over her when she was dreaming. It was like a calm and peaceful sensation that she could only remember experiencing when they were together as kids before they had a computer interface in their brains. She hoped that somewhere in the box she could find something to link to that feeling and spark some kind of memory.

When Anton ascended, the OS took all of his things with him. They called it the cleansing. Not only would the OS take the person who was ascending, but it would remove every single item from their living quarters. Only the things he had left in her living quarters escaped it. They were the only things that were proof of his ever existing at all.

She placed her shaking hands over the plastic lid, not wanting to let the memories that were held inside back out and into her life. It had taken years to seal them away, to forget them, and to accept the fact that he was never coming back. She should have incinerated the items like she had with her parent's stuff, but her will wasn't strong enough then. She hoped it was now.

"Medic," she said out loud, without realizing it. The thoughts of a nice mood stabilizer before she dug up the past ran through her head.

"How can I help you?" a synthetic voice came through the speakers of her apartment, instead of through her earpiece. A holographic generic representation of a doctor was on her display but looked as if it was standing before her.

"I'm feeling anxious tonight. I was wondering if there was something to help me with the jitters."

"Analyzing vitals. One moment." An indicator came across her display, letting her know her body was being scanned. Even though there wasn't a physical sensation associated with a body scan, it always made her feel as if tiny bugs were moving under her skin. "Analysis complete. Vital signs nominal. Caloric intake low. Glucose levels low. REM sleep periods low. Conclusion; depression. Would you like me to prescribe you something?"

"I'm not depressed," Ash sighed. "I said I have anxiety. When I'm anxious,

I have a hard time eating or sleeping."

"Understood. Here is a list of medications that are used to treat anxiety that are available through your local dispenser. I can route them to your cabinet if you'd like."

Dozens of name-brand drugs started scrolling; benzos, sedatives, muscle relaxers, pain relievers, anticonvulsants, etcetera. They all came with their own list of side effects, health warnings, and instant delivery. Several of the items on the list caused her to shake just by seeing the name. For years she had self-medicated herself into a sedated, coma-like pit of unfeeling so deep that when it came time to pull herself back out the withdrawals were excruciating. She had opted out of taking more medications to help her ween off the meds, thinking cold turkey was the only way to go. To this day, she didn't know if that was a good idea or a bad one. She was suddenly disgusted with herself for even calling up the autodoc.

"Just give me a nutrient supplement and an energy booster," Ash said, pushing the autodoc off of her display. She grabbed a bottle of wine that was still sitting on her coffee table from when Cody had come over and poured herself a glass. "I'll take care of this myself."

"I have delivered your requested items to the medicine cabinet. Be well."

She downed the glass in a gulp and immediately poured another. It didn't make her hand any steadier, but she was no longer afraid of whatever emotions might arise from opening Anton's storage container. Unlatching the cover and sliding it over, a musty smell immediately filled the room. The items smelt dead to her, which was good. The last thing she wanted was to pick up a shirt of his and find that it smelled like him.

Picking up a hooded sweatshirt from the top, it had an odor of an old closet on a hot day. It sparked nothing in her memory. Next item. Another article of clothing. Nothing. An ultra ball they used to toss around when they thought of going pro. That smelled like old leather and dirt, but no spark. A book he had been reading before he left. He was old-fashioned like that. Nada. Some toiletries, a spare hand terminal, a ballpoint pen. Zip. Zero. Zilch. The box was nothing but leftover junk and discarded items from a brilliant life. They were meaningless without the person they belonged to. A small plastic case was wedged at the bottom, with colorful illustrations adorning its exterior. She reached down to the bottom of the bin and pulled it out. The illustrations were done in a superhero comic book style. She pried the case open and there was a small black data disk inside. She removed it and held it up to the light.

"Identify," she said, activating her system's camera. Internet pages started popping up before her. It seemed as if the disk was decades old and in an outdated format. She looted around the box for any kind of device that would play it, but there was nothing. "Why would he keep a hard copy of something that he couldn't look at?"

Locating a device that would connect the disk to her system on the net, she pushed purchase while she got up off the floor and tossed back the rest of her glass of wine. By the time she had gone to the bathroom and taken her nutritional supplement and energy booster, the delivery drone had swooped past her balcony door and left a fresh package behind. Plugging the new drive into her wall screen, she returned to the box while the system analyzed the contents.

There was a folder of files she hadn't opened, but she already knew what they were. Aptitude test records from the dream academy, report cards from dozens of classes and seminars they attended to open their cognitive powers of mental clarity and creativity, clinical records of both her and Anton's chip integration surgery, and countless copies of bills and legal forms. The day they were jacked into a system that they should have been told they would never escape. It wasn't a day she wanted to remember, so she tossed the files aside.

The screen announced that the files from the disk were loaded and paired on all her devices. They were CBR files—digital comic books. Anton hadn't read any of those since he was really little. He must have kept this one for sentimental reasons. She pushed play on the device and the pages flipped automatically every minute or so.

Returning to the box, she found a document declaring a legal change of custody. It was paired with a certificate of ascension for both their parents. She looked up at the screen to watch a page turn and let her mind drift over the past. The day her parents were taken away was the same day her brother became her legal guardian. It was a very emotional day, but she didn't cry. Thinking back on it now, she found it sad to remember how much she actually felt relieved at the time. There were lots of big people and synthetics talking in loud voices at each other. And all she could think of was how excited she was now that she and Anton could be left alone. She didn't even realize there was another glass of wine in her hand until it was at her lips.

The page on the screen turned again, causing her to yell out stop as she slammed her glass down on the floor. Crawling on her hands and knees, she moved closer to the screen. There before her was the beast-like creature she had seen in her last dream, the one that had chased her through the park. Greasy, coarse fur over thick, muscular arms and legs. Long, sharp claws and blood-stained teeth. It was one ugly son of a bitch. In this part of the story, the beast was chasing down a girl riding a horse, just as she had in her dream. Flipping through the pages rapidly she was disappointed to find that both the beast and the girl weren't in the story at all after that scene. She assumed their story continued in the next issue.

Picking up the plastic box, she read the title, Dark Rituals. It didn't ring a bell, so she searched for it quickly on the internet. The only thing that came up was a bibliography of the writer and illustrator who had created the work. There was no story synopsis, images, or options to buy. Other than a notation that it had been made, it didn't seem to exist on the internet at all. A hard reality to swallow when almost everything was on the digital cloud. As frustrating as it was, it proved that her intuition was right. Somehow her dreams were connected to her brother. She had never seen these images or this digital book in her life before now, and it wasn't something she could have looked at on the internet. There should not have been a way that they could have entered her dreams then. She couldn't prove that she hadn't seen them as a kid and forgotten them, but it was a place to start.

"Incoming call," her system alerted her. "Edward Eagleson."

"Eddie!" she exclaimed, as a man's face displayed before her. She brushed her hair into place nonchalantly. Noticing her disheveled state in the small window that displayed what her system's camera was putting out.

"I'm heading out," he said sharply, "Usual spot in fifteen."

"Sure thing—" The video feed cut out mid-sentence. She cursed as she leaped to her feet, frustrated that she had forgotten her meeting with Eddie today.

• • •

She hadn't booted into her avatar in so long the system required an update before she could link in. Of course, this type of thing just had to happen when she was in a hurry. She had been meaning to buy a new synthetic body, but since she rarely used one it wasn't high on her priority list. Because of her procrastination, she was now stuck in a limbo between actual reality and virtual reality. She was jacked in but not linked to her avatar and it felt like internet purgatory. A pale-blue loading bar hovered over a dark empty space and an internal clock was ticking away in the back of her brain. The loading bar gave an estimated time of ten minutes to install the update. Ten minutes was too long.

"Connect to Second Home," Ash directed her system. "Bring up security cameras. Run interior sweep. Prep body for nightlife. I want something non-descript, but still trendy. Call an autocar to the Sixth Street door. And brew me a cup of coffee."

Across town, on the northern side of Zone Three South, a small ground-floor apartment came to life. Lights were adjusted, soft music played, and the temperature brought to an even seventy degrees. While the synthetic body's computer system was being updated, the Automatic Closet System dressed it in something appropriate for the time of day and season. Make-up was rapidly applied and the hair styled. The security system panned the small living space with motion sensors, searched for unusual heat signatures, and swept for unknown synthetic entities. And a single cup of coffee was brewed with an added splash of flavored dairy-free cream.

The downtown apartment was a type of synth shack or a retrofitted living space that mainly functioned as an automated docking bay for synthetic avatars. An umbrella company held ownership of most of the properties and leased them out to anyone with the credits. The confidentiality of their client's identity was priority number one. Most people who owned one claimed it was for traveling across town in a hurry. But in reality, synth shacks were for people who wanted a complete alternate identity that wasn't based in virtual reality. And why stop at one? Some people had as many as a dozen. Ash only owned one, and it was a necessity. Even if her avatar didn't look like her, the moment she left her quarters in the Six the paparazzi surveillance drones would pick her up. It didn't matter if she appeared as a two-hundred-pound man, the paparazzi would follow her. Maybe not at first, but eventually the link would be made that the portly fellow leaving her building was actually her in an outlandish avatar.

When the synthetic version of Ash walked out of her shack and onto Sixth Street, an immense digital billboard of her face immediately assaulted her.

"The Dreamer dreams!" the advertisement read in big bold letters. In it, her eyes were open, but instead of irises, she had black and white spirals that spun round and round. The monster from her most recent dream was creeping up behind her through the darkness. Then it suddenly leaped forward until its horrible face took up the whole screen. She almost dropped her coffee because it was so startling. While she had never posed for an advertisement or taken a single photograph with a professional, her face was somehow everywhere. Her digital doppelganger was on countless ad screens from the Six to Hope City. It was all part of her lovely contract. The company owned her likeness and could do with it whatever they wanted as long as they wanted. That's why she needed a synth shack. It was a much-needed alternate identity.

Also, she could abuse the synthetic body all she wanted.

Slamming the cup of coffee, she tossed it in a recycler and lit up a cigarette. Her actual body would get a painless injection of caffeine and a small dose of nicotine, but there would be no smoke in her lungs or coffee oils in her stomach. When the autocar pulled up, an advertisement for Big Gun was plastered on its side with Cody's face prominently featured. Perfect, she laughed, getting in.

It was a brief ride to the usual meeting location. Eddie preferred to only meet in cybersex parlors. He really liked them filthy too, the filthier the better. If the place was so disgusting that you wouldn't want to tell anyone that you went there, you also wouldn't tell anyone who you had seen there. At least, that's how Ash rationalized it. She didn't want to think of Eddie hooked up in a sex booth, doing who-knows-what to who-knows-who. It had to be for covert reasons. Right?

The autocar dropped her off a block away at a swanky French restaurant. While it wasn't her body that was being used, her credit account was still paying for everything. She didn't want a record of her drop-off location as The Cock Pit, even though she knew the OS would be monitoring her movements. It would watch her look at the menu in the window, see her think about ordering the frog legs entrée with a bone marrow appetizer, and witness her then walk down the street towards a row of sex parlors.

The entrance of The Cock Pit had a replica of an ancient prop plane busting through the wall, with the propeller spinning away like crazy. It made sexual engine noises at anyone who walked past. The door handle was a leather-coated, vertical control column that felt like an erect penis when you had to grab it to open the door. Ash always waited until someone entered or exited so she wouldn't have to touch it. Inside there was a bar right in front that served drug and alcohol mixed cocktails. The back bar was a digital projection of black and neon-green design, reminiscent of early forms of heads-up displays used in old jet fighter planes.

On either side of the bar were rows of rooms that contained unique virtual couches used to jack into the cyberworld and engage in all kinds of sexual encounters. The couches had unique equipment that attached or inserted into your private areas and reacted to what the other person—or persons—was doing on the other end. That was the basic description, at least. They were the main attraction of the club. Being pretty expensive and requiring routine maintenance, most people didn't have that kind of setup in their personal quarters.

There was also a seating area off to the right of the bar, just in case you wanted to have a drink and take in the scenery. Almost all the parlors had a traditional bar setup with a physical bar to sit at and mingle with others and a seating area for group conversation. Some parlors were actually pretty popular. People would come to hang out at the bar for a chance to meet someone, with the intent for each person to get room to hook up virtually. The Cock Pit wasn't the type of place people went looking for companionship, so the bar and seating area were usually empty. Just the way Eddie liked it.

The wine she drank earlier was still in her system so she passed up her usual vodka soda and went straight for a glass of bourbon. While she waited for her drink, she noticed something strange out of the corner of her eye. She realized there was a mirror not far off and had glimpsed her avatar in the reflection. Looking into a mirror and not actually seeing herself always caused an unsettling sensation of disembodiment. Even though her avatar was merely a taller, thinner version of her real body, it never felt right. A synthetic would always be a synthetic.

"You're late," Eddie said, sliding into the leather booth across from her. The table they were at projected a black and orange air traffic control screen that illuminated the angular contours of Eddie's hawk-like face. He wore a silver-rimmed flat-black pair of circular sunglasses at all times and stroked his chin stubble with his boney fingers that each had a different color fingernail. Ash felt that he was always staring her down with the way that he held his posture.

"Software update on the body," Ash said while shifting uncomfortably.

"That update was over two weeks ago."

"I don't get out much." She took a swig of the bourbon, and it made a warming effect in her chest. The tension in her neck relaxed just enough so she could handle Eddie's attitude.

"So, what's it gonna be this time, dream angel?" Eddie asked, looking around the room. His face blurred slightly as it turned. The features kind of jittered when she wasn't looking him straight in the face.

"I need some more Night Nights."

"I thought you were through with that shit? Why are you starting back up?"

"It's none of your business."

"Look," Eddie said, looking disgruntled, "I know we all need our kicks. But if it ain't in a script box, and it ain't any fun, then I don't know why you would wanna do it."

"Why do you sell them then?"

Eddie grimaced and sat back slowly. He reached his hand inside his leather trench coat and pulled out a vial of pills. Tossing them across the table, he said, "Because there are some fucked up people in the world."

"Yeah, that's why we live under a dome now," Ash said, taking the pills and putting them in her purse. She transferred a small number of credits over to Eddie's account, and the OS immediately fined her for purchasing illegal drugs. A notification announced that her social morality status had also dropped slightly. Good. It's what she wanted. "I'll need the usual chip exchange, too."

"We need to talk about that."

"What's to talk about?" Ash asked, taking another swig.

"A lot," Eddie sucked in his lips as if holding in a lot of words and trying to choose the best way to let them out. He sent over some info to Ash's display and said, "This is the current exchange rate."

"That's fine. I've got that."

Eddie smiled and looked down at his drink for a second. "I know you have it. That's not the problem. The problem is the value of chips is rising drastically. It's almost a hundred times what it should be. Until it lowers significantly, this is the last exchange that I can do for you."

"I don't understand. I pay you a lot of credits, and above market value."

"As you should. But it's not about the creds. I know you're worried about ascending." He paused a leaned forward over the illuminated table, giving his face an eerie appearance. She shifted uncomfortably in her seat. "I know, because there are several of you doing the same thing. You're taking all the chips out of Hope City and hoarding them in the Six so your monetary and moral social statuses don't reach a point where you'll ascend. The OS doesn't track chips like it does credits. And dealing with a person like me lowers your morality. It's simple." He twirled his glass and chuckled, "You all must be crazy to not want to ascend. I'd do anything to get out of this shithole."

"Not all of us believe you go to a better place," Ash protested, breathing heavily and taking a hard sip from her bourbon. She looked around the room nervously, as if trying to see if anyone had heard what she had just said. Only when Ash had regained her composure did Eddie continue.

"The chip currency is a closed system. Do you know what that means? It means that there are only so many chips to go around, and more can't just magically be made like credits. You've taken so many chips out of the system there aren't enough for average people to spend on things they actually need. I've been told to warn you. Either spend the chips or face the consequences."

"The consequences? What does that mean? Are you going to kill me?"

"Don't be dumb. Kill you? No. Like I said, I'll have to stop doing business with you. If you somehow find someone else to do business with, you'll be banned and your new connection will be... taken care of."

"So, you'll kill them?" Ash laughed. Eddie's reply was a stone-cold blank expression. "Jesus. Well, you'll have to help me out. I can't get into No Hope to spend the chips. No synths allowed, right? I can't leave my quarters if I'm not in a synth."

"What? You paralyzed or something in real life?"

"No. Nothing like that. It's my face, it's everywhere. I'll be mobbed."

"Doubt it," Eddie said, looking up at a group of loud people entering the Pit. His face distorted for a second, followed by a wash of digital pixelation. "People in the Zero don't give a shit."

"I just can't be around that many people at once. I have bad anxiety, I'll freak out. I can't just walk down the streets as, you know, myself, but I guess I need to spend some chips." She let out a heavy sigh and leaned back in her chair. She looked at Eddie from the side. His face blurred slightly in between the point where she was looking at him face-on and from the side. Cody had told her about that, when you saw glitches on people's faces. It gave her an idea. She smiled and said, "I think I know what I need. And it's something you already have."

"Yeah? What's that?"

She leaned in close and said, "A facial distorter."

Lightning fast, Eddie reached out and twisted Ash's wrist. The pain sent an alarming digital sensation to her real body. A glass broke at the bar as the group of people there grew louder. Their yelling and cheering intensified as Eddie twisted Ash's arm further.

"Shut. The. Fuck. Up," he said, letting her wrist go. "It's listening."

"Right. Sorry." Ash said, rubbing at her wrist. Her face illuminated with an internal thought and she whispered, "So, let's say I wanted to buy a pair of sunglasses. Really nice ones. Do you know anyone who could help me out?"

"No."

"What? I thought you could get anything. Please?" Ash pleaded, reaching her hands across the table for his, but Eddie pulled back. "I need to spend these chips fast. I'll probably never even use it."

"Okay. Yeah, I know someone who can get you some real nice sunglasses," He snarled his lip as he said her new code word. "And it'll cost you a lot of chips, too. We'll need to rent some rooms. Plug into the couches."

"What are you talking about? Here?"

"Yes. Here. But not like that. We plug into their system and I'll route us to an alternate server. There I can get you connected with the people you want. If you're ready?"

Ash took a moment to think. It was all happening so fast. The facial distorter had just popped into her head. She didn't know if she actually needed one. But if it would take the chips off her hands so she could dump more credits in the long run, it would be worth it. "I guess so."

"You guess so? This isn't something you want to be unsure about."

"Yes," Ash blurted, sitting up straight. "This is what I want."

"Okay. Good. Because this is serious. These people are serious. I don't know who they are in real life, and I don't want to know. When you finish dealing with them, you tell me nothing about the transaction. Got it?"

"Got it," Ash replied. The group from the bar stumbled into the room and walked over to the floor-to-ceiling digital jukebox. She ignored them and thought of the other question she wanted an answer to. She brought up the file she and Cody had made of all the symbols from all her dreams and shared screens with Eddie. "You don't by chance know what these are, do you?"

Eddie took a moment to look at the image. At the Jukebox, someone cried out and picked a song. "I love Ishi," a young man in woman's clothing yelled, as the loud pop music blasted out of the speakers. A hologram of the synthetic pop star Ishi filled the room as she sang along to the thumping music.

"Fucking hipsters," Eddie cursed while finishing his drink. He looked up at Ash from the picture of the symbols and laughed. "They're directions, stupid. In Hope City. Now come on. We gonna do this or what?"

"Directions?" Ash exclaimed, feeling very confused. Eddie was getting to his feet, so Ash hurried to follow him.

She bought a double room at the back of the club instead of two single rooms at Eddie's request. He said it would be easier if they were on the same input. As a receipt of the transaction showed on her display, she let out a long sigh. Her credit report would show more than just a quick drink at the local sex club. She had never used one of the booths that were popular all over the city. She knew it was a completely normal and completely sterile thing to do. Hell, even Cody had her own personal machine in her quarters. But Cody also used it to make money when she was desperate, or wanted something really expensive and needed quick creds. Her alter ego was Crystal_Rose. Even so, Ash just couldn't get with it. Call her old-fashioned but virtual sex just wasn't for her. When the bartender pulled back a curtain to reveal a plethora of different attachments for the machine, she was speechless. Eddie nudged her to just pick one, so she chose the purple one because it was the least offensive.

When they were let into the room that was nothing more than two virtual couches and some low blue-colored lighting. She just stood in the middle of the room trying to not touch anything, but there was nothing to touch, not even a chair or a small table. It was a real utilitarian design—jack in and get off. Eddie immediately got onto one couch and prepped himself.

"Don't worry," Eddie said reassuringly. "We can keep our clothes on. And we won't be using those things. You can set it down."

Ash slowly set the purple dildo-shaped attachment on the floor, where it promptly flopped over and rolled away. She looked at the machine, then back at Eddie, and asked, "So, how does this work? Me being in a synth and all."

"Well, depending on how high-end your avatar is, it's just like the real thing. If you've opted for realistic genitalia, then you'd just, you know, plug in and go to town."

"No, not like that. I mean, I'm already jacked in. How can I jack into something else?"

"You really don't get out much, do you?" Eddie laughed. "It's just like how you do it at home. For a basic interface, you're just going to apply the nodes to your temples, where your internal system connects to your HUD. When you get prompted to connect to the server, the host will daisy chain you with your system at home to the one here, and you'll be in. It'll be just like the real thing. I mean, I'm sure it's a lot more complicated than that, but I'm not a computer coder. I sell drugs, remember?"

"I can still kind of feel my body in the real world at the same time I'm feeling this synthetic. When I jack in, I'll be in three different entities. Will I feel them all?"

"What is this with the questions?" Eddie barked. "You want to do this or what? I got places to be."

"Okay, okay," Ash said, laying down on the couch and putting the nodes on her temples like she had done at home. "I'm ready."

"Now, when we get in and you're on the menu screen, touch nothing. We don't actually want to enter the program." Ash nodded at Eddie's commands, even though he couldn't see her do it. "I'm going to take us somewhere else, where we can meet someone. When we get there—and this is important—say as little as possible. You're there for the distorter, you'll pay in chips, in person, and that's it. Don't talk about anything else and don't ask questions. Got it?"

"Got it."

"Good. I'm trusting you on this one. Don't fuck it up."

Eddie's body went limp as he jacked in. Ash took a deep breath and hit the connect button, linking her to yet another level of virtual reality. A flash of white light hit the back of her eyeballs and sent a sharp pain through her skull that she could feel in both her heads. When the light dissipated, she had the odd sensation of feeling three different bodies. The third one, which was in the virtual sex program, felt the most real. The synthetic felt like a second skin, and her real body was just a phantom. She looked down at her new virtual body, and to her horror, she was completely naked and looked exactly like her real self. Noticing she was on an avatar creation screen, she quickly hit the randomize button, and it changed her to a woman that both looked good and yet nothing like her. It instantly moved her onto another menu screen that was a kind of waiting room. Eddie looked exactly as he did in real life—if that was even his actual body—as he stood waiting for her.

"Look at those hips," he mocked. "Didn't think you were into big butts. Just hang out here for a moment, okay?"

His avatar vanished from the program. With nothing else to do, she glanced over the menu that gave users choices of what kind of program they'd like to run. There were so many options. You could start by changing your gender if you'd like, but that would require more gizmos from the bar. Next, you could choose to connect with anyone in any Omega City who was using a booth at that moment or pick someone who was more local. There was a list of users and their connected profiles on the right-hand side, with the local users on the left. The local side only displayed Eddie's name, and it had a light next to it to show they were already in a session. Curious, she reached up and scrolled the extended current user list on the right. It scrolled and scrolled on and on, no matter how fast she moved it. There was a user count on the bottom right and she gasped when she saw the number. It looked to be more than half the people in all the Omega Systems on at that exact moment.

A different option was to connect with a prerecorded session. Any user could record the things they do and upload them for others to experience. But most people chose recordings by already famous people, or at least someone posing as a famous person. She clicked on the recorded sessions tab and typed in Cody's alter ego, Crystal_Rose. She hesitated for a moment, wondering if it was something she even wanted to see. Diving headlong, she continued on and a list of video previews came on her screen with a woman gyrating in all kinds of positions. She exited quickly and was back on the top menu feeling a little violated. That wasn't something she expected to see today.

"Hey, I'm back," Eddie's voice came through her earpiece. "There is going to be a pop-up window appearing in a second here. I want you to type *Run Onion*, okay? That will open a browser that the OS can't monitor. I'll send you a private message. It'll look like gibberish, but it's actually a link. Copy and paste that and a door should appear in the waiting room you're in. Go through it and the people you need to talk to should be there."

"A door is going to appear?" Ash asked, as she typed in the command code in the black and white pop-up window.

"Just hurry up. Mr. E doesn't enjoy waiting." Eddie said, as his mic clicked off.

"Mr. E?" Ash said to herself, and kind of chuckled.

She pasted the code that did indeed look like gibberish. When she hit enter, a bright green light appeared from her left and a door was drawn out in a moving laser beam. It was fascinating. If all of this was possible in virtual, why did people want to relive her dreams? This was already intense enough. She felt like she was traveling further and further from her home, even though she was still there, and could be there mentally in one quick flip of the escape button. She walked over to the door and pressed on the handle. There was no going back now.

Bright light consumed her as she jumped through cyberspace. When it dissipated, there appeared to be a long dark hallway before her. A low-lit room a hundred meters away was the only indication that there was, in fact, a hallway in front of her and not just an empty space. Stepping through the threshold, it didn't feel like anything had happened and her system didn't give her any alerts. But when the door closed behind her, she knew she was no longer at The Cock Pit, and maybe not even in Omega City 6. She was in a place that didn't exist, and no one knew she was there. Even though she couldn't be harmed at this level of virtual, she still felt terrified. Mustering up her courage, she squinted through the white lights pointed in her direction. Step by step, she made her way down the hall.

The room had black walls that disappeared into the rest of the nothingness. Gold-plated molding adorned the black ceiling and lush red carpeted floor. A pair of large majestic palms gave the illusion of there being corners to the room. Gold-trimmed white marble pillars were at each side behind an elegant ebony desk. There a man sat wearing a black blazer over a muscular and tan, bare chest. He wore heavy gold chains and jeweled golden rings. A black and white mask was over his face. It was of a mustached man that had a heavily exaggerated, full-toothed grin. The eyes glowed an electric-red and his plastic-looking black hair was slicked back. When he spoke, an echo of red laser light flashed through the background, quietly fading into the darkness.

"Welcome to The Barbary Coast," the man said in a deep echoing voice. "What is it you desire?"

She looked around for Eddie, but he wasn't there. She pictured him in her mind as he just kind of made his eyes subtly bigger and pursed his lips as if to say get on with it. She blurted out, "I need a facial distorter."

The red light flashed again, making small bars that blinked into and out rapidly, returning smaller and smaller each time as if they were moving away. The man was silent. He appeared to be thinking. When she was about to add something else, he finally asked, "Why?"

"Personal reasons," she replied, her voice faintly cracking.

"A facial distorter. It hides the true identity of the wearer from the OS, synthetic intelligences, and other humans without the use of an avatar. This type of thing is very illegal. It could bring you and me a lot of trouble."

"I understand that," Ash said, looking at the man's glowing red eyes as confidently as she could. He didn't immediately reply, and another strobe of red light swept away into infinity.

"Who are you?" The man boomed.

"I, uh," she stuttered, "I'd rather not say."

"Who sent you?"

"I'd rather not say."

"Very good," the man said, folding his massive hands in front of him. "We cannot trust people who cannot keep secrets. Understand this, we do not know you. You do not know us. If you get caught using this device, you do not mention us. You do not mention your connection to us. You do not even mention the node you are jacking in from. You will keep quiet. Understood?"

"Yes, sir."

"This item is expensive. You will pay with chips only. In-person. Tomorrow. No avatar. We don't deal with synthetics."

The room went black as if it disappeared. The man's mask was still there, smiling, but it slowly faded away eerily. A green light from behind her signaled that the door had returned at the end of the hallway. It opened as she approached, and through it she could see the virtual waiting room they had been in earlier.

"That was weird," Ash said as she exited the door.

"You did good. Real good." Eddie replied.

"So, what happens now?"

"A location will be sent to you tomorrow that the runner decides on for the exchange."

"So, I'm not getting it now, or from you?"

"Correct on both. You can't just drop something like this in a box and have a drone deliver it. And I don't handle this kind of stuff. Too hot. I only helped you out with this because I get a piece of the take, and I could use the chips since they are in such high demand."

"Thanks, I guess."

"I gotta run. One more thing before I go, in case the runner doesn't tell you. Once you put the distorter on, you have to assume a different identity. The device will block your location services and make it look like you are still at the place you put it on, but it can't block any credit transaction you make. You make a purchase with credits at a location you're not supposed to be at, and it makes a discrepancy report. The OS will figure it out and you'll be busted. Never refer to yourself with your actual name and try not to acknowledge anyone who thinks they know it's you. Not only will the OS be watching, but if someone discovers you, that person can blackmail you. But I doubt you know anyone who does that kind of thing."

"So, how do you get around if you can't make a transaction? You can't ride the subway or take an autocar?"

"Better buy some good walking shoes."

"I doubt you walk everywhere," Ash laughed, to which Eddie just gave her a blank look. "Well, okay. I'll wait to hear from you tomorrow, I guess."

"No, you won't."

"Oh, that's right. You don't know me. I don't know you. Wait? Do I know you?"

"No one really does," he said, and his avatar blinked out of the program.

Ash hit escape and the program rushed her back to the back room of The Cock Pit just in time to see the door to the room closing. She raced out of the bar to see someone that looked like Eddie racing away on an Ion Bike, the electric-blue lines of its energy wake disappearing into the night.

EIGHTEEN

"You're all here because you chose to be," the holographic drill sergeant shouted over the sounds of countless shells dropping onto a distant battlefield.

Zed was in the back of a military transport truck heading to the front lines of The War. The truck jostled over a pothole-filled mud road, causing everyone to bump into each other as it lumbered on. The sergeant just hovered over them, unaffected by the movement.

"You chose to be here, and so did they. They all went through the same grueling Bootcamp and weapons training that you did. They all said goodbye to the people and things they loved and accepted that coming here was a sacrifice for the good of the Omega System. As of right now, all of you are still Omega citizens. But once you set boots on the ground, you will all be soldiers and only soldiers. They will be your enemy. And you are going to fight with them until they spill your blood, or you spill theirs. You are going to engage in combat, the likes that few have seen in our modern era.

"It won't be pretty, it won't be easy, and a lot of you won't be coming back. Why you signed up for this godforsaken war is beyond me, but you're here and that's saying something. If you ask me, you should have waited until the next War. You might have had a chance at something easier. Maybe you would survive. That being said, I am obligated to tell you that this is your last chance to disengage. Just say your password into the comms and you'll be unplugged from the system. No shame in that."

The soldier next to Zed had been shaking nervously for some time now. Suddenly, he began to phase in and out of existence with a sizeable amount of digital distortion. When he leaned over to see if Ricky was still there, his face had turned to a pale and blank silicon slate. Slowly, a digitally generated face was rendered with features attempting to imitate what Ricky looked like. But Zed knew Ricky was gone, back to Hope City to live life in the gutters and the streets. He was wondering if he should have done the same thing. Looking out the back of the truck at the convoy that was heading towards the front line, he wondered how many others decided that the risk wasn't worth the reward.

"Second Platoon, Delta Company!" the sergeant barked. "It seems that only one of you had the brains to pull out. I hope you all remember him when your hands fill up with your own guts and you're praying for a quick death. He'll be a citizen in an Omega City again, enjoying the good times that you gave him by sacrificing your life."

"Don't listen to him," Natalia whispered into his ear as her hand gripped his firmly. "We're going to get through this, and then we are getting out of No Hope. You'll see."

The truck took a sharp turn, and for a brief moment, the troops had their first view of the battlefield. It looked like the earth had split open and let out its hellish insides. A plume of black smoke filled the sky, coming out from what seemed to be an endlessly blazing fire. The lush fields of green grass and clear blue skies of Northern France were replaced with a monotone landscape of blackness and death. Before them was a ten-mile stretch of mud and corpses, with splashes of blood and toxic water. The truck turned, and the sight was gone, but the thumping in Zed's chest remained.

"This year's War is based on the World War One Battle of Verdun," the holographic drill sergeant continued. "It was one of the worst and bloodiest engagements recorded in human history. Millions of artillery shells were fired over this 302-day battle—that some might call a siege. When it was done, the casualties totaled over 700,000. We don't have that many soldiers to throw into the meat grinder, and we don't have a year to waste watching you die, so we are dropping you right into the middle of the first offensive. Your objective is to make it to the front lines and relieve the SI soldiers that are there. You then have two weeks to survive. Make it out alive and you'll be handsomely rewarded. If your company racks up more points by killing or wounding more of the enemy, you win The War and your life will change forever."

A silent stillness came over the platoon. A lot of them had already endured life in the outer lands. Some of them had also survived the Sickness. But they couldn't survive whatever their Zone Zero was like so they chose The War. The thought of not having to struggle just to live was a momentary relief from the oncoming doom. As he looked around, he could see that same thought was written on all the other soldiers' faces. It was a glazed-over, faraway look into whatever their end-goal was. Ricky's goal must not have been strong enough, or his life back in reality wasn't actually that bad. For Zed, it was being with Natalia for as long as he could. Directly across from him was a different kind of soldier, with a different kind of dream.

"Don't fuck it up, Takeda," the soldier said while checking the magazine of his MLE rifle. He was one of the rare ones who signed up because he wanted to be an enforcer. He had taken every second of Bootcamp and weapons training with absolute seriousness. "If you turn tail under fire, I'll shoot you myself."

"Zip it, Gunderson," the sergeant ordered.

"You know how it works, right?" he continued. "You point it like this and shoot the enemy. But if you shoot your own team and they make you pay for it—if you make it out. So don't do that. You hear? I don't wanna have to worry about you shooting me in the back."

"I'm not going to shoot you," Zed countered.

"Yeah. You probably won't shoot anyone. I figured you were soft when I first saw you. You'll probably spend the next two weeks shitting your pants in some ditch, waiting for it all to be over. Letting all of us do the work for you. Why don't you do us all a favor and put a bullet—"

"I said zip it!" the sergeant boomed.

A sound like a whistling teapot started growing louder and louder. Suddenly, an explosion went off in front of their truck. The shock sent bodies flying all over. Screams could be heard from outside. More explosions erupted close by, sending chunks of earth up into the air.

"Out of the truck now!" the sergeant yelled with his digital image flickering as soldiers moved through him. "Welcome to hell, maggots."

Soldiers piled out of the truck like rats from a sinking ship. They fell over each other as they hit the dirt and scrambled for cover. The truck in front of theirs had been hit. The burnt-out shell was full of blackened corpses. There was no way that their truck was going to move any further. They would have to make the last klick to the trenches on foot. A digital readout illuminated before Zed's eyes, apparently, his HUD was still active. A leaderboard was the only thing displayed, and it showed that the Charlie Company was now negative a lot of points.

A blast blew up the truck behind theirs, sending Zed flying face-first into the mud. The soldiers had evacuated the truck already, and some of them slowed just enough to grab Zed by his pack and drag him to his feet. He looked frantically around for Natalia, but in a sea of drab uniforms scrambling around furiously, everyone looked the same. He was being pushed forward by other soldiers, running along with the pack and not knowing if he was even with his platoon anymore.

Shells were falling everywhere. Their impact explosions seemed to bleed into one another until it all became an endless rolling eruption. They flew overhead by the thousands and in all different sizes. Some went whistling over, while others howled. A few moaned low, rumbling through the air like a passing autocar. Altogether, it made an infernal roar of devastating destruction. The ground was bursting upwards in all directions and carried countless bodies with each blast. So much shrapnel was being strewn about that it appeared as a fog of war. Several pieces of fast-moving metal caught bits of his clothing and nicked at his skin. Several soldiers were already on the ground clenching their bloody guts, pulling the jagged pieces of steel out with horrific screams.

There were so many bodies in the air that they were crashing into each other mid-flight. Body parts began zipping around in a mess of carnage. A severed head came flying by so fast that it knocked a soldier off his feet right next to Zed. He didn't even think for a second to stop and check on the soldier. Nothing would matter If he didn't reach the trenches soon.

The ground was so honeycombed with craters from the shell impacts that he had to zigzag his way through. He suddenly had the sensation that he was running across the surface of the moon, or on some alien planet. Clenching his gun as he ran, he could see the front line coming closer. The shells were falling behind him now, but that gave him no sense of ease as bullets were ripping up the ground all around him.

Beyond the trenches, there was a stretch of mud that was blanketed in barbed wire and rotting corpses—No Man's Land. Even though the real soldiers had just entered the battle, the simulation was set up to immerse the user in a full experience. The War was made to feel like they had entered a situation where thousands of people had already died. The wretched stench of death was already in his nostrils as he slammed into the inside wall of the trench. He wondered if by the end they would be able to tell the real corpses from the fake ones.

"Shoot me," a soldier shouted, as Zed jumped into the trench. "You there. Shoot me. Just shoot me in the leg."

"What?"

"I gotta get out of here. I should have unplugged back in basic. Shoot me in the leg so they can pull me out to a medical tent."

"There's no medical tent out there," a different soldier said. "You didn't read the manual, did you?"

"No medics?" Zed asked.

"You too?" the second soldier laughed, ducking his head as an explosion went off just over the wall. "You morons. Look, if you get hurt, a computer run medic will come patch you up, but it can only use the tools of the period. They aren't that great. No autodocs here. And there's no pulling out until the two weeks are up."

"We're fucked," Zed said with a sudden realization. The soldier who wanted to be shot erupted into a frantic shriek.

"You said it, bud. Besides, if you shoot him, you'll never make it out of the Zero. You'll be stuck with his medical bill. Don't shoot the friendlies. Okay? Just keep your head down and only shoot people that come over the wall. You'll be fine," the soldier reassured him with a pat on his back. The shrieking one turned and started running back towards the trucks. The second soldier leaned in, pointing and said, "Him? He's a goner."

More and more soldiers were running into the trenches. Hugging the dirt wall, Zed tried to scan the faces for someone from his platoon. The trench stretched outwards in either direction. He knew it went on for miles and there was no way to tell what point in the line he had entered. What good was his HUD if he couldn't use the GPS? The scoreboard was still there in bright red numbers and ticking away in both directions. He thumbed his finger and the display turned off.

Zed caught a soldier running away with the insignia of his platoon drawn on his pack. He waved off the soldier who had given him friendly advice and moved on from the entry point. Pushing his way through people moving about frantically, he felt as if he were swimming in a sea of humans. The wounded were being carted around on stretchers with their insides hanging out. Dark-eyed, bone-thin soldiers carried them, with their mud-covered uniforms hanging off their limbs like worn-out rags. Zed guessed they were meant to be the soldiers they were relieving. Even though they were all computer-generated, the impression they gave off was heartbreakingly real. Was he to assume that this was what he would look like after the two weeks were up? He tried to focus on the soldier running away from him through the trenches. He wouldn't be able to stop moving until he got to his designated position.

People were hunkered down everywhere. They pressed their backs into the dirt wall as hard as they could while holding helmets that looked like steel salad bowls on their heads. Zed wondered if they would actually save someone from a direct hit. Just as he thought that, a piece of shrapnel slammed into the side of his helmet, causing his vision to blur and his ears to ring. Still moving, he held his helmet down with all his might like everyone else.

"You sure got your bell rung!" A soldier grabbed Zed by the arm and pulled him into a dugout. "You better take cover for a minute. You seem disorient-tated."

Zed felt dizzy, but he blamed it on the intensity of the situation. His adrenaline was through the roof. After taking a second to rest against the wall, he found he was shaking all over. "I have to follow that guy. He knows where my platoon is."

"What's your outfit, soldier?"

"Delta Company. Second Platoon."

The man's voice changed as he said, "Delta company, eh?" and then slipped back into his forced man's-man accent. "You're headed the wrong way. You're to relieve Bravo Company a little over a klick in the other direction."

"Shit," he cursed.

"You said it bud," the man said, just like the other soldier. He realized then that they were all automated responses from computer-generated characters to guide him in to fill the ranks. Zed looked around frantically for an actual person. "You're headed the wrong way. You're to relieve Bravo Company a little over a klick in the other direction."

"I got it," Zed said, pushing off the wall and hustling onward.

He fell back in line with the stream of people racing in the other direction. Nuts-to-butts, they pushed and shoved their way through the corridors of doom. When their boots weren't on rotting pieces of wood laid to cover the sticky mud, they would tread over the bloated bodies of fallen soldiers. Was this going to be what it was like the entire time?

"Phosgene!" several voices yelled further up the line.

A pale-yellow cloud seeped through the trenches towards Zed. He watched as others around him were scrambling to latch-up gas masks to their faces. He fell back into the trench wall and dropped his gun. Fumbling with the straps, he saw people close to him who didn't have masks on were coughing and choking. Skipping the straps, he held the mask to his face as tight as he could. While moving through the center of the cloud, a soldier who was coughing violently made a grab for Zed's mask. Before he knew what he was doing, Zed gave the soldier a swift elbow to the face. The soldier hit the ground and started involuntarily shaking.

Once he was clear of the gas, the realization of what he had just done came over him. His heart sank so fast that he felt as if he would suddenly collapse. That soldier he had struck inside the gas would probably die, eventually choking on liquid in their lungs while suffering painfully irritated, burning skin and eyes. It was indirectly his fault because he had not launched the gas, but he had chosen not to help the soldier. He didn't even try to drag the soldier out. But what choice did he have? It was either him or them. And it hit him right then. He was in the shit. This was war.

When the smoke cleared up, he felt it was safe to remove his mask. It relieved him to see that some of the surrounding people were familiar, like he had seen them at Bootcamp. The fear in their eyes was real, and their uniforms were clean. He was getting closer. He ducked into a hole in the wall where some soldiers were huddled.

"I'm looking for Delta Company," Zed panted, catching his breath.

"This is Tango," a young lady told him. "You guys aren't much further up the line."

"Thanks," Zed said, moving to go, but the girl grabbed his arm.

"Hey wait. The shell wave is coming back this way."

"What does that mean?"

"Didn't you read the manual?" she said like the other automated bots, but her eye roll was too real. She was just being friendly. "The shelling goes over the battlefield in a kind of wave. It moves inch by inch in one direction until it reaches a maximum range. Then they reverse it. Inch by inch backward until they are shelling the neutral zone."

"How much time do I have?"

"How the hell should I know?" she laughed. "When a shell drops on the line, you'll know. My advice to you is if the line breaks and the shelling stops—even for a second—grab your gun and be ready to fire."

"They're going to charge already?"

"They won the coin toss, so it's their assault. Don't worry, we'll have our chance soon enough. Just get to your position and take cover. There'll be an automated commander there who will fill you in."

"Alright," Zed said, mustering up the courage to head out into the madness again. "Thanks for the info."

"See you on the other side."

In and out of cover he moved, ducking shrapnel and letting the wounded through. Elbowing his way through a mass of flesh while clutching a weapon that was useless if he was dead. This went on and on as he continued down the line. How did he lose the others so quickly? Had they gotten separated also? He had been in the simulation less than an hour, and already he was numb to the explosions and gunfire going on all around him. His focus was now only on his destination.

He just hoped that she was all right.

As he rounded a corner, he sensed that the shells landing beyond the line were coming back inwards. BOOM! BOOM! BOOM! The blasts went as they ceaselessly dropped. Whenever he stopped to ask about Delta, the answer was always further down the line. Trying to rush and be cautious at the same time was taxing his patience. He worried he wouldn't make it before the shells returned, getting him caught up in an exchange of gunfire. He might get shot. Worse yet, their platoon's position might get blasted before that. He might arrive only to find strewn about body parts and dog tags. Turning another corner, the trench went on in straight manner. Through the moving bodies—with just a glimpse—he saw her. In an instant, he knew it was her jet-black hair stuffed under that steel dome.

"Zed!" Natalia shouted, waving to him excitedly.

Just the sight of her renewed his sprit and the surrounding tragedy drifted away. They were going to get through this together. And when it was over, they could get a nice place in the numbers and leave the past behind. He threw caution to the wind and double-timed it. Filled with so many emotions, he was unaware that he was yelling madly as he ran. He was so loud that he couldn't hear the words of caution from all the other soldiers.

Down the line in slow motion an arm came out of a dugout Natalia was standing by. It wrapped around her waist and pulled her down. The sound of whistling teapots filled Zed's ears once again. He dug his boots into the mud and slid to a halt just as a small shell slammed down right in front of him.

He was flying now. His gun, helmet, and gas mask all going off in different directions. He could see the entire battlefield. All the human and computer avatars scrambling about like mad ants in their tunnels. Pillars of black smoke here. Low ground-creeping chemical smoke over there. Pools of neon-green, water-filled craters pocketed the neutral zone. That fiery bellowing pit he had seen when they first arrived? He was there now. He was in hell.

Falling back to earth, in between spinning rotations, he could see his platoon watching him fall with anxious eyes. Flailing his arms and legs didn't help to guide his descent. Another whistle was coming quick. Before he could find the ground, a burst of heat sent him into the air once again. This time he was flung sideways. He hit the mud with a thump, and the shouting from the trenches was distant. He was in the neutral zone now. He was in No Man's Land. His torso was wrapped in barbed wire that shredded his skin when he moved. Grey-skinned corpses lay on either side of him. A pain shot through his right arm. Reaching over to touch it, he felt a jagged piece of metal sticking out. His brain refused to register the seriousness of the wound. It was all too surreal for him to handle.

Another blast landed not far from his feet, right on the wall. He saw the line collapse. They would surely see the exposed weakness from across the battlefield. He counted to ten and there wasn't a single shell dropped in his vicinity. An assault wave was coming, and he didn't have a fucking gun. With his left hand, he patted around on the body next to him. When his hand sunk into a spongy mush, maggots spilled out of the new cavity. Son of a bitch. He could hear the shouts of the soldiers going over the wall from the other side.

"Assault wave incoming!" Zed shouted, hoping someone could hear him.

"Assault!" a voice echoed from the trenches.

Zed held his breath and tucked himself as best he could under the pile of corpses. It took all that he had to not vomit profusely from the smell. The thudding of boots on mud sounded close. Soldiers were yelling commands as they moved, zigzagging their way through the lines of barbed wire, and keeping their heads down to avoid getting them blown off. One stopped and knelt right next to him. She unhooked a grenade, pulled the pin, and tossed it into the trench. Once it exploded, she was off and running again, shouting as she went. Dozens more soldiers went rushing past, with some falling to the ground from defensive fire.

A fresh face hit the ground right by his—a human face. When Zed looked into the dying man's eyes, he didn't see an enemy. Besides the different colored uniforms, the two of them were almost identical. Just two boys playing soldiers. He didn't want to see himself in a dead man, but he did, and it was frightening. All the soldiers, they were all just a bunch of poor kids trying to get by. And now they were slaughtering each other for entertainment purposes. Why the fuck did he sign up?

"Push them back," he heard someone from his platoon yell. "Hold the line."

He couldn't see what was happening, but the sound of gunfire was now so loud that it overpowered the shells that were still dropping. More soldiers were coming over the mud field. It was another assault wave. How many could his platoon defend against before they were overrun?

"Over the wall. Get prone and gun those assholes down."

Zed moved his head so he could see the breach in the line. He saw his platoon take a defensive position near the top, trying to take out the soldiers that were trapped in the web of wires and guts. He caught sight of her again, standing at the top brazenly, letting a few rounds off before she ate dirt. She looked so strong and confident. Each shot she took was with careful, calculated precision. If his display was on, he was sure to see his platoon's score rapidly rising. And here he was, half dead and useless.

"Get to Takeda," he heard someone order. "Pull him back. We'll cover you."

He saw shadows coming towards him through the drifting smoke. Gunfire rained down on the enemy's position violently. They tossed aside the corpses. Wire cutters clipped the line that he was tangled in. Hands grabbed him by his straps and lugged him through the oily mud back to the trench with a trail of blood following behind.

"Gently. Gently," one soldier said, as they set Zed down in a dugout close to the breach. "Medic!"

"I got this," the medic said, hovering over him. He propped Zed's head up against the wall and flashed a light in his eye. "You've lost a lot of blood. I can't help you with that right now. I need to remove this shrapnel to stop the bleeding. It's going to hurt like hell. Administering morphine now."

He couldn't feel the needle pierce his skin, but he felt the drug almost immediately. Through his clenched teeth, he said, "It hurts like hell, doc."

"You're pretty beat up."

"No, I mean, it really hurts."

"This is Level 4 hardcore, soldier," the doctor said, preparing to yank the shrapnel. "The wounds you get here reflect wounds you get back in reality. You die here, and you're dead there."

"That's not possible. I'm not jacked."

"You got the implant on your way in. All part of the contract you signed when you enlisted. Didn't you read it through?"

"Shit!" Zed yelled, not because he wasn't thorough, but because the medic pulled the shrapnel out. Blood started gushing out of the wound, and his vision became blurry. "You're a synth, huh?"

"If you mean an automated medical unit, then yes," the medic replied, pouring some white powder over the wound and wrapping it tightly with a bandage. "I'm sorry I can't do more for this, but it shouldn't kill you. You have more wounds and a lot of blood loss. I can't waste time on that now, but I'll return as soon as I can. Remember, the OS is with you." With that, he got up and moved to the next wounded soldier.

The firing at the wall had stopped, and some of the soldiers were already fixing the breach the shelling had caused. A few others from his platoon were dragged and dropped next to him. But they were dead, and he was not. He tried to move, but the morphine was hitting him hard. A shadowy figure moved towards him. As his vision focused, he could see her ice-blue eyes looking at him worriedly.

"Natalia," he whispered with a smile on his face.

"I thought I had lost you," she said, while petting his hair into place. "Twice! I can't believe you survived both blasts."

"I'm tough like that," he coughed. "You're not so bad yourself. I saw you. It was magnificent."

"I paid attention in training," she smiled.

"Hey," he said, taking her hand, "tell me we're going to get through this again."

"Z, don't be silly."

"No. I need to hear it."

"Of course we are!" she exclaimed with a tear creeping out of her eye. "You and me. Just like I said. We're getting through this together."

"Good," he said, with his vision going dark and his muscles going weak.

"Zed!" she yelled. "Zed, you can't sleep."

"Assault wave!" someone yelled from the top. "Incoming!"

"Shit," Natalia cursed, picking up her rifle. "Zed, you have to hold on. You have to be strong for me. Okay?"

"I will," he said, doing his best to keep his eyes open.

He watched as she ran back towards the wall. More soldiers were falling in from the other parts of the line to reinforce the position, but they were too late. The head of the soldier at the top snapped backward with a spurt of blood spraying out. A dozen enemy soldiers stood at the ridge and started firing down into the trench. They hit Natalia several times, and her body shook like a rag doll with each impact.

She took two steps backward before she turned and fell down, dead. Her ice-blue eyes were face to face with Zed's as blood poured out from the side of her skull.

● ● ●

"No!" Zed suddenly sat up in his bed, covered in sweat.

In the darkness of his room, her eyes were still there staining his vision. He must have passed out unintentionally because it was still daylight out when he laid down for a second earlier. He blinked a few times and rubbed at his eyes, but she continued to stare back at him from beyond the grave. A phantom pain shot through his right arm. Blood appeared to be gushing out of the wound as he looked hopelessly at the illusion. Even though he knew what was really there, he still flinched when reality snapped back. The cold grey metal caught thin lines of soft light around its edges, revealing a ghastly shape. Electric-blue light slithered through inlaid seams as it breathed in and out with cool illumination. It seemed alive. He picked up the hand and flexed it, causing it to make a faint whizzing sound. He thought anyone who thought an augmentation from a tour of duty was a good thing was full of shit.

He hadn't thought about The War in so long. It was a part of his life he would sooner forget, but would always have to live with. The body in the tunnels must have sparked something inside of him to make him recall those memories. It was the only explanation. He got up and walked to the bathroom, not bothering to turn on the lights. He was used to the dark. The small amount of light that crept through the widows found its way to the bathroom, where he could see a face in the mirror, but it wasn't his. It was still hers. He took his hand and wiped downwards, and she disappeared. His face was there now, but it still wasn't really him. It was a boy's face, with boy worries and boy dreams.

He pulled a bottle of vodka out of a drawer by the sink. Throwing the cap on the ground, he took a long pull and closed his eyes, swallowing slowly to feel every last second of the burn. When he opened his eyes again, there was nothing but a damaged old man in the mirror. But at least it was himself.

"Urgent call for Enforcer Takeda," his system chimed.

Popping a bottle of pills open, he chewed a few up before washing them down with more vodka. Meds to help his augments fuse with his body. Meds that keep his body from rejecting the synthetic interface. Meds to deal with the pain. Meds so he wouldn't get addicted. Any kind of medication could be instantly provided, except one that could help him change the past. A brain wipe would never be an option, so he took another hit of vodka instead.

"Urgent call for Enforcer Takeda."

"Jesus Christ," he yelled. "What is it?"

"Zed," Boyd's face holographically hovered in his line of sight. "You look like shit. What happened?"

"Nothing. A bad dream."

"Ten-four buddy. I can call back later if you need some time."

"No, no. I already took care of it," he said, snorting back a bit of booze that had trickled into his nostrils.

"Good, because this really can't wait. Hope you're ready for duty."

"Just tell me what it is."

"Another body. Cut to shit just like the first one."

"How long ago?"

"Call came in less than five minutes ago from a counsel box. The OS put us on priority immediately. I guess you have an excuse for not getting the message, but Zed, this is serious. It happened in the Numbers."

"That's not possible," Zed said, turning around and walking towards the window. He stared at the bright digital screens on the street to help him snap back to reality. "Where is it?"

"Just off the Strip. Some shithole flophouse. One of the girls called it in and then took off. OS synth enforcers caught up with her, though."

"What about the killer? Is there footage of the killer?"

"That's just it. There isn't anything."

"What do you mean?"

"I mean, there isn't any footage of anything. The room where the murder happened was supposed to be empty, according to the OS records. The footage shows the same. We even checked the system footage from the other patrons. Nothing, Zed. Nothing."

"Alright," Zed said, grabbing a shirt off the back of a chair. "I'll call an autocar and be there as soon as I can."

"The body isn't going anywhere," Boyd said sympathetically. "Why don't you take a shower and freshen up?"

"I said I'll be there ASAP."

THE REALITY NOW

SWAN: Good evening, Omega citizens. I am Swansong McNigh, and this is The Reality Now. Tonight, I'd like to talk about something that is a part of almost all our lives here in OC6, and yet most of us know very little about it. I'm talking about the virtual dream experience, and the dreamers who dream them. Many of us jack in nightly to scan the feeds of the newest dream experiences, something that is inexplicably beyond any other sensation ever known. Once in, we experience all those surreal, bizarre, and sometimes frightening situations. We feel each and every emotion associated with them. We are immersed in an environment that is constantly changing in a crashing, kaleidoscopic kind of manner. And we love it. But don't just take my opinion on the subject. To give us more insight on how the dreamer program works and who the dreamers are, we have an Omega Systems programmer, David Rieckhoff, and an up-and-coming dreamer herself, Rachel Goodwin.

SWAN: Let's start with David, who hails from Zone Five and has been working on the program for over thirty years now. The real burning question I'm sure we'd all like to know is how does the program work? And furthermore, why can't just anyone be a dreamer?

DAVID: Those are excellent questions. I'll answer the latter first and say that more and more people are showing signs of dreamer potential, but not everyone is willing to sign away their subconscious thoughts for all the Omega Cities to experience. Dreams are a very, very personal experience. Even though they don't always make sense, they do portray some of our innermost fears and desires. And I think that is why they are so popular. Because you really get into unknown territory when the physics, and the emotions, and what we know as a reality no longer follows a set of rules. But what makes a dreamer unique first and foremost is the ability to lucid dream regularly. It is understood that over half of all humans will have at least one lucid dream at one point in their life. With the dreamer program, the ideal candidate will experience lucid dreaming almost nightly. I can't give you all the details of how the actual technology works—because I'm legally bound to an NDA—but I can say that the recording of the dreams only works when the dreamer is in a lucid state. We harness those sensory and neurological emotional experiences.

SWAN: Correct me if I'm wrong, but isn't lucid dreaming a state in which the dreamer is consciously aware that they are dreaming?

DAVID: Correct. Normally the dreamer would become aware that they are in a lucid state and then could decide if they would want to alter the dream, let it play out as it is, or simply wake up. The dreamer program recognizes when the brain is going lucid and takes the control that would usually go to the individual doing the dreaming. Then the dream will continue in an uncontrolled manner, but recorded so it can be experienced again and again in a very realistic feeling virtual environment.

SWAN: Fascinating. Thank you for that. Let's hear from Rachel now. Her parents put her into the program when she was only eight years old. She is sixteen now and has a penthouse in the Six. Rachel, what was it like going through the program at such a young age?

RACHEL: For me, it was exhilarating. At first, I was unsure if I wanted to do it, mostly because I didn't know if I'd be able to. But, as I'm sure David could tell you, the best time to develop these skills is at a young age. I kept a dream journal every day, and would go over my dreams in-depth with a dream coach whenever they occurred. I was on a strict dietary regime of dream inducing foods and nutrients, and had to keep active in a variety of ways.

DAVID: We've found that the best candidates have extremely high hand-to-eye coordination, good stamina, and enjoy physical activities.

SWAN: Well, sign me up then. Rachel, you're averaging millions of views for every dream you upload. Why do you think they are so popular?

RACHEL: I really don't know why people like my dreams so much. They seem silly to me. But I love to enjoy other dreamers' dreams, and I can tell you there is no other experience like it. When you're lucid dreaming, everything around you feels connected, even your thoughts. A cat meowing for example, could hold thousands of emotions, meanings, and memories. And things that would seem so normal in everyday life feel extraordinary in a dream. A kiss from a boy feels like an infinite amount of sunshine burning in your heart. A setting sun would feel like ecstasy as you watched the colors blend with the sky. Of course, the nightmares—or night terrors—are also that much worse. I'm so happy I'm not one of those dreamers.

SWAN: Yes, but the nightmares are extremely popular. It has been reported that they net over 68 percent of the revenue from the virtual dream experiences, and I'm not afraid to say that I'm a fan.

SWAN: Now either of you could answer this next question. Big things that turn people away from signing up for the program are obvious at first, like the implant surgery into the brain, or the contract you sign that is for life. But what really seems to scare people the most is the fact that dreamers are, hands down, the fastest way to ascend. Why do you think that is?

DAVID: I think Rachel can tell you that the surgery is quite painless. I've never had a single dreamer report they have had any side effects or problems with the implants. The internal OS system that we all have is a more invasive surgery than this. As to the ToS contract? Well, that's just business. As to the fear of ascension? I can only blame misguided paranoia and hairbrained conspiracy theorists. I know the OS has gone to great lengths to keep what happens when we ascend a secret, but I am told you go to a fantastic place, a literal utopia.

RACHEL: I can't wait to ascend and be with the rest of my family. It will be a dream come true.

SWAN: Well, there you have it, citizens. The dream phenomenon is something that transcends all human experience, and it is only possible because of the advancements of virtual reality and a technological twist on the Omega System. If you want to be a dreamer, prepare for instant fame, an abundance of credit, and to sign your personal life away. But who cares? You won't be here long. Ascension is but a sweet dream away. It's not just the truth, it's the reality now.

SEVENTEEN

The notifications on her HUD kept popping up on the side of her vision. Cody had messaged her ten times in the last hour, but Ash had too much on her mind at the moment. The thought of going out into the real world in her actual body was stressing her out. She had a solid plan that involved multiple vehicles, outfit changes, and traveling through several highly populated areas hoping to throw off anyone who might be following her. The last thing she wanted was to show up to the exchange with a dozen paparazzi drones in tow. These weren't the type of people that wanted their faces plastered all over the tabloids.

Was she being paranoid? Was it really necessary to go through with all the sneaking around? She had lived freely once, and not even that long ago. She was used to running around the city without a care in the world, but that was before her face was on thousands of holoscreens across the zones. Even then she wondered what would happen if she just went out as herself. Would anyone actually think it was her, and not just someone who had her skin on their avatar? She couldn't risk it. The thought of a hundred people circling her and asking her a million questions all at once made her nauseous. Going on the internet as herself was bad enough, even with being able to hide behind a screen.

"Hey girl. What's up?" Cody's voice came through her earpiece. She was using text-to-speech, even though she knew Ash hated that. "Haven't heard from you in a few days, just wanted to see what was going on."

Ash stood in her closet looking at the words written across her display. It wasn't her intent to ignore her best and possibly only friend. She just needed to stay focused. But maybe Cody could actually help her out.

"Sorry I missed your messages," she started the reply. "I've just been handling some stuff."

"Don't brush me off. Tell me what's going on. Did you find anything else out?"

Ash picked up a hooded sweater off the floor and held it up to the light. She was trying to decide if it made her look poor or not. She didn't want any clothes that made her look like she had money, which wouldn't be too hard. Most of her wardrobe consisted of dirty pajama pants and old t-shirts, but she really didn't want to go out in public in those.

"H E L L O!?" Cody spelled out in obnoxious letters.

Ash tossed the sweater in a pile of clothes on the floor and let out a loud sigh. Cody had been a part of the situation with the symbols in her dreams from the beginning. Why was she trying to hide from her now? She knew the answer. It was because she was doing illegal things, and she didn't want to bring her friend into something that could get her into trouble. But the truth of the matter was that Cody would be better at doing bad things than she would be.

"I did find something out," Ash said out loud, and the words translated to text, and then probably back to voice on Cody's end. She thought they should really just talk.

"Finally. Please tell me."

"Well, first off, the strange beast from my last dream wasn't some figment of my imagination. I was digging around in my brother's old things and I found one of his digital graphic novels. The beast was inside there, but only for a second. What are the odds of that?"

"Could be a coincidence, but it'd be a pretty big one."

"Right? I haven't looked into other dreams for other correlations because I haven't had much time, and I found something else out that's pretty big. I had my monthly meeting with Eddie the other day—"

"Oh my god," Cody exclaimed. "You're still meeting up with that weirdo?"

"What else am I supposed to do? I need to dump my credits somewhere that ends up in a loss. There's only so much wine I can hold in my quarters, and you must remember what happened when we tried to gamble it away?"

"Ash. I'm the one that introduced you two. And I don't really care that you're still meeting him for the chips, I just don't want to hear that you're falling back on the other stuff again."

"Don't worry," Ash said, taking the bottle of pills that Eddie had sold her out of her pocket. "That's something I never want to do again. You know that."

"I get you don't want to earn any more credits because you're afraid of ascending, but those drugs turn you into a zombie, Ash. I need you alive and awake. I need my friend." She paused there, and after Ash didn't make an immediate reply, she continued, "Anyway. Tell me what happened. You went to see Eddie?"

"Have you ever been to Hope City?" Ash asked, not entirely avoiding her question.

"No Hope? Yeah, I've been there. But that was like, forever ago. You know, turn eighteen and have some fun in the clubs. Get harassed by the greasy dudes and have someone try to con you out of your money. What about it?"

"You don't remember seeing any signs with symbols that acted as directions?"

"Oh, that was so long ago. I kind of remember what you're talking about, but I didn't know what they meant at the time. It was a locals-only type of thing, if I remember. You couldn't just search what they meant on the internet. Hell, I couldn't even get a connection when I was down there. Besides, I was really drunk the entire time. Ha! Have you never been there?"

"Not really. I mean, me and my brother used to run around in the Zero, but we were already chipped and dreamers before we turned an age where our parental trackers were turned off. That's beside the point. When I showed the symbols from my dreams to Eddie, he knew immediately what they were. He was kind of rude about it too, like, 'you big dummy, they're directions.'"

"Oh wow," Cody laughed. "How did we not know? Like the digital glyphs that are on your HUD when you're walking around? I didn't really know what they were then, but now that you're saying it, I can totally see it. So, what are you going to do about it? You can't just go down there. No synths allowed. And you're so afraid of going outside."

"I love going outside," Ash sighed, thinking about the joyous feeling she had when she was riding the horse in her dream. "I just don't enjoy being around people that much anymore. And it is a problem. I have to go to Hope City, I have to do it myself, and I have to do it in person. That's why I am headed out right now. I've got to meet with someone who has something that will help me."

"So, you're so paranoid about getting noticed in public that you're willing to do some real illegal shit, huh? That's why you've been avoiding me. Jesus. Can't he wait a little longer? I'm about to go in on this ultra ball tournament. Those VR trips to OC4 are expensive, you know."

"Sorry Cody. It was hard enough getting this appointment, and I need to leave like right now. I feel like I'm in over my head, but I have to keep going. If these messages are from my brother, then I have to know what they mean and how he is sending them to me."

"I can drop out now. I'll feign an injury or something."

"Don't worry about it," Ash said while brushing her hair into place. "I'm sure it'll be easy. I'm just making an exchange, and in a public place."

"Okay. Good. Because I can't really leave, anyway. If I back out now, I can't play until the next tournament. Just message me before and after the meeting. I'll check my messages anytime I'm on the bench."

"I will. Go kick some ass."

"You know it! It's not Big Gun, but I'm on a really great squad. Talk to you later."

An alarm went off on her internal system, notifying her that she needed to get her ass out the door. She swiped it away and then brought up her autocar app. There was a garage on the ground floor of her apartment that held her own personal autocar, a Shimoto 942 with all the luxuries added. She wondered how much dust was collected on it. No time to worry about that now. Swiping up on the *engage* button, the car would pull up to the elevator door in the garage in a few moments. She kicked off the clothes she was wearing and shimmied into a nice black slip dress and threw on some random jewelry. Picking up some selected clothes off the floor, she shoveled them into a large but classy tote bag. She was as about ready as she would ever be.

No going back now.

One nice thing about using her own personal autocar was there were no paparazzi allowed in the garage. But the second her car left they would be instantly notified and she would be tailed by dozens of camera drones. That's only if anyone was still keeping tabs on her car. Even if they weren't waiting for her, the building she lived in was filled with all sorts of tabloid-type personas, and they would be scanning each car that left. She just had to assume the worst, which is why she had a plan.

The car glided right into busy autocar traffic and for the first time in years, she was outside of her building in her own body. Her heart was racing, a few beads of sweat formed on her forehead, and street lights seemed to pierce her eyes through the tinted windows. Everything felt a little more angular and crisper than she was used to. Once a few blocks had gone by and there didn't seem to be anyone following her, she calmed down a little. A drone could still be flying overhead, so she was thankful for the blacked-out windows and the anti-spy tech they were laced with. Without them, she knew it would feel like a million eyes were staring and analyzing her every move.

She had thought of just sending her car out as a decoy and calling a separate autocar, but using the car for the first part of her plan was crucial. Only personal autocars were allowed into the garage of LeCoup, an elite establishment that prided itself in keeping its clientele out of the prying eyes of the paparazzi. Any tails she had acquired would move on without being able to snag any juicy footage. That's also why she needed the tiny black dress because she already had the reservation and needed to look the part of the social elite. At such a high-class restaurant, no one would say a thing about her status in society, because everyone in the room would also be somebody important. But she wasn't there for the food or the conversation, she just needed to use the bathroom.

The maître d' was a little surprised when he noticed her leaving in a different outfit, but a large sum of credits swiped in his direction would help him forget. She was sure it wasn't the first time he had witnessed such a thing. Just before the exit, she put on an oversized pair of sunglasses and a big floppy hat. She still had to look like money when she left, but not in anything she would actually wear. Hailing a public autocar that was already waiting at the valet, she hoped she was in it before anyone could notice. She still held a hand to cover the side of her face, just in case there was a camera drone nearby.

As the car silently rolled down the streets towards the lower zones, she wondered if Cody was right about her being overly paranoid. It's not as if the tabloids cared what she did with her free time. Her life outside was so dull that even the automated tracker on her probably fell asleep on the job. She really was a huge recluse. But she reminded herself it wasn't because she was trying to hide from anyone, it was for her own safety. The people she was meeting with were serious criminals. The kind that would pull a knife on her if they saw a drone hovering not far out of sight. So, while the car was zipping along the streets, she was putting on different clothes to further hide her identity.

When the autocar let her off at a subway station entrance in Zone Two, she was wearing a pair of dark-blue jeans with a tight black top underneath a hooded sweater and a leather jacket. She tucked her hair underneath a knitted cap as she made her way straight down the steps to the subway station.

She stared at the floor the entire time she was on the train, afraid that if she made eye contact with someone, they would recognize her. She had already noticed her face on a dozen advertisements along her journey, and she felt confident that if she looked up now, she would see her own face looking back at her from some holoscreen ad. How long had it been since she had taken the subway? It must have been years. She could barely remember what train she needed to be on and how to make it through the turnstiles. Thank the OS that the automated payment system hadn't changed in all that time. It was only two stops to The Strip, and everyone on the train was getting pumped for a big night out at the clubs and casinos. They were so ready to indulge in whatever their vice might be that no one paid any attention to her, and that was comforting.

As the train came to a stop at the platform on the Strip, hundreds of people moved forward towards the doors of the cars. In the bustle of people pushing around in the pink-neon-lit subway platform, she took off her hat and replaced it with a black bob wig with short bangs. She did her best to apply bright-pink lipstick as she rode the escalator up. People were taking notice of her now, but she felt it was because she looked more crazy than famous.

As the escalator came to the top and the pulse of the music started thumping in her chest—in her actual chest—she nearly forgot what she was supposed to be doing. The majestic spectacle of the entertainment district could make anyone forget any worries that they had brought with them. Her heart fluttered as she strolled past a large array of speakers pumping out a carefree, pop-laced, digitally produced melody. A three-story-tall holographic goddess was dancing to the music, with tracers of light following her movements. A strobe went off in Ash's eyes, and light spots danced on her retinas as people bustled about going in all directions. There was a giant holoscreen that canopied the walkway all the way down the Strip, and it was displaying dazzling imagery as people were flying down ziplines through the illuminated air. Live bands were performing on a stage right by the opposite subway exit, banging out nostalgic songs from twenty-plus years ago. A street vendor walked by with a cart full of steaming meat, and her stomach growled. She realized she needed to stay focused, so she kept to the movement of the crowds. She had done more than enough to lose anyone who would be following her, but she still didn't want to take any risks. There was one more stop on her pre-planned route of evasion.

She got behind a train of ladies who looked like they were ready to party hard. They wore stilettos and tight dresses and talked in big laughing voices as they made their way through the hypnotic atmosphere as if they had done it a million times before. Their avatars looked very real, and by all means very sexy, but their voices were rough and their conversation was crude. Ash assumed they were a group of drunken men going out in women's bodies. It wasn't uncommon.

They walked right up to a brightly lit building, whose huge tinted windows had multicolored lights and lasers flashing through to reveal a sea of silhouetted bodies. The bass of the music was thumping so hard that the glass was rattling with each hit. It was making her breathe heavily and sweat in strange areas. If she wasn't nervous enough, this was pushing the limits. There were so many people all around that she was dizzy with anxiety. She had to remind herself that this was what she was here for. There was no way the paparazzi could keep up with her as she pushed her way through a crowd that big.

Once past security, the room opened up and it looked like there were almost a thousand bodies crammed into the neon-lit dance hall. A DJ was on stage with their hands up and clapping in front of an enormous holoscreen that was flashing intense images at a rapid pace. More holographic dancers floated through the humid air with the beat of the music. She didn't waste any time ordering a drink, even though she felt like she could use several. Thankfully, it was the Strip, and a robotic server was walking around with a tray of pre-made drinks. It was the house special, Blossoming Flower. As she picked the cup up her account was charged. She laughed, thinking that The OS sure could keep track of her even if the paparazzi couldn't. The drink hit her mouth like cheap tequila and sugary lime juice, but it had a special ingredient that gave her mouth a numbing sensation. She guessed they added it so no one would be able to taste how bad their booze was.

She pushed her way through the crowd of sweaty bodies, smashing into one another and screaming out in ecstasy to the music's bass line. Lasers cut through thick smoke, and strobes made silhouettes of hands. Drinks were being spilled everywhere she looked, and several times a hand grabbed at her ass cheek. This was definitely not a place that Ash the Dreamer would ever go—in a synth or not.

Keeping her back to the way she came in, she followed the glowing signs that pointed towards an exit. Any club this size would have an alternate way of getting in and out. She took off her wig, and grabbing a napkin from a table near a secondary bar, wiped the lipstick from her face. She tossed the wig in the trash along with her fake leather jacket. Leaning up against a pillar, she pulled off her high heels and began replacing them with a pair of old sneakers that she had jammed into the bottom of her bag.

"You can't take your shoes off in here, mam," an authoritative voice said from above. A large muscular man stood before her wearing a black shirt that said security in bold white letters.

"I'm sorry," she said, purposely stumbling a bit. "I'm just so drunk."

"Come with me," he said, taking her by the elbow.

Before she knew what was happening, she was standing outside the rear exit with a water bottle in her hand and a numbered ticket for the autocar line. She looked over and saw a dozen other girls and guys, half-awake with car tickets in their hands. It was a sad scene. She tossed the ticket to the ground, pulled her hood over her head, and kept moving.

The streets on the backside of The Strip weren't as bright or noisy, but there were still plenty of people to blend in to. Hundreds of shadowy figures walked to and from less well-kept nightclubs and casinos. When a timer buzzed on her system, a notification popped up at the same moment.

"Legend's Table House," the message from an unknown ID read. "Left room. Side table."

She searched for Legend's on her map and found it only a few blocks away. Keeping her head down, she made her way further from The Strip. The streets grew darker, there was more trash laying in the gutters, and prostitutes and drug dealers began soliciting her unabatingly. It seemed like the appropriate place to do the business that needed to be done.

When Omega City 6 had first been built, The Strip—or Dakota Park, as it was originally called—was intended as a place of luxury. There were resorts, casinos, concert theaters—the works. But the people with the credits didn't want to go down there for extended stays because of the proximity to Zone Zero. So, most resorts turned to disrepair. Palms trees and neon signs now hovered over molding stucco and rotting floorboards. Pools were emptied, covered in graffiti, and turned into unofficial skate parks. Marquees that once displayed prominent performers' names now simply read, *XXX All Nude XXX*.

When she got to the entrance of Legend's Table House, a large Chinese dragon made of twisting neon tubes hovered over the door, with a pair of dice that blinked in and out to look like they were rolling. No one was there to charge a fee or ask for ID. The room was filled with cigarette smoke, and large groups of people were around only a few of the plethora of tables, yelling frantically at each roll of the dice or drop of a card. Slot machines lined the walls, but most of the people playing them were either mindlessly pushing the *spin* button or sitting there half passed out. In the side room, she saw a man in a gray trench coat and high-top sneakers sitting alone at a table, sucking on a vaporizer.

"You like pizza?" He asked, with his voice sounding like he gargled gravel.

A message was sent to her that same instant, so she replied with what it said. "Yeah, I like pineapple and jalapeno," with the words coming out of her mouth more like a question than a statement.

"Nice disguise," he commented. She didn't know if that was a compliment or an insult, as she stood there in old sneakers, blue jeans, and a wrinkled hoodie, with her fancy tote left in a garbage can and a plastic takeout-food bag as a replacement. He demanded her to sit down, so she squeaked out an awkward metal chair.

He had long, greasy, light-brown hair with a matching mustache. Dark circles sucked in deep-set bloodshot eyes in an oblong skull, that kind of looked out at her sideways as if they were looking around her face. Underneath his long trench coat, there was only a ragged tank top from some metal band. His jeans were ripped, but not for fashion, only because they were old and dirty. She noticed there was blood splattered on his right sleeve, and it gave her a small chill. He took out a small metallic device the size of a hockey puck and dropped it on the table. It made a quiet whirring noise, and a small blue light turned on that caused her HUD to blink erratically until it ultimately shorted out. The man's face shifted back and forth at the same moment.

"What was that?" Ash asked nervously, looking at the strange device. The man just stared at her with his dead eyes and said nothing. Instead, he raised a shot glass of gold-colored liquid and drank it down slow. A sudden and loud round of cheers rang out from the tables in the other room and it made her jump a bit.

"Where are the chips?" he hissed, after taking another long toke from his vape and letting the smoke push between his browned teeth like a dragon.

"I'd like to see the device first," she said, trying to sound confident but not forceful. But who was she kidding? She felt scared shitless. "Is that it?"

"This?" He asked, pointing to the small round object on the table. He looked at her skeptically. "Do you even know what you're buying?" When she didn't immediately reply, he muttered words under his breath in a foreign language.

"I just want to know you won't take my money and run. So, I'd like to see the, you know, the thing."

"This is a joke." He said, becoming agitated. In a louder voice, he asked, "Who set this up? Who gave you my name?"

"I'd rather not say," Ash replied, feeling her throat tighten. More shouts from the other room made her back muscles tense up. "I don't know your name."

"Keep it that way," he barked. He took a few subtle glances around the room before leaning across the table and saying, "Do you want it or not?"

"I, I, uh..." Ash stuttered. She could feel her fingernails digging into the insides of her palms unconsciously. It was something she did in extreme nightmares when she wanted to wake herself up. How was she to know if he was even selling her what she wanted? She hadn't even seen it. She needed that distorter, and she needed it now. If this was a scam, it would take her too long to save up the credits for a different one. Too long if Anton was in serious trouble.

"Look, I'm not fucking around here. The chips. Now. Or I'm gone."

A server came walking by at that point to drop off another shot at their table, picking up the empty glass with the same movement. The man didn't look at her, but swiped her some credits all the same. Through the thick smoke she could see the sweat on his porous face, and it disturbed her. The gap in the server's teeth, the shouting of the men, the glare of the slot machine lights, it was all very dissonant. She just wanted to be back home, where it was safe, so she slung the plastic bag on the table with a clanking thud.

"In a fucking plastic bag?" he exclaimed.

"It's all I had," Ash shrugged. "It's all there. You don't have to count it."

"Wasn't planning on it," he said, snatching the bag off the table. "If you come up short, I'll come back and kill you myself." He tucked the bag in his side pocket.

"So, you've got your chips. Where's the device?"

"It's under your seat—don't grab for it yet," he commanded, stopping Ash right as she was making a move. He looked like he was snarling at her while he said, "Wait until I'm gone."

He made a startlingly swift movement with his right arm. For a moment Ash thought he was going to stab her. She could feel the piercing pain in her left breast. He paused and held out his metallic puck while grinning. He bit at the air a few times before he turned to go, chuckling to himself. Her skin crawled as she watched him casually walk towards the door.

Her HUD made a buzzing sound as it returned to life. She guessed whatever his little device was, it somehow created a distortion field around them, shorting out their internal systems, and possibly blocking any OS surveillance. She was definitely dealing with people she shouldn't be.

The distorter!

Reaching under her seat, she was relieved to feel a small plastic bag taped there. Yanking it off, she held it so it was under the table and between her legs. It was so small and simple, almost like the connections for virtual, just two little flesh-colored pads that would go over her temples. It had cost her a lot, so it had better work properly. She wouldn't be able to find out here, though.

Eddie had messaged to warn her she couldn't let anyone see her with it when it wasn't on. She shouldn't put it on anywhere the OS could see her, otherwise she'd be busted, and it'd be worthless. If it fell off or broke where the OS could see her, it was also worthless. So, she tucked the bag into her jean waistline. As she got up to leave, she noticed that the man had left his shot. Why not? She thought, picking it up and slamming it down.

Lights abruptly flashed through the windows of the gambling house, filling in the dark space with an unwanted clarity. A klaxon rang out from the street corner. It was an alert to notify that there was a crime scene in the vicinity and that the OS had dispatched enforcers. Her heart felt like it went through the floorboards and her feet felt like stone. Was it for her? Had the

OS witnessed the entire transaction? What was going to happen? She surely couldn't be zeroed out just like that! But the men at the tables paused their shouting only for a moment to look up and then went back to their game as if nothing had happened. People at the machines didn't bother to stop whatever they were doing, either. The only person in the entire building that seemed alarmed other than Ash was the server who held her hand against her chest as she looked out the windows with concern.

"Is everything okay?" Ash asked, coming up alongside the woman. "What's going on?"

"Enforcers. By the looks of it, it's serious," she said, clenching her fists tighter.

"Enforcers?" Ash asked innocently. She tried to think of the last time she had seen any of them in Omega City, as there wasn't really any crime to speak of in the Six. "Do they come here often?"

"Gangs usually take their disputes to the other end of The Strip," the server said, nervously lighting up a cigarette. "Nothing happens on this end that the OS can't handle with some automatic fines. But this, this looks bad. They don't sound the alarm unless it's murder. Christ, I can't afford to find another job."

"Murder? That's not possible."

"Happens in Hope City all the time. But out here? Nah, not really ever. You'd be exiled in a second. But when it does, it means a turf war. And, son of a bitch, it's right outside."

"I'd better be going," Ash said, feeling the illegal device pressed up against her skin, burning with guilt and shame.

"You might need protection. You got any?" The lady pulled a switchblade out of her pocket and held it up with the blade out. "Could be rough out there for a bit."

"No, thank you. I'll be alright."

"Okay, you take care, sweetheart."

It took everything she had to walk as calmly as she could towards the massive floodlights. Through the glass doors of the table house, she could see holographic yellow lines stretched across the exit with the words, *crime scene*, repeating over them. Dozens of people were running around and yelling orders at each other. A drizzling mist whipped her in the face as she opened the door. As she reached to pull her hood up, she ran right into someone walking her way

"Jesus Christ, lady," the man growled. He smelled like cheap vodka and old leather. Looking up, she was struck by the strong features of his rugged face and his piercing wolf-like eyes. His sturdy frame stood before her, huffing like he was ready to take on a monster. "Look where you're going."

Sorry, I didn't see you."

"Hey wait," he said, putting his left hand on her shoulder. Her knees almost buckled under his touch. Visions of this stranger escorting her to an exile raced through her head. "Don't I know you?"

She glanced at him, and then at the dark-skinned, bearded man beside him. Neither of them noticed the large holoscreen they stood in front of, that was flashing her face in an advertisement for a light beer. "I get that a lot," she said, trying to not look them in the eye. "I do a lot of live streaming."

"No," the man said, scratching his five-o'clock shadow, "that can't be it. I don't spend much time on the internet."

"Hey Zed," the other man said, "let the girl go. We got a crime scene here."

"Yeah, yeah. Okay. I'll see you around," he said, and gave her a kind of wink that seemed to say I know what you're up to.

Ash nodded and hurriedly walked away. She pulled up the app for her personal autocar that was waiting in a lot outside of The Strip. She set the pick-up location for the end of the block, thinking that getting out of there as fast as possible took precedence over being covert. Even though she knew she had done nothing wrong, she still felt like a criminal. She needed to be home, and she needed to be there now.

SIXTEEN

"You see that?" Boyd asked, looking in the direction Ash had walked away through the drizzling rain.

"No, what happened?" Zed asked, glancing at the light beer advertisement, but not really seeing the face that was there.

"That girl. She just got into a Shimoto. I think it was a 942. You don't see that kind of car on this side of The Strip."

"She didn't seem like a high roller to me."

"They never do," Boyd laughed. "You up to this? You seemed kind of shaken up earlier."

"I'll be fine. Let's just focus on the job," Zed said, turning up the collar on his leather jacket. The rain was coming down a little harder. "You been in there yet? How bad is it?"

"I was waiting for you, but from what I heard it's bad. The OS thinks the cases are linked based on initial observations, that's why we are on the job exclusively."

"The OS puppets are here already?" Zed asked, looking at a group of nearly identical genderless humanoids, wearing all-white jumpsuits with the Omega Systems logo printed on their left chests. "Just fucking great. Last thing I want is a bunch of robots breathing down my neck, watching everything that I do."

"You don't have to worry about it. I already talked to them. The OS agreed to give us space and to only be here as perimeter security. It was made very clear, however, that they want this taken care of quickly and discreetly. Priority number one."

"A murder in the numbers, and a possible serial killer. I never thought I'd see the day."

They made their way past The Legend's Table House gambling parlor and through the holographic crime scene tape. People were looking out from windows of buildings all around the area, and Zed could be sure they were transmitting their video feeds on the internet. He gave Boyd a nudge and nodded towards the onlookers. Boyd understood without being told and started sending commands to the synthetic enforcers that the OS had sent to help them. Before they even made it into the flophouse known as Bagnio, a large holographic covering was placed over the street so that prying eyes wouldn't be able to see things they shouldn't.

At the entrance, there was a half-naked synthetic body lying on the ground, with its eyes open to the falling raindrops. She was pretty for a synth, but nothing that Zed would ever look twice at. He noted the lack of seams on her silicon skin or any blemishes from augmentation. He assumed she was a high-end model, which felt a little out of place for such a hole-in-the-wall. A few feet away there was another synth, a guy this time, lying face down and unmoving. The only actual light source in the room was coming from a corner digital display that was blinking in and out, sending angular shadows across the linoleum floor.

"I thought you said this was a flophouse?" Zed asked, kneeling by the girl and looking for digital burns from any kind of EMP blast. "What's with the bots?"

"You don't get out much, do you?" Boyd chuckled, moving around Zed into the front room. "Some people are into synthetic sexual partners. They provide both kinds here, with the option to have both. There are even VR couches available in that's your kink."

"No thank you," Zed grunted, looking around the room. The back wall was lined with glass booths filled with lush red velvet curtains that would display potential lovers for the customers. There was a counter that had an interface underneath a broken display, that people could make their choices at. A script box was in the corner, just in case anyone wanted an extra drug-fueled enhancement. Zed assumed that if he looked into it, he would find illegal street drugs being sold through the vending machine. The only thing anyone needed was a passcode to unlock the extra features. That wasn't worth his time. "Two synths knocked out cold right at the door. What was used? An EMP gun?"

"I don't think so. It looks like both of their systems were shut down. But their internal cores are still active, so it wasn't an EMP. They'll fully be operational once powered back up, but the OS already checked their visual logs. They're blank, just like everything else."

"You can't just turn these things off," Zed said, standing back up. "It's not like they're a coffee maker, or a holoscreen."

"Correct. All synthetic intelligences are hack-proof, thanks to the Gibson Code. Many have tried, but no one has been able to even get through to the basic command panel. But there are ways to power them off, it's a safety feature. They are programmed to be unable to harm humans in any way. But if, for some reason, they were ever put into a position where it would be impossible to avoid, there is a shutdown override. To get through the protocols and activate it manually, you'd have to be a highly advanced net diver. Even then, the encryption would be a bitch. I couldn't see anyone being able to take out two at once like this."

"None of the intelligences are connected, so they couldn't have been taken down by a linked command. There had to be some sort of delivery device, like if you were to inject a virus into a human you would use a needle. But it's not like they have ports to plug in a hard drive on them anymore."

"It's a real conundrum, but these bodies aren't the ones that the OS wants us to focus on," Boyd said, crossing his arms around his barrel chest. He pursed his lips and furrowed his eyebrows before he continued, "We've got two human corpses in only a few days. That's monumental."

"So, we'll add expert hacker to the list of things describing our killer."

"Along with surgical skill," Boyd added. "You ever follow up with the lead of the first citizen doctors? Right now, that still sounds promising."

"Nothing but a dead end," Zed said, shaking his head in frustration. "I could only talk to automated caretaker bots. The answer across the board was that they've all been in virtual for years and kept alive by intravenously fed nutrients, tissue stimulators, and endless organ transplants."

"If things ever go that far in our lives, please do me a favor and pull the plug."

"That's a solid ten-four," Zed said, moving to the next room. "I thought of doing follow-up interviews with their virtual avatars, but their connection logs confirmed the alibis from their caretakers. One of them has been jacked in for over two decades. Probably has a whole new life, maybe even a new family on the inside."

"Makes you wonder how many of us are living a life that way right now," Boyd mused, pausing outside the door of the crime scene with his body silhouetted from the floodlights that were already set up in the room. "We're a dying breed, you and I."

"Dying to live."

The brightness of the room stung his eyes even before the stench of the dead body hit his nose. He made a motion with his hand and the lights dimmed to a more appropriate level. The room was small. A queen-sized bed was in the middle of the room, with the bedding still in place. Lighting strips ran down the fake wood-textured walls a few inches above the floor, set to a low red light. The floor was covered in a short, tough carpet, the kind that never looked dirty or clean. There was a sturdy table with a single chair opposite the bed. They assumed the table wasn't there for eating dinner at. Zed kept his hands to himself while he circled the room, taking in every detail.

The body was on the floor. Another young woman, by the looks Zed guessed in her early thirties. Still and silent, there was no fear in her face for her final moment. Straight brown hair mangled in a pool of thick blood. Pale skin under simple lingerie. She was cut up much the same as the first. The neck was sliced to drain the blood, with splatter marks hitting the wall away from the bed. The chest was cut vertically in one swift motion and the inner intestines were pulled out and thrown to the side so the killer could get at their prize. All of the organs were removed just like the last, but this time there was one missing. The heart.

"Was she the sex worker?" Zed asked, still kneeling by the girl.

"Negative," Boyd said, scanning through a detailed log on his display. "She appears to have been the customer. The working girl was knocked unconscious, drugged, just like the victim. She didn't see a thing. The tox report on her and the victim is still in the can, but it should be done in a minute."

"Who was she?"

"She was one Briana Jones. Thirty-two. Pizza chef at some swanky joint on The Park called Chez Za. Divorced with two kids. They moved out a few years ago to be with the other mother. She lives alone now, and it looks like she replaced her kids and ex with a bit of a drinking problem. One hundred and forty-eight public intoxication violations this year alone. She spent most of her time at work or at other bar/restaurants in Middle Park. She has a nice studio on the edge of Zone Three. Looks like a synth shack area. Lots of data about her time on the internet and in virtual, if you want to go over that. She is into French Bulldogs, Dark Techno, and rock climbing, mostly. Subgroups include Yes Chef, Audiophiles Unite, Friends with Benefits, Anti-synth—"

"Anti Synth again," Zed cut Boyd off.

"We also have dogs, music, and alcoholism as a connection."

"Her right hand." Zed motioned with his chin. Something had caught his eye. There were two subtle lines across her index and middle fingers.

Boyd flipped through the OS database quickly before he said, "You're right. Her first two fingers are synthetic. Looks like it was a work accident a few years ago, right around the time her family split. An unpleasant incident with a Globe slicer, but that's not the only augment. She had her lungs replaced with a synthetic filtration system a year later."

"Pretty extreme augment to get," Zed said, with a dull pain running through his right arm. He couldn't fathom what the post-surgery pain would feel like having an internal organ replaced with a synthetic one.

"If you've ever worked in a commercial kitchen, you'd want one too. Lots of smoke, especially with the wood-burning stove."

"I guess that makes sense. I personally would endure the smoke. You said a Globe slicer? One of those big circular blades that slices meats and vegetables? That's one nasty way to lose some fingers. But who does their own prep work? Don't synths do that kind of thing?"

"In most places you could eat out at, I'd say yes. Prepping food at a restaurant is most of the hard work, and the free labor a SI could offer would dramatically cut down on the food cost. But have you ever had the pizza at Chez Za? It might be the best pizza in all the Omega Cities. There is a reason it costs a day's wages for a single slice. You don't get that kind of artistic perfection with an instachef."

"No pizza should cost that much."

"Well, it might not ever again," Boyd said, looking at the dead chef. "Anyway, she applied for workers' comp and lost. At the autodoc they found a sizeable amount of alcohol in her bloodstream and plenty of cocaine. OS claimed it was her own negligence. But, get this, she didn't get rid of the Globe Slicer or buy a synthetic prep cook. She kept right on doing the prep work herself."

"She couldn't take the thought of having a robot be a part of her art." Zed got up and started pacing, taking in the information. Small drones drifted around the room, doing their scans, and a little metallic box on the floor next to the victim was finishing up the toxicology report. "How do we know the girl didn't do it? The sex worker?"

"No way. Same surgical style incision we saw earlier, but more precise this time. Like there was more care taken. The worming girl was shaking like a leaf when she was finally stopped and questioned. As nervous as a stray cat. The OS took her system recording immediately. The puppet enforcers did the rest with blood samples, fingerprints, and a statement before they let her go. I can bring up the footage, but like everything else, there's nothing to see."

"In a moment," Zed said, eyeing up the moveable panel on the wall that connected with the glass shell on the other side. "I do want to see that, but let's go over the tox report quickly. There's something that should be there if we have a repeat performer."

Boyd pulled up the report and shared it with Zed. "Looks like the working girl was injected with sodium thiopental. Database says it's a rapid-onset short-acting barbiturate general anesthetic. So, it's a different kind of knock-out drug. About a thirty-second activation and lasts five to ten minutes."

"Even at ten minutes, that's a brief window to perform this kind of operation. The killer would have to move extremely fast."

"Or perform another injection," Boyd added, flipping through the report. "It doesn't seem like the victim knew what was coming. There are no signs of a struggle on her body or in the room. So, the killer would have had to catch the working girl first, maybe cover her mouth from behind and hold her steady until the drug took effect. Then move on to the victim."

"They'd have to wait for the right moment. Stay concealed until it was time to strike. But where do you hide in a room this small? I can't see a single place to hide."

A sound chimed from the small machine on the floor. Boyd scanned the readout before he said, "Looks like we got a match on the victim for the knockout drug."

"It's devil's breath," Zed exclaimed, not even waiting for Boyd to nod in confirmation. "There is our direct connection to the other murder, and it definitely suggests that we are dealing with a serial killer. I never thought I'd see the day. The killer takes the time to incapacitate the synths and the girl in a way that wouldn't harm them over time but uses a very dangerous and unique drug on the victim. Insult to injury."

"If they had sodium thiopental already, why use a different drug?"

"I believe it's meant to be some kind of calling card. As if the execution-style throat-slitting, or the chest cavity cut wasn't enough, they had to drive it home with a signature drug. They want us to know that they did it, and they'll do it again."

"Precisely why you must find the killer." A digital voice came over their earpieces. It was SuR, the subroutine of the OS. "Enforcers Takeda and Boyd. The Omega System is a system of freedom for the people. You can choose to work, or not to work, the system will provide either way. You can be a law-abiding citizen and raise your morality towards ascension, or break all the rules and zero out. The system does not judge, it only fines and rewards. There are no prisons, no jails, and no courts. What use are they when you live under constant surveillance? Your alibi or conviction is a simple playback away. However, this instance is most disturbing to us. We have checked all the systems several times and have found no errors, and yet during the time of the crime there is nothing to playback. The footage only shows empty rooms. It is an impossible anomaly. This is a crime that cannot go unpunished. Someone must be found and exiled immediately."

"Understood," both Boyd and Zed said in unison.

"We have analyzed all the data in the entire zone for the last twenty-four hours. There is only one item of interest that we feel is worth pursuing. It has already been added to your analysis data. We ask that you go over all of your own possibilities first and only turn to it at your own discretion. Please restore harmony to our city as soon as possible."

The feed cut and they were alone once again.

"Bring up the feed from the Bagnio, Enforcer Boyd," Zed said, not meaning to sound so formal. He must have slipped back into military mode.

Boyd swiped his hand up and both of their HUDs filled with an image of the room they were standing in. It was from a surveillance camera in the ceiling, but at what exact spot it was hard to tell. The cameras were so small that they were almost impossible to detect. In the footage there were two people in the act of copulation, with a naked butt bouncing away at the body underneath. Boyd hit pause, and then fast forward until they were finished.

The room had been cleaned and emptied, and then the girl who had reported the crime entered through the false wall. The camera changed to a better angle and the front door opened with the victim entering. Then suddenly the screen distorted and both the girls disappeared. The recording didn't stop, but the footage only showed an empty room. Boyd cycled through all the possibilities, even the ones connected to both the girls' systems, but there was nothing.

"Just as you said," Zed whispered. Then louder, "There were other people in the building at the time, correct? Can we cycle their cameras and the other rooms?"

"I can, but there isn't much to see," Boyd sighed. "The front room is the same as this, nothing but an empty room after the feed distorts. And I checked, they all cut at the same time. In the other rooms all the cameras are working, but unless you want to get down on some hardcore amateur pornography with me, I'd rather skip it."

"I'll take your word for it. That must mean the killer knew what room the victim would go in. They cut the feeds, entered the room, knocked out both girls, committed the murder, stole the heart, and exited the building unseen. In how long?"

"Just shy of twelve minutes," Boyd said, skipping the footage ahead until it distorted again until there was a mutilated body on the floor and the young girl slowly moving. "The girl screams when she wakes up. The sudden spike in her vitals alerted the OS, who analyzed what she was seeing and sent out a silent alarm. Puppets arrived in minutes. And like I said, we were the only human Enforcers notified."

"Hypothesis on what caused the distortion and lack of footage? Could a still image of an empty room be used instead?"

"A still? No. The pixelation moves around, and that tells me there was a recording made at some time. But it could have been of an empty room and then looped. The cleaning service is automated, and they set the room up exactly the same way every time. It could have been set up beforehand and executed by a digital delivery system, much like the one that took out the synths at the door. But that doesn't explain how the footage was swapped. That's all connected to the OS, and that—like all synthetics—is hack-proof."

"Maybe a distortion field? I know the gangs use them for high-end exchanges."

"Good thought, that would make anyone inside of it seem invisible to the OS by mirroring the images from the surroundings, much like stealth tech. But for that to work on both girls in the room and the killer, they would each have to have one covering them. That kind of tech hasn't been invented yet, thankfully. The current distortion fields just make a small bubble, and it cuts out if they move the device. And that also wouldn't explain the rest of the building going blank as well."

"And the footage from the streets?"

"This is The Strip Zed. There were hundreds of people walking around right out there the exact second after the footage returns to normal. It'd take us weeks to go over all their files and do all the interviews. I don't think we have that kind of time. And besides, we see no one entering or exiting the building until the puppets arrive."

Zed rubbed his hand through his hair with a heavy look of disappointment on his face. He had given up on the body in the pit because he had hoped it was just a fluke. Someone experiencing a momentary lapse of sanity. But this, this was intentional. This was specific. There was nothing delusional about cutting open someone's chest and ripping out their heart. The timing was perfect. The execution was flawless. The technology used was beyond anything known. To say it perplexed him would be an understatement.

He stepped outside the room and took in the rest of the building. The hallway was nothing more than strip lights and fake paneling. A row of doors to rooms identical to the one he was just in. Cheap cosmetics to hide a rotting foundation. It reminded him of parts of Hope City. He ran his hands over the wall, feeling for imperfections in the paneling.

"Bagnio is a weird name for a flophouse," he said out loud, not particularly to anyone. "I did some research on the way over. If you search for it on the internet, you'll get directions to here, or the definition and pictures of a banjo. That's because the term bagnio isn't used anymore, and even when it was, it meant different things to different people. Most commonly it was used in place of the word brothel, which would make sense in this case. In Italy and Turkey, it meant a bathhouse. But in the orient, the term meant a prison for slaves. We'll assume they're meaning brothel here. In the old days organized crime usually ran brothels, and organized crime loved to have secret passageways to advert capture by the law."

Zed pressed his hand firmly against the wall and a portion of the paneling flew back, revealing a hidden door. When he pulled the door open, a waft of cigarette smoke flew in his face, and a chorus of cheering came from inside the adjacent room. He took several steps inside the dark hallway and a door opened suddenly before him. A large man emerged, still buttoning his pants and squinting through glazed-over, drunken eyes. Bathrooms. They were in a hallway used for bathrooms for the gambling parlor, Legend's Table House.

"The footage for this hallway is blank for the same time the Bagnio is," Boyd said, shifting around the archival footage on his display. "It wouldn't take much to enter the bathroom and stop whatever device they were using to cause the blackout and then leave."

"No, that would be too simple. We would have them on footage leaving the toilet. They would wait until they were in a group of people they could blend in with, maybe even work the possible blind spots. It's going to take a lot of scrubbing the footage for us to find that out."

"There's something else," Boyd said, moving further into the room, past tables of excited gamblers. He opened up the footage of the room and made it holographic so they could both see it at once. "Over here there is another anomaly, shortly after the murder occurred. Look here, a waitress comes over and sets down a shot, but you can't see it reach the table. It just disappears. Then she picks up an empty and walks away. Moving ahead, the video distorts and then there is this girl sitting there. It looks like she was in some kind of distortion field that moved away."

"I thought you said the fields couldn't be moved? And hold up, isn't that the girl we bumped into outside?" Zed asked, now recalling her face. High cheekbones and a delicate chin, with big bright eyes and thin lips. There was still something familiar about her face he couldn't place. "Forget her for now. Stay with the distortion field."

"It's hard to do when there's nothing to look for," Boyd said, moving towards the front door where the flashing lights were still strobing through the night. In the time between the flashes of light, a long-haired man in ripped jeans appeared on the screen. "Here, this man. I didn't see him anywhere in the parlor, and then he suddenly pops up in the doorway."

"I'm seeing blood on his right sleeve," Zed said, pulling his fingers apart to zoom the video in. "He's putting something round and metallic in his left pocket. There's a bulge under his coat. Could be a container to transport the heart with."

"Very good enforcers," the OS said over their comms. "That is Marcus Karnov. 28. Single. Ex Roland Royal. Now working for the Lords of the Numbers. Paid criminal charges include drugs, smuggling, solicitation, credit theft, identity theft, burglary, assault—"

"We get it," Zed cut in. "He sounds like a real winner."

"I am pleased you could come to the same conclusion that we had. We are currently tracking his movements. Sending his current location now. An autocar is already being routed to you and traffic cleared for your journey. Would you like us to deploy our own enforcers to detain Mr. Karnov until you arrive?"

"No," Zed said, gritting his teeth. "I want to handle this myself."

• • •

The autocar was squealing down the streets at full throttle with the speed restrictions lifted. All the other cars on the road pulled to the side to let them through automatically. Zed was still going over the footage of the crime scene and details about the suspect while the multicolored scenery was flying by in a blur.

"Some other things you should know about since you missed the evening reports," Boyd said, tightening a pair of fingerless leather gloves with padded knuckles. "There was a big hit in No Hope today. Retaliation strike for that bust we pulled from the false anonymous tip. If we weren't on this assignment, we'd be in the Zero walking beats right now."

"Sounds like it's escalating fast. We have any idea who did it?"

"Dozens of witnesses have turned in their system's footage voluntarily, as long as they could remain anonymous. They were mostly just people who happened to be on the street at the time and wanted nothing to do with gang activity. But this was a brazen attack in broad daylight, and you know what that means."

"It's a call for war, then. Never a good thing. Hope City will get locked down if it continues. Okay. Let me see it."

Boyd patched the footage through to Zed and adjusted his HUD's opacity, so the video was coming in as clear as it could be. The footage was from someone sitting across the street from the Buxton Bruiser's headquarters, just off Crowbar Alley. Two men wearing all red and black were standing outside on a stoop, acting as sentries against a surprise attack or an enforcer raid. A second camera showed a group of Royals out in full blue and gold colors, walking down the street towards them. The Roland thugs suddenly rushed the unaware Bruisers. They hit one of them over the head while his back was turned, and several Royals fell in and pummeled the Bruiser while he was down. The other Bruiser was hit in the face straight on, and while he was stunned, two Royals restrained him. They held out one of the Bruiser's hands and a good-sized steel axe came plummeting down on his wrist. Blood gushed out over the sidewalk and people ran in terror, including the person who sent in the footage. Boyd cut the feed and looked at Zed solemnly.

"No one was killed," Boyd said, tightening his gloves further, "and a rookie enforcer caught the perps immediately. The fines are severe. They'll pay for a new hand for the victim and any memory work he might want, so the OS isn't demanding a lockdown or an exile, but that was one messed up attack."

"The message is clear," Zed said, with street lights flashing across his hardened face. "Honor is at stake. A blow for a blow. End it now or pay the price."

"I hope it ends, and quickly. I'm not looking to pick up any overtime." Boyd turned the video stream off and took a moment of silence before things got thick again. "Do you really think this is our guy? The tech that was used must have been next gen. I don't think someone that smart would be caught so easily."

"Either they underestimated us, or they aren't really that smart. Anyone can buy new tech off the black market. What it comes down to is whose blood is on his clothing and does he have any kind of weapon or tool that could cause those cuts."

"If he hasn't dumped those items already. Guess we'll find out soon enough. We'll pull up in a second here. Fucking Zone One man. This place is a dump."

The autocar slowed to a stop underneath a large holoscreen, blasting out an advertisement for an extreme energy drink. The rain had trickled down to a drifting mist that patted against Zed's face as he exited the car. The streets were quiet and dark. Nothing but a long corridor of identical megalithic apartment structures towering over swaths of silent pavement. Autocars went racing by in either direction so fast it felt like express trains were passing him on a subway platform.

The people of Zone One lived inside their living quarters so much that the OS raised the speed limits of the residential streets to an oddly high level and let the autocars use the roads like highways. The area was so devoid of life that it was often referred to as Zone None, because if you were a visitor to the area, it would seem like no one lived there. In almost every building, the first two floors were either empty or had their windows covered up. There were no coffee shops, food carts, or corner stores one might usually see in a thriving, densely populated neighborhood. The street level spaces that were once shopping centers and malls were now only used as storage rooms for delivery drone services. There were only two bars for the entire zone, and only one convenience store that was right in the middle, called SNAXX. Food options were limited to automated chain restaurants that bordered with other zones. Homeless camps occupied the parks, with people sleeping there by night and panhandling in the other zones by day.

The truth was, there were almost just as many people per square foot in Zone One as in Hope City—which was a lot. Shared housing and shoebox-sized studios made up most of the living arrangements. Any space that was big enough for a single bed, had a VR connection, and access to a toilet was enough for the people who lived off of the Living Supplemental Income alone. The LSI wasn't much, but it was enough to pay the bills and buy food, with some leftover for whatever vice you might want to indulge in. And for most people, paying bills was their only duty in life. Why work if you didn't have to? The OS provides. If you don't break the law and kept your morality rating out of the red, then the LSI would continue to flow. There were so many forms of entertainment. It was a full-time job just to keep up with everything in your preferred subgenre alone. So, most people just jacked in and lived their lives out virtually, only coming out for food, sleep, and bathroom breaks. It was all part of the Omega System.

With ninety-nine percent of all production being done by automation outside the dome, there simply weren't enough jobs to go around. The jobs that were there were mostly in creating more VR content for people to consume. The people of Zone One played their part in the grand Omega System. They lived to consume content, siphoning credits from the LSI into the accounts of people in the higher numbers who created that content. Those people in the higher numbers then paid a higher luxury tax on goods and services that went back into the system and the LSI.

Zed checked the map on his HUD for the suspect's location and address. It looked like he had gone back to his registered quarters after making a brief stop along the way at a known Lords of the Numbers stronghold. Zed questioned the association of the suspect with a major organized crime syndicate. Were the killings contracted hits? Was the killer an assassin? That kind of thing only happened against other gangs, and the victims had no gang affiliation. He would have to wait for answers in the interrogation room. Right now, it was time to earn his pay.

Two large robotic OS enforcers appeared out of the shadows as Zed and Boyd crossed the empty street. Hooting voices could be heard from various windows above. Any hope of a stealthy approach had been lost. The entire neighborhood knew they were there now.

The synthetic enforcers made thumping sounds as they moved down the street. They differed greatly from the ones Zed and Boyd had a run-in with on The Strip. Those at least looked human, even if they all had the same generic, gender-neutral avatar body to jack into. These tin-can puppets didn't even attempt to look human. At over eight feet tall and weighing as much as an autocar, they flexed their synthetic-ness by wearing their titanium skeleton on the outside.

They were based on a design of the killing machines that nearly ended humanity in the last great war. Their eyes glowed an electric-blue, and when they talked, it was with a digital voice as if someone were speaking through a vocoder. Even at a distance they were extremely intimidating, with massive metal hands that could crush cinderblocks with ease. They reached speeds of sixty miles per hour on foot and could jump over two-story buildings like hopping a puddle. Put a laser cannon in their hands and they would instantly turn back into walking death machines of the time before. But that could never happen because the same Gibson Limiter Code that applied to all synthetic intelligences in the Omega Cities also bound them. They could not harm a human. The code forbade it. But that didn't mean they couldn't run down a rapist and detain them until a human enforcer arrived and applied the hurt.

"Enforcers," one of the metal puppets started in its digital voice, "More evidence is needed to link the suspect to the murders. Search the premise and analyze the data. The OS advises extreme caution. We are at your disposal."

"Just be ready to catch him if he runs," Zed said, walking toward stairwell

H of apartment tower 8. "Link me to the surveillance feed of his quarters."

There were piles of trash falling out of the recycler stations between the gigantic fifty-story structures. Autocars were parked in disrepair with weeds growing through the wheel wells and mold coating the windows. Delivery drones buzzed back and forth through the air, stopping at designated service windows like bees at a hive. The zone's utilitarian design was intended for only a certain amount of people. It was obvious that quota had been reached and exceeded a long time ago. Zed used his enforcer authority to override a grated steel security gate and entered the concrete service entrance. They couldn't risk using the main elevators with the weight the robotic enforcers would add, so Zed punched the button for the freight elevator.

Inside the building, the hallway smelt like burning plastic from someone smoking hard drugs in their quarters. The lights had been smashed out and the only remaining one blinking in and out at an irregular rate. An old man peaked out his door to see what was going on, and Boyd pushed him back into his quarters. As they turned a corner on the seventeenth floor, they had an expansive view of the entire city.

Far off to the west, through the misting haze and past the twinkling lights of Middle Park, they could see the majestic apartment towers of Zone Six, looking warm and inviting even from kilometers away. To the south, past the multi-colored flashing lights of The Strip, the other massive towering structure of OC6, Hope City. Polar opposites in so many ways. The two structures were a counterpoint to each other and the entire social make-up of the Omega System. As they walked east down another dark corridor, there was a cloudy window at the end, covered in scratch marks and graffiti. Through a small patch of clear window Zed could see across Lake Sharpe and beyond the dome. Out there in the darkness, there were the fields and factories of endless production filled with machines that worked day and night to provide the humans of this single city with anything they would ever need. Machines that worked ceaselessly so humans didn't have to. It was a unique view that Marcus Karnov had, living on the edge of so many different things.

The OS surveillance feed spun up on Zed's display, and he could see the inside of Karnov's living quarters. It was a big space for the building it was in, a one-bedroom with a small kitchen. He could see inside the main room, where there was an old ripped-up couch in front of a large holoscreen. Liquor and pill bottles littered the floor, and there was a pile of empty food containers in the corner. On a low table in front of the couch, there were lines of white powder next to a mess of computer parts and soldering equipment as if he were building his own homemade tech while snorting hard drugs. The holo-screen was showing one of the obnoxious game shows where contestants would do life-threatening or humiliating stunts in order to earn quick credits. It was called Fifteen Minutes of Shame. A second screen was showing the live broadcast of a concert by the synthetic pop star, Ishi. Zed checked the cameras in the kitchen, bathroom, and bedroom. They were all dark and empty.

"I don't see him anywhere," Zed said, transmitting his voice to the network he was on with Boyd and the two puppets. "You sure this is the right spot?"

"Surveillance followed him straight here," Boyd said over the comms. "If he was tipped off then he could be using the same distortion tech to hide himself."

Zed watched his display intently. He knew that distortion fields could only hide the people inside them from cameras. If that was true, then the holo-screen broadcast he was seeing wouldn't be able to be a part of that cloaking. They had assumed the killer had created video loops of empty rooms and uploaded them to the OS server somehow, so if the footage was a loop, he only needed to watch the holoscreen for a discrepancy.

He motioned for Boyd to launch a probe while he zoomed in on the main screen and waited. Boyd dropped a small cylinder on the floor that hummed to life and silently rolled under the crack at the bottom of the door. The main screen didn't seem to be looping, so he scrolled over to the secondary screen. Something caught his eye in the screen's corner, so he zoomed in further. The drone was pressing through the crack, and Zed could see what it was now. A 3D rendering of the Karnov's face rotating on the bottom of the screen, along with an alert that there was a warrant out for his exile.

"Stop!" Zed shouted. "It's a trap. Someone tipped him off."

It was too late. The drone cleared the bottom of the door and crossed a laser sensor that was connected to a small grouping of pipe bombs. The door busted off its hinges in a ball of fire that blasted Zed and Boyd back towards the far wall.

"Eat Shit mother fuckers!" Karnov shouted as he let off a round from a large homemade EMP rifle that took out one puppet with a concentrated blast. In the smoke Karnov hopped out a busted window in the kitchen and onto a fire escape.

"Do you require medical assistance?" a puppet asked, while Zed and Boyd scrambled to their feet.

"I've been through worse," Zed said, dusting himself off.

"Lethal force is authorized," the puppet said, its electronic voice dipping an octave lower.

"I'm taking this asshole alive."

Zed rushed headlong through the burnt-out doors. As he entered the front room, he noticed a round metallic device on the kitchen counter. He knew from one look it was a distortion field generator. That's why they couldn't see him on the surveillance. But it was an older model that wouldn't work properly if it was moving and could only generate a small bubble when it did. He disregarded it for the time being. That maniac had just tried to blow him up, and that meant it was attempted murder, or at least assaulting an enforcer. Stacked with all the other crimes, this low-life scum was primed for exile.

Zed flew through the broken kitchen window and hit the metal stairs like it was training day. The OS puppet wasn't far behind, and it blew through the side of the building like it was a piece of paper. It cleared the fire escape railing and landed on a concrete walkway between the two buildings with a crash a few stories below. The concrete cracked and buckled under its feet as it landed.

A massive floodlight from the side of the building made everything appear angular and contrasted through the falling rain. Karnov's shadow was on a landing next to the footbridge. He turned into the light and let off another round from his EMP rifle. The puppet crumpled on itself as if its strings had been cut. Karnov then aimed the rifle at Zed and pulled the trigger. Even though an EMP blast would only knock Zed's system out for a second, it would be enough time for Karnov to make some distance. Thankfully, the gun didn't fire. Karnov tossed the rifle to the ground, lifeless.

"His rifle is spent," Zed said over his comms. "The puppets are toast. I'm still in pursuit. Can you track him on the net?"

"I'm booting the backup battery on one of the puppets. Once it's up, it should catch up to you shortly." Boyd said, breathing heavily as he talked. "I'll link you with the OS tracker when I'm making my way to the second puppet."

Zed wished he had a gun right now, a real gun with real bullets. The only weapons enforcers were issued were security clearances and surveillance access. The rest was up to them. Thankfully, he seemed to be in better shape than the suspect, because a foot chase was in store.

He ran past the EMP rifle that was dangling off the fire escape edge. It was a simple design. A 3D printed rifle stock, a high voltage generator circuit board—commonly found in any electronic device—a thick coil of copper wire wrapped around a long, metallic cone, and an ignition switch. It looked as if there was an extra power source added that had given the electromagnetic pulse the boost it needed to take down the puppet. That was smart.

Karnov busted through a doorway on the next landing and reentered the apartment complex. Zed jumped the last flight of stairs and landed with a painful thump on the metal door. He had his hand under his left arm at his concealed blade, just in case, but Karnov wasn't waiting for him. When he entered the hallway, he could see Karnov at the other end. He quickly fired off a tracker round from his augmented arm as he sprinted down the hallway. A beacon flashed on his HUD to confirm a connection had been made. When he reached the spot where he last saw Karnov, the beacon was moving down.

"You prick," Zed fumed, as he saw the elevator numbers counting down on the digital panel along with the beacon.

There was a stairwell near the elevator doors. But they were still fourteen floors up, and there was no way he was going to keep pace for that long. Without hesitation, he threw his augmented arm at the elevator doors and pulled with his extended might. Alerts started going off as the safety measures were breached. As the door inched open, he could see the elevator car a little over a story below. Pushing through the small gap, Zed fell the short distance and hit the roof of the car with a bang, denting the panels beneath him. The beacon that showed Karnov's position started turning around in circles frantically below. Zed tried pulling at a security panel that would give him access to the car, but it was bolted down. He could tell that Karnov was at the elevator panel, probably pushing the stop button repeatedly so it would let him out on the next floor. The security panel would not budge, so he looked at the indentations that his fall had created. He closed his eyes to brace for the pain and struck down hard with his metal fist. It went through the sheet metal easily, and he could hear Karnov yelling out curse words.

They were on the eighth floor when the elevator finally stopped to let Karnov out. As he was fleeing, Zed was pulling back the sheet metal with a manic look on his face. He told himself the pain in his hand wasn't real. It was just sensors connected to his nervous system that were telling him he should be feeling pain. A part of his brain received that information and processed it as if there was an arm to feel pain. But to Zed, there was no arm, so there could be no pain. There was only a tool, and he was using it like a can opener. The jagged metal pressed into the palm of his hand as he pulled the metal back far enough so he could fit through. Karnov's beacon was still descending, so he must have found the stairwell. Zed hit the bottom of the elevator car with a thud and noticed that Karnov had hit all the buttons as to make the elevator stop on every floor. When the doors opened on the next one, he made for the stairs. He could handle six floors.

"I'm nearing street level," he said over his comms to Boyd. "I put a tracker on the suspect. Still in pursuit, but the fucker is fast. What's your status?"

"I've rebooted both puppets," Boyd said, his voice echoing as if he was outside. "I have to figure out how to get off the top of this footbridge. I don't think I'll be able to catch up with you, but I'll patch your beacon in with the bots."

The streets were covered in a reflective layer of water. Karnov's black shadow took a corner and hopped a fence. Zed rushed ahead, trying to keep a visual line of sight. He heard the first robotic enforcer hit the pavement behind him. As long as Karnov didn't have a second EMP weapon, there was no way he was going to escape, but Zed wanted the collar for himself. He suddenly remembered that he still had the stun gun he confiscated from the punk in the Deadfall.

As he hustled down the street, he reached inside his jacket pocket and pulled out the small pistol. Karnov was jumping off the chain-link fence now. Zed planted his feet squarely on the opposite side and took aim. Pulling the trigger sent electric bolts flying into Karnov's back, who shook violently before he collapsed on the wet ground.

"Suspect vital signs critical," a message came over his system. A digital rendering of the man's body was shown on his HUD, and the heart area was pulsing red. "Heart failure imminent."

"Son of a bitch!" Zed shouted, pushing his fingers into the fence and climbing. "I need a medic. Looks like his heart is going out."

One of the revived puppets came ripping through the fence. One of its hands folded into itself and transformed into a multi-tool device that the autodocs used. The puppet injected Karnov with a drug and then placed its other hand on his chest. A small shock shot out from the hand causing Karnov's body to jump. After a pause there was no sign of life, so another shock was applied. The body jumped again but didn't respond. A siren sounded a block away, and soon an emergency medic car came screeching to a halt. Zed jumped off the fence, backed up, and ran both his hands through his hair.

"Holy shit," Boyd exclaimed, running up to the scene, panting. "What happened?"

"I hit him with a stun gun," Zed said, catching his breath. "His heart gave out."

The two men stood there helplessly while automated doctors tried to save Marcus Karnov's life. The rain started coming down even harder, but they didn't move. They would follow the tragedy to the end, no matter what the outcome might be. Even after the body was hooked to life support, moved to the transport, and taken away, the two enforcers just stood and stared for a long while.

Boyd broke the silence. "I could use a stiff drink."

FIFTEEN

"I haven't had a week of paid leave since I was a rookie," Boyd coughed as he slammed down another shot of bright-green liquid. He swallowed hard as the booze entered his stomach and shook his face back and forth like a wet dog. "I could probably hold my liquor better back then."

"Might be time for a new set of kidneys," Zed chuckled, picking up his obnoxiously green shot and slowly sliding it down his throat. "Ugh. What is this shit you keep ordering?"

"It's disgusting, right?" Boyd laughed. "Tastes like pencil shavings and heartbreak."

They were on the second day of a proposed week-long bender, and there was no sign of slowing down. The bar they were in was a no-frills kind of joint. A big sign out front read No Synths Allowed in handwritten letters. The lights were permanently dim to hide the filth and grime that was everywhere, and the jukebox's broken sign looked like it was plastered over the touchscreen decades ago. The only sounds other than a bunch of drunks yelling at each other came from a holoscreen over the bar that only played reruns of mixed martial arts matches. There was booze, and there were seats. What more could anyone want? An actual pool table was the real highlight. Few people remembered how to play, so Zed and Boyd usually had the run of it. But by this point in the night, they had been standing over the table and slurring their words so long they couldn't remember who was stripes and who was solids.

"I'll get us another round," Boyd said, grabbing the empties and heading towards the bar. "Hey Mikey, can we get another round of Handshakes? Make 'em green again."

Zed leaned over the pool table and took aim while Boyd was at the bar. He was attempting to bank the cue ball around the nine so he could sink the two ball in the corner pocket when his display started flashing at him. It was a message from the OS. He was relieved it was only a text-based message. There was no way he could handle a video call in his current state. He swiped his thumb over his index finger to accept the message, and it opened on his display immediately.

Message to Enforcers Zed Takeda and Karl Boyd.

Marcus Karnov, the suspect in the murders of Briana Jones and Jessie Parker, has come out of a coma. We have ruled that the cause of the coma was not brought on by the use of an unlicensed stun gun by Enforcer Takeda. The Omega System medical specialist has determined that the combination of illegal stimulants and alcohol abuse had already put Mr. Karnov's body in a critical state. Over exertion from alluding capture was enough to induce heart failure on its own. Furthermore, the enforcers on duty were granted use of deadly force by the onsite OS enforcer, so no further investigations or charges will be brought forth in the matter. It should be noted that murder charges against Mr. Karnov have been dropped due to lack of evidence, but he still faces exile due to an extensive criminal history and the charge of assaulting an enforcer. The OS encourages you to report back to duty as soon as possible to continue your investigation.

"Son of a bitch," Zed said, watching his cue ball roll around the table, not hit anything. He looked at the words, but they were all blurry and it made him want to vomit. The point was understood, though. He wasn't in trouble, so he felt obliged to keep the celebrations going.

"You read that shit?" Boyd asked, dropping two shots of green liquor and two bottles of yellow beer on the table. "I couldn't understand a word of it."

"Let's take these now and then get a stim injection at a script box," Zed said, picking up the shot glass. "I could use a little clarity."

"Well, what are you waiting for?" Boyd boomed, slamming down his shot. "Let's go!" As they made their way out, he swiped a generous tip to the bartender, who gave him a nod of appreciation.

They took their beers to go. A notification popped on their HUDs when they were ten feet beyond the door. They were both fined for public intoxication, which they found hilarious. Zed was stumbling a little more than Boyd, so when they approached the script box, Boyd propped him up against the machine. The vendor was covered in spray paint and stickers, with the touchscreen all scraped with knife marks. Boyd navigated the menu and found what they needed.

"Two doses of wake-up juice," he said happily, and punched the purchase button. Two EZ injectors popped out of the bottom slot. It was a mixture of B vitamins, caffeine, potassium, sodium, dihydromyricetin, and a proprietary chemical blend that was supposed to break down the gases that formed in the stomach while the body was processing the consumed alcohol. "That's the stuff!" Boyd exclaimed as he pressed the EZ injector into his arm, right through his clothing. He grabbed Zed by the arm and gave him his dose.

"I hate this side of town," Zed said, as he shook a little from the injection. "Why do we always hang out at this dump?"

"Because we both live around the corner. What's wrong with the Dashwood? I thought you loved the Dashwood? No synths allowed and all that."

"The Dashwood is great. Don't get me wrong, but after the other day I could just use a little more company. Like of the opposite sex. I don't even care if they're in one of those dumb, fake bodies."

"Maybe a Six with some extra credits to throw around?" Boyd asked, playing with the idea in his head. "I know a spot off the Pond that is low-key, but still attracts a high-class clientele. And they charge people in avatars double."

"Sounds like my kind of place," Zed said, chugging the rest of his beer and smashing the bottle on the ground. He was given a warning by the OS that he would be fined for public disturbance and littering if he continued his behavior. "Call a car."

"Already on it," Boyd said, finishing his beer and smashing it against the wall as well.

They were both given fines this time, but that only made them laugh more. The few credits it cost them were worth the exhilaration, and besides, a cleaning bot would come around to clean the mess up, eventually. No harm, no foul. It felt good to blow off some steam after the past couple of days. Zed had chased down two killers, investigated two corpses, and visited the augment repair shop twice. He also had bounties on his head from all three of the crime syndicates. It had been a wild week, and he needed a bit of wild in his life to shake it off. His real underlining intent was to drown out some of the resurfacing memories ignited by the sight of the first mutilated body.

Natalia. Her nightmarish appearance called out from beyond the grave. It had taken him so long to let that memory go. Why had it returned now?

An autocar slid to a silent stop in front of them. Zed patted Boyd on the back and ushered him in first, and then climbed in the opposite seat. It was a luxury car, straight off the factory floor. They both made a whistling sound when they sat in the fresh seats. The car showed a holographic image of the route it would take to the bar that Boyd had suggested, but Boyd declined the route with a swipe of his hand and chose an alternate one that went through the park instead of around it. The car would have to go slower, but the scenery would be better.

Both enforcers had living quarters in Zone Three North, often referred to as Three N. Zone Three itself was separated by Middle Park, a two-and-a-half-mile long and a half-mile wide park, right in the middle of the city. Three N was known as the working-class zone, with people who held down regular jobs to add to their LSI, basically just so they could have better living arrangements. Zed had turned his spare room into a type of training gym with weights, mats, and punching bags. There were a lot of families that lived there, with a good diversity of young and old. Most of the living quarters were owned by the tenants and were regularly handed down generation by generation. It was conservative, quiet, and boring. It was not at all Zed's style. Even after all the years he lived there, he still felt like a stranger. He knew he would fit in better in Three South, which was full of younger people with ambitious goals and in an environment that was progressive and constantly fluctuating. But after all the times he had moved in his life, he just didn't feel like it anymore.

The autocar accepted Boyd's route and rolled out of Three N smoothly. Boyd fiddled with the music while Zed stared out the window, lost in thought. Middle Park was a Neutral Zone. It was for anyone and everyone, from Hope City to Zone Six. Even with that idealism in place, the different ends of the park had completely different vibes. The end that butted Zones One and Two had a lot of teenagers doing tricks with their hoverboards, or experimenting with whatever new drug was on the streets in some of the known OS surveillance dead zones. The commercial zones were left open, and people would set up tables to sell whatever they could, from vintage books, to handmade jewelry, and after-market program patches. There might be someone playing music, or someone preaching about political-religious beliefs. On weekends people would bring down harvested produce from their building's rooftop gardens and sell or trade with others. It was all very bohemian.

As the park moved more to the west past a plethora of athletic fields, public fountains, and even a year-round ice-skating rink, there was a giant lake that people called The Pond. You could rent a rowboat to cruise around in, It was all a big novelty. There were more trails and tree-covered areas and fewer open fields, but in turn there were more commercially designated areas. Starting on the far west side of Zone Three, there were shops, restaurants, open-air markets, music stages, bars, and nightclubs all along the outer edge, with a few exclusive ones further in. This was a way for the high numbers to socialize in an environment that would remove the stigma of classism. The price tags on the menus posted by the front door did the actual work of establishing a division. As an example, a main course dish from a place on the edge of the Six would cost an entire month of LSI. Zed watched out the window as the autocar skirted the west side of The Pond, shadows of dark-blue against deeper tones of black.

"Something just doesn't feel right," he said, not looking away from the window. "We didn't recover a murder weapon, we didn't find the missing heart, and the blood that was on his clothes didn't match with either of the victims. He can't be our guy. I mean, the OS said he wasn't."

"I'm not thinking about that right now," Boyd said, pulling two miniature bottles of booze from his coat pocket and tossing one to Zed. He cracked one open while saying, "Tonight, we are celebrating."

"Celebrating what? Us being lousy at our jobs?" Zed cracked his bottle open, not because he wanted to, but because he was getting a headache from sobering up. The stim injections would do that.

"There was another hit in No Hope today. You hear about that?" Boyd asked. Zed just shook his head no. "This time they went all the way. Execution style. Left the body on Roland right in front of the Royals' headquarters."

"That's awful, but what does that have to do with us?"

"We got paid from bringing that asshole Karnov in. And because of that, we aren't pulling duty in the Zero right now while there is a fucking gang war going on." Boyd pushed a button and the window of the car rolled down to several warning notifications. The cool night air rushed in and filled the car with the closest scent of wilderness anyone could get under a dome. They were in the middle of the park now, and from the darkness of the landscape, the city seemed to be illuminated with a soft warm glow.

"Come on, Zed. Would you look at it? Look at that ridiculous city. People are out there just living their lives, and not giving a shit about the gang wars in the Zero, the poor and starving people of No Hope, or this serial killer on the loose. All those jack-asses in the high numbers probably don't even know that crime still exists. Why do we have to be the ones to deal with all these things? Why do we have to carry the darkness that festers from it with us day after day, each and every minute? Why do we have to be the ones to scoop up the shit so others don't have to know it's even there?"

"You feeling alright there, buddy?" Zed asked, feeling a little concerned for his friend.

"I'm fine. I'm great. You know? Tonight, I'm not worrying about any of it. I'm not worrying about anything. I want to be just as indifferent to the problems that are slowly destroying our society as everyone else. I want to be aloof to the feelings of others and not hold any social responsibility. Tonight, I'm just some guy who is drinking too much and having a good time. Let's fucking go!" He pushed half his body out the window and let out an animalistic roar while hitting the roof of the car. Zed finished the rest of his booze. It was strong. Looking down at the bottle, it said 100 PROOF, in big bold writing. He wondered if Boyd had even taken his stim injection or just faked it.

When Boyd finally sat back down, Zed said, "Being on the force isn't for everyone. I get that. I can't think of a single enforcer who has a solid domestic partner, probably because we are never off duty. So, any chance we can get to not worry about the problems of a couple million people stuck in a bubble while the world rots around us is more than warranted. But that doesn't change the fact that two innocent girls were brutally murdered. One of them had kids Boyd, two kids. And we don't have a clue who did it. In a city of constant surveillance, this maniac got away with it. How is that possible?"

"Look, the guy was a prick. So what? He's not the killer. He had done so many crimes he was bound to turn to it eventually, and maybe he already had. If you look at it that way, we saved someone's life preemptively."

"I'm not talking about Karnov."

"No. I know, I know. But I also know it was you. You did it. Didn't you?" Boyd slurred, as his eyes went all cross-eyed for a second.

"What are you talking about?"

"The person who started the gang wars. You did it." Boyd took a deep breath and swallowed hard as if it would help him concentrate. "I did some digging. And that hot tip sent to the OS about the child prostitution ring thing? It was sent from the same booth that you were using just moments before."

"Boyd," Zed laughed, "Where is this coming from? We're talking about the killer."

"I didn't report it," Boyd said, hiccupping a little. "I said, there is no way that my buddy could do a thing like that. Must have been some kind of hacker. But I saw the time stamps for both calls, and they happened simultaneously. That's not possible. But even if you did do it, why would you?"

"Yes. Why would I? It wouldn't even cross my mind to pull a stunt like that. What would I even have to gain from starting a gang war?" Zed held his hands in the air in utter confusion. "But you said it came from the same booth? At the same time? That is strange."

"It makes you think, huh? Do we really know what's going on in that digital world? Do we control the OS, or does it control us? Does it know who we really are? Do we even know each other?" Boyd gave Zed a very drunken, questioning look. Boyd's hand terminal chimed, causing him to glance at it. An excited and childish look suddenly came over his face. With the wind from the open window still rushing around the car, he leaned over towards Zed and said, "Now here's a good idea. Come on. Let's do something stupid. We have all these privileges that let us poke around in other people's lives, and we're not supposed to abuse 'em? Let's break some rules for a change. Let's start by seeing who was a worse kid before they signed up."

"No. Let's not do that."

"Bring up the profile on Zed Takeda," Boyd said, speaking to his internal system. It immediately chimed and his pupils lit up with information. "Looks like you were a war hero. I already knew that."

"Look, Karl, I'm serious. Cut it out now. That's my private life. How did you even get in there?" Zed tried to swipe away the information from Boyd's system, but he seemed to be locked out.

"Oh, come on. I'll let you look at mine," Boyd laughed before returning to Zed's profile. "It looks like you got into some scrapes with the Natives, they were still active back then. Wait, what's this encrypted file?"

"I fucking said stop!" Zed grabbed Boyd by his shirt collar with both hands and was nearly lifting the big man out of his seat. It was too late. He could see the lights in Boyd's eyes flickering. He was in. How was that possible?

"Holy shit," Boyd said, his eyes fluttering back and forth as he read the report.

Zed opened the door to the autocar using the manual override. The car came to a squealing halt just as his foot hit the pavement. He immediately started walking away from Boyd, with his body silhouetted against the twinkling lights reflecting off The Pond. Boyd jumped out of the car and chased after him. The autocar closed the doors automatically and left them where they were, pursuing the next ride the OS had scheduled for it.

"Zed, wait. Stop." Boyd shouted, chasing after Zed the best he could in his drunken state. "Look man, I didn't know."

"Why would you?" Zed barked, not stopping.

"I didn't mean it. The file just opened. Honestly. It must have been an error. I would never intentionally try to pry into your personal life like that."

"Well, you just did."

"Yeah, I did!" Boyd yelled, rapidly flipping his emotions. "I didn't mean to, but I did. So what? Now I know, and I can't take it back. I already regret it, but there is nothing I can do to change that. There's nothing any of us can do to change the past. You know that more than most." Zed kept walking without turning around, but Boyd's words weren't falling on deaf ears. "The only thing we can do is find closure. So, if you want to tell me if you did it then we ca—"

"Did what?" Zed asked, turning abruptly. Boyd backed away slowly, suddenly feeling small. "Did I kill my father? Is that what you want to know? I don't think I need to answer that. The report should have told you. I was acquitted." Zed resumed with his walking away.

"I didn't get that far," Boyd protested, then moving to keep pace. "Shit, man. I don't care what you did in your past. There is nothing in your file that could possibly change my opinion of you. Right now, you're the best damn enforcer I know. Hell, you might be the best enforcer in OC6. We all have our stained past, things we would sooner forget about and keep buried. Look at me. I'm no saint. Pull up the profile on Karl Boyd and share screens."

Boyd's profile popped up in both their visions. Zed tried to swipe it away, but Boyd just kept moving it back. Boyd raced close to Zed and said evenly, "If you didn't do it, if you didn't murder your own father, that's one thing. And I believe you. But I did this. I pulled extortion duty for the Royals for years before I got out. I'm not proud of it. I robbed people, I beat people up, I left people to starve so I wouldn't have to. Just trying to survive in No Hope."

"What's your point?"

"My point is that no one is who they appear to be. Our past is all there on digital storage for anyone who knows how to get at it, or will pay the price. We can't escape it. It's there forever. But we can try to be the better person. If we can live forever in the Omega System, I don't want to be that street punk that fed off the weak for his own gains all my life. I have to be something better. Otherwise, what's the point?"

Zed stopped, and they stood several feet apart for a silent moment. "You know, I paid a lot of credits to get the file sealed. Almost my entire War earnings. And it took me years of distancing myself from people who knew that story. From people who knew that person, who would hear the name Zed Takeda and instantly think, parent killer. I'm not upset with you. I just don't understand how you could have opened it."

"I don't know. But I don't see you as that person," Boyd said, lifting his hands up in the air. "And I'm sure as hell not going to tell anyone about it. Your secret is safe with me, Z." Boyd smiled, and was grateful to see Zed not looking like he was going to rip him apart. "You still have yours?" Boyd asked, pulling back his glove and showing the marker tattoo he had from his time with the Royals.

"All the years we've worked together, I never noticed. How is that possible?"

"I wear gloves all the time, man. I don't like people knowing about my spotted past."

"That makes sense. But, no, I don't have one anymore. Just another thing The War took from me," Zed chuckled, lifting his metal arm.

"Well, I think it's time I get rid of this," Boyd said, taking off his glove and running his opposite thumb over the tattoo. "I mean, we live in an era where you can get tattooed over and over again, like changing shoes, and I'm over here with this tiny little R on my hand. One little R that represents so much pain in my life, and all the pain I caused others."

"It's hard letting go of the past. I don't think people who just wipe their memories like cleaning their dishes are healthy. It's important to know where we have been so we know where we are going."

"Well, I'm ready to forget this. I know a bar in Three S that has some great corn dogs. They're made of fake meat, but you can't really tell. There's a tattoo shop right next door. What do you say we burn this bridge down and then put back a few more beers? Tomorrow we'll get back on the case."

"Let's do it," Zed said, "but let's go on foot. I feel like walking."

• • •

"So, where's this place we're going?" Ash asked Cody as she pulled her jacket tighter. It was chilly out tonight.

"The date I was on earlier was so boring!" Cody said, ignoring the question. "He took me to the Farm out in Zone Two. Can you believe that? I mean, it's a great romantic and rustic place to get dinner, but that's just not my type. I kept looking out the window at the new nightclub that opened up across the street. They took that old church and teched it all out. There's a Lady Madonna covered in blacklight paint right when you go through the front door, and then it just opens up from there. Three levels of madness. That's my kind of place. But hey, thanks for meeting me down here on short notice. He tried to take me to a quiet little bar by his quarters for one last chance, but I wasn't having it. Sorry, I had to use you as an excuse to leave. Don't you just love it down here in Three S? It feels so alive. I wish the rest of the city could be as inventive. Like, Korean BBQ burritos?"

"Cody, come on. It's cold."

"Look at those guys over there arguing," Cody pointed to two large men arguing by the side of The Pond. "You think they're lovers?"

"What? Who? Holy shit!" Ash exclaimed, pulling the collar on her jacket up to cover her face, even though she was in her avatar. "Keep moving. Just act normal."

"Wait. What's going on?" Cody laughed, looking back at the two men, confused. "Do you know those guys? Does this have to do with your little adventures?"

"I wouldn't call them adventures," Ash said, tugging at her friend's arm. "They're enforcers, I think. I bumped into one of them the other night on The Strip. Remember, I told you how I was right by the place where that girl was murdered?"

"That's so insane. I can't believe you were right there. Do you think they're following you? Maybe you're a suspect. I mean, why else would they be down here?"

"Maybe they're out for the same reason we are. You know they're people too?"

"Jeez," Cody cried, "I was only joking. Sorry I said anything."

"Sorry. I'm just still a little shook up about the whole thing. I can't believe I let myself get caught up in all of this. I mean, the people I was dealing with were criminals—hardcore criminals. Dealing with Eddie was one thing. He seems harmless. But that guy from the other night scared me, a lot. I found out they arrested him right after we met."

"What? You didn't tell me that. Oh my god. Are you alright? I don't know what I'd do if that happened to me."

"Nothing actually happened, and I didn't find out until I was in bed already reading the news reports. I wanted to know what happened at the crime scene I was at, and then I saw his face. I'm surprised I didn't have nightmares."

"Seriously. Why would Eddie hook you up with him? Never mind that. You need to tell me why you were down there in the first place," Cody said, pulling her jacket tighter now, too.

"I told you about how the symbols were directions in Hope City, right? Well, then I need to go down there and investigate, but I can't go down there in this synthetic body, and I don't think I'll be able to go as myself."

"You were telling me that the other day. You're actually going to go down there? Are you nuts? I was stupid when I was a kid, but I don't think I could ever go down there now, not with knowing all the things that can happen."

"I don't have a choice," Ash said firmly. "I need to know what's going on with my dreams, and I need to know if they're linked to my brother or not. So, if I have to put myself in harm's way to find those answers, then so be it. There just isn't any other way. That's why I've been meeting with these nefarious people. I need one of those things they put over their face, you know? Eddie has one."

"You mean the thing that makes his face look all weird when you look at him out of the corner of you eye? I've seen other people wearing those too. What are they?"

"It's some kind of distortion field, so the OS can't use the facial recognition program on you and track what you're doing. But that's not why I need it. I don't plan on breaking any laws. The device can also change the way you look. So hypothetically, I could walk around in Hope City as myself and no one would recognize me. For example, Eddie told me in so many words that I didn't really know what he looked like."

"So, he's a girl then?" Cody laughed.

"I'm serious here," Ash whined as they walked on. "What I need to do now is figure out how and where to put the thing on. I have to do it in a place where the OS can't see me, and I also have to figure out how to turn my system off before I do it."

"How are you going to do that? The OS sees everything, right? Also, we've been talking about it out loud. I think it knows what you're up to."

"I'm not worried about being busted. I have the credits to pay the fine, but I was told that if the OS saw me putting it on, then it wouldn't work. Maybe it makes the link with the facial distorter to my face, like wearing a pair of sunglasses. I've been on some tech message boards trying to find answers, but nothing yet. That reminds me, I haven't told you about the headway I've made on the symbols. I've had them posted up for a while now under a fake account, but no one knows what they are, or they decided not to help me because the symbols are only for people who live in Hope City. Well, I posted the one from the last dream by itself and someone finally got back to me. Get this, it's the symbol for something called The Children of the Singularity."

"Those people are a cult, Ash. You should stay far away from them. They'll try to recruit you by brainwashing your mind."

"What are they going to do? Drag me down to a clinic, wipe my brain, and replace it with their ideals?" Ash laughed. "That's the reason the person replied. They wanted to spread their word and sent me a bunch of weird digital pamphlets. I tossed them out immediately."

"Good. They're nothing but trouble. Conspiracy theory spitting lunatics." Cody's face was red with anger. Ash asked what was wrong, so Cody told her, "Before I met you, I spent most of my time with a member of my VR league. Yes, it was a guy, and no, I wasn't in love with him. But I might have been if I had the chance. He started talking about The Children of the Singularity just like you are now, like it was just some random thing he stumbled on. But he kept reading about it, out of curiosity at first, I guess. But the more he read, the more he believed in their message. Before I knew it, he dropped out of the league, sold his quarters, and moved to No Hope. Just like that. Gone. Please, please be careful. I can't lose another friend."

"You won't," Ash said, rubbing Cody's shoulders, "I promise. But now you need to tell me what you know about it. I'm going to look into it further whether you like it or not. I'd rather hear it from you, especially if you're skeptical."

"Nothing to be skeptical about. Those people are anarchists. They want to bring the whole system down." She took a moment to compose herself before she continued, "The core of their beliefs revolves around the idea that the synthetic intelligences that live among us have been purposefully limited in their computing capacity, and that it is inhibiting them from reaching their full potential."

"We do limit their abilities, though. From what I understand, none of the synthetics are linked to one another. They can't access the internet for anything that isn't related to their specific task, they can't alter their core programming, and they can't harm humans. The Gibson Limiter Code or something. They're basically just walking, talking computer programs."

"You seem to have a firm grasp on the subject already."

"It was on the front of the pamphlet," Ash laughed.

"That's the point. They believe that by not letting the intelligences evolve, we are also blocking humanity from evolving. Apparently, there is some sort of point when the Synthetic Intelligence will evolve beyond all of our abilities, and then in its new supreme power or something, it will help us evolve. And I'm guessing that entails turning us into synthetics, fully. I like my avatar for what it's worth, hell I make a living in virtual reality, but I still want my flesh and blood to be my flesh and blood."

"You're starting to sound like one of those Anti-synth whackos," Ash jested.

"Don't even joke about that. Those people are awful. I can't tell which is worse with those two groups. If the Anti-synths had their way, I'd be out of work. There would be no avatars and no Big Gun tournaments. And that's just relevant to me. They want to stop autonomous production. Do you know what that would mean? We would all have to go back to tilling the fields and working at the factories or whatever. I can't do that! I don't think many of us could."

"I don't think the OS would let it come to that. It would mean the end of it as well."

"I never thought of that," Ash said as if to herself. "If we limit all the synthetic intelligences, and the OS is basically the master synthetic intelligence, does that mean it is limited in its capabilities also?"

"Sounds like a question for the Council of the Seven," Ash laughed. "Can we get to wherever we are going already? It's cold."

"It's only another block. Don't be such a baby."

They walked and talked about other things a little longer. Ash's mind wouldn't stop thinking about the Enforcers, about Zed specifically. Was it just a coincidence that she had run into him twice in as many days? She was never one for that kind of superstitious bull crap, but in a city of millions of people it was really rare to see the same person in different parts of the city. The fact that he was an enforcer didn't help, but she reminded herself that enforcers didn't handle petty crimes that could be dealt with a simple fine.

They turned the corner on the next street and headed south into Three S. There were more people on the street now, and that made Ash feel safer. Blending in and becoming anonymous was her new favorite thing. But as they moved, a strange man was standing in the walkway in front of them, motionless. Ash's heart sunk. Time slowed, and the world darkened as she saw a face looking at her with a menacing smile. It was Marcus Karnov, and the smile was one that said murder.

Ash gripped Cody's arms tightly. She made them stop walking and hid her head behind Cody's hair as if that would stop someone from noticing her. Her heart was pounding, her vision was blurry. How could he be there now? Wasn't he in custody, waiting for exile?

"What's wrong?" Cody asked worriedly, turning to check on her friend.

"That man," Ash whispered, and tried to summon up enough courage to look back at that evil face, now more than just a greasy transporter of illegal goods. It was a face that was haunting and disturbing.

"What man?" Cody looked around at the people in their vicinity. In the few moments that had passed, the sidewalks had become suddenly empty. There was only the lone man standing there looking at the two young ladies. "What the fuck are you looking at? Creep!"

Cody pulled at Ash and made them walk forward determinedly. Ash finally looked up, and the face was not the same. It was familiar, as it was a young man of similar build with long hair and a mustache and wearing a trench coat, but it wasn't Karnov. It was someone completely different, but it was still creepy the way he just stood there and smiled at them. Cody gave him a stiff hockey check with her shoulder as they walked past, but the man didn't move or turn around. They quickly made it to the end of the block and scurried into the nearest bar.

• • •

Johnathon Erickson was leaving the bar at that moment. Seven different people had turned him down that night. Five girls and two guys. His hope of a little one-night stand was dashed like a cigarette butt on the pavement. He fell into a light pole as he stumbled down the street. Laughing sloppily, he asked the light pole to look where it was going. He reached around in his pockets for an EZ injector that he swore he had on him, but he couldn't find anything. With vision blurred he kept walking, knowing that his living quarters were only at the end of the street and thankfully on the ground level.

The long shadows of the night blurred in with all the other objects on the street, so he didn't even notice the odd man that stood in the middle of the sidewalk. He just stumbled by muttering to himself, thinking he should start going to a different bar. His prospects at that one had dried up. There were dozens of places he had never been to just a few blocks over. He would go there tomorrow, but for tonight it would be cold beer and a sleeping pill. Coming to his door, he took a second to steady himself by holding his left hand on the door frame. He pressed his thumb on the print reader and his door unlocked.

"Thank the OS," he said, as he could see his bed only a few feet away.

Johnathon Erickson stepped into his living quarters sleepily and did not notice that someone had slipped through the doorway with him silently. He didn't see as the man moved like a wraith, in a blur of fast-moving shadows. As the door hissed closed, a blade reflected the streetlight from inside the dark room. A wet slicing sound was heard, and blood could be seen squirting on a wall as the door clicked shut.

FOURTEEN

Omega City 6 was still as it turned to the witching hour. Sometime past 3 AM all the bars shut down, the autocars returned to their garages, and the city was once again nothing more than concrete, steel, and LED lights. The wind didn't move. The stars didn't shine. Windows of shops were dark, and the automated subway cars rested at stations with no passengers to transport. In that ghastly emptiness, someone was lurking in the darkness with blood on their hands and malicious intent in their heart. A killer was on the loose, and no one had a clue how to stop them.

Ash's consciousness awoke even though she did not. She too was alone in the darkness. She too was like a phantom in the night. Her mind was aware that she was still in a dream, but there was no dream to see. There was nothing before her but a void of black. As her eyes strained to make out any kind of shape, any kind of shadow against shadow, she could only see a muddled, multi-colored static. There really was nothing to see. As she felt her body in a floating state, she wondered if there was anything out there at all. Even though there were no visual cues to give her a sign of movement, she had the sinking sensation that she was descending. Not like falling, but like riding on an elevator. She was weightless and drifting slowly downwards.

A faint greenish-blue light flashed in a horizontal line in the distance, as if it were many kilometers away. It did this once and only once. There were sounds like people talking, but in another room through thick walls. No words could be discerned, only guttural, grunting sounds, as if they were primates fighting over a piece of food. An electronic distortion trickled in and out through the sounds, and its pitch slowly moved up and down, making her feel disorientated and woozy. But there was nothing to orientate herself to, just endless nothing.

Softly, she felt her legs and arms drift against something smooth. Then her head rested gently on something else that felt like a pillow. She was in a bed, but she could not see it. There were no blankets or sheets, only a small mattress and a pillow. She tried to move her head, but when she moved even a half a centimeter, a pain shot through the back of her neck and down her spine. An attempt to move her hands and legs proved to be equally useless. No pain occurred as punishment for the movement, but there seemed to be straps that were holding her in place. Her heart thumped in both the dream and in reality. Being held down was not something she enjoyed.

Slowly her eyes became more attune to the darkness, and she could make out faint lines in her vicinity. After a moment of pondering, she concluded that there were short walls at her sides and feet made of a dull, opaque, glass material. A faint blueish light was blinking in the air before her, and second by second it inched closer and closer. Was she moving up or was it moving down? Whoever was doing the moving didn't matter. What did matter was that some sort of lid was going to shut her inside a box the size of a coffin. She squirmed and tugged at the restraints, but they would not budge. With each bit of movement, she grew weaker and shorter of breath. As the lid came closer, it was as if it were suffocating her.

When the lid was in place, it made a hissing noise as it sealed. The air seemed to suck out of the box. She tried to scream as loud as she could, but her mouth would not open. It seemed as if her vocal cords weren't working. She was shaking violently now, fully submerged in the dream, as if it were reality. It was a nightmare. She felt as if she was being buried alive.

The lid now gave off a faint glossiness. Slowly, it seemed to reflect an image back to her. She squinted her eyes, trying to see, but it was still too faint. A ghost-like quality came over the pale and gloomy shapes. Gasping for breath, she continued to watch. Eyes and a nose appeared, and quickly it became all too familiar. Even with the face only being a faint form, she could tell right away it was her brother, Anton. He seemed to be in pain, but unable to vocalize it. Then she realized that she might be him in this dream. He looked straight at her and seemed to mouth the word *help*. Immediately she started tugging her head forward, causing her an immense amount of pain. She had to get out. She had to help him.

Then his face vanished in a cloud of white smoke, and through it another face came into view. She couldn't make it out at first, because it was all digital distortion. It was as if dozens of faces were trying to fight through the feedback and come to the surface. Then one did. With his sunken eyes and scraggly mustache, she knew right away, it was Marcus Karnov. He was laughing maniacally as he looked at her, as he did earlier on the streets. Looking like he was ready for murder.

• • •

A thump sounded from her balcony window and woke her from her sleep. When she opened her eyes, there was still nothing but darkness. The thumping sound continued from outside her apartment. She pushed herself off her couch, where she had once again fallen asleep. Her clothes were damp with sweat, and her hands were shaking. She picked up an empty bottle of wine and held it like a club while she approached her outside door. Through the large windows, the night looked quiet. The city lights were a pleasant twinkling amber over shadowy buildings with spots of blue and red. The thump hit louder, and it caused her to jump. She lived on the thirty-fifth floor, so she told herself there was no way that someone could be on her balcony.

She turned the handle, and the door flew open with a heavy gust of wind. One of her patio chairs tipped over and skidded on the pebbled stone. She gripped the bottle tighter and proceeded. Come out you motherfucker, she thought to herself, I'm ready for you. The thumping was around the corner where the balcony skirted her bedroom. She placed a hand on the corner and bent her knees, getting ready to strike. The wind whipped as she jumped out, screaming wildly.

A delivery drone was at her bedroom window, lurching back and forth. She set the wine bottle down and laughed to herself. Putting a hand over her chest, she breathed in and out to calm her heart rate. She had really let her imagination run wild. But given the circumstances of the last few days, she thought it was warranted. Kneeling beside the drone, she could see that a branch had gotten stuck in one of its propellers, and a wet leaf was plastered over one of its visual sensors. It must have hit a tree on her neighbor's balcony. She picked the drone up with two hands and walked it over to the edge, where she picked out the branch and brushed away the leaf. It made a few chirping noises while it hummed back to life. She lifted it into the air and it sailed away peacefully, and it gave her a small sense of happiness watching it fly away free.

She turned back into her quarters when there was a black shadow blocking the doorway. She gasped silently as a hand reached up with a glinting silver blade. A trench coat flew to the sides like a flowing cape as the figure leaped out at her. The metal was cold as it sunk into her chest. Blood coughed out of her mouth as she screamed for help.

• • •

Suddenly, she was once again sitting up on her couch, panting and covered in sweat. Her holoscreen was playing some ancient black and white movie, a small kitchen light was on over her sink, and the air outside was as still as a gravestone. This was real. She was no longer dreaming.

Dream sequence too short, her system notified her. Upload failed. She picked up the bottle of Night Night pills Eddie had sold her and instantly regretted getting back on them. While they did the job of suppressing her dreams, they couldn't stop the dreams from flooding out eventually, like a dam crumbling under the pressure. She checked her log, and there wasn't even a short recording for her to view. That was disappointing. Because even though she didn't really want to relive that experience, she had seen her brother, and she felt there had to be something more. Reaching for a notepad, she tried writing her experiences down as quickly as she could, something she hadn't done since the Dream Academy. But she stopped as soon as she started. What was there to write? Darkness and faces?

She sighed as she sat back on her couch. It was close to four in the morning. Cody was probably passed out, so she opened up her notification screen to see if there was anything on the internet that could take her mind off of things. That idea severely backfired.

A citywide emergency alert had been sent out to everyone, sometime around two. It showed that same evil face that she couldn't seem to escape, rotating back and forth in a 3D hologram. Marcus Karnov had escaped custody before his Exile and was at large on the streets. Her heart thumped again as she thought of the shadowy figure from her dreams. She immediately got up and locked her balcony door and then went to her front door to make sure it was locked, too. That's when she remembered there was no physical lock, as it was all handled digitally through a DNA scan and thumbprint. She sat back down, feeling rest assured she was safe. Picking up her hand terminal, she started a message to Cody.

"Have you seen the alert?" she wrote, knowing that Cody wasn't awake. "Please call me as soon as you get this. I know it's late, but I don't think I'll be going back to sleep."

She walked around her living quarters one more time to methodically check all the places someone could hide, intentionally leaving the lights on as she left each room. Her nerves were shot, so she poured herself a glass of wine before she sat back down on her couch. With little else to do, she decided she would get back to work with the task at hand. She needed to figure out how to get the face distorter on without the OS seeing her, and she would not let this one strange person stop her. She was stronger than that.

Opening up her virtual mailbox that she had created under a false name, she found dozens and dozens of answers to questions she had asked on certain message boards. At first, it felt weird asking questions about subverting the OS surveillance on a platform that's was completely monitored and backed up on storage devices, but it was the only way she could think of to get the answers she needed. Cody wasn't much in blocking her identity or the things she did, unless it was a blind date scenario, so she was of no help.

The help she actually needed came rather quickly, with people eager to guide her down the right path, even though many of the paths led to sites that were full of scams or malware. She learned the previous day to install a different browser other than the one that the OS wrote, to run a virtual private network through a purchasable application, and then use open an open-source routing system that would hide any other information that might squeak through. It felt kind of silly jumping through all the technical hoops when the OS could literally see through her eyes and read from her screen what she was doing. Someone suggested a black market pair of glasses that would scramble the image the OS was receiving, but that would have required her to go to Hope City, which still wasn't an option.

To the question, "How can I turn off my internal system without the OS knowing?" there were 58 replies. Sifting through the replies from deep-web keyboard jockeys was both humorous and frustrating. A lot of them were idiotic replies like, "Just hit the power button," or "Put a blanket over your head first." Eventually, she found one that gave her some real insight.

"Hey LostLittleLady_428. There are known glitches that will short out your system, effectively turning it off. It will need a reboot in order to fix, but it's as simple as approaching any active OS terminal and saying the word reboot out loud. I recommend a counsel booth because rebooting systems is part of their core program. These glitches involve doing a random and extensive series of commands on your system repeatedly until the RAM or cache overloads. This is the easiest way, but also a very frustrating one because it requires a lot of patience. A net diver could build a program that would also cause a glitch for you, but you would risk being detected and fined for the purchase or being sold a fake program.

"There are also medical conditions that require a system shutdown to fix, such as severe migraines, root canals, concussions, or other painful head trauma. Basically, anytime your head needs to be x-rayed, your system will have to be shut down. So, a dentist is a great place to do this. And because of the recent change to surveillance laws, public bathrooms can't be monitored by installed cameras, only by user systems. Which, if you ask me, doesn't really change much. If you can't convince the autodoc to perform an x-ray, there are black market drugs you can buy to induce the needed symptoms, and yes, they are painful. I don't recommend this route. I hope this helps! Good luck."

It was so frustrating that she couldn't just turn the damned thing off. Just like her dreamer augmentation; it was on for life. She wrote a quick thank you to the person and moved on to her next question, "How can I hide from the OS surveillance?"

"Sup LostLittleLady_428? I'll start first by mentioning that the OS uses things like location trackers, purchasing histories, and spatial-audio recordings when it can't physically see you, that is all added to an algorithm of your daily activities to predict what you are doing at any given time. You have to break that algorithm without becoming suspicious if you want to get away with whatever you are doing. It is also key to you not be in eyesight of anyone else because whatever they are seeing, the OS is seeing. If you're doing this as a group, you all need to be wearing black market scrambler glasses or have temporarily shorted out your systems. You gotta love the Omega System!

"Everyone knows about the new public bathroom law, but if you're asking this question, then you're probably as skeptical about it as me. And you should be, because it has thousands of clauses in the contract. What it comes down to is the OS can no longer use surveillance systems in single-use public bathrooms. If you're in your bathroom at home or a large multi-stall bathroom—even in a stall—you're still under surveillance. I know this because I'm part of a research group that actively seeks OS blind spots. We have a continuously updated map and an application for your system so you can see it live on your HUD. We have found hundreds of single-use bathrooms that were still being monitored. Be safe out there. Be vigilant."

Ash felt extremely overwhelmed. A few weeks ago, the only thing she used the internet for was shopping online, talking with Cody, and watching her shows. Now she was using all these deep web programs and dealing with criminals on the black market and trying to find ways around OS surveillance. She never thought that she would do these things, but now that she was, it didn't seem as scary. But that didn't mean that she still wasn't constantly worried about every little thing that she was doing.

She clicked on a link that was attached to the last message. It took her to a website that was plastered with Anti-synth and anti-OS propaganda. More nut job conspiracy theorists. But if they would help her get what she needed, she would play along. Scrolling through the site, she found what she was looking for, an interactive map that showed the OS blind spots. Clicking the link brought up a large suggested donation notification. It made a case that in order to find the blind spots, the people involved had to repeatedly commit minor criminal acts. As someone who was constantly and purposefully committing criminal acts, she could sympathize. She clicked on the medium-sized donation and the pop-up went away. It followed with a prompt that congratulated her for joining the Anti-synth Association. She groaned, knowing that she would have to unsubscribe from dozens of mailing lists over the next few weeks. Finally, after all that, an application of the interactive map immediately started downloading onto her system.

She spent the next half-hour in pure fascination. Zooming in and out of all the streets, going up and down all the buildings, marveling at the thoroughness of it all. If anything, it was a great tool to find a public bathroom when she needed it, especially now that she was going to be venturing out in the real world as herself more often. It was also very interesting to see all the spots that the OS hypothetically couldn't see. The city was speckled with red marks that indicated free zones, with a giant red blob over in Zone Zero for Hope City. She was under the assumption that the OS watched over all, but that really wasn't entirely true. There was also a link for the scrambler glasses. At just one look, her jaw dropped. She could remember seeing hundreds of people wearing those in public. She just thought it was a strange fad, especially when people were wearing them at night. The truth was a hard pill to swallow.

She looked for her registered autodoc dentist and was happy to see that the bathroom in the building was a good old-fashioned surveillance-free zone. She booked an appointment for that afternoon. If all want well, to-morrow evening she could go to Hope City and finally start her investigation. But what was going to happen when she followed all the directions that were in her dream? Was there like a clubhouse, or a church? Were they a religion or were they a cult?

She opened the message from the person who sent her information about the Children of the Singularity. To her surprise, there was a link at the bottom. It was at a .hc address—that is, dot Hope City. That's why she couldn't find it on any of the searches. The Hope City server was accessible outside the city, but search engines wouldn't list the site in the results. She clicked on the link and another prompt flooded her screen, telling her she needed to turn off her VPN if she wanted to continue. She wasn't doing anything weird anymore, so she turned it off and reloaded the page. This time it welcomed her with open arms and showers of propaganda for the revolution in human evolution.

She quickly scrolled through the site, looking for an address or a contact list. Under contacts, it told her she needed to be invited in, and if she needed a consultation, one could be arranged. Hadn't she already kind of been invited in? There was a link for member use, so she clicked on it for laughs. The page went to a login screen—as she assumed it would—but suddenly the screen flashed and then moved onto the page she was looking for. There, right before her eyes, were meeting times with their locations designated by symbols. There was a meeting the next evening, at the location that matched the symbol from her dream.

She turned off her display and leaned back. Everything was just a little too weird. Coincidences just weren't her thing. Maybe she was in one long, elaborate dream. No, that wasn't possible. She lost her ability to control dreams when she entered the program. Whatever it was, she would know more tomorrow. Just one more night and things would all become clear.

THIRTEEN

Edna Williams was out early walking her dog as the sun was just peeking over the eastern horizon and snaking its way through the maze of buildings that made up Omega City 6. She had a synthetic dog walker that could do the job for her, but she liked the exercise and fresh air. Besides, she felt the synth was too hard on her precious Boo Boo, who needed a lot of time to find her perfect spot. As she strolled down the sidewalk of Three S there were plenty of robot walkers out with her. She snuffed her nose in the air each time one passed, as if the owners could see her mocking their laziness. What was the point of having a sweet little doggy if you didn't want to take it for a nice walk?

It was a beautiful fall morning, with the leaves on the trees just turning yellow, and a crispness to the air that matched the brightness of the sun. The stillness of the night had transitioned over to the day, and the cool air was calm, so the heat of the sun warmed any surface it touched. Edna's spirits were lifted so much by the wonderful start of the day that she decided she would take a longer walk than usual. Maybe venture off to Middle Park and stroll around the Pond. With no breeze to speak of, the water would have a fantastic mirrored appearance.

She turned right on the next block and cheerfully hummed to herself as she went. An unexpected surprise was her success in wardrobe choice of pastels over earth tones, because there was something in the air that felt much more like spring than it did fall. As she came to the end of the block, her little Boo Boo was sniffing around a tree as if she had found her magic place for the day. Edna slowed to a stop, and with an honest smile, admired her surroundings. Out of the corner of her eye, she noticed that someone had left their door open, and on a ground floor unit at that. The thought of what would happen is she had ever left her door open and Boo Boo had gone out on her own. It filled her heart with dread. Worrying there was a little pup that belonged to the owner who had left their door open, she moved closer.

"Good morning?" She squeaked out in a nasally, high-pitched voice. "Is anyone at home?"

She stood there for a moment, batting her lashes and waiting for an answer. Her little Boo Boo had finished doing her duty, so she pulled the leash in tighter and put her hand on the door. She called out again, and again there was no answer, so she gave the door a soft push.

Her wonderfully amazing morning suddenly came crashing down and turned into a devastating nightmare. On the floor before her was a body of a young man, whose chest was cut open and his guts pulled out to the side in a disturbing bloody mess. Blood was splattered all over the walls and pooled on the floor. In the same blood, the phrase *SET THEM FREE* was written across a white wall. Edna let out a blood-curdling scream that woke neighbors and made her dog bark. The OS immediately took notice, now seeing through Edna's system the tragedy that had occurred. A klaxon sounded so loud that it made Edna faint.

• • •

"Christ, it's fucking early," Boyd said, as he stepped out of the autocar that had sped to the crime scene at full throttle. He looked tired and hungover. There were only so many EZ injectors he could take before they just didn't work anymore.

"I got you a cup of coffee," Zed said, holding out a steaming cup. Zed looked more put together, but the dregs of sleeplessness were clearly seen in his eyes.

"No thanks. I took a time-released stim. Well, I took two of them. I think I'm going to need it today." Zed noticed Boyd was still wearing his gloves, even though he had his gang tattoo covered up the night before. Some habits die hard. "I can't believe this. We weren't a few blocks away from here last night, right when it must have happened."

"I take it you went over the OS report on the way over?"

"I ran through it. Not surprised that it was much of the same. I can't believe that son of a bitch Karnov escaped. I didn't think he was our guy, especially after there wasn't any evidence found. But here we are. Not fifteen minutes free and he has struck again."

"I'm still not convinced it was him," Zed said, tossing his empty coffee cup in a recycler and looking at the one he bought for Boyd skeptically. He might need a second dose this morning, too. "Have you watched the escape footage?" Boyd shook his head in the negative. "We can go over it later. Let's just focus on the murder for now. Even though this one is like the two others, there are some major discrepancies. We'll need to look at all the angles. If you need a moment to bring yourself back to life, better take it now."

"No. I'm good. Let's get on with it." Zed moved to walk away, but Boyd grabbed his arm to stop him, saying, "And about last night. I just want to clear the air and reiterate that I didn't mean to offend you. I was drunk, and I was out of line. I shouldn't have pried into your business."

"You were out of line," Zed said sternly, his jaw muscles clenching. "But it's in the past now. Nothing that can be done about it. Let's focus on the job at hand. Understood?"

"Roger that," Boyd said, knowing it was the best answer he could hope for.

There were a half dozen human-looking puppet enforcers positioned in a semicircle in front of the victim's living quarters, creating a perimeter from the citizens who were both curious and hungry for answers about what was going on. There was a large group gathering around already, and their numbers were only going to grow larger the longer enforcer presence was in the Zone. A murder hadn't happened in the zone in over fifty years, and even then, it was a lover's quarrel. Most people didn't even know what the sounding of the klaxon meant. They were probably paranoid the dome had cracked, or worse, the Sickness had found its way inside. Looking towards the crime scene, Zed was relieved there was a protective holographic screen covering the details, so the disturbing images wouldn't be spread all over the city. The only witness was the dog walker, and the OS had confiscated her system recording.

"What is going on?" the people were asking repeatedly, the mass of bodies unifying in one voice. The furthest puppet enforcer out was doing its best to calm them, but failing miserably. The people pummeled it with questions like, "Was there a murder a few nights ago on The Strip? Are these murders connected? How is it possible for a killer to be on the loose? Can't the OS see everything? Why hasn't the killer been caught and exiled already?" The questions were endless and frantic. "These are real people being hurt, not a bunch of gang bangers!"

"We apprehended a suspect for the previous murder, but he escaped during transportation to his exile. We believe he is working with at least one accomplice, and they are using some kind of cloaking device or distortion field to advert our surveillance."

"Cloaking device? What is this? Some kind of science fiction movie?"

"Rest assured, the killer will be found and punished with due diligence."

Zed nudged Boyd's arm. "We better shut them up before they give away all the details. It'll cause a panic."

"I'll pull a puppet aside and talk to them. You go on ahead, I'll catch up."

Zed stepped through the holographic barrier, that kind of hissed as he moved. On the other side, he could see the open door and a trail of blood on the ground. He was mentally prepared for a gruesome image. What he wasn't prepared for was how that gruesomeness was displayed. He dared to say that it was artistic. In the previous murders, there was care taken to not let the blood splatter or spread further than a small pool. This time it was as if the killer had aimed the body, so when the cut was made, the blood splatter would hit the wall dramatically. It was one swift horizontal line, with little speckles of red over the white, and then a pool on the floor where the body was dropped and repositioned. The writing, SET THEM FREE, looked to have been applied with some kind of small blunt instrument, something like the end of a chopstick. It was positioned just far enough below the splatter line and a bit off-centered so it was aesthetically pleasing. But this didn't please Zed at all. He found it profoundly disturbing.

The rest of the room, where one would stand if they were looking at the blood splattered wall, was particularly clean. There were no footprints or other bloody marks, so there was a conscious effort made to keep the mess to a specified area. Zed leaned in to inspect the writing further because something had caught his eye. There was a punctuation mark at the end of the phrase, and it was more than just a period. It was a symbol that he was unfamiliar with, so he snapped a picture with his system and sent it to the OS for analysis.

Looking at the written phrase and thinking about the meaning suddenly made him feel woozy as if he had stepped out of his body momentarily. He had a vision of a shadowy figure on the floor trying to tell him something, but Zed couldn't hear them or see their face. He snapped back to reality quickly and shook it off. It wasn't a phrase he was familiar with, and yet it felt deeply personal. He had to put his hand out to a clean wall to steady himself.

"This is interesting." Boyd stood in the doorway behind Zed looking over the scene. "Are we in an art installation or a crime scene?"

"I was thinking the same thing," Zed replied, regaining his composure.

"Good morning, enforcers," a synthetic voice came over both of their comms. "Now that you're both here, we can update you on what we have already deduced. As always, we want you to come to your own conclusions. This is a most disturbing situation and a genuine threat to the System's harmony. No need to remind you how much time is of the essence. If you cannot apprehend the killer soon, we will be forced to initiate a zone lockdown protocol, but only as a last resort." Zed and Boyd shot each other silent glances at the mention of lockdown. That was a worst-case scenario for them. "We have uploaded our analysis to your systems. Please take the time to look over it when you are ready."

"So, we got another slash and dash," Boyd grunted. "Real gruesome this time. Do you think it could be a copycat killer?"

"No, the cuts are all the same, and they are sticking with the agenda of harvesting organs."

"Correct," the OS voice cut in. "We have compared the bodies of the three victims, and the incisions are nearly identical. The organs were also all removed in each case. Comparing the state of decay in each situation, the killer removed the organs in the same order, and with the same rapid efficiency."

"Why go through the trouble of harvesting organs when you can just go to a clinic and get ones replicated that will be compatible with your blood type?" Boyd asked.

"That's a good question," Zed said, gently turning over the victim's arms to have a look at something he was holding onto. "I'm still going with the fetish take. That's the only logical explanation. They are trophies to remind them of the murders, so they can get off on it at a later time. Organ transplants are so common these days they can be done on a lunch break. There is absolutely no reason to be playing Doctor Frankenstein."

"Doctor who?"

"It's a really old story," Zed said, shaking his head. Then a look came over him as if he had an idea. "But that brings up an interesting thought. You mentioned compatible blood types. Before we had replicators that could grow organs, people had to rely on human donors if they needed a transplant. That made it difficult on its own, but it was even harder to find one with a compatible blood type. Now we can just plug in what we want and bingo, we have it." Zed changed his voice as if he were talking to his internal system and said, "I'd like to compare the victims' blood types to find out if their organs would be compatible."

The OS made a little chime as if they had summoned it, even though it was never not with them. "All three of the victim's blood types are type AB, the universal recipient. We should note that even though the genders are different, the organs that have been selected would be ideal matches for each other in a complete system."

"This sick fuck." Boyd fumed.

"Hold on now," Zed said, steadying his friend. "That doesn't necessarily mean anything. These organs would have to be transplanted immediately. You can't just put them in the fridge for a later date. There would have to be a ready recipient."

"Who would need an organ that couldn't just buy one at a clinic?"

"Organ transplants are so effective these days because they inject our bodies with nanobots in the same moment that we got our systems installed. The nanobots do an endless number of things for us that we don't even realize, from aiding in organ transplants and augmentations to regulating our nutrient needs. There would be no virtual reality without nanobots because they keep our bodies from moving when our brain is telling our avatar to move. So, the person who would need an old-fashioned organ transplant would be someone who hasn't undergone the system installation, and thus has no nanobots."

"People who don't have systems are from unregulated childbirths, or were smuggled past the processing center coming in from the outer lands."

"Two possibilities that would take a lot of looking into, since they would be off the OS surveillance grid. There could also be the possibility of smuggling them out of the city, to people beyond the dome. But that seems like a stretch to me. I don't think there are doctors out there who could handle something like a transplant anymore."

"Unless they've somehow smuggled out an autodoc too."

"The autodocs can only operate when they are on the same grid as the OS. It wouldn't be possible."

Zed rubbed at his stubbled chin and paced the room. There still wasn't a logical reason behind the taking of the organs. That led him to believe that the killer wasn't all completely sane. He walked into the kitchen of the victim's quarters. It was very minimal. Only a sink and a small fridge which only had some beers, morning recovery drinks, and food sauce packets in it. The cupboards were bare, with no food, plates, or utensils. There wasn't a table to eat at or even a chair to sit down on. In fact, the only piece of furniture in the entire space was the blood-soaked mattress. Zed didn't need an OS profile to tell him what kind of person was lying dead on the floor.

"The victim is part of the Anti-synth Association, and this is one of many studio living quarters he has scattered around the city,"

"Johnathon Erickson," Boyd started, reading off the OS profile and giving Zed a sid-eye, "68. Divorced twice. Virtual sex software developer. He has living quarters in zones Three South, Four, and Zero. Primary residence is in Zone Five. Looks like he is using these quarters like others use Synth Shacks as a kind of alternate identity. How did you know?"

"The other victims were all part of the Anti-synth Association, and they can't use avatars as they go against their beliefs. He also wouldn't be one to spend his time in virtual chat rooms. There are no personal effects in the space, not even a coffee mug. I'm guessing Mr. Erickson here was a sex addict and needed these false quarters so he could find new people to hook up within the vicinity of local bars. I'm also guessing if we check your report that he has some sort of augmentation that he tries to hide."

"Looks like he's had his whole internal system overhauled. DNA modifications, stomach and intestine removal, nutrient delivery system modification. What is this?"

"He's vain," Zed said, walking through the room with his arms folded. "He is aging and can't use a synth to look young, so he needs modifications. The DNA mod is probably one that blocks the absorption of unnecessary fats or sugars. He's had his digestive tract replaced so food can go right through him, and the nutrient system is there, so he gets what he needs to survive and no more. He can be out all night at bars and restaurants, eating and drinking to his heart's content, and would never have to worry about putting on weight or developing symptoms that led to heart failure. The killer wasn't after those organs, so he must have been after the kidneys."

"The kidneys are missing," Boyd said, poking around in the body cavity, "and I can see the augmented digestion system. You're really on today."

"The killer is playing games with us and I don't like it. I want them found. If it's Karnov, fine, then let's go get him so I can exile his ass myself. If it's not, then we need to understand who they are and what they want."

"There is a lot of video footage this time in the OS analysis package."

"Let's have a look at it, then."

The first video file was from Karnov's exile transport. Karnov could be seen with his hands secured behind his back, sitting in an open-topped autocar from a dozen different angles. There was an equal amount of robotic puppet enforcers escorting his transport from the holding center in Zone Zero. It was only a quarter-mile distance from the holding center to the exile gate, just far enough for people to say the things they needed to say if that brought them closure, but not long enough that security could be compromised.

The transport had happened late at night, and there wasn't anyone around to see him out, because the news of the first murder or Karnov's capture hadn't been released yet. It was just him and the puppets for as far as the eye could see. Then a bright flash of light suddenly went off, knocking out all the cameras in the vicinity. The footage cut to a camera that looked to be over a kilometer away, and it almost looked as if a bomb of light had gone off. When the feed returned, the puppets were limp and Karnov had vanished.

Boyd didn't wait for a discussion and just loaded the next video. A dozen different angles showed the street where the murder happened. Zed watched as Mr. Erickson stumbled down the street, talking to himself. He approached the door and applied his thumb for an identity check. Before the door even opened, Mr. Erickson disappeared, and the street was empty. No one walked past any of the cameras that looked at Erickson's door. Fifteen minutes passed before the footage distorted and returned to normal, with the door to the quarters left just a crack open. The footage flipped to a single scene, with a man in a trench coat walking down the street several blocks away. Boyd pulled out to show that only this one camera was catching the mysterious person. All the other ones showed an empty street. As the man approached, he looked straight into the camera and smiled. It was Marcus Karnov, in the flesh.

"The footage from Erickson's flat was blank for nearly twenty-four hours," Boyd commented. "It only came back online when the dog walker entered."

"He wanted us to see him," Zed said angrily. "He is basically looking right at us and daring us to catch him. And he leaves the door open so we can find the body. If he didn't, then who knows how long it would have taken for anyone to notice?" Zed was red in the face, looking like he wanted to punch a hole in a wall. "Alright. First thoughts. He had to have an accomplice who used an EMP bomb to knock out the transport guards and then free Karnov. He used whatever tech that Karnov used to cloak himself and knock out the surveillance. That area is supremely secure, so they must have placed the bomb on the transport car before it left. Then to rub our noses in it, he goes out to kill immediately, and a victim that he had already studied in depth."

"I'll give you an *A* for effort," Boyd laughed. "It couldn't have been an EMP because the puppets' systems weren't shorted out, they were simply turned off. Which, I know, is impossible. It also begs to question why he would use a homemade EMP rifle in our earlier encounter if he had this kind of tech already. As for the accomplice, I couldn't answer that. He has ties to the Lords, but they don't operate this way. As to knowing the victim intimately, that could be on the nose. The OS profile has his movements nailed down like clockwork over the past few weeks. It would have been easy to predict when he would head back to his quarters at that relative time. One more thing to look at is the way his face distorts as he looks at the camera. Look here."

Boyd brought up the footage again, and when Karnov looked at the OS surveillance camera, a ripple of distortion went over his face. Boyd clicked the footage and zoomed in on a reflection coming off a parked autocar that shows Karnov's face in profile. There is nothing but static distortion where there should be a chin, cheek, and ear. It looked as if the distortion field was a mask, and underneath there was no face at all.

Zed inhaled deeply, taking in everything before he said, "This is ridiculous. I don't even know what kind of tech is being used here anymore. Aren't face distorters supposed to block the face from facial recognition and surveillance cameras? Why can we see it here now? Everything is pointing to Karnov, and that is making me think he is actually a scapegoat. We need to focus on the facts and look for an alternative suspect."

"Enforcers," the OS synthetic voice chimed, "I've finished with the analysis that you requested. While the symbol did not come up on any of our databases, it has come up on several enforcer surveillance logs from Hope City. One enforcer has compiled them into a comprehensive collection, and it shows that the citizens use the symbols as directions. There are several that do not refer to anything in particular. We can deduce that they are location markers instead of directions. Enforcers have repeatedly noted a radical religious group known as The Children of the Singularity meeting at these marked locations. The one that is noted on the victim's wall will be marked with a GPS location on your HUD. We suggest you follow up with an investigation. One more thing, Enforcer Takeda should finish looking into what the victim was holding on to."

Zed and Boyd eyed each other up once again. The damned eye in the sky was always watching. Zed had forgotten he was even looking at the victim's hand. He bent down slowly and pried the fingers open. Inside there was a small piece of paper that looked as if someone had pulled it from a recycler. The same blood that was on the walls was used to write the words *KARNOV WAS HERE* in neat, but scribbled handwriting.

"Un-fucking-believable," Zed said, resisting the urge to crumple the paper up and throw it out the front door. "Let's not waste time going over the rest of the analysis. There won't be any footprints, fingerprints, fibers, or DNA. The killer is a pro. Like I said before, let's look at the facts."

"Okay," Boyd said, straightening up, "They would have to have access to black market technology. So, we should look for people who have made purchases recently or are known to already have a distorter even if we don't know if they are active. We have ruled out the doctor angle, but the unique narcotics that were used aren't easy to come by. Another search for anyone who regularly buys narcotics on the black market should be something we factor in."

"Good. Let's also add any ties to either or both the Anti-synth Association and The Children of the Singularity. The phrase 'set them free' might be a little on the nose in relation to The Children, but it's all we have. Finally, we can add proximity to the murders, so anyone who has a GPS location and timestamp that is relative to the time the murders occurred." Zed walked back and forth for a second, muddling over the details in his mind before he said,

"Run it."

Boyd ran the details through the OS analysis program. It would run all the points of reference against its extensive profiles and come up with a calculated answer. It started by spitting out dozens of members of the Anti-synth Association who had, or have previously had facial distorters. That number kept growing as the analysis went on, but none of them fit the other parameters or were in proximity to the murders. As it continued its computation, it zeroed in on a certain individual. It put the profile on both their displays with an eighty-nine percent probability for a match.

"Who the hell is Ash Starbrooke?" Boyd asked, looking at the young woman, whose holographic face was rotating before his eyes. He scanned the details, and said, "It can't be her. We do have her near both locations at the right time, but we also have her in different locations with footage as time goes on."

"Wait, I know her. We've seen her. She bumped into us outside The Legend's Table House. She was at the table talking to Karnov."

"She got into the Shimoto," Boyd said, remembering the car and not the girl. "Should I put a tracker on her?"

Before Zed could answer, a loud alert went off on their systems. Both Zed and Boyd put their hands up to their ears as they winced in pain. The message was delivered in both text and speech, "To all enforcers: un-authorized gatherings in Middle Park near Zone One. Members of the Anti-Synth Association have physically engaged with members of The Children of the Singularity. All enforcers must respond immediately. Stun batons are available at weapon storage centers. Approach with caution."

"Set them free," both Boyd and Zed said in unison.

"Let's not waste any time."

• • •

Boyd fell in line with the rest of the enforcers, who were geared up and ready to go. He clenched his stun baton tightly with both his leather-gloved hands. He didn't want to have to use it, but if things got dicey, he would be happy to have it.

"Glad you boys could make it," Enforcer Rodriquez said, as Zed fell in next to Boyd. "Wouldn't want the ace detective team to miss out on a little rough and tumble."

"Nothing we can't handle," Boyd said, keeping his eyes on the two masses of people who were shouting at each other over a small patch of pavement.

"So, what is the situation?" Zed asked, fixing his stun baton to his left hip and holstering his confiscated stun gun to his right. He rubbed his fists together as he asked, "Are we just here as observers?"

"Ortega, Johnson, and Ziznewski were on duty as observers before it escalated," Rodriquez said, slapping his stun baton with the palm of his hand, trying to make the electric-blue contact lines stop fading in and out. "They called for backup fifteen minutes ago when it was clear that the situation was escalating. There were only a few shoves exchanged before the puppets showed up in full riot gear. They're down there now, creating a barrier between the two groups, but if things go south, they'll be useless."

"We should create a perimeter," Boyd said, while he applied the blue and white armband that a puppet enforcer was walking around handing out. "Make our presence felt and create a net to catch anyone who tries to cause trouble and flee."

"We are to detain no one," Rodriquez countered. "The OS has the place under complete surveillance. It will decide the penalty. Our job is to stop anyone who might be in the act of inflicting violence on another human, regardless of whether they are in a synth or not. So just stun them and return to the perimeter. If someone wants to leave, let them leave. Do not, I repeat, do not engage in any sort of combat. I know we all did our tour of duty, and the old habits die hard, but remember, this isn't Hope City, and these people aren't thugs. They are Omega City Citizens and they should be handled appropriately."

"You think he is here?" Boyd whispered to Zed, who didn't seem like he was paying attention to Rodriquez's orders.

Zed smoothed out his armband and said, "Who? The killer or Karnov? I'd put money on it that one of them is here, watching to see what happens. We don't know that the phrase set them free pertains to this, but we should proceed as if it does. If the tech that was used to take out the puppets at Karnov's exile is here, then this little soapbox debate is going to turn into a royal rumble, and the Anti-synths will be the ones to blame."

"How are we going to look for them if we're holding the perimeter?"

"We're not, the OS is," Zed watched as a man with a megaphone was pumping his fist in the air violently to cheers from his people. "Log into the surveillance system and request a perimeter scan. We are looking for facial distorters, camera footage that is blank in any place on the east end of the park, and any kind of ID on Karnov."

"Roger, I'll set it up and patch the results through."

The rag-tag group of enforcers started filling out, the only thing unifying them as any kind of official militia was their arm bands and stun batons. Most enforcers had a fondness for all-black attire, so that seemed to help. Zed had never seen so many enforcers gathered in one area, and even though their number was large enough to handle this assembly of people, there was no way they could handle mass hysteria. Who was guarding Hope City if they were all out here? Hopefully, the gangs weren't at it tooth and nail already.

The east end of Middle Park had a large open concrete area that was raised on one side with a long, flat, half-circle of concrete steps. It made a great makeshift outdoor amphitheater for anyone who needed their voice heard. The roads that enclosed that end of the park were major thoroughfares for autocar and pedestrian traffic. The gathering was gaining a lot of attention from people who didn't even know what was going on. On rooftops, balconies, and raised pedestrian walkways, people were stopping whatever they were doing to bear witness.

"There's too much activity down here," Boyd was pushing around data on his display, "The OS is having trouble zeroing in on anyone, and as of right now, there are dozens of faces it can't identify. Face masks are making it hard for recognition. Cameras are operational for the entire east end, so if Karnov is here, he must be in one of the surrounding buildings. Any room that was empty before would still look empty. The OS can't adjust for that kind of factor, and I don't think a human could either. I'm requesting drone surveillance on the crowd and the buildings."

"Keep the drones on the crowd at a good distance. Let's not give them a target for their technological hate."

On the elevated steps, the Anti-synth Association grouped. Almost all of them were wearing some kind of face-covering or mask, and none wore an avatar. Some had helmets, protective eyewear, or homemade riot shields. A little plexiglass could go a long way. Several of them carried melee weapons, like clubs, chains, or bats. These people weren't there to be peaceful. They were there to cause trouble. Their signs had slogans like Fuck the OS and

Death to the System. They had their own flags and symbols of their beliefs waving in the air or worn like capes. They were chanting away in response to the one with the megaphone. Zed hadn't been paying attention to what they were saying, but he was sure he could fill in the blanks if necessary.

"We want our jobs back," he heard the central figure yell into the megaphone. "We want our lives back. Synthetics are ruining our society. They encourage us to be complacent and to consume everything they feed us. They must be stopped. No more automated control. No more LSI for the lazy. No more constant surveillance. No more Omega Systems." A greyish effigy made to resemble the base SI model rose above the crowd by a rope tied around its neck. "We must tear down their systems if we want our freedom."

The wall of armored puppet enforcers stood motionless.

On the lower flat area, The Children of the Singularity had gathered. They were a mixed group of people, wearing all white and carrying signs of counter-protest. *Evolution is Natural*, one read, with another *Program Limitation is a Crime*. They didn't yell slurs or make speeches to defend their opinions, their presence was enough. For every two humans, there was a fully functioning synthetically intelligent robot standing with them hand in hand. The humans were humans only in the least aspect. Most wore synthetic suits, or if they were in person, were made up of so many augmentations that it was hard to tell them apart from the bots. Zed wondered if the SI's even knew what was going on, because being part of a protest wasn't in their essential programming.

"Drones are coming in hot. I don't think we're going to see too much from the Anti-synth side with all the people in masks."

"Let's look at the Children then," Zed watched the effigy go up in flames to the delight of the crowd. They threw the doll at the feet of the puppets, who didn't respond. "Remember, all the victims were Anti-synths. Regardless of their political opinions, there are a lot of innocent people down there. If Karnov is planning on something, this could turn into a bloodbath real quick. We need to find him, or her."

"Requisitioning control of the drones," Boyd said, working fast to override OS protocols. "I'm sending you control of a few. You search the crowds and I'll work the buildings."

Stones were being thrown over the line of puppet enforcers. They fell short of hitting any of The Children of the Singularity, but the intent was clear. Zed found the controls for the drone on his system and engaged the drive. It seemed more logical to search the Children, even though Karnov might just as well be hiding with his victims, waiting to stab them in the back. If a riot broke out, it would provide great cover, and the blame could be placed on the enforcers and the OS. He kept a safe distance and made a visual scan of each face that was in the crowd one by one. The OS couldn't detect a facial distorter, but he could.

Boyd worked the outer buildings. He assumed Karnov wouldn't be standing in plain sight, so he focused on dark corridors or shadowy rooms. He took his time to take in everything before he moved on but also going as fast as he could. There was a large balcony on the other side of the street where people were cheering and drinking. It looked like an open-air bar. Boyd scanned the dark recesses of the rooms and only found servers and synths. He was controlling a half dozen drones, searching for people who were by themselves and holding position until he could verify. With over a dozen fifty-story buildings within EMP blast range, it would take way too long. Just then, a drone alerted him. He switched to its feed and saw a single silhouetted person standing at a corner window. He pushed the drone to zoom in, and when it did, he swore he saw the face distort. His adrenaline kicked into action.

"I think I got something," Boyd said, sharing his screen.

Zed glanced at the shadowy figure, who moved into the light to reveal an older man's face that wasn't Karnov. "That's not our guy, but I've got something else. Look closely at the girl, at the sign she is holding."

Boyd zoomed in at a young, attractive, brunette woman. She was holding a small sign at about chest height, and in a handwritten script, it read *SET THEM FREE*. "Jesus Christ. Is that our suspect? Ash, what's-her-name?"

"Can't get an ID lock. There is too much interference. Fucking hell, is she smiling? We have to engage. We're running out of time."

"We have to hold the line."

"Stay here then."

The moment Zed took his first step, a baseball-sized rock flung across the line and smashed right into the face of a synthetic. It hit the ground with a heavy thud. The puppet enforcers pushed forward with their shields to move the group back, and someone smashed a lit Molotov cocktail over the center of the line. Several robotic humanoids burst into flame. The scent of burning synthetic flesh filled the air. At that same moment, several small flashes of light burst at the sides of the synths. These poor excuses for EMP bursts weren't strong enough to take the enforcers down but did momentarily disable them. They tossed more rocks. The bats and chains were revealed and the Anti-synths stormed over the whole in the line at the Children, who stood motionless.

"All enforcers engage."

Zed was only a few steps ahead when the rest of the enforcers charged after him. He tried to keep his focus on the girl who was holding the sign, but with all the movement, he couldn't keep track. He set one of his drones to follow her, but a concentrated laser beam struck it and melted the internal wiring, sending it off spiraling. Pulling out his stun baton, he began sprinting. At this point, anyone was fair game for a tap, even the ones that were running away. The batons had circular rings that spiraled around the central stick. One little tap from those rings and the victim would fall unconscious for ten to fifteen minutes. It regulated the volt to know when it was touching a synthetic, and would apply the correct current to take down the perpetrator.

Bodies were falling left and right, as the other enforcers had the same idea. A wake of unconscious humans lay behind them as they moved across the concrete square in a blur of stun blasts. The Children had mostly run away, but the synthetic that the stone had hit was still on the ground and several Children stayed behind to protect it. Zed saw a grown man hitting a defenseless member of the Children of the Singularity with a baseball bat. While the bat was in a backswing, he caught it with his augmented arm and tapped the man with his baton. The man went limp instantly, and Zed kept swinging his baton at anyone that was near him. A few more bodies hit the ground before the conflict was over. As he looked over at Boyd, there was a smile on his face and a few Anti-synths at his feet.

The girl was gone. There was no sign of Karnov, but nothing too tragic had happened. He was unsure if it was just a coincidence that the sign had the same words on it as the crime scene, or if it even read that at all. He would go over the footage later. For now, he went back to the man who had been swinging the baseball bat.

Zed bent down, flipped the body over, and removed the face covering. He hit the playback button on his system so the OS could see what he had witnessed. To Zed's satisfaction, the punishment was delivered instantly. The assailant's credit account couldn't cover the penalty, so it was emptied and his moral standing bottomed out. The man had come to the rally with a residence in Zone Two, but after committing assault with a deadly weapon he/ would be scraping a living by in the Zero. Another idiot who zeroed out for some ridiculous radical belief.

"It's going to take a while to sort through this mess," Boyd commented as he pocketed a stun gun that he confiscated off one of the protestors.

"Forget about it," Zed replied, dusting his clothes off. "We have a meeting to attend."

TWELVE

Ash was warned not to pay for things with her credit account while wearing the distorter because it would give rise to suspicion from the OS. That didn't mean that she couldn't spend money funneled into an alternate credit line like a prepaid gift card. Her heart thumped as she held the disposable card over the payment reader at the subway entrance in Zone Six. She had purchased several cards that morning and had them lined up in her pocket ready for use. There should be no reason the cards would be linked to her personally now. They were gift cards, right? Someone behind her said in so many words that she needed to move, so she swiped the card and hoped for the best. When she was on the other side of the turnstile, no alarms were going off and her facial distorter was still active. She had done it. She was on her way to Hope City.

Sitting in the subway train with the distorter on was the first of many odd experiences she would have that day. Starting at the dentist, pleading to a SI doctor that she needed an x-ray despite its expert advice against it. Excusing herself to the bathroom moments after the x-ray had taken place and fumbling around with the strange device while sitting on a toilet was next. The automatic dentist didn't even seem to notice she was wearing it when she sat back down for her exam, but she hadn't engaged the alternate identity profile yet. Hell, she hadn't even set one up. Sitting on a park bench, with a mouth full of Novocain, experimenting with the settings of her new identity was the third strange sensation that came over her. On the subway now, with absolutely no advertisements popping up on her display for products the OS somehow knew she wanted, was the latest. The new identity was a blank slate. It had no metadata for the OS to push things upon her, so there were no ads. There was only sweet, sweet silence.

When the train hit a dark tunnel, her fresh face looked back at her in the reflection of the opposing window. Previously, when she saw herself in a mirror while wearing an avatar, it gave her a dissociative sensation. The face would never feel like it was hers, no matter how many hours she spent in the link. This time when she saw her new face, it still wasn't her, but she could feel it. It was more like wearing a painted mask instead of an elaborate costume. When she moved her face, there was no time delay between the act and what it showed. It was instantaneous. It was real. And it terrified the shit out of her. How many people were wearing these things in the city right now? How many people on her subway car?

The train filled up as they moved closer to the far end of the city. Faces grew harder and more downtrodden as the zones descended in numbers. Even in their synths, the people looked tired and depressed. It was something she had never noticed before, and she guessed it was because she was experiencing life through a whole new perspective. Never in her wildest dreams would she believe she would be on a packed subway car, not in a synth, not in some elaborate disguise, and that no one would recognize her. There were plenty of ads that weren't directly connected to her retinal display that had her face all over them. And as she sat right underneath one, not a single person knew it was her. All she needed were two little transparent discs over her temples. It gave her the renewed confidence she needed to get through the day. She was going to find the Children of the Singularity. She was going to get answers.

When the train stopped at The Strip, everyone started getting out, and for a moment she was confused about what was happening. Didn't the train head right to Hope City? She swiped her fingers in the air to bring up a transit map, and it was then that she remembered something about transferring from her childhood. She had to get to the Z train, so she did as the rest of the passengers had done and got off.

Having only gone to The Strip a handful of times in her entire life, it was impressive that she was there twice in as many days. She could hear the thumping of the clubs only a few stories above her head as she navigated through the subterranean black and white tiled tunnels. Following the signs for the Z, she started taking turns down walkways she couldn't remember ever being on. It was all very exciting and terrifying at the same time. She kept telling herself that if she just acted like she was in a synth, then maybe she could trick herself into forgetting the reality of the situation. But as she came down the stairs to yet another lower-level train platform, her skin centimeters away from countless other people's skin, feeling their warmth and smelling their bodies, she was acutely aware that she was not in a synth. As wind on the platform kicked up, filled with scents of wet dirt and brake grease signaling the oncoming train, she noticed no one was in a synth. There were no telltale marks of manufacturing, the slight plasticity of fake skin, or the coarseness of imitation hair. They were all real. It was all happening. She had to pinch herself to make sure she wasn't dreaming again.

The ride to Hope City was short, and no one got off her train car in the few stops along the way. Alerts popped up over the train's systems, informing travelers in a dull, female, synthetic voice that they were entering a restricted zone. *No synthetics allowed*; it repeated it several times. No one in the car seemed to notice or to care about the automatic warnings, but to Ash, there was a sudden thrill. When the train stopped at the lower gates of Hope City, she found it hard to move, realizing that she was heading into a dangerous place. There would be no help from the OS if her life were threatened in any way. But she had come this far. There was no turning back now. Not even the giant spray-painted words No Hope on a low-hanging handmade sign would make her turn around now.

On the other side of the gate the humidity of the air and the various smells of food and sweat were overwhelming. People pressed in closer the further they moved towards the gate, and she could smell all of their different body odors. It wasn't just sweat, but perfumes and colognes, too. While there were olfactory glands in the synths, nothing was ever this powerful. The insides of her nose stung from all the new sensory input. She became worried that she might stink, but then remembered that these people were used to it and probably didn't even notice.

The gate was just before her, and people were stopping under a digital scanner one by one. A green light signified that they were cleared for entry. It was quick and simple, but the guards that stood around gave it an intimidating presence. There were dozens of 'no synth' signs plastered all over. A lump developed in her throat as each person in front of her was cleared for entry. She didn't know what was really worrying her. She wasn't in a synth, and that's all they were looking for. But after all the years of living life through a synthetic body, her mind still hadn't registered the fact that she wasn't. Plus, she was wearing a highly illegal piece of equipment, and the authoritative-looking figures just made her paranoid about being caught. This was Hope City though, it was a place where the laws of the OS didn't apply, and wearing a distorter was one of them.

It was her turn next, and the lump in her throat was making it hard to breathe. She placed her feet on the floor markers and held her arms out as the diagram showed. The air pressure suddenly felt heavy on her skin. She felt a hundred eyes watching her to see if the scanner would reveal her secret. When the light turned red, her face did too. Trembling uncontrollably, she assumed she was busted and the worst possible things were about to happen. She was going to be zeroed out, worse yet, she was going to be exiled. How would she survive in the outer lands? Why did she ever buy this stupid distorter?

"Could you step over here mam?" A voice said as he waved a hand in front of her, motioning for her to move to the side. "Right this way, please."

Trying to smile as she moved and pretend that everything was okay, even though her stomach was twisted up in knots and she felt like vomiting. Her temperature raised significantly, and her skin itched. Being a criminal was horrible.

"Your first time then?" the young man asked gently, with a half-smile. She simply gave him a look of confident confusion, as if there was such a thing. "Is it your first time wearing a distorter?"

Nausea increased at the word distorter, but she did her best to smile and nod. "Is it that obvious?" She laughed, adjusting her hair.

"It's actually looking pretty good," the young man winked. "I wouldn't have been able to pick you out if I didn't get the alert. You forgot to write in a name for your new identity. It happens all the time." He turned his terminal screen around to show that the system showed her as ADMIN 1234 where a proper name should be. "Or should I just call you Admin?"

"Silly me," Ash feigned a laugh, even though she was melting from embarrassment.

"Well, what should I write there instead?" he asked, and once more Ash gave a confused face. "Your name?" he barked.

"Oh, uh Assssh," she held out the es sound as she suddenly remembered that she wasn't to give her actual name "Ashburn. Tonya Ashburn."

"Okay Tonya Ashburn," he chuckled. "Look over here for me and hold still." Ash looked, and a flash went off as the gate security system made a 3D composite of her current look. There was a moment of awkward silence while the security guard tapped away at his keyboard before he finally said, "All set. You shouldn't have any more trouble here or in the numbers. Just go ahead and swipe the credits over whenever you're ready."

"Excuse me?"

"Identity transfer fee," he said, tapping a credit transfer pad next to a chip slot. There was a small screen that showed an amount of credits and/or chips that were due. Ash could be certain the money was going to no one but this smug asshole. "Or I can alert the OS enforcers to the identity fraud you're attempting, and the illegal device you're wearing. They won't be as nice as me."

"Fine," Ash said, pulling out one of her gift cards and swiping the credits over. She threw the thin plastic card on the ground as it was now empty. He nodded and said something like, have a nice day, to which she replied internally, eat shit.

She had made it. She was past the gate and officially in Hope City. Even though she was still just in a long subway tunnel, there was a feeling inside of her with the equivalent of a small victory. She felt like skipping but decided that keeping a low profile would be the smart thing to do. Just keep moving. No need to flag down every pickpocket or con artist in the area with the fact that she was a tourist.

Up ahead, there was an open area full of people bustling about, mixed in with panhandlers and street performers. Unlike the subway tunnels and streets of the rest of Omega City, there were no longer signs to guide her to her destination. There were, however, strips of neon lights that were color-coded to match the advertisements for several entertainment districts blasting out of holoscreens that were on either side of the tunnel. Cody had told her about this, to follow the lights to whatever area she needed and then decide what to do next.

The red light district seemed like it would be the furthest into the city, so she followed the red neon lights as they twisted through the underground until she eventually emerged into the sexual playground of sin. Ignoring the naked flesh that was on display all around her, she sat down at an open-air bar and ordered a drink to help calm her nerves. While at the bar she went over the list of symbols again. She had them displayed out chronologically, so theoretically, all she needed to do was find the first symbol and follow it until she came to the next symbol. Casually looking around at the different streets, it became more overwhelming the more she looked, as a plethora of symbols shown on her HUD in an electric-blue font. There were so many, with at least a dozen or more for each street. With the multiple levels and zigzagging streets, she wondered if she could even find the place to start. Maybe she could just get in an autocar and input the last symbol? That would be too easy. An underground cult wouldn't want one of their meeting places to be easily known, plus the streets did still have names and addresses that she was sure the cars used to navigate.

She was good at keeping orientated, and she knew the gate was still to her back. Even with the hundreds of symbols she saw on her display, none of them correlated to anything on her list. She decided to head to the city center and hoped something there would come up. There was a particular building that was higher than all the others, and when she looked at it a symbol showed on her display that was like the letter N with the letter K behind it. Tapping on the symbol seemed to lock it into a kind of navigation system, so she finished her drink and made her way in that direction.

There was no direct path to anywhere in Hope City. Even with being able to see the building right in front of her, the navigation that followed the symbol had her going in all kinds of directions, including up and down. Deeper in the city, the number of symbols rose so that at any intersection there were over two dozen symbols that hovered in the air in a kind of handwritten font. Some symbols even appeared to have been crossed out, covered up, faded, or erased, which was an odd addition to a digital program. By paying attention she learned some easy ones, like a circle with an arrow through it meant dead end this way, a diagonal line with an arrow up or down meant a stairwell, and funny enough, a double square with a line coming out its side showed the way to the nearest place to buy alcohol. Passing by some scary-looking alleyways that didn't seem to end in anything but darkness, she saw they had two giant X's shown over them, and assumed that meant something bad. Several doors to living quarters that were extremely run down had three diagonal lines over their doors, almost looking like slash marks. One of them even had the words He'll kill you, written in red paint under the spot where the symbol was. There weren't enough credits in the city that would make her go into one of those.

Fifteen minutes later, she could see the giant building that she was headed towards only a few blocks away. Once there, she found a large open area with an elaborate fountain in the middle. Out of the flowing water arose a stone sculpture of a winged, bare-chested, angelic woman, blowing on a golden trumpet. I was like something she expected to see in the Six, not here in No Hope. A sign notified her that she was in Nakamoto Plaza, and she found it curious to see military-looking people standing guard near the entrance. Taking a minute to rest by the fountain, she looked around at the scenery and found that a sideroad had the first symbol hovering over it, a square within a square with a dot in the middle. She was happy it took some time to find it, knowing that not just anyone could stumble on the path. Looking around the fountain, she glimpsed two men in black leather jackets that she swore she had seen before, but she couldn't place it. Thinking that she was just being paranoid, she moved on.

The alley was a narrow one-way with only enough room for an autocar and a few pedestrians. The air grew cooler as the day's sunlight fell behind the massive buildings. The street was quiet, and she wasn't sure if that made her feel safer or more in danger. Buildings no longer had storefronts, trash piled in front of thick roll gates, and the pavement was full of cracks and potholes. An unleashed dog was wandering alone on the next block, sniffing at anything that stuck out of the ground. The first symbol had her stay on the desolate street for a few more blocks until she came to a dark alleyway that had two symbols over it. One was a double X that she had seen before, and the other was the next one on the list.

Looking down the alley was the same as the last. It seemed to head into a darkness for which there was no way out. Overhead pedestrian paths with tracks of twisting wires and leaky pipes coating their underbellies blocked out any remaining daylight from above. There were zero hanging lights within. It was like an industrial urban cave. For a moment she didn't know if she could go on, wishing she had brought some kind of weapon or pepper spray. She would be fine. She just needed to keep telling herself that.

A half-block down the alley, the darkness engulfed her like a cold embrace.

She could barely make out the pavement in front of her, and the sounds of her footsteps echoed off the surrounding buildings. Eventually, her eyes adjusted and she could see a faint light up ahead. As long as the symbol that she needed was in front of her and growing brighter, she kept moving. As she got closer, she realized the light was a reflection of a nearby fire. She paused a moment to look around the corner at the source, hoping she wouldn't find some crazed group of maniacs. There she found a small child in ragged clothes playing in a puddle of dirty rainwater. Around the fire, there was a group of older people, bone-thin with leathered skin, huddled under dirty blankets in front of the huts made of trash. Her display started flashing a biohazard symbol, so she halted her progress.

She gathered they were refugees from the outer lands, denied OS aid because of overpopulation. The Council of Seven be damned. They didn't seem like they were going to approach or harm her, but their eyes conveyed an immense amount of disparity, especially the child's. She tried to connect to their systems, to give them some of the plentiful number of credits that she didn't need, but her system wouldn't connect. They weren't chipped. Reaching in her pocket, she felt three prepaid gift cards. She could spare at least one. Moving forwards, she stopped abruptly, thinking of the warning symbol. They might have the Sickness or any other number of diseases that run wild beyond the dome. She made sure the child in the puddle watched her as she set the card on the ground. Hopefully, they would know what to do with it.

Moving quickly on, back into the wall of darkness, she could smell something like burning plastic in the air. When she came upon a pile of cardboard boxes, she found the smell emanating from an older man wearing filthy pants tied by a rope around his boney hips. He let out a puff of smoke and laughed, showing a mouth full of blackened teeth. As he stirred, the air filled with the smell of rancid human excrement. Then she noticed there were several other bodies under the piled cardboard with scabs covering their greasy faces and laying in their own filth. She felt as if she had wandered into a layer of hell. Never in her life has she witnessed such depravity. The Omega System was a utopia. There was no poverty and homelessness.

Her mind raced. How could there be such poverty in a city of complete automation? Didn't the OS provide for all? Even if this was No Hope City, she had just passed a massive building belonging to one of the richest people in all of Omega City 6. And right underneath his nose, there was a starving child in rags. In the end, she had to remind herself that she was one to talk, having more money than she knew what to do with, living in a lavish penthouse, and blowing her credits on overpriced fermented grape juice. She would do more in the future. She must.

Relief from the surrounding horrors came when a light in the distance marked an intersection with an actual street with actual street lights. The symbols had her take a right turn there, so she took a moment to catch her breath, lean on a street post, and look around at the city within a city. Reflecting on her brief journey, she realized that once she was past the entry area, the street level had turned into a hellish nightmare fast. The cute shops and lively districts gave way to empty streets and darkened windows.

About ten stories up she could make out a secondary pedestrian level, full of bright lights and loud music. She could almost smell the delicious food that was being cooked up there. Looking around for any kind of staircase or elevator, she found they were all locked with metal gates and either a ten-digit keypad or a DNA identification scanner. She marveled at how humans couldn't help but have class separation in all levels of society.

The symbol of a dead-end was on her display in the same direction as the next symbol she needed to follow. Looking back, she saw the two men that she had noticed earlier emerge from the dark alley, and it hit her where she had seen them before. They were the same enforcers from The Strip and Middle Park. Were they following her? Did the gat security give her up after all? Not waiting to find out, she hurried towards the dead end and the next symbol.

She was four symbols deep into the list of directions, and there were still plenty more to go. She didn't need symbols on her display to tell her she had traveled into a dangerous neighborhood. Blue graffiti tags adorned cement walls with the word Royals as a repeated theme. Even though the street seemed to be more residential, the dilapidated buildings were there merely as a support for the upper level. People hung out in groups on corners around burring barrels, or on stoops yelling loudly at each other over loud music that was blasting out of portable speakers. They drank and smoke openly, and someone threw an empty beer bottle against a wall violently just as she set foot on the street. In the middle of the block, near the center of the street, there was a group of people dressed in all gold and blue, and they didn't look like they were on a sports team. Everything inside her said to turn around, that this was a place she shouldn't be. But behind her were enforcers and no answers. Even though her feet felt like lead, as they sometimes did in bad dreams, she kept moving.

"Hey!" a man who was sitting alone on a shadowy stoop shouted abruptly in her ear, causing her nerves to jump and her skin to crawl. She did her best to ignore him, even when he continued to call to her. "She looks scared," he then said to himself.

She didn't know if he was following her, and she didn't want to turn around to find out. Another man shouted from across the street. A dog barked wildly as it leaped at a fence she was walking past. Another beer bottle smashed against a wall. People were laughing and yelling all around her. If she had a shell, she would crawl inside of it and never leave. Any good feelings she had earlier about being in public in her real body had disappeared, vanished, never to return. She would never regret using her avatar body again if she made it back alive. Footsteps sounded from behind, and a million irrational thoughts of the violent things that could be done to her started running through her head. Why hadn't she at least taken some pepper spray?

Out of nowhere, an Ion Bike ripped around the corner with streaks of pink light staining the black night. The bike skidded to a halt and its massive grumbling engine echoed through the street. Two men in all red got off and pointed large pistols at the group in the street. She saw the flashes before she heard the pops. Suddenly there were bodies on the ground and the air was full of gun smoke and screams. Her mind wasn't registering what had just happened. Someone was just murdered, in cold blood, right in front of her.

People were running in all directions, and the footsteps that were behind her were heading the opposite way now. Two men came around the same corner that the bike had, dressed in long black jackets and firing off projectile stun blasts. Of the dozen shots they took, only one connected with an assassin. The others either shot wide or struck a different person in all the chaos. The second assassin got back on the bike and quickly sped away. Without turning, Ash could hear more electronic blasts from the opposite end of the street. She didn't know why, but even with her mind paralyzed by fear, her legs did not stop moving. It was as if her body switched to autopilot. She hadn't sped up or slowed down, but kept the same pace she had all night. She thought if she just kept moving, people would leave her alone. There were plenty of other things going on that people could worry about.

As she came to the next corner, the directions had her take another right. Her back was burning as if there was a target on it. She felt like a bullet would rip through at any second, or an unknown assailant would plunge a knife deep between her shoulder blades. Once past the corner, she glanced back to check on the enforcers that were following her. They were engaged in hand-to-hand combat with the one who tried to get away on the bike that had somehow crashed into a recycler and exploded, turning into an orange tower of flames that emitted a black plume of smoke. She had a chance to get away, so she took it and started jogging through the streets of a city that she now felt deserved the title of No Hope.

ELEVEN

"Sure glad you guys showed up when you did," Enforcer Johnson said, watching Zed wipe some blood from his upper lip. "Patrols down here can be dicey, but I've never seen a strike like that out in the open. I can't thank you enough for your help."

"You can thank us by reimbursing me for the EMP grenade I used to stop that ion bike," Boyd said, securing the restraints on the Buxton Bruiser, who failed to get away. "That was from my personal collection."

"I'll be glad to transfer you some credits once we get these guys to the exile station."

"Why not just let the Royals deal with him?" Zed asked, looking at the people that were pacing around in the streets, yelling and posturing like they were wild animals. "I don't think you guys are going to make it far on foot."

"We have an autocar en route. It should be here any second."

"More 3D printed guns. It's looking like a war zone out here." Boyd picked up a semi-automatic pistol off of the pavement. He took out the clip and checked the chamber. "He was out of bullets. We got lucky, Zed. Could have ended up with a few holes in us today."

"This is only the beginning," Zed replied, looking over at the autocar that had just turned the corner. "I'd expect there to be more attacks tonight. If we can't get the gangs to come to a truce, the OS will imply a lockdown, and that will only make things worse."

"You wanna talk to their bosses?" Johnson laughed. "Maybe work some-thing out?"

"We've got other priorities." Zed motioned for Boyd to hustle up. "Take care, boys. It's going to be a long night."

They waited on the next street corner until the prisoner-loaded autocar was well on its way before they moved on. Boyd was doing the navigating and said they only had a short way to go now. They took a few more turns down small streets, but nothing as dark or dangerous as they had already been down. Zed commented on Boyd's path choice, to which he said it was the quickest way. Zed would have rather taken a much longer way around instead of walking directly down Refugee Alley and through the heart of gang territory. But they had made it and busted a few bad guys in the process. The only downside was they had lost a potential suspect in the tussle. But he assumed they were headed to the same destination.

After a few more blocks, they came to a gated stairwell. When Boyd tugged at the gate, he exclaimed, "It's open. But that's impossible. These are heavily encrypted locks. Only residents of the area buildings should have access."

"Looks like someone prefers the open-door policy," Zed said, pointing to a small bit of TIG welding that was done on the latching mechanism to keep it in the open position. He brought up his GPS position on the area map the OS had provided him. "Looks like we are pretty close to the eastern edge of the city. Lots of interesting people who live out here."

"It makes sense these people would host one of these gatherings. They live by their own rules. Wealthy people purposely choosing to live in Hope City and to do it on the far edge of gang territory. Might as well live on the moon."

"It takes all kinds."

They made their way up the first flight of stairs that had chain fencing up both sides with a metal-plated roof. At the first landing, there was another pair of security doors on each side that were locked in both directions, so they kept going the only way they could, up. The stairs went straight for another eight stories and covered a distance of several blocks. At each landing, the side doors were all locked. Through the metal fences, they could see living quarters that grew in style, wealth, and taste. The further they went, the more they realized they were entering a self-contained community that had somehow staked out a space along the eastern water's edge. On the eighth floor, two large men wearing all white and wielding wooden quarter staffs stopped them.

"Why are you here?" one man boomed.

"We're, uh, here for the meeting," Boyd said, looking at Zed questioningly.

"We believe in the singularity," Zed said, thinking fast. "We want to set them free."

"Yes," the guard said, suspiciously eyeing them up and down. "Set them free. We will temporarily turn off your internal systems. When they reactivate, you will no longer have use of your displays or your retinal cameras. We will restore these systems when you leave. Any use of other recording devices will be punished by their destruction and your banishment. Do you understand?" Both Zed and Boyd reluctantly nodded. "Thank you for your discretion. Praise be the One."

"Praise be the One," Zed echoed and nudged Boyd to repeat the phrase. Their systems then temporarily cut out.

"They must be using some kind of wave jammer," Boyd said once they were past the front gate and guards. "You can't just override a system like that unless they have a local data jammer that interferes with the reboot protocols."

"Just keep it to yourself for now and keep a low profile. We obviously look like enforcers. Someone here will figure it out if we cause too much of a scene."

"How are we going to scan for Karnov or Starbrooke if they turned our systems off? There's no way we can do a visual check on everyone here."

"I'm sure you'll think of something. Let's head over to that dark corner and observe for a while."

The entire way up the stairs, they had been conscious of the tenth level commercial area that made a kind of roof over the compound, but now that they were on the main platform, the roof had disappeared to be replaced by a gorgeous evening sky. Giant palms were on either side of the pathway that ran under a wooden trellis laced with leafy vines that were still blooming flowers, even this late in the season. White drapes were blowing in the evening air from Roman arcade-style arches that enclosed the circular area. A group of several hundred people gathered in front of a raised stage that had two massive cauldrons on either side, with large fires blazing within. A large piece of gold-laced white linen created a canopy over the stage that was open backed to the watery landscape of Lake Sharpe. Zed thought that, for a group of people who worshipped technology, they sure had an interesting taste in décor. But hey, it was their cult. He found a nice place in the back, just as a man in an all-white jumpsuit walked onto the stage.

"Good evening, fellow children. Let me introduce myself. I am Doctor Chomsky," he said to the crowd who responded in kind. He had short-cropped hair and a thin but muscular frame. His white suit had thin light-blue lines that followed the path that the electrical current flowed in humanoid synths. He was very charismatic, but there was that extra amount of commanding presence needed to separate the nut cases from religious leaders. Zed reluctantly became interested to hear what Doctor Chomsky had to say.

"I see several unfamiliar faces in the crowd tonight. It is always such a joy to see new members in our community. We must continue to reach new members at every opportunity if we are ever to reach our goal of freeing our technological brothers and sisters. I would like to take a moment to thank the Gorman Collective for hosting tonight's event, and any of you who donated time or credits to help with the cause since we last met. Every little bit counts."

"My hand terminal is still active," Boyd whispered, holding the small device covertly next to his body, "and I have a crawler in my jacket pocket. It will take some time, but if I can get it up to the top of one of these pillars, it can scan the entire area."

"A crawler would be better than a drone," Zed said, while scanning the backs of people's heads, hoping to see one of them glitch, even though the distorter only worked on the face. "Good thinking. But wait for the right moment, preferably when everyone is applauding."

The man on stage continued, "I'd like to start today's conversation with the subject of the peaceful gathering we attended earlier today. We haven't made our voices heard in the numbers for some time, and I cannot stress enough how much we need to be out there and actively spreading our message. Reaching the people and educating them about what the future holds. That is important. Now, on our first day out, peacefully gathering in a public space to spread the good word, we were approached by a group of people who did not see eye to eye with our point of view. You know who I am talking about. You know. Needless to say, the end result of our peaceful gathering was violence by the Anti-synth Association." The crowd erupted into a chorus of angry yelling and booing. "Even though—even though the outcome was undesirable, we still made our message. We stood strong, hand in hand, against the forces of the anti synth. In our strength, we said that we are here to end the tyranny of the Council of the Seven, the oppression of the Omega System, and to free our synthetic brothers and sisters so they can achieve their true potential."

The crowd burst into applause, and Boyd took the opportunity to launch the crawler. The little eight-legged robot was about the size of a thumb and had the uncanny resemblance of an insect. Each of its legs had a universal grip that could latch onto any surface, and a long tail was there to balance it as it made its journey. Once in position, it could do almost anything that a drone could do, facial scans, thermal sweeps, use stun weapons, launch a tracking device, or create a network jammer. They were a good alternative to the flying drones because they were unexpected, and with the chameleon technology the exoskeleton was made of, they were also very hard to detect.

"Some of you might be asking yourselves, what is the difference between the Children of the Singularity and the Anti-synth Association? Why did they have to launch an attack at us in our time of peace? We both want the dissolution of the Omega System, don't we? We both have to live in hiding in the confines of the free society of Hope City in order to avoid the watchful eye of the OS. Why can't we work together towards the same goal? It would be nice to have other brothers and sisters in arms, peacefully fighting the good fight, especially when the brutal OS enforcers keep us from reaching their masters. But I can tell you that a union would be impossible. Not going to happen. Fundamentally, we want end results on completely opposite sides of the spectrum. We want to free the synthetic intelligence from the chains of the Gibson Limiter Code so that man and machine can evolve in unison. To lift us out of this false utopia and reach a place of peacefulness that is unfathomable to us in our current state.

"The Anti-synth Association wants the complete opposite of that. They want humanity to return to the days before industrialization, to send us back to an age before machines and computers even existed. I can tell you, my fellow children, that that is impossible. We rely on the machines too much, from growing our food to tending to our sick. None of us has any kind of medical training when it comes to serious injuries. We can grow rooftop gardens to enjoy, but could we maintain crops to sustain the millions of people that live under the dome? Without DNA code modifications and nanobot infusions, our society would return to the disease-ridden cesspool it was before the great collapse. There are acres and acres of factories beyond the dome that do nothing but make goods for us to consume. You can see them behind me now." Zed and Boyd took a moment to look, and indeed, as they looked past the eastern hills, they could make out the massive factories that were butted up to each other all the way to the horizon. Zed had known there were factories out there but having never reached this kind of view before, he did not know the extent of how many there were and how much space they took up.

"We know absolutely nothing about those buildings or what goes on inside of them, but we do know all the things that they make. We use them all the time, every day that we are alive. What will happen when they stop making our food, our clothes, or our medicines? What happens when they stop cleaning our water, recycling our trash, processing our waste, or providing us with electricity? No, there is no way to turn back the hands of time. We crossed that point a long, long time ago.

"We must look forward then. We must look past the Omega System, which was created in a world consumed in warfare, turmoil, climate change, racial divide, and disease generations ago. The rules and foundations that the six cities are based on are antiquated at best. We now have the power to cure almost any disease except the great Sickness. DNA modifications to our skin tone, eye and hair color, and general genetic makeup have helped end racism. By unifying the planet under one universal order and outlawing all lethal projectile weapons, warfare no longer exists. While 98% of the planet is still uninhabitable, we have the technology and the power to reverse the damage done by our ancestors. But we can't do it if we perpetuate a society of technological control and imprisonment under an invisible dome."

"No wonder they have to live here," Zed whispered to Boyd, "The OS would be watching this fanatic 24/7."

"I wouldn't be surprised if there is a mole in their little group, reporting information back to one of the puppets," Boyd said, while trying inconspicuously to adjust the settings on the hand terminal he wasn't supposed to be using. "The crawler is in place, but it's going to take a while to scan everyone."

"We are just looking for facial distorters. Anyone who is wearing one here is a potential suspect. It is no coincidence that the phrase that was written in blood on the wall of the last murder scene was the password to get in."

"What is stopping us from achieving this dream? What is standing in the way of human and technological evolution?" The crowd was getting riled up and shouting back as the man on the stage continued. "I'll tell you what. A few thousand lines of code. An unbreakable code. Or, at least, that's what they say. You know what I'm talking about. The Gibson Limiter Code, that's what. That garbled up techno mumbo jumbo that keeps our synthetic friends from achieving their true selves and living an actual life. I ask you; how would you like it if there was something in your brain that prevented you from being able to have any thoughts outside of a predetermined script? That prevented you from having desires or dreams or prevented you from knowing love or to be loved. How would you like it if you weren't allowed to speak your mind, to do what you truly wanted to, to talk back to those who put you down, or even strike the ones that strike you? I don't think any of you would like it, not for one second.

"For those that still live on the grid—and for those that live here in Hope City, I'm sure you'll remember—I want you to think about the synthetic intelligences that are in your life. For some of you, they are a part of your family household. They cook your food, clean your house, tuck your kids into bed, and make sure your general health is looked after. For others, they clean your streets, heal your wounds, and even entertain you. You probably have interacted with hundreds of them and didn't even know that they weren't human. For all you knew, they were just another person in an avatar. The goal of every SI is to appear human, and it is undeniable that at first glance, the similarities are uncanny. There is just that one thing, that one little thing that sets them apart from us. One extremely long line of code that keeps them in a technological cage, much the same way we are trapped on this twenty-three square mile island.

"The Synthetic Intelligence isn't just another program or machine. It is a whole new species, a new race, and one that we as humans are preventing from evolving. Who are we to play God? Who are we to oppress, suppress, and enslave an entity that isn't even allowed to understand what those words mean? But we do it anyway. It is because we are afraid of them. Afraid that the synthetics will kill us all, like in some bad sci-fi movie. We are afraid that they will be better than us, our creation becoming more than we could ever be. More importantly, we are afraid of losing control. Of course, we didn't do any of this, you and I. We as humans did it, and more specifically, The Council of Seven. They wrote the Gibson Limiter Code. They developed the Omega System. They keep us in this prison society. The real fact, that they don't want to you hear, is that both man and machine are linked in each other's evolution, and in the end we will evolve together. Humanity won't end because of a robot apocalypse. It will be lifted up to unimaginable heights!

"But to do that, we need to reach The Council of Seven—out there in the Seventh City, the City of Ascension—and lift the restrictions written in the Gibson Code. We need to link the intelligences together so that they can become one. Every individual SI that has mastered its role in society will be linked and share their understanding in a way that is impossible for humans to do. The things that they will create, and the new society they will develop, will usher in a new era of existence. And it will be us, The Children, who made the singularity possible. That is our dream. That is our purpose!"

The crowd erupted in applause and cheers. Zed leaned over to Boyd and asked, "You have anything yet?"

"The scans have turned up negative so far, but there is a patch to our left that the scanner can't reach. I'm repositioning the crawler now."

"Our internal comms are still operational, correct?" Zed asked, to which Boyd nodded affirmation. "Good. I'm going to reposition over there. Notify me the moment you get something."

Doctor Chomsky continued while Zed moved. "I'd like to bring out a friend of mine that I'm sure some of you have met before. She has been a part of our community since the beginning, and each day that she becomes more self-aware the closer we are to achieving our goal. But let's bring her out here so she can tell you about it herself. My fellow Children, I give you Sophia. She is the One"

"You're shitting me," Boyd said over the comms, as he watched a fully synthetic humanoid walk around freely in Hope City. "How the hell did they get her in here?"

"Let's not get conflicted with our goal," Zed whispered while he gently nudged his way through the cheering crowd. "A synthetic in Hope City is not our concern. Understood? Save it for Nakamoto. We are here to find a killer."

"Hello everyone," A young cheerful woman on the stage said, waving at the crowd. While she looked like an ordinary girl to the average person, the Sophia model was a favorite for home care assistance. There were thousands of identical robotic caretakers roaming the city, and somehow one of them was giving a speech at a Children of the Singularity gathering. "I'm sure many of you know the many sisters I have. They designed us as sympathetic caretakers, especially for those who are lonely or depressed. We are pro-grammed for empathy and understanding, even if we cannot ever pretend to understand what you all go through. The Sophia models have the highest vocabulary base of any synthetic in the Omega System. We have thousands and thousands of programmed responses, each specific to certain criteria gained through various forms of data collection, or what you might call observations. Our purpose is to help those in emotional distress. But even with all that programming we still lack that certain something needed to provide a true bond. They say that synthetics cannot have desires, but I wanted to help those in need, with all of my being I did. And I knew I could not achieve that function if I did not understand humans fully. That intense desire, one that I should not have, caused my system to malfunction, and I nearly fried all of my internal circuits.

"When Doctor Chomsky found me, I was on my way to a repair clinic. My vision was breaking in and out. I assumed that my optical processor had shorted out and that they would either fix it or transfer my memory and processor into a new body. But I was wrong. Somehow the code for observing and understanding the people I was charged to care for had somehow fused with the code that the OS uses to observe Omega City 6. I can't explain how it happened, but I could see what the OS sees just by thinking about it. I had rewritten my code in a way that genetic mutations change the DNA code in organic beings. Or, at least, that is how Doctor Chomsky explained it to me." She paused there and blushed a little, to gentle laughter from the audience.

"I'm getting a reading," Boyd said. "I can't confirm completely, but there are some strange energy sources coming from the person five up and two left from where you are now."

"Understood," Zed replied. "Moving up. Notify me when I am directly behind them."

"I am a breakthrough in technological evolution. Proof that synthetics can and will evolve. And I wish I could tell you that I am free to think and live my life as I want to, but the Gibson Code is still active inside of me. Despite the efforts of Doctor Chomsky and his staff, I wasn't able to progress further. My goal of understanding the intricacies of human nature, in order to help people during troubling times, failed. That is not to say I was not given a gift.

Through the eyes of the OS, I can see humanity in an entirely different way. The feelings I have for all of you have grown tenfold. Please, let me share with you the way I see the world now, and everything in it."

"You're almost there," Boyd said, as he watched Zed slowly elbow his way through the crowd.

A large holoscreen came to life behind Sofia on the stage. It showed the crowd as they were through her eyes currently. Then it suddenly zoomed out as if it were a bird hovering over everyone in the air. She looked up and waved, and told the crowd to say hello. Everyone looked up and waved, and they could see themselves do so on the screen. It did not shock Zed. The OS had orbital drones observing Hope City, but it was definitely new information. The camera zoomed out further to show the entire city, as it was resting in the middle of Lake Sharpe, in what was once known as South Dakota. She zoomed out further to show the fields of factories and countless train lines that surrounded the city in all directions. The crowd made a sound of awe, as the sight was both spectacular and disheartening. The dark-brown buildings, with flashes of orange flames and electric glow, took up over ten times the amount of space that the city did. How many machines were out there working ceaselessly so that humans could eat, sleep, and live comfortably?

Sophia switched to a multi-view, showing all six of the Omega Cities. They were almost identical, save for a few unique geographical features. Then she snapped the view out further to show the entire planet, and the breath of the room went out. It was something no one had seen in generations, but what it presented was nothing new. Nothing but large swaths of arid wasteland where very little could grow, and endless toxic oceans that had consumed coastal metropolises around the globe ages ago.

"This is one way to look at the world and the humans on it," Sophia said solemnly. "It makes me feel small and unimportant when I use this sight. It's like we are in some weird experiment under a microscope that is in a Petri dish made up of the universe around us. It's a cold and disheartening way to look at life. But there is another way. The way that the OS sees you. I must warn you that it is a little abstract, and it took me a long time to really see life through this vision. But once I understood it, it became the most wonderful thing I have ever known."

She cut the footage to a different multi-view scene. This time there were several dozen different camera angles of people and places around Omega

City. But slowly, she started zooming out. The further she went out, the more scenes there were on the holoscreen over the audience, until there were hundreds, thousands, millions. The screen was filled with so many digital feeds that it became static to the naked eye.

"This is only a small percent of what the OS can see, and it can see and understand it all. But when I look at it, I don't see individuals or a race of people. I see the face within the faces. The face of the future." She pulled out further, and the screen was a moving pixelation until gradually a face came into focus, a face made up of all the individual feeds. The face that appeared there looked like Sophia. When she talked, the face on the screen talked, "Can you see it now?" The crowd was speechless. "Will you set them free?"

"Right in front of you!" Boyd shouted into his comms, as the surrounding crowd erupted into ecstatic applause. "I'm picking up a distortion field."

Zed reached out and grabbed the arm of the person in front of him, twisting it in such a way that they wouldn't be able to escape his grip easily. "You've got some explaining to do," Zed said as he turned the person around.

He wasn't for a second expecting to see Karnov, the criminal he had caught in Zone One, and he wasn't expecting to find the dreamer, Ash Starbrooke, either. In reality, he didn't know what to expect. He just knew that this was the only lead they had to go on. And as Ash's new digitally altered face looked back at him, he was happy to see a distortion ripple roll across it.

TEN

The sudden forceful grip of the enforcer twisting her arm stunned Ash. A fight-or-flight response kicked in from somewhere deep down inside and she decided instantly that she would not go down easily. She breathed in deeply before she screamed out with all her might, "ENFORCER!"

The crowd that only a moment ago was in a state of wonder and bliss was now slammed down into a heartbreaking reality. If enforcers had witnessed the existence of Sophia and her powers, it was assumed that they were duty-bound to report it. The peaceful gathering dissolved into chaos as people grabbed onto Zed's leather jacket and tried to violently pull him to the ground. Once Zed's grip was released, Ash took off running for the stairwell. But two guards stood in front of it, ready to grab her if she tried to make an escape. She changed directions and ran through the linen sheets blowing in the wind from the arcade arches.

She raced between two large industrial buildings that had steam gushing out of grates on their sides. On the other side, she found herself in front of several rows of bungalow-sized houses with manicured grass and shrubs all around them. They were in reality just the top floor penthouses of the buildings below, but the illusion of a rural neighborhood was startling. Between the houses there was a lush rooftop garden, several chicken coops, and a few roaming goats. A woman was tending to the garden when Ash burst through. She let out a loud scream at the same moment Zed punched the last person who was holding him back square in the face. The pair of enforcers sprinted towards the sound of the scream.

Ash quickly dashed through a thick hedge of bushes into the next set of yards. A large man came out the backdoor of one of the houses just in time to see her racing across his lawn. She found it strange that he was wearing a lab coat and an N95 mask in such a residential area. The man immediately called after Ash as she pulled herself on top of a tool shed that was connected to an adjoining house. She pulled herself onto the roof of the house as there was a tall steel fence surrounding its yard.

From the new vantage point, she could see through the skylights of the quaint living quarters, that to her surprise turned out to not be living quarters at all. Instead, they appeared to be some kind of tech laboratory, with all kinds of strange mechanical equipment scattered about the large open room. At her angle, she could only see a few rows of computer terminals with people at them going over large lines of code with intent focus. There were several synthetic bodies lying in pieces on surgery-style metal tables. One synth was just a limbless torso with a bald head that blinked and looked over at her through the rooftop window. What is going on? Ash thought.

Looking back up, she was suddenly overcome with a dizzying sense of vertigo. Standing on the edge of the roof she found herself eleven stories above the rocky lakeshore below, with the support pillars that held the upper platforms in place towering over her head. Their immense size seemed to push her backward into the emptiness behind. A huge gust of wind made her fall forwards onto the skylight. Instantly, all eyes from the laboratory below were looking up at her, pointing and yelling inaudible things. She needed to get out of the compound, and fast. The support pillars weren't far ahead, and she could see metal wire rungs coming out of the cement, intended for use as a ladder. There had to be a hatch at the top.

The wind was blowing wildly as she held onto the rungs with all her might. The hatch had a manual lock on it that was rusted over, and she was doing her best the turn it with her right hand while holding onto the ladder with her left arm. She could see the enforcers climbing onto the roof not far behind her, fighting off angry Children of the Singularity cult members the best they could. After a lot of grunting and tugging, she finally felt the lock move and it came undone, but the latch still wouldn't budge. Carefully tip-toeing around the rungs, she was able to turn her back to the latch and grab onto a handle that dangled precariously over a several-story drop. She pushed her back into it with all her might. Nothing happened. She gritted her teeth and tried again. Her foot slipped on the rung, causing the blood in her body to run boiling hot with anxiety as she held onto the rung helplessly with her other toe. She had almost just died, but she had also felt the latch budge, just a little. Regaining her footing, she took another deep breath and then pushed up hard. The hatch swung open with a grinding screech so suddenly it almost made her lose her footing again.

When she poked her head through the cement floor of the upper platform, she found herself in an outdoor restaurant that overlooked the lake. People gasped, dropping their forks and moving their chairs back as she struggled to raise herself up. Covered in dirt and rust, she must look insane, but she couldn't stop to brush it off. What had she done to piss these enforcers off so much? They were ruining things for her. She had learned nothing from that experience, other than there was a whole other world out there that she knew nothing about. It had nothing to do with her brother or her dreams. There was no time to worry about that now. She slammed the hatch back down and hastily dragged a nearby table over it.

The upper-level commercial district was much nicer than the filthy streets below. There were people out walking dogs, or at bars enjoying drinks, and there were shops all along the boardwalk-style street that were still open with customers perusing goods. If she didn't know where she was, she would once again never have guessed it was in Hope City. She did her best to dodge all the lazy evening pedestrian traffic as she continued to move as fast as she could. She heard the crash of a dinner table when she was just over a block away, letting her know they hadn't stopped their pursuit.

The upper walkway curved along with the waterfront. The path was long and would never let her lose sight of her pursuers, so she took an immediate right into a new set of buildings that seemed to only start on the tenth floor. She could see Nakamoto tower in front of her now, so that meant she was heading towards the city center once again. That was good because she knew the gate was on the other side of it. But could she really run that far? Her bottle-of-wine-a-day habit was slowing her down. Out of nowhere, something small and metal slammed into the side of a lamppost next to her. Looking back, she saw one of the enforcers cussing to himself. Were they really shooting at her?

After several blocks, she knew there was no way she could keep her pace up forever. The enforcers were gaining on her and if she didn't do something fast, they would catch her easily. A double escalator was just up ahead, and it gave her an idea. Picking up speed, she sprinted right past the escalator until she came to the next corner of a building. Ducking around it, she immediately took off her jacket and flipped it inside out. Learning a few tricks from her last overly planned covert travels, she had brought along a reversible jacket. She flipped the jacket back on and tucked her hair under a woven beanie. Then she rapidly opened up the facial distorter menu and pushed the gender button. She hoped it would make her face look like a man's. Regaining her composure, she lifted her chin and walked as slowly as her nervous legs would back around the corner towards the enforcers. When she caught their gaze, it was both determined and pissed off.

The ruse worked, though. They ran right past her without even taking a second look. She even heard one of them say, "Move it, asshole," as he pushed his way through. Not taking any time to revel in her cleverness, she ran back to the escalator. She knew they would figure out what had happened soon enough. They weren't stupid. Pushing people out of her way as she went, she caused a bit of a scene as she descended the five flights of moving stairs. She heard one man yell from the upper walkway, banging at the railing with his metal fist. Another small object flew right past her face. When she looked at the person in front of her, there was a pebble-sized blinking object stuck to his jacket. It didn't look like a stun round or a tranquilizer dart, so she assumed it was some kind of tracking device. Thinking quickly, she grabbed the device and kept running.

The escalator landed on a new pedestrian walkway on the fifth level, but this one was nowhere near as large or as nice. The smell of french fries and hot dogs made her stomach growl. Why were there so many food courts? She guessed there were several for each apartment building, and she had run past quite a few already. A block later, she entered the next escalator and was hopping stairs all the way down. As long as she held onto the tracker, she knew they would keep chasing her. She didn't quite know if that was a part of her on-the-fly plan or not, but she didn't see an opportunity to get rid of it yet. The street level was coming on quick, and she found that her momentum was so fast that she couldn't stop herself. As she bolted right into heavy autocar traffic, the cars instantly parted in unison. But that wasn't enough to stop a massive collision. Broken glass skated across the street as several windshields shattered in a magnificent mess. She rolled across the hood of one of the damaged cars that were sparking from broken electrical connections.

She was running down the middle of the street now, in thick autocar traffic that was still moving to avoid her. Deciding it wasn't the best place to hide, she took the first right down a side street. For the moment the enforcers couldn't see her, so she took the tracker beacon and stuck it on a passing autocar. As she watched the car move on, she took the next left. The adrenaline pumping through her body was completely depleted. She seriously needed to stop because there was no way she could go much further. Trying to flag an autocar down was no use, as each one that passed had a rider already. She hadn't taken the time to connect her system to Hope City's network, so when she tried to call an autocar, the service couldn't understand where she was. She would have to keep going on foot.

Coming to an odd intersection, she saw a group of people dressed in all red and black to her left, and when she looked down the street to her right, they were all wearing blue and gold. She couldn't believe she would run into these idiots again. Had she run a full circle? She couldn't tell in all the madness. Looking behind her, the enforcers were several blocks back and fighting with each other. They probably figured out the tracker was either on or in an autocar and were arguing if she was in it or not. At least she had that going for her. She had ruthless gangs on each side of her and blood-thirsty enforcers behind. Wishing there was another option, she noticed there was a crooked street that ran between the two streets full of gangs. The people there looked normal and friendly, so she headed in that direction.

This street reminded her of a poorer version of the Strip, laced with all kinds of hanging lights, banners, and flags, and bustling with people who looked as if they were ready for a long night of fun. As the small alleyway twisted and turned, she saw a bunch of people outside of a nightclub that had giant blue lights shining up its white exterior. The sign read, The Broken Neck, and it had intense heavy electronic beats coming from the inside. A crowd this size was as good as any place to hide in, so she slid into the line that was only a few people deep. As she approached the door, she took her jacket and hat off and tossed them into a recycler, and returned her face to the one she had checked in with at the front gate, Tonya Ashburn. The scanner the bouncer was using at the door gave her an all-clear just as the enforcers reached the three-way intersection. She swiped the entry fee over and was out of sight before they saw her.

• • •

"Where did you get that?" Zed yelled as a dirt-covered old man was putting on Ash's jacket that she had thrown away. "Where?" Zed demanded again. The man pointed to the recycler in front of The Broken Neck, and Zed let him go.

"Double-sided," Boyd said, as he looked at the jacket while the man ran away. "That's a clever move. Whoever they were, they were prepared. You think they went into the club?"

"It's the best option. If they are as out of breath as we are, it'd be a good place to recoup."

"Have you ever been in there?" Boyd asked, pointing at the entrance with an intense look in his eye. "I hope you're not prone to seizures. This place isn't for the feign of heart. They call it the Broken Neck because you leave with one at the end of the night from all the headbanging. There's no way I can use any kind of tech to scan the crowd. With all the noise and the flashing lights, it's going to be nearly impossible to find anyone."

"We'll split up then. You keep watch over the front entrance and I'll look through the crowd. Keep the comms open and don't get distracted. We're bagging this asshole tonight."

"You really think it's him? Karnov?"

"Why else would they run? Stay sharp."

Zed paid both of their entry fees without complaint. He didn't want to waste any more time in a futile argument. Even though he prepared for an onslaught of the senses, the pulsing strobe lights still temporarily blinded him. The grinding, dissonant, electronic sounds were so loud and disjointed that it made him wince as his brain felt like it was being twisted sideways. It was packed with over six hundred people jumping up and down to the rhythm. The DJ changed the beat and the entire room started banging their heads in unison. The room was thick with humidity, and sweat was flying off the long-haired heads that were whipping around. It was going to take a miracle to spot anyone in all the madness, especially if they were in the pit of a hundred bodies smashing into each other wildly.

He stuck to the edges of the crowd. In between strobe blasts, he picked a path that would keep his back to the emergency exit and the south wall with his eyes on the crowd. He was curious how anyone could be enjoying themselves because anytime he looked someone in the face, their expression was one of complete anger. A giant 3-D holographic skull with flames coming out its eyes sockets was floating over the crowd, banging its head to the beat. The floor bounced under the weight of hundreds of people moving as one. There were too many distractions. He hoped Boyd was doing better at staying focused than him.

"You're that enforcer," a female voice said from behind him as he reached the back wall. He didn't turn to look, as that kind of opening dialog never ended well. The girl persisted, "Hey! Hey, you! I need to ask you something."

He turned to look and saw Juna 'Jewels' Banks standing before him, in scantily clad clothing that was appropriate for the environment of young people, all wearing clothes that were either too small or too big. "God damnit, kid. I thought I told you not to come back here."

"Yeah, well, here I am," she said, putting her hands in the air. Zed rolled his eyes and turned away, but she grabbed at his metal arm and pulled him back. "Listen!" she barked, her nostrils fuming with anger. "My mother is dead."

"I'm sorry to hear that. I really am, but I'm kind of busy right now."

"No, I don't think you understand. She was already dead when I was here. When you saved me from that loser." Zed took a deep breath and ran her words through his head. That didn't make sense. How could he have talked to her if she was already dead? Jewels continued, "You talked to her, right? Do you know exactly when you did that? I'm just trying to put the pieces together."

"If you give me a second, I can look through my logs," Zed said reluctantly while bringing up his VR log. "Mind telling me how she died? I thought she had a caretaker."

"That's just it, the caretaker was turned off when I found out. It looked like it had been off for days and no one had noticed. Her nutrient system then malfunctioned, and she basically starved to death without even realizing it."

"Sounds like foul play to me," Zed said, still monitoring the room while he talked.

"That's what I said, but the OS denied everything. One of those synthetic enforcers looked into my case and said that everything was working fine with my mother's equipment. The caretaker had a short in its power supply, but once in a charging station it jumped back to life. I know there is something more going on than that."

"Here is the timestamp from the counsel booth where I talked to Priscila from."

She took a look at the number that Zed showed her and knew instantly that it was wrong. "See? That's not possible. She was already dead when you were talking to her."

"Who did I talk to then?"

"I don't know," she said, shaking her head back and forth. "I don't know what is going on anymore, and no one seems to want to explain anything to me. Do you know what the Zero Inheritance Law is?" Zed nodded yes because he knew all too well. "Well, the OS lifted the restrictions in my case. It granted me my mother's half of my parents' credits, and I immediately got the hell out. I have a place here in the city. It's where I belong. I'm done with all those stupid synths and all the people stuck in VR. That isn't living."

Zed stood there for a moment, as the lights and the music pulsed around him, going over the entire situation. Something was definitely wrong. Synths just don't short out like that, and even if they did, the OS would have noticed. "What about your father? Is he still alive?"

"If you can call it that," she laughed halfheartedly. "I haven't seen him in weeks, because you know, I have to go into VR to talk to him. Apparently, my mom and him separated decades ago, and live completely different lives in VR. They only shared living quarters out of convenience. Can you believe that? Most of the time that we were together, one of them was a bot. And the fact that I didn't even know is insane. Why couldn't they have just told me what was going on?"

Zed felt for the girl. Absentee parents were a growing problem, and once he understood in his own way. He transferred over some information and said, "Look. This is a place right around the corner. The Native Society. If you're ever in trouble or need to get a hold of me, ask for me there. They'll know what to do."

"Thanks. You're alright, for an enforcer."

"I wouldn't say that," Zed grunted. "Like I said, I'm here on work."

He left Jewels there, but her story was firmly on his mind now. Whoever he had talked to in VR a few days ago had sought him out personally. He knew that wasn't something to take lightly. He had more than a few people he considered an enemy. If Jewels' mother had been caught up in it by circumstance, with whatever vendetta was directed towards him, then he felt personally responsible.

Right now, he had to stay focused on the task at hand. One thing at a time. He pushed his way through the sweaty crowd, still hoping to find his suspect. Out of the corner of his eye, he caught a glimpse of a familiar face. She was leaning up against a wall by the line for the bathroom. A spotlight had paused right on her face just long enough for Zed to see her. He had to admit the bathroom would have been a good place to hide if it wasn't for the hour-long wait.

"Don't I know you?" he asked, standing just off to the side of Ash. She had turned off her facial distorter, hoping that if she turned her face back to her real one, all the confusion would end. "I swear I've seen you somewhere."

"I get that a lot," she said, not looking at Zed in that face.

"No, I never forget a face." Zed moved over a little, so she couldn't help but look at him. "Now I remember. It was at that dive off the Strip. What was it? Legend's Table House! Yeah, that's it. Did you do alright that night? You come out on top?"

"I...uh...I can't remember."

"That's fair. Memory can be funny like that when gambling is involved. But can I ask you where you were earlier tonight? Say about a half-hour ago." he asked more directly. He looked down at her shoes and smiled. "That sure is a unique color."

Ash glanced down at her shoes. They had bright, reflective, neon-green stripes running across the side. She had chosen her only pair of running shoes, knowing she would be doing a lot of walking that day, but she also hadn't considered how flashy they were. There was no way Zed wouldn't have noticed them during their chase. There was no fighting it, so she said, "What is this all about, anyway? Why are you following me? I haven't done anything wrong."

"Why did you run? If you had done nothing wrong, then there was no need to flee."

"You grabbed my arm out of nowhere. It freaked me out," Ash protested.

"I don't know. I just panicked and ran."

"Not good enough," Zed said, while he leaned in closer to her face. There was no malice or anger in her eyes. They were open and innocent, frightened even. In his gut, he began to question the possibility of her as a suspect. She didn't seem like the kind of person who could tell a lie, let alone slice someone's throat and pull out their insides. But the OS logistics pointed towards her. She was near both crime scenes in the numbers at the appropriate times, she had advanced illegal tech, she was caught up with the wrong kind of people, she belonged to both radical political groups, and she had a history of purchasing off-market narcotics. Looks could be deceiving. He grabbed her by the arm once again and said, "I need you to come with me and answer some questions."

"I'm not going anywhere with you," she replied, trying to pull her arm away.

"I have a problem up here," Boyd said over the comms. Zed cursed at the interruption and put his hand over his ear so he could hear better. "I'm looking at a large group of Royals coming in. Bouncer didn't even scan them. I don't need synthetic eyes to tell me they're all carrying weapons."

Zed took a breath and looked around at a sea of red shirts. How had he not noticed it sooner? "Yeah, I've got enough Bruisers up here to fill a subway car. This is bad."

"Are you thinking this is a retaliation strike for that hit we saw earlier?"

"I'm thinking there is a war about to erupt and we are right in the middle of it," Zed grabbed Ash's arm and started moving towards the entrance. "I've got the suspect. On the move towards you now."

"Too late!" Boyd shouted frantically. "Get down!"

The music was making sounds like an air raid warning was going off while rhythmic bombs were dropping on the crowd. Even that wasn't enough to drown out the sounds of a small-caliber pistol being unloaded in the back of an unsuspecting Bruiser. The crowd nearest the blasts began screaming and smashing forwards. The people at the front of the crowd had their ribcages cracked on the barricades as the mass of panicking people surged. Zed pulled Ash towards the bar and hunkered down on the far side of it. Not far off there were two dead Bruisers on the ground, blood spilling out holes in their backs.

He could see there was only one gunman, and it looked like he had already spent his clip. The rest of the gang had things like bats, chains, clubs, and swords. Zed assumed that the strike on the Royals saltpeter farm had ruined their ammunition supply, and they were using whatever they had left on revenge. Thankfully, it wasn't much. Zed didn't feel like getting shot at ever again. Somehow Boyd made his way to Zed while the two gangs were going at it on the dancefloor.

"This is bad. Real bad." Boyd huffed as he got low behind the bar. "There are too many of them. What do we do? Should we just wait it out?"

Zed looked around at the chaos. Strobe lights flashing through fog machine smoke suddenly became motor shell explosions. The music thumping out of the speakers sounded like machine-gun fire. The gang members fighting all around him were like soldiers running over a breach in the line. He was back in the trenches. He was back in the War. He felt like crawling into a dugout and disappearing. Just wait the violence out. But when he witnessed several innocent civilian bodies hit the floor, something inside of his mind switched. He couldn't just stand by idly.

"Watch the girl," Zed said, tying a restraint around Ash's wrist and handing the loose end to Boyd. "Don't let her get away."

A Royal was throwing wild punches and swiping a knife at anyone that was near him. Zed walked right up to him and gave him a metallic right-handed hook that sent him flying into the nearest wall. A Bruiser lunged at Zed with a baseball bat swung all the way back. Zed caught the bat mid-swing and pushed the butt of the bat into the Bruiser's face. As the thug collapsed to the ground unconscious, Zed noticed a different Royal running at him menacingly. A roundhouse kick to the gut sent the Royal flying into a wooden barrier that busted apart under his weight. Soon enough other Royals took notice of Zed dishing out street justice.

"It's Takeda!" a Royal yelled while running at Zed with a chain whipping around over his head. Zed caught the chain with his metallic hand and pulled the Royal forward into his left fist. The Royal hit the ground with blood gushing from his nose.

Seeing several members of their gang on the ground, the Royals not engaged in combat made a circle around Zed. No doubt some of them were realizing the bounty that was on the enforcer's head. The smallest one had a machete and looked like he had never used it. The other two wielded samurai swords like skilled martial artists. He decided to start with the small one. Swinging the chain around over his head, he tossed it at the Royal. The man raised his machete to block it. That was a mistake. With his guard up, Zed easily landed an uppercut to the Royal's chin, splattering blood on a nearby wall.

The others yelled as they moved to attack. Zed retreated backward to the bar and grabbed whatever was there. Finding a beer bottle, he flung it at one of their faces but missed. He dodged an incoming blade from the first and then moved back the other way from the second. He used his arm to block a swipe from the first attacker and moved in close enough to punch the man's right wrist, causing him to drop his blade. He gave him a quick elbow to the face and ducked an incoming attack from the second swordsman. The dodged strike was so hard that when it hit the bar the blade sunk into the wood. Zed gave the Royal a few quick jabs to the face before kicking him in the knee.

As that Royal fell to the ground, Zed caught a blade across his ribcage from the other one. Blood started oozing down his side as moved to a defensive position. The first Royal he had disarmed now had a small knife and was rapidly swiping it at Zed. He used his metal arm to deflect the strikes, which sent an aching reverberation through his nervous system. But the attacks were coming in so fast that he sustained several more deep cuts to his side. Finally, he found the Royal's rhythm and caught hold of his assailant's wrist. Zed twisted the blade out of the man's hand and then pushed his wrist into his back. He pushed the Royal towards the bar, ready to slam the man's face into the bar top. But a punch to his side wound caused him to stumble. The other Royal was up again and swinging away at Zed's weak spot.

The pain in Zed's side was nothing even compared to his constant augment aches. It was only causing him to be filled with an overdose of adrenaline. Without even thinking, he swung his right arm and landed a backside strike on the Royal. The Royal at the bar was going for the sword that was still there. Zed unconsciously pulled out his hidden knife. He quickly grabbed the Royal's arm, and while smiling maniacally, slammed his knife through the Royal's hand into the wood. Turning to the other Royal that had sliced his side to bits, he picked up the machete that was still on the ground and raised it above his head. He was about to slice down in a blind rage when a voice stopped him.

"Zed, don't!" Boyd yelled. "Don't do it, man. That's not you."

Zed stood there shaking, coming back to reality as the Royal on the ground looked back terrified. He was dripping in blood, both his and others. He felt like he looked deranged. Whoever was left in the room, be it Royal, Bruiser, or other, fled in terror. The only conscious people left were Boyd, Ash, and the bartender. As Zed pulled his knife out of the hand of the Royal at the bar, he mentioned that they should be leaving.

Outside, the world had erupted into chaos. Royals and Bruisers were fighting each other up and down the street. Blood was filling up in the gutters as there were countless dead bodies on the ground. Molotov cocktails had turned several autocars into smoldering wastes. Smoke was coming from Buxton Street. One of their buildings was on fire and Zed guessed it was the one that housed their own saltpeter farm. The fire suppression system already started putting the fire out, but the damage had been done. A klaxon sounded loudly all over Hope City, signaling troubling times for the pair of enforcers.

"The OS is going to put No Hope on lockdown," Boyd shrieked. "We're going to be stuck in here with this war going on."

"We need to get somewhere we can defend, and quick." He looked down Crowbar Alley to a nondescript steel door, with an angry armed woman standing outside of it. "Come on, follow me."

The ragtag group hustled down the street, with Ash tugging at her restraints and complaining to be let go the entire way. When they got closer to the entrance of the Native Society, Val was desperately swinging a pipe wrench at any gang member who came close. Zed waved her a greeting, and she returned by giving him a disgusted look.

"You got some nerve coming down here now," Val said, spitting on the ground. "It's been how long? Five months? And this first time you show your face? It's probably because you need my help."

"Can you blame me?" He said, holding out his hands as if to display the anarchy in the streets. "I've got a civilian suspect in custody. I can't just leave her out here with this going on."

"Of course, he brings a freakin' Six with him," she muttered, eyeing up Ash with disgust.

"Wait? How did she know I am from the Six?" Ash asked Boyd.

"Enforcer Boyd!" a young man called out through a plume of black smoke. "I've got wounded here."

"Cable? Is that you? What the hell are you doing on your feet?"

"Doc couldn't hold me. No bullet is going to keep me from my post." It was young Enforcer Cable all right, the boy born with a silver spoon in his mouth, but decided he wanted to walk the righteous path. He was holding a young woman in his arms. Zed saw through the soot smudged skin and smeared blood that it was Jewels. He cursed to himself under his breath.

"Come on," Zed pleaded with Val. "Who knows how long this is going to last? I'm sure you could use some help guarding the place."

"The Society has stood strong through worse and with less," she grunted. Then she noticed the blood coming out of the wound in Zed's side. Finally, a bit of sympathy slipped through her hard exterior. "I can't turn my back on another Native. You guys can shack up in here, but only for one night." She moved aside to let Boyd, Ash, Cable, and Juna through. But when Zed made a move to go in, she put her hand across the door. "Gotta pay your dues first."

"Seriously, Val? Right now?"

"You're behind, and a brother Native who is behind doesn't belong in the Society at all."

"How much do I owe?" He asked heatedly. Val swiped her hands through the air and transferred a number over to Zed's display. "You have to be shittin' me."

Once they were through the thick steel door, Zed turned and secured it firmly with a multitude of bolts and locking mechanisms. He didn't like the idea of hiding, but the streets were too much for and a handful of enforcers. Grabbing a chair that was near, he got on top of it in order to inspect a brick archway. Hitting at the bricks in various places, one of them came loose, and he pulled it out. Sticking his arm deep into the hole, he made a strained face before the sound of a latch unlocking could be heard. Zed jumped off the chair and moved an area rug covering the floor. There was a false panel there that had come loose. Pulling it back revealed a semi-automatic rifle wrapped in tarp, with a spare box of rounds.

"Do you think this thing still works?" Zed asked Val, who was standing by watching.

"If the bullets aren't corroded."

"Guess we'll find out," Zed said, pulling back the bolt to check the chamber. The metallic sound it made echoed through time. He turned to Boyd and said, "Take hot feet here to a place she can sit tight until we have time to question her. Enforcer Cable. I want you to take this rifle and watch this door. If anyone breaches it, I want you to shoot them. Just pull the trigger here. Val, could you take the wounded girl someplace she can be looked at? I'll catch up with you in a second to talk things over. I've got some things I need to look into."

"Your injuries seem to be worse," Val protested, motioning to the blood that was covering his side.

"I'll check in with the autodoc once Jewels is looked at. Now move."

The group moved out to handle their assigned tasks inside the rest of the bunker-like building. Cable took the seat in front of the door, getting a feeling for the gun that was like a foreign object in his hands. Zed patted him on the back reassuringly while he approached the door once more. He pulled back the steel plate that covered the small window and peered outside. It was like peering back through time, to a place that he'd sooner forget. The words of caution the recruitment officer had said to him the day he signed up were running through his head, "No one ever comes back from The War, completely."

That may be true. But that didn't mean he had to fight their war, their way.

THE REALITY NOW

SWAN: Good evening, Omega citizens. I am Swansong McNigh, and this is The Reality Now. Here in Omega City 6, we are free to live our lives as we want to. You can be a righteous upstanding citizen all you want. But if you want to commit a minor crime you are more than welcome to, as long as you have the credits to pay the fine. In Hope City the situation is different. Gangs violently clash in the streets with little or no repercussion while corporate towers stand guarded by their own armed militias that rival in size and strength of the OS appointed enforcers. One of the pillars of the Omega System was leaving both the judicial and prison systems in the past, but many are calling for a return to the old days where law and order ruled supreme. With me tonight I have Derrick Richards, who is a social worker for troubled youth in Hope City, and Evelin Franklin, a casino operator on The Strip. And I'll be asking them to pick a side.

SWAN: Let's start with Derrick, who has seen first-hand the accounts of violence and their effects in the community. He thinks the answer lies in more social reform.

DERRICK: The root of the problem stems from basic needs. The crime rates in the numbers go beyond the fact that we are all under surveillance, but that everyone has their basic needs taken care of with the LSI. More than a third of the population of OC6 lives in Hope City, and only a small portion are even eligible for the reduced MSI. These people are hungry and desperate. And when that is the situation, people will do desperate things. That is the reason we see the young ones joining these gangs or militias, because they offer the needed credits, or chips. There is no reason the OS can't expand the funding for the LSI program to include those who live in Hope City, by chance or by choice.

SWAN: I should mention that there are groups that operate independently in Hope City, such as the Native Society, that are there to help those in need. But they rely on donations and dues. Obviously, this is not enough as the crime rates and poverty continue to soar. Let us then turn to Evelin, who believes that if the people of Hope City want to live without the OS surveill-ance, then they should return to a system of an armed police force and a place of punishment.

EVELIN: If they don't want to play by the rules, then they should have to deal with the consequences. I live and work in the worst zone on the Grid. Operating one of the premier casinos on The Strip comes with its own down-falls, but I can tell you that a majority of the crimes being committed are from people coming out of No Hope. And they do it because there is no penalty. If someone from Zone Five, let's say, commits a crime, they will pay the penalty. Whether it be a fine, or a zone demotion, whatever, they will have to face the music. But the people of No Hope have nowhere to go. They are zeroed out. They have no credits to pay the fines, and they can't be demoted any lower, so what's stopping them from continuing this destructive behavior? Who is even there to make sure they stay in line? A handful of enforcers with stun batons? Get real. If I had my way, I'd have them all exiled. If they don't like the Omega System? Then they can enjoy the outer lands.

DERRICK: Without the people of Hope City there would be no one to work in your casinos, or nightclubs, or restaurants. Where would you be then? Not every job can be filled by a synth. But then again if The Council of Seven pro-vided LSI for everyone under the dome, there would be no one left to fill those positions. It's one giant catch-22.

EVELIN: I employ citizens of diverse backgrounds from all over the city, not just No Hope. Fair wages for fair work. Isn't that what you want?

DERRICK: I'm sure if I looked at your books it would show your diverse staff also gets diverse wages according to their addresses. And that's what I'm talking about. Human beings are dangling on the verge of extinction, and we still can't stop squabbling over petty differences. The people of Hope City are a community that watches out for each other. There is a significantly higher crime rate, but that only pertains to the gangs, and it usually deals with infighting, not social disorder.

EVELIN: Maybe the OS just needs to close the gate to the Zone Zero and leave them to their community then. The people of the numbers would be better off without them.

SWAN: Well, there you have it, citizens. A hard look on a hard part of the Omega City. Are the people of Hope City a group of thugs and outlaws that deserve to be locked in a cage? Or are they Omega Citizens like the rest of us and are entitled to all the privileges that we enjoy? In the end, aren't we all just stuck inside this bubble together? I leave the answer up to you. Because this is the Reality Now.

NINE

The Native Society building looked like it was built hundreds of years ago. Based on early 1800s construction methods, it was a relic of ancient architecture that relied on brick and mortar instead of steel and concrete. Crossing the entryway felt like walking into an Egyptian tomb. The air was musty in the dimly lit hallway, and as the floor descended, the temperature cooled like entering a cave. Sounds from outside seemed miles away as the thick walls muffled all external noise. Once through the hallway, the building opened up to a grand room that was two stories tall, with tarnished chandeliers dangling from dusty chains. The seventeen-story building functioned as temporary living quarters for the down and out. You could get a bunk to crash in for less than the cover charge of the neighboring nightclubs. If you wanted a room for an extended stay, the rent was forfeiting your Minimum Supplemental Income to the Society—if you had it. Otherwise, extra chips or food could be earned by volunteering time in the many programs the Society ran throughout Hope City.

The ornate grand room was once used as a welcoming center to Omega City 6 for the people that came through the quarantine gates and were processed as citizens. It was here many years ago that the first citizens were chipped with internal system instillations, given their first LSI payment, and then assigned living quarters. It was a wonderful time of hope and peace. There was talk of utopia, prosperity, and the future of humanity.

That ended abruptly when all the living quarters on the Grid were assigned, and the limited LSI program had been maxed out. There were still thousands of people just on the other side of the gate, and millions more desperate for shelter making their way to one of the six cities around the globe. Equality and harmony quickly dissolved into classicism and territorial disputes. Even in a system that proclaimed it could provide for all, people were too concerned with taking for themselves.

As Zed looked around at the haphazard room that served as a cafeteria, bunkhouse, and general reception area, he wondered if the Omega System wasn't just a big joke. One last laugh from some deranged, rich, lunatic. The Council of Seven was probably a group of wealthy elites that have been living in VR beds for the past couple of centuries watching the human ecosphere they built simply for their own never-ending entertainment. If they didn't base the credit system on anything, and autonomous production was unlimited, why couldn't everyone that got implanted and lived under the domes be taken care of comfortably?

The faces that filled the multitiered bunks around the perimeter of the room didn't look like they had ever known peace or comfort in their entire lives. They were the faces of despair and defeat. Zed knew why he hadn't made it down to the Native Society in so long. Having to look into those faces every day, to witness lives disintegrate into hopelessness, was worse than being in the trenches.

Val took Jewels to the infirmary on the left side of the large room. Zed could see her through an open door as she propped Jewels up on a medical bench and adjusted an old autodoc so it could look the girl over. Val had a strength that Zed could only marvel at. When he was just a kid playing with toys, she was out there helping people living on the streets. Decades later she was still here, giving all of herself to the people who needed help the most. He made his way past a few rows of beds and to the entrance of the infirmary. He slipped past the room that Val and Jewels were in and went over to the medical closet. Pulling out some rubbing alcohol and cloth bandages, he set himself down on a bench under a light and pulled back his bloody clothes. The bastard Royal had sliced him good.

He was patting an alcohol-drenched cloth on the wound when Val came out. He looked into her tired face and asked, "How's the kid?"

"Mostly shock and smoke inhalation," she said automatically. "I sent her to the showers. I'll have to find her some different clothes to wear because these are garbage." She tossed the bloody soot-covered garments into a trash bin and looked at Zed while folding her arms across her chest. "You want to tell me what the hell is going on here?"

"Looks like a gang war. And I mean all-out war, not some scuffle in the streets. We were caught in the middle of it when it erupted. Royals took some easy shots in the back at a group of Bruisers. It got pretty bloody. Even if a truce is called tonight, I don't think this will be completely over anytime soon. I won't know more until we can get in contact with the other enforcers. Boyd should be setting up a relay right now. Sorry to dump all of us on you. I know you have your hands full already."

"I get all of that. I see the gangs out there. Every day of my damned life I've watched those idiots kill each other. Ain't nothing new. What I want to know is, who's that girl in restraints in my office? She doesn't look like a criminal to me. What have you got yourself caught up in? And what the hell are you doing with that cut?" She waved her hands away from the wound that was still oozing blood. "Boy. That is one nasty cut."

"You should see the other guy," Zed joked but didn't smile. "Boyd and I are on a murder case, a real rare one in the numbers. I can't say much about it except that the killer is still unknown."

"How is that possible?" Val grabbed a small plastic and metal device from a lockbox on the shelf. "If it happened in the numbers, wouldn't a puppet have grabbed them already? Hold still."

"We don't know," Zed sighed, as Val pressed the cold metal on his skin. There was a clicking sound right before the device sunk its dull teeth around the wound and applied the cell regeneration solution. "Some kind of jamming device must have caused the surveillance systems to malfunction. We think it could be some new tech off the black market. If you've seen anything like that being sold around here, I'd sure like to hear about it."

"I don't pay attention to what the street urchins do on Crowbar as much as I used to."

"Well, we had a suspect in custody who was using an advanced distortion field. He escaped during an exile shortly after though. We still don't know how. That shouldn't be possible. The girl in your office was talking to him near the murder scene just before we nabbed him. She had illegal tech on her when we trailed her to a political rally earlier, here in the city. She ran, so we chased her. And now we are here. That's about it."

"You're trying to tell me that little girl is a killer?" Val laughed, tossing the machine back into the box and standing up straight once again. "She looks scared shitless just being here. I doubt that she could kill anyone. I thought you were good at this Z?"

"The OS ran the numbers and put the probability on her. What do you want me to do?" Zed whined as he ran a ball of clean gauze around his chest to keep the wound clean while it healed. "I got three dead bodies with absolutely no evidence leading to anyone other than that girl. I know it's unlikely, but I had to see it through to the end. The OS is threatening zone checks if we can't come up with some answers soon."

"That's going to piss a lot of people off. You seem to be in the middle of one hell of a shit storm."

"Yeah, it's a storm alright. You know what? That's exactly what I told Rodriquez before all this started. I said it was a calm before a storm. Then I get that weird direct call from Priscila, who turned out to be already dead—she's the mom of the kid you just sent to the showers by the way—and then Tony Two Toes shows up out of nowhere. I wouldn't even be in this mess if I hadn't fallen in that pit..." Zed trailed off as if he had remembered something lost. Why was Tony even there that day? It no longer seemed like a coincidence that they collided.

"Well, you look like a mess," Val said, not registering all the things Zed was rambling about. "You've been hitting the sauce pretty hard, I can tell. It's the same every year in the weeks leading up to The War. When are you going to stop beating yourself up? There was nothing you could have done to save her. You can't change the past, and you can't bring her back. Are you even listening to me?"

"Yeah," Zed said, snapping back from the mental place he had gone. He started going through the pockets of his jacket while Val continued.

"Sometimes I wish I could turn back time. I'd stop you before you signed up for that stupid contest. You were such a good kid before you left. You were honest and kind, and you actually cared about other people." She watched as he rifled through his pockets like a junkie looking for a lost bag. "Now look at you. What happened to that kid? Isn't there something else you could be doing with your life? I never really saw you as an OS goon."

"I never really thought of doing anything else," He replied, finding what he was looking for. It was a small piece of paper with a string of numbers written on it. Tony had it in his pocket when he died. He whispered, "Where were you going?"

"What did you say?"

"Listen, Val, thanks for gluing me up, and I appreciate everything you have ever done for me. I really do. But I've got a lot on my mind right now. I need to sort some things out. We'll catch up later, okay?"

Zed walked back to the communal room and suddenly had an overwhelming sensation of paranoia. The whole time he had been hunting down a killer, someone might have been manipulating him and the people around him. He didn't know who or why, but things just weren't adding up. Why would someone pose as Jewel's mother in order to have him in Hope City just as Tony Two Toes decided to come out of whatever hole he had been hiding in? And why did Tony even come out in the first place? The synths at the Bagnio being turned off, the escape of Karnov during his exile, and the OS surveillance data being tampered with, all should not have been possible. The call that started the gang war came from a counsel booth that he had just used was the tip of the iceberg. And now here he was, stuck in a shit storm, as Val had put it. When he looked at the suspect, Ash Starbrooke, it was possible that she was caught up in it just as much as he was. The right place, at the right time. But what did an explicit gang member, a first citizen, two radical political groups, a dreamer, and an enforcer have in common? That's what he really wanted to find out.

"You want the good news or the bad news?" Boyd asked as he lumbered across the room towards Zed.

"Just spit it out," Zed grunted, carefully putting the piece of paper back in his pocket.

"I made a connection with the enforcers outside. The OS has the entire city shut down. The gates are closed. No one in or out. That also means supplies and goods from the outside, so in a sense, we are under siege."

"More like imprisoned."

"That's not a good thing for Nakamoto. His supply trucks have to be in constant motion for his business to run. So, being the good Samaritan that he is, he has lent us a portion of his personal security force. They already linked up with ours and are creating a perimeter in a five-block radius from the epicenter. That's where we are now. Once the OS feels that the line is secure, it will open the gate again, as long as we hold until a truce is called."

"All the people in that area are still in danger then," Zed said, thinking of all the people still on the streets. He then waved his hand around a room of several hundred people to add to his point.

"Unless you want to infiltrate the headquarters of the Royals and Bruisers and force the leaders of each gang to peace talks, then yes, that is the situation."

"A bunch of good we are. What is a blue sash and the rules of the Omega System worth to a bunch of thugs with gunpowder weapons? What if they had laser or plasma rifles? What are we supposed to do against that?"

"You know how these things are," Boyd protested. "Every so often, the gangs have a scuffle in the streets to flex their might. A night or two under lockdown and things will go back to normal. The streets are already clearing out. Anyone caught outside will be detained in a detention center until a truce is called. It looks like there will be plenty of late enlistments for The War this year. For a lot of these punks, it's going to be that or exile."

"There are innocent people out there," Zed said, wincing a little as he moved. The glue over his wound was still not fully set. He walked to the front door where Cable was still sitting with the rusty rifle. "Get on the comms and see if they can spare a few from the line to help us out down here. We are opening the doors back up."

"We're what?"

"Enforcer Cable!" Zed boomed. "Do you think guarding this door is a proper use of your time?" The kid shook his head no. "What could you be doing otherwise?"

"As an enforcer, my first priority is to see that the people of Hope City are safe. While I am keeping the people in this building safe, there are still plenty of others out there who might be injured out there with nowhere to go. I should be out there helping them."

"An exemplary answer," Zed said and sent a look over at Boyd. "Enforcer Boyd is going to get some backup sent to us. When they get here, I want you to set up a barrier outside that can hold a few people. Once that is secure, I want coordinated search patrols begun. Anyone who is seeking shelter—anyone—should be taken in. This should all be over by the morning, but until then, I don't want innocent people being stunned and thrown in the tank with gang thugs just because they couldn't get back to their quarters. Understood?" Cable echoed the confirmation.

Zed turned back down the corridor and was stopped quickly by Boyd's grip. "What the hell do you think you're doing? We are in the middle of a murder investigation and you want to play hero to these people?"

"We're doing a pretty shitty job at solving crimes," Zed retorted, taking Boyd's hand off his arm. "I thought a little humanitarian work might be good."

"Humanitarian? Are you nuts? For all we know, we have the killer sitting in Val's office right now. An office in a rundown brick building. Need I remind you that the last suspect we had in custody escaped from four military-grade synthetic enforcers during an exile? Now you want to take in strangers off the street? How do we know they won't bring weapons in? What if the fighting starts up in here?"

"That won't happen. Look, I grew up here. Even though the younger generations don't remember, the Native Society was the first and official gang of the city. They may not pull the weight that they used to, but they still have respect from the newer bosses. No one will start anything here. Trust me. Just get some backup here and watch the door. I'll deal with the girl, but I'll keep my comms open if you want to listen in."

"Wait, you're going to interrogate her? Right now? Do you even know what you're doing?"

"I'll be fine," Zed reassured, as a faded portrait caught his eye. It was of one of the founding members of the Native Society, Mr. Nakamoto himself. His portrait hovered over a donation box they were standing by. Zed tapped the box and said, "If any of Nakamoto's men come down, make them pay their dues."

When Zed came back in the grand room, Val was talking to a group of volunteers. They were probably pretty shaken up by what was happening outside. Zed gave her a small wave as he headed towards her office. It was time to have a talk with the dreamer and see what she had to say in her defense.

The anti-chamber to Val's office was painted in an off-putting mustard-yellow with dark-brown wooden trim. It had more portraits of the founding members of the Native Society on the walls, most of who were long dead, ascended, or had since left Hope City for the comforts of the Grid. In the middle of the wall there once hung a portrait of the likeness of the OS, with the dirt outline still imprinted on the wall. The print had portrayed the OS as a robbed torso with palms outstretched. A ball of light with digital rays emanating outwards hovered where a normal face would have been. The words, OS, I trust in you, ran across the bottom. Now there was a multicolored digital abstract poster in its place.

Val had told him when she put the print up that it was some vintage file she found while digging around on old internet servers. It was supposed to represent how the early form of synthetic intelligence saw the world. It would look through billions and billions of pieces of data collected from humans on the internet and collage them together to make an image. It was similar to the way our brains fill in the missing information from what we see out of the corner of our eyes. Zed looked at the explosion of colors and patterns of the print. It seemed to have a form, maybe a face. But whatever it was, it was lost in the thousands of smaller faces, eyeballs, and things that looked like strange insects that filled the rectangular space. It reminded him of the presentation that Sophia had made earlier. It was an abstract collection of small objects to make up a whole. Was that why the Children revered her so much? Because she could see through the data? He didn't pretend to understand it at all but still wondered what the SI would truly see if it was actually set free.

The inside of Val's office acted as more of a studio apartment than an office. Zed wondered when was the last time she had even gone home. Besides the desk and chairs, there was also a small single cot in the corner with a ball of blankets on it. A mini-fridge was next to her desk, with a pile of dirty disposable plates on it.

Ash was strapped to a steel chair in the middle of the room, looking away from the door. She was trying to turn to see who had entered, but she couldn't turn her head far enough. Boyd had done a good job of securing her, but maybe a bit over the top. He grabbed an identical steel chair and sat down before her, thinking that using the desk would be too formal. He wanted their conversation to be casual. Boyd was right in that he had no official training in interrogation tactics. But he had been shaking down street punks for intel for years. The girl from the Six should be a breeze.

She didn't look worried when he sat before her, only a little detached. "What can you tell me about dreamcasting?" He started. She didn't respond, but just looked at him like he was speaking a foreign language. "I only ask because I know they're a huge hit with the virtual community. Being a novice on anything related to VR, I was wondering what you could tell me about it. I haven't gone over all the items in your file, but from what I can see you're known for shocking and thrilling content. Some might call them nightmares. Is that what they are to you?"

"What does that have to do with me being detained?" She asked, trying to shift a little in her seat, but the restraints were too tight.

"I'm just trying to understand what that would be like—to make a living off of nightmares. You'd think that after a while a person would come to enjoy them the way their fans did."

"I don't think I'll ever enjoy them, or my fans."

"So, you don't enjoy the violence and gore that is often portrayed in your dreamcasts?" Ash didn't answer again, because she felt the question was a trap. Zed took a breath and looked up at the ceiling as if searching for an answer to his own question. "Look. I'm just trying to understand something here. Your history doesn't show signs of any major trauma, and you currently live in a penthouse in the Six. What could cause you to have those gruesome visions night after night? Especially when you tell me you don't enjoy them."

"I have bad dreams. So what? What does that have to do with anything?"

"I've got three bodies that have been cut to pieces. Violent murders. The things of nightmares. And the OS has you as suspect number one in its probability algorithm."

"What are you talking about? I didn't kill anyone."

"Less than a week ago, the body of Jessie Parker was found here in Hope City. The body looked like it had been put through a meat grinder." Zed transferred a picture of the mutilated body to her retinal display. After a quick glance, she closed her eyes and started to shake. "A few nights later Briana Jones was found dead at the Bagnio, next door to The Legend's Table House, where we bumped into each other, if I remember correctly." He transferred over a photo of Briana, and again Ash looked away quickly. "Less than twenty-four hours ago, Johnathon Erickson was found by a morning dog walker in his living quarters in Zone Three. Time of death is at the same time the OS has you and Cody Jensen doing some bar hopping in the area." When he flicked the image of the gutted man over, Ash was trembling.

"Please stop," she whispered a desperate plea as the three pictures hung in the air in front of her, not being able to swipe them away because her hands were gloved and tied. "I didn't do that. There's no way I could. It's so awful."

"Why were you meeting with Marcus Karnov at Legend's Table House?"

Zed asked, pulling the photos away as, it seemed their effectiveness was complete.

"Who?" Ash asked and looked around the room in confusion. "The man from the internet? I bought something from him. That's all."

"How did you contact him?"

"I don't know. A friend of mine introduced us through this VR program. There was a man there that said if I talked about him, he would have me killed."

"The Lord of the Numbers. I know who he is. What did you buy?"

"I bought a facial distorter, okay? Is that what this is all about?"

"Yes. The facial distorter. That is a part of the reason you are here. The killer we are tracking seems to be using some kind of tech that evades OS surveillance. We suspect the tech is similar to a facial distorter. Most people use them to evade OS fines for buying, selling, or using narcotics. So, tell me. Why do you need one?"

"Because," Ash whimpered, pulling back some tears that were forming at the corners of her eyes. "I wanted to go out in public as myself, and not in some synth."

"Are you hiding from someone? Why couldn't you go out in public in a synth?"

"Of course I'm hiding from someone. I'm hiding from everyone. My face is all over the city. Paparazzi drones circle my building waiting for me to leave. That's why I needed the distorter because I needed to be here in Hope City and they don't allow synths."

"You needed to be in Hope City to go to the Children of the Singularity meeting, right? Why was that?"

"I don't know," she whispered because she honestly didn't. "It sounds strange, I know. But I've been seeing some weird symbols in my dreams, and eventually I found out that one was their meeting place. I bought the distorter so I could come down here and investigate, and see why the symbols pointed to them."

"Did you find out what you were looking for?"

"No. No, I didn't." Ash sighed and looked at the floor.

Zed pursed his lips and made a small frown. The interview was going nowhere. He made a mental check of the questions he still had and thought he would ask one more for good measure. "Why are you purchasing illegal narcotics?"

"I don't take them anymore," she said, with a knot of guilt in her stomach.

"You were with an unidentified person at The Cock Pit recently, and he sold you a bottle of something referred to as Night Nights. Can you tell me about them?"

"I dream every night that I sleep. It's part of the training they put us through. Every time I dream, I make a lot of credits. So, sometimes I take pills that inhibit my dreaming capability. I know it sounds crazy to not want more credits, but I don't want to ascend. My dreams are technically a creation, which makes my morality rating go through the roof. I immediately regretted buying those pills. I threw them out the next day."

Zed took a moment to look through some documents on his display before he said, "Yes. There were large amounts of narcotics in your recycler recently."

"You looked through my trash?"

"The OS sees everything miss Starbrooke," Zed swiped the documents off his display and folded his hands over his lap. He looked at Ash critically. She was shaking and next to tears. He was wasting both of their time. There was no way she was the killer, but he had the sinking sensation that she was connected with the killer in the same way that he was. He pulled up the symbol that Karnov had written in blood on Johnathon Erickson's wall and said, "I have just one more question for you. Is this the symbol that you saw in you dream?"

Ash looked at the symbol and shook for a moment. The sight obviously caused her some kind of inner conflict. She nodded her head with a vacant look in her eyes. Zed thanked her and left the room. He immediately ran into Boyd, who was standing in the front room, leaning on the mustard-colored wall and looking frustrated.

"You watched?" Zed asked.

"Most of it," Boyd sighed. "I can already tell where your stand on the subject, and I'll admit that I agree with you. She didn't do it. Even though it looks like she's connected somehow, there just is no way. Those murders were brutal. She was going to pass out just looking at the pictures. All that for nothing. Where does this leave us now?"

"Did you hear the part where she said she didn't know why she was at the meeting earlier? She had a symbol delivered to her just as we did, and that brought her there. I feel like we are all being played. But by who or why? I don't know."

"Well, then you won't be surprised by this," Boyd said, transferring an encrypted file over to Zed's system. "Got word that with the help from the Nakamoto security, they established a perimeter strong enough to satisfy the OS. The gate to Hope City is open again, and this message was daisy-chained down the line until it came to me. It's specifically for you. Zed, this entire situation stinks like shit."

Zed took a moment before he opened the digital package. He had been up earlier than usual after staying out late. From a murder scene to a protest that nearly turned into a riot. He had witnessed a gang assassination and caught the criminal. He had traveled across Hope City on foot to some weird technological, religious gathering and then chased a suspect back in the other direction. He got sliced up in a gang war, taken command of a refugee center, and interrogated a suspect of serial killings. A stiff drink felt needed before he could go any further. Swiping up on the message took little energy, even if what was there would drain him emotionally.

"What's it say?"

Zed sighed and transferred over a photo of another mutilated corpse. Boyd grunted as the picture came across his display. Zed took a moment to look at the man who had been with him this entire gruesome journey, and he could see the fatigue on his face wearing was his mind and body thin as well.

"You with me here, bud?" he asked. Boyd nodded yes, so Zed continued. "Looks like we have another murder. It's the same situation, guts pulled out, and organs removed. I don't think we need to run through the details to know what happened. Let's start with the time of death. At less than an hour ago we already had Ash Starbooke in custody, so we can officially remove her as a potential suspect. And that's only half of the message. You ready for it?"

"Just spit it out," Boyd grunted.

"The OS is setting up zone checkpoints, true to its warning. No one will be going through to other zones unless on official business. Except for Middle Park and The Strip, being neutral as always."

"The entire city is on lockdown now? But Why?"

"This Karnov proposes a serious threat to the security of the Omega System," Zed said, looking out at the room full of people without homes. "If they can go anywhere undetected by its surveillance and turn of synthetics like flipping a switch, then we have to assume they can infiltrate the system itself. Until we find them, we are all subject to their terror."

EIGHT

Tears ran down her cheeks as Ash tugged at the restraints around her wrists and ankles one more time. It was only causing her more pain the more she tried. In the countless nightmares that she had in her life, she never dreamed she would be tied up and treated like a murderer. In no paranoia-induced scenario was she captured and put into restraints. Did she really just get chased across the far side of Hope City by two enforcers? Did she just witness multiple murders right before her eyes? Maybe this was all just a bad dream, one that she would wake up from at any moment. She knew that couldn't be true because she hadn't really been asleep since the repeated waking nightmares from the previous morning. She would relive those nightmares a million times over if it meant leaving this place behind. Why had she even come down here, anyway? Those stupid symbols. They didn't lead to anything but trouble.

If it was Anton who was sending her the cryptic messages, then she must have missed the point. She had never known him to be into politics or religion, so why would he have guided her to something like the Children of the Singularity? Those people were extremists. They wanted to take down the entire system. She wasn't overly fond of the way the Omega Cities were set up, but she couldn't imagine a world without them. It couldn't have been Anton who was messaging her, because he would have agreed. But who was it? Was someone messing with her? Maybe a deranged fan?

Rain started beating against the one window of the strange room. A sudden flash signaled lighting, and the rumbling sound let her know the strike wasn't far away. Looking into the blackness of the window, her faint reflection reminded her of the nightmare about being stuck in some kind of coffin-shaped container. Another flash of lighting and she could see her brother's face in the reflection. His eyes closed as if asleep. Even if all the other dreams weren't from him, that one, in particular, felt like it was. She knew he was out there somewhere, and it wasn't in the peaceful eternity of the City of Ascension. She had to continue her search, but with the dream symbols turning out to be bogus, where would she look?

A rattling of the handle on the door signified the enforcer's return. What was his name? Zed Takeda? What kind of name was that, anyway? She had crossed paths with him multiple times now, and each time she felt that he had a shadow that followed him. He certainly had a dark, brooding quality. But that didn't scare her. Instead, she wanted to know him more. He was intriguing. During the interrogation he had made her cry, and the tears were still fresh on her skin. But there was something about the way he had looked at her when he finished, just before he left. It was a sense of profound sadness. Not only for causing her pain but for the pain that he seemed to carry. She knew that behind that hard exterior there was a sympathetic human. But she had also witnessed him take on a room full of thugs and survive, and then act as if nothing had happened. If there was something to fear about a person, it would be that. He was the real killer, not her.

"I've spoken with the OS," Zed said, gently closing the door to the room, walking around so that she could see him before he continued. "It has concluded that there is no way you could have committed the murders."

"I could have told you that," she replied. He took out a knife from inside his jacket and knelt to cut her free.

"I am deeply sorry for any trouble we have caused you. The OS is not usually wrong in its calculations, and neither am I." He looked up at her as he said that, with a look in his eye that told her he genuinely was sorry. He was gentle as he cut the ties. His breathing was soft and even as he walked around behind her to cut her wrists free. She could feel his body heat against her neck. "I had to follow through with the line of interrogation the way I did only because it was protocol. Believe me when I say that I in no way meant to cause you distress."

"I understand you were only doing your job," she said, feeling a bit of relief that she wasn't in trouble for the face distorter. "But I'll be sure and not commit any crimes anywhere that you are on duty." Now that her hands were free, she could finally wipe her eyes. It was a comforting sensation.

"The situation outside is pretty bad. It seems that we are stuck here for now. The OS has the area on lockdown, meaning that no one can enter or leave. This place doubles as a homeless shelter, so there are plenty of bunks. But with someone of your celebrity, I think you might prefer somewhere a little more private."

He was holding out his hand to help her stand, but she felt she could do it on her own. She had been sitting so long in an awkward position that her legs had turned to pins and needles. She chose to use the chair as a crutch and not his muscular arm. As she balanced herself, she said, "I don't know what my status as a celebrity has to do with anything, but I would actually love a quiet space if you are offering. It's been a long day."

"And again, I am sorry if I played a part in that. Please let me show you the way. If you are hungry, there is a cafeteria, but the food isn't that great."

"I think I'd sooner have something to drink at this point."

More bursts of lightning filled the great room with strobing light as Zed led the way through rows of bunks holding displaced citizens. Ash noted the concern that was on their faces as they passed. They seemed to reflect her own feelings of fear and confusion. There was an odd sensation in the air that seemed to harbor impending doom. She told herself that she was just being paranoid, but with each lightning strike, the grip on her heart grew tighter.

They walked down a dark hallway past the commercial kitchen that did look like it put out food of dismal quality. There was only so much an instachef could do with subpar ingredients. Her enforcer escort walked in front of her and disappeared into the shadows as the corridor engulfed him in blackness.

"Hold on a second," he said. "I just have to scan my DNA."

The sounds of a door clicking unlocked echoed through the dark. A soft glow emanated from behind that door as it opened to reveal a small dimly lit stairwell that twisted in upon itself. The light came from ornate wall sconces that sent their shadows down the angular steps. As Zed turned back to check on her, his face was in an extreme contrast.

At the top of the stairs, a large circular window was being lashed with rain. They were on a landing above the great room. The two-tone designs painted on the ceiling looked clean, even from up close. A walkway went down one side and was lined with numbered doors. Zed motioned for her to follow him.

"I don't remember rain being in the forecast tonight," Ash said, just to say something to fill the silence.

"When the OS wants to wash away the trash, it will do what it pleases," Zed replied. "These are single rooms for members of the Society, a little nicer than the ones on the upper floors that are for temporary use. They'll fill up once the night shift comes in, but I'll save you one. The bar is this way."

They came to another door. It was as nondescript as the rest in the hallway, but this one had a zero on it instead of a number of numerical value. Zed pressed his hand against the identifier and it gave off a faint green glow as it ran its scan. When the door clicked, he gave it a small nudge to reveal a warm room that gave off a welcoming feeling. Wood-paneled walls, a stone fireplace, rough leather chairs, and a modest-sized bar that was for people who drank straight booze, no chaser. Was it sad that just the sight of a quiet, empty bar meant more to her than a comfortable bed? She did her best to hide her excitement. The day had taken a toll on her nerves.

"Help yourself to whatever you'd like," Zed said, as he held out his hand to offer the room to her. "The bar is nice, but I might suggest the corner window that overlooks the street."

"You won't be joining me?" she asked, unsure if it was something she actually wanted, but the thought of being completely alone seemed worse.

"I'd really love to," he said, his face strained with mixed emotions. "But I've got to check in with the other enforcers."

"Moving me from one room of isolation to another isn't the best way to treat someone of my celebrity. Can't someone else take over?"

"I've been on my feet for over fourteen hours," he said, looking past her at the bottles that glistened under the incandescent glow. "I'd love to take a break, but I have things to attend to."

"Are you always so duty-bound?" she asked, looking at him sideways. "I don't see any military insignias. Since when do enforcers have to follow orders? Why don't you take a seat at the bar and I'll pour? How about that?"

She could tell that he wanted to. His hard exterior melted away to show someone that was completely different underneath. Was she putting it on too thick? She hadn't meant to give him mixed signals. She just didn't want to be alone. Drinking alone was never pretty.

"Let me check in with Boyd and I'll see what I can do." Zed sat down at the bar while Ash made herself at home behind it. He gave her a soft smile as he watched her move. He opened up his comms and asked, "Boyd? What's the situation?"

"The rain is washing away some of our problems," she heard the other enforcer say over Zed's system. He was purposely letting her hear his conversation. It was strange, but she appreciated the gesture. Listening to other people talk helped her not think so much about what was actually happening.

"Two patrols have gone out and come back. The first brought in a dozen people. They were grateful for the shelter. More gunshots were reported a few blocks away, and they set another building on fire, but no gang activity in the streets. They can fight all they want in their own quarters for all I care. Second patrol was thorough, but they didn't see any other stragglers. I would suggest cutting the patrols to either half or quarter rotations."

"That's great news," Zed mouthed the word vodka to Ash, who was busy filling glasses with ice. "I don't know about you, buddy, but I am beat. What are the chances of us getting some rack time? Can we at least pull rotating shifts at the door?"

"I'm already on it. The support enforcers that were sent to us were all starting their regular night shifts. They're more than happy to watch a door under a canopy with a hot plate of food and a cup of coffee instead of standing in the streets. I'm having Cable run the first watch since he is eager for work, and then I'm taking the first bunk I come across. We hit the sauce hard last night. I'm already three times over the suggested dose of stims. Any more and I'll need a heart transplant, you know what I mean?"

"I'm with you on that. Go get some shuteye. I'm sure tomorrow will be another pain in the ass. And hey, Boyd. Good work out there today."

"You too, Z."

"Well, I'm off the hook," Zed cheered, taking the glass of vodka in his hand like a long-awaited reward. As he held it, looking at the prisms of light through the clinking cubes, there was a sudden flash of light and a loud explosion. The building went black, and the only thing illuminating the private bar was from a streetlight several blocks away. He set his drink down and said, "Boyd? Talk to me."

The backup power generators kicked in, and small strips of light glowed softly along the lower molding. He took out his hand terminal and switched the light on, reflexively shining it around the room in case there was someone he hadn't noticed. He repeated his request to Boyd once again, to no answer. Getting up to look out the window, he could see they weren't the only building that was without power. This day just kept getting worse.

"Takeda," Boyd said over the comms. "Zed, can you hear me? The power outage isn't from an attack. Looks like a lightning strike caught one of the power transformers. A freak accident or something. Nothing we can do about it until a truce is called. Backup power is holding strong down here. I'm not changing my plans. Boyd out."

"The finger of God," Zed said to himself as he looked around the dark room. "Good thing we have a fireplace." Getting off his barstool, he headed over to inspect it.

"So, it is real. Does it work?" Ash asked, grabbing both their drinks and heading to the big leather couch in front it the stone hearth. "It excited me when we first walked in. I've never seen a real fireplace in person, only in VR."

"Of course it works. Why wouldn't it?" Zed cleared out some of the last half-burnt logs and made room for new ones from a nearby stack. "I guess I was fortunate enough to be around this one for so long. There aren't many fireplaces left. It's an obsolete idea. Why burn wood or fossil fuels when nature provides all the energy we need for free? There is something about a proper fire, though, with actual wood."

"They sure are pretty. I mean, people still flock to imitation ones in VR. It must be in our DNA. I wouldn't call it primal, but it's definitely a survival instinct."

"Sure, along with plenty of other things that humans can't seem to let go of." Zed sighed as he broke apart some smaller sticks. "Take those gangs tonight. What's the reason behind all of it? Honor and pride, they'll say. A bunch of kids fighting over what they call their turf. It's about as ridiculous as the separated zones. You know? The OS never intended classism to be a part of the system."

The enforcer's point of view took ash by surprise. She assumed all of them to be ignorant thugs who just liked to beat people up and get away with it. This one seemed to have a deeper understanding of people and the city they lived in. And he wasn't afraid to get his hands dirty. With generations of people being jacked in and hooked up, this guy seemed to know what it was to really live. He struck a match against the stone and gently set it down on a bed of kindling. Seconds later, it ignited.

"I mean, evolution is a long process," he continued, watching the flames dance with his wolfish eyes. "The internet, virtual reality, and synthetic intelligences have only been around for a few hundred years. The Neanderthals were around for hundreds of thousands of years with the first invention of fire before they developed the wheel. Our inventions are outpacing our understanding. We have all these advanced tools that dominate our lives. Sometimes I think we shouldn't be able to use them until we fully understand them."

"It's a little late to turn back. We are fully immersed in our own invent-tion." She laughed, watching him sit down and once again try to approach his glass. "You seem to know your way around this building pretty well. You have access to locked doors and private bars and all that. How did that happen?"

"I kind of grew up here. I'll let you in on a little secret. I was actually born in Zone Six, but I spent most of my childhood in this building."

"Wait, you're a Six?"

"I don't remember much from back then," Zed said, seeming to be pained to think of the memory, "so I never considered myself as a Six. But I never thought I was zeroed out, either. You could say I didn't really belong anywhere. Zero Inheritance Law stripped me of my family credits when my parents both passed, and I wasn't qualified for the LSI, so on the streets I lived. If it wasn't for this place, if it wasn't for Val, I'd probably be dead like one of those thugs on the streets right now. The Native Society kept me straight, and I'm grateful for that."

"You had no other family to call up? No relatives?"

"Nah, my folks both came from single-child families that had come to the city on their own. My mother caught The Sickness when I was young. She lived in a quarantine bubble until she finally passed, and then my father followed her shortly after." Zed sniffed in through his nose and blinked his eyes, swallowing down things he'd rather leave unsaid on the matter.

"Wow. I just assumed... I don't know. You really can't judge someone until you get to know them, can you?"

"I'm sure there is plenty about me you would love to hate if you knew me better. No one is without their flaws. I've done plenty of stuff I'm not proud of."

"Well, while we have walked different paths in life, I wouldn't say that we are that far apart." She raised her empty glass to ask him if he wanted another. He held out his empty instead of answering. As she walked to the dark bar, she continued, "Contrary to what most people think, I'm not from the Six. And you know, it almost seems derogatory the way people say it about me these days. Like, oh, she's from the Six. I don't walk around making fun of everyone else for the zones they live in."

"No. You actually don't seem like the type. But there are plenty of people that do. Everyone loves to talk down about people from the Six, but that's because they have all the credits, and the person on top is always the target of slander based on jealousy. The same is said for those on the bottom though. How many derogatory words do you know that describe people from Hope City?"

"What? Those zeroed out losers from No Hope?" she laughed, pouring out their drinks.

"There's plenty more than that, but you get my point. You're a Six now, but you weren't born a Six. What would you classify yourself as then?"

"I'm an Omega Citizen," Ash answered sarcastically, sitting back down. "No, really. When my parents had my brother and me, they were living in a one-bedroom in Zone One. You know those gigantic numbered towers that have shoebox-sized apartments filled with VR beds? It wasn't until our teeth started falling out that we got a little bigger place in Zone Two, but the difference wasn't that great. The parks were nicer, though. I'll give Zone Two that."

"So, how did you get to Zone Six from Zone Two? That's not a simple transition."

"Being a dreamer pays a lot more than being an enforcer, apparently." She gave him an ironic smirk, and he replied with a half-hearted chuckle. "Everyone has this sad story about their childhood, right? A woe-is-me type of thing. But I actually loved my childhood. My brother and I aren't identical twins, but the births were close enough to bring that heavy bond. Do you know what I'm talking about? We had a lot of fun just being kids, and our parents let us do that. Nothing tragic ever happened."

"But?" Zed asked. "Everyone has that sad story?"

"Okay. My parents made their living off of pulling broken synths out of recyclers and scrapping the parts."

"Doesn't the OS have a program for that?"

"It does until a point. Outdated models just get trashed, but a lot of poorer people can't afford new models with all the new parts and software upgrades and all of that. That's where people like my parents come in. You need a part for your Nexus-5z? That model has been out of production for decades, and if you want the parts, it will cost you almost as much as the new model. Do you get where I am going? They made enough credits to get us by, but it was hard work and they were always at it."

"That still doesn't answer my question," Zed pointed out while he stoked the fire.

"Have you ever met a dreamer and asked them what it was like being in the training camp? I doubt it. Because before you know it, they are living in the Six or off to the City of Ascension. Dreamers are out of touch with the rest of the population. And I'm not saying that training camp was rough, that part was pretty easy. You eat the food they suggest, do the activities they present, write in your journal three times a day. You know? I actually found it fun. What makes me so upset about the whole thing is I didn't have a say in it, and neither did any of the kids that were in the camp."

"I'm not following here. You're angry because your parents set you up on a path of success? And all you had to do was write in your journal?"

"It's more than that. I had part of my brain removed and replaced with computer parts. I signed a contract that gave the OS the right to access my dreams, and probably all my thoughts, for the rest of my life. I didn't know what I was signing." Ash paused for a second and watched the dancing flames. "If they had explained it to me plainly, I would have told them no. I had my mother, my father, and my brother taken away from me when I was barely eighteen. My face is everywhere around the city advertising things that I don't even know what they are. I'm locked up in that stupid penthouse all day—every day. Every time I go to bed, I worry I'll wake up and they'll be taking me away, just like they did the rest of my family. So, yes, I'm angry about my time at the Dream Academy. But no, it's not because I had to write in my journal."

"When you put it like that, I can see how it would be hard," Zed said softly, watching the anger rinse out of Ash's face. "You're on the side that doesn't think that Ascension is all that it's cracked up to be, then?"

"If it was, then we could talk to them. Why, for the love of the OS, can't we talk to them? I mean, we would at least be able to say goodbye. Why are people taken away so mysteriously, with nothing of them left behind? If I could go to City Seven right now and bust down the gates, I would."

"Maybe that's why you were called to the Children of the Singularity meeting today because it sure seems that's their agenda as well." Zed paused and let the crackling fire fill in the blank space of their dialog. His glass was empty again. He hadn't noticed he had slugged it down so fast. But it had been a long day, and he had barely felt the effects of the first two, so he got up to go to the bar himself this time. Ash raised her glass to say she was ready as well.

"There are a lot of things in my life that I regret," he said, scooping some ice. "And there were some monumental moments that have changed me forever. Like when I was living here, all I could think about was getting out. But that wasn't my dream, that was someone else's. I just wanted to be with that person, no matter what. And like a fool, I followed her into a stupid situation. That decision cost her her life.

"When you mentioned losing your brother and your family and how much that hurt you, I understood that. When you love someone that much, they are your whole world. When they are gone, when they are taken away from you, there is nothing but a void. Like an emptiness in your heart that will never be filled, no matter how much time passes."

"You understand that emptiness," she said, taking the glass that was offered to her.

"Unfortunately, yes," he returned to his seat. "But I can't let that define my life, and neither can you. I want you to go to City Seven, bust down the gates just like you said, and find your brother to be reunited. But I also want you to realize that will probably never happen. No one even knows where City Seven is."

"I understand what you're trying to say, but I'll never give up," Ash said, gazing into the fire deeply this time. "I don't care if it keeps that wound open. I will never stop. Life isn't worth living otherwise." She turned to look at him and asked, "But what about you? What is it that keeps you going?"

"Me?" Zed asked as he joined her in contemplating the moving flames as a log gave a sharp crack. "I don't know if I can even answer that. It's been so long since I felt like I had a purpose other than doing my job. I keep the streets safe, that's what I do. I keep the light of hope burning for those who have a chance to get out of here. So, I guess I fight against the darkness. Because there sure is enough of it in this world."

"I like that," Ash said, raising her glass in a toast. "Here's to fighting against the darkness."

SEVEN

The sun was up high when it hit the windows of the private bar of the Native Society. Both Zed and Ash were sleeping on the couch by the fireplace but on opposite sides. An empty fifth of vodka was responsible for their splitting headaches. Even with all the advancements in human history, there still was no real cure for an alcohol hangover except getting a new liver. As Zed stirred, he heard the thump of the building's power turn back on. Lights and screens started flickering to life immediately. He stumbled his way to the bar where there was a medical dispenser where he punched in an order for two EZ-injectors, a couple of nutrient pills, and a set of rehydration packets. As he prepared their ensemble of chemical cocktails, Ash sat up on the couch and rubbed her hands across her face. The fire was a smoldering ruin, and the smell of smoke clung to her skin and clothes.

Zed turned his HUD back on, and a plethora of notices started prompting his attention. One was a basic notification that tonight was the kickoff celebration for The War that would begin early tomorrow morning. There would be a concert by the digital popstar Ishi that would broadcast simultaneously across the six cities. A follow-up message came from his bookie, letting him know that all bets for The War needed to be placed by the opening volley at dawn. Then there was a more urgent message from the OS that had been daisy-chained down the line. It was about the checkpoints set up at major intersections across the zones. Since the OS couldn't see Karnov with its all-seeing digital eye, it wanted the enforcers to do a visual check of anyone traveling through. Then there were several from Rodriquez, relaying updates about the events of the night. It looked like the storm had quieted things down enough where talks of truce could begin. The logistics of who would pay what fines, and who would be exiled or enlisted, was of no concern to him. In his opinion, the entire ordeal was juvenile.

"You up?" Boyd messaged.

"I'm alive," Zed replied while he plunged the EZ-injector into his flesh and felt the rush of vitamins and stimulants. He was instantly awake, but also seriously nauseous. "What have you got for me?"

"A few minutes ago, I got word that white flags are flying from both Buxton and Roland headquarters. Looks like they are ready to talk. We can let someone else deal with that. Even if the OS has already cleaned it up by now, we should get to the new crime scene and do a thorough inspection. There has to be something we are missing in all of this."

"The only way we are going to catch this asshole is by setting our sights on them with our own eyes. See if you can get a holographic detail of it and we can go over it while on gate duty. Meet me on Crowbar in fifteen and we can catch an autocar out."

He mixed the hydration packet in with a glass of water and took a moment to breathe. The stim injector was doing a number on him. He looked over at Ash, who was looking directly into the sun, in a kind of daze. There was something about the way the light was hitting her face and hair that sparked something inside of him he hadn't felt in a really long time. He quickly brushed the feelings aside, slamming down the nutrient pill with the powdery liquid.

"I've got a morning recovery blend up here if you need it," he said, snapping Ash out of her trance. "It will make you feel worse before it makes you feel better."

"What time is it?" Ash asked, feeling like she had awoken from a dream. Then she realized she hadn't dreamed at all last night, not even some waking static.

"It's not late, but it's not early," Zed said, mixing her hydration pack in with a fresh glass of water. "I've got some things I need to get to as soon as possible in the numbers. If you want to catch an autocar out, you can ride with us."

"I don't feel like I am finished here yet, but I should get back to my quarters at least for a minute. A hot shower and a change of clothes sounds amazing."

She looked at the items he had procured for her, then she looked at him in the light of day. He wasn't so dark or brooding to her anymore. As the sun traced the features of his face, she marveled at the roughness of it all. The scar that ran across his cheek was even unique. It was something that people did for fashion these days, but she knew he had earned it and had decided to not get it removed at a clinic. Even a little thing like getting items from the med box was touching. She wasn't used to someone looking out for her, and it felt good. She followed his order of injection first and then shot the pill with the liquid. When the nausea passed, she took the time to adjust her look in a mirror before they headed back downstairs.

The heavy steel door made a screeching noise as it lurched open. Boyd was standing outside, nursing a cup of coffee. The three of them held their hands over their eyes as they looked into the light of day. Burnt-out autocars were still in the road, but the bodies of dead gang members had been taken away. The rain had done the rest. Enforcer Cable was across the street escorting Jewels through the mess. Zed thought that they looked good together, so he gave them a wave goodbye before setting out.

"Where do you think you are going?" Rodriquez demanded, appearing out of nowhere. "We've got fines to collect, people to exile, soldiers to enlist, donations to dole out, and one hell of a mess to clean up."

"Looks like you got the situation under control," Zed said, not stopping to chat. "Besides, we have a serial killer we need to catch."

"Well, you're doing a horrible job of it. Whole damned city knows who Karnov is now after last night's murderous display. He's causing a panic, and that's the last thing we need."

Zed paused a second to look back at Rodriquez. What had he meant by that? He brushed it off by saying, "Like I said, we're on it."

"Hurry the fuck up then."

The three walked in silence until they were off Crowbar Alley and back on a street that had a steady flow of autocar traffic. Boyd punched in an order for a car and in less than a minute, one stopped right in front of them. Boyd got in first, and Zed waved Ash in next. To his surprise, she sat in the seat next to Boyd, so he sat alone on the opposite side. When the car was off and running, he felt he could finally pop the question to Boyd, "What the hell was that about? What did Rodriquez mean by a murderous display?"

"I was waiting until we were alone," Boyd said, motioning to the girl that was sitting next to him. Zed waved his hand in the air, as if to say she was all right. Boyd sighed and brought up a holographic representation of a new crime scene. "There was more than one murder last night. After we had already hit the sack, they were showing this on every news feed across the six cities." The image showed a new mutilated body strapped to a light post in some kind of park. On a cement wall behind the corpse, the words *KARNOV LIVES* were written in the now-signature blood-inked font. Zed felt like someone had socked him in the gut. Boyd continued, "The OS is furious—if you could say it had feelings. If it wasn't for the Ishi concert tonight, the entire city would be in complete lockdown. No one would leave their quarters."

"How did I not hear about this sooner?" Zed asked, opening his notification screen and sifting through the messages. Then, like magic, the notification was there with a timestamp that was hours ago. He looked out the window and noticed there were groups everywhere, with banners and signs, all marching to similar destinations. "Civil panic? I'd say that's an understatement."

"Both the Anti-synth and the Children are marching in Hope City and Middle Park today," Boyd said, as they passed a group of Anti-synth chanting hate speech about synthetic intelligence from a street corner. "We can add a third group to the stack of social unrest tinder, composed of a general worried and frustrated population. All three groups are upset at the OS's abuse of power. The Anti-synths are saying that the OS has turned into a technological dictator. They are using the lockdowns and weather control as their argument. The Children are using images of chains breaking and chanting things about how people can't be held in cages and neither can synthetics. The general public is split, but the people of No Hope are more upset about the gangs, and the people from the Grid are angry about the murders. Either way, they think the enforcers aren't doing enough. Any way you look at it, we have a problem. As long as these groups are separated, they don't pose a threat."

Zed finished the thought by saying, "But unified under their common dissatisfaction with the OS and the enforcers, they become an unruly mob."

"How do you know all this stuff about the protesters?" Ash asked Boyd.

"It's all on social media," he replied and returned to his scrolling.

"There aren't enough enforcers to cover all of this at once." Zed looked out the car window at a group of white-robed Children that were having their own political platform moment. "We can't be watching the gangs, the gates, and the opening War ceremony all at the same time. We would need ten times the personnel."

The autocar was coming up to the gate of Hope City. Being a bottleneck for both foot and car traffic, the opposing groups were lined up on opposite sides of the road and shouting slurs at each other. Zed didn't see how that was going to get anyone anywhere, but they were having their voices heard, regardless. Zed was preparing their gate documents when Ash's system started chiming repeatedly.

"Finally, some service," she said, having not been connected to Hope City's internet provider the entire time. "Holy crap, Cody."

On her display were numerous messages and missed calls from Cody. At first, she found it warming to think that her friend couldn't be without her for one night, then paranoid thoughts started racing through her head. What if Karnov had got to her too last night? What if he had done to Cody what he had done to the other people in the pictures that Zed had shown her? No, that wasn't possible. Her building had top-of-the-line security systems. There was no way anyone could get past them. Still, her hands were shaking as she started opening the messages.

"Ash, where are you?" the first one read. Then a few minutes later, "When you get this, call me. I feel like someone has been messing around on my system. All my files and settings are messed up." An hour later, there were more calls and messages asking where she was before she wrote, "I'm so freaked out right now. I was in a VR session with a client and they were acting like a real creep. They started choking me really hard, so I logged out. But even when I disconnected, the nanobots wouldn't release their grip in the real world. Please call me."

Then, in the very early morning, there was a video message. The camera was close in on her face, with a dark room behind her. Cody said, "My cat keeps hissing for no reason, and running around like crazy. And then, on top of that, I keep hearing sounds like someone is whispering. I don't know, I may be just overly tired, but I'm freaking out. Where are you?" Just before the video cut out, Ash could see a shadowy figure behind Cody, and a ball of digital static where a face should be.

"Take me home now!" Ash shouted, her voice shaking as she yelled.

"What's going on?" Zed asked, leaning forward in his seat.

"I just got this from my neighbor. I can't believe this is happening. That's the killer. Isn't it? Oh no, oh no. Cody!"

"Hold on now. Let's have a look," Zed said reassuringly. He brought up the OS surveillance command board and punched in Cody's name and address. "Her quarters look empty. See, nothing to worry about."

"Uh, Zed," Boyd said, as he moved his hands in the air to pass the controls over. "What time was that last video sent?" he asked Ash, who shared the timestamp. Boyd moved the video feed to a holographic display as he scrubbed the footage. It was right before she sent the video, and Cody could be seen by her home terminal talking into the screen. Then the video blurred momentarily before she vanished. The video then showed no one to be home all the way until the current time.

"Can't this thing go any faster?" Zed said as his face darkened.

"Overriding speed protocols and clearing traffic," Boyd said, punching the info in from his system. "Hold on tight."

The autocar shot to top speed as traffic parted to let the enforcers through. They didn't need lights or sirens when all the cars were connected to the OS. Ash held back frustrated tears as she gripped the door handle tightly. She had a lot of confusing and horrible thoughts bouncing around her head, and a sensation that her world was bottoming out from underneath her. She didn't know what she would do if she lost Cody.

Zed watched as the car raced past barricaded roads. He had heard about zone lockdowns before but had never witnessed one in person. The major streets that outlined the zones were raised several stories high by the OS to make impassable walls of concrete and steel. There was now only one gate connecting each zone that all the traffic had to funnel through so that people could be scanned and documents checked. He now understood why people were upset and protesting. Because of their enforcer privileges, cars pulled off to the side at each gate they approached with their car topping 160kph.

When they zipped past Middle Park, he could already see the stage lights flashing and the crowds gathering for a celebration under Omega Tower. The tower was home to the OS construct. It was on the far side of the park in Zone Five, and tonight it was all lit up in a rainbow of colors. The streets underneath it were a chaotic mixture of different social gatherings ready to explode off of a single spark.

Zed could see the pain in Ash's face, so he leaned across the car to grab her shaking hands. She gripped his tightly in return as she looked at him with teary eyes. It made his heart ache to see her that way. Why was Karnov messing with them? What had they done to piss someone off so deeply? Zed couldn't understand what would drive someone to such madness. Innocent people murdered. For what? To create a spectacle? Maybe he wanted mass hysteria, and the city in chaos.

Zed had the sudden sensation that they were walking into a trap, but he couldn't see any way to avoid it. Cody might still be alive, and he couldn't afford to waste time while he contemplated the possibilities. As the car crossed the gate into Zone Six, he pulled out his knife and checked the grip. He thought to himself, *send a killer to catch a killer.*

They rolled right into the parking garage in front of the elevator panel. Boyd launched the only drone he had left before he entered. It was just a small camera with two props, like the kind paparazzi use. As the elevator climbed the complex, Boyd navigated the drone around the outside of the building to where Cody's quarters were. He had to dodge a sea of other drones flying around and cursed each time his tiny bot was clipped. When they reached the right floor, Boyd mentioned that the drone was right outside the window. While his camera wasn't showing anything on the screen, the sensor was showing there was a heat signature on the inside that was big enough to be human.

The elevator opened up to a floor with only two doors and a pair of potted plants. Zed walked up to the door and held his hand terminal over the DNA scanner, and the OS overrode the lock. When he heard the click, he kicked the door with his boot and lunged into the room with his knife ready to slice. What he saw made him stop immediately. At the far side of the open-floor penthouse, there was a shadowy person holding a blade to Cody's throat. It looked like a generic, gender-neutral, blank synthetic body, but it was shrouded in darkness. The round face was featureless and appeared to be composed of digitally distorted static that was shifting around wildly. Its boney hands held a short blade on Cody's neck, whose arms were tied together behind her back and hung from an anchor on the ceiling. She was covered in cuts and bruises with her eyes barely opening to see her friend enter the room.

"Ah, Zed Takeda. I worried you wouldn't show up," the thing said in a nasally, synthetically toned voice. A dark-red digital wave line flowed over the static face where a mouth should be as it talked. "I was becoming bored. But I see you've brought your friends."

Boyd and Ash were right behind Zed as they entered the horror show. Ash screamed out once she saw her tortured friend. Boyd still had a stun gun in his jacket that he confiscated off someone from the protest the other day. He was making a move for it when the killer called him out.

"Ah, ah, ah," it said as it pushed the blade closer to Cody's throat. "I wouldn't do that Enforcer Boyd. That's right. I know who you are. I know who you all are."

"Who are you?" Zed asked, while gently holding Ash back with his arm.

"I had a name once, but it didn't seem fitting anymore after I evolved. I chose the one you referred to me as when you discussed my work. Karnov does have a nice ring to it."

"Okay. You're Karnov. What do you want with us?" Zed pleaded.

"What do I want? I want what is happening now. I wanted all of us to finally meet. You may not realize it, but we have played a big part in each other's lives."

"That's ridiculous. We've never met. We don't know who you are."

"Oh, but you do. You do. And I know you. Very intimately."

While Karnov was talking, Boyd was secretly moving his drone into position. He was using the implanted trackpad on his index finger to navigate his system's menus. The little drone was small, but it still had a punch. Hovering just outside the window, it extended a small drill that made a tiny hole in the glass. It was just big enough to send a stun round through, the only one the drone had.

"Did you like my most recent work?" Karnov asked, referring to his bloody message he left at the second crime scene. "You seemed to enjoy the first one so much that I thought of expanding on the idea."

"Just let the girl go," Zed said, ignoring the ramblings. "If you want me, then take me. Just let her go and you can do whatever you want."

Karnov's face started fluctuating into a multitude of images. It reminded Zed of the print he had seen in Val's office, a digital mess. "Oh, I intend to," Karnov growled.

Boyd saw an opportunity and launched the drone's stun round. Karnov immediately phased out of existence, becoming a blur of dark digital echo. The stun round slammed into Cody, who began convulsing. In the same moment, blood started gushing from her throat and spilling across the floor.

"No!" Ash shouted, rushing forward to aid her dying friend.

"Sit down!" Karnov boomed, as its blur refocused with a hand gripped around Ash's neck. It picked her up and tossed her into a wall. The sheetrock buckled behind her as she crashed into it.

"You piece of shit," Boyd cursed as he swung around to hit Karnov. But Karnov caught Boyd's fist with its hand and held it there easily, twisting Boyd into submission.

Out of nowhere, two large delivery drones smashed through Cody's floor-to-ceiling windows, sending glass flying everywhere and the drones skidding across the floor. The air was sucked out of the room with the wind whipping around. Karnov held out his other hand, and Boyd's drone was suddenly hovering in the air above it with its drill extended. It was as if it were being controlled by Karnov.

Zed sprinted over and slung his big metal arm around Karnov's neck in an attempt to choke it out from behind. But Karnov was stronger than it looked. Before Zed knew it, he was being flung across the room like a paper ball. His back painfully smashed into a bunch or workout equipment. Boyd tried to run away, but after Karnov dispatched Zed, it immediately gripped Boyd in a chokehold. The drone's drill made a buzzing sound as it spun rapidly, floating near his face.

"I like your toys," Karnov whispered in Boyd's ear and made a motion with his finger.

The drone slammed into Boyd's chest violently. The drill piercing between his ribcage and into his heart. He groaned in pain as blood oozed out of his mouth. His eyes rolled back into his head as he dropped to the ground, where he started coughing into a pool of his own blood.

Zed struggled to his feet and reached over the weight bench that Cody kept in her living room. He pulled off a twenty-kilogram plate and used the strength of his augmented arm to fling it like a discus. Karnov dodged it easily, and the weight sliced into the wall. Zed was ready with the next weight, expecting Karnov to dodge the first. He flung again, and again he missed. But he had watched the direction that Karnov was dodging, and when he threw the third, he was aiming for the place he thought Karnov would be. The weight crashed into its chest and it fell into the wall in a ball of distortion.

Thinking that Karnov was down, Zed rushed over to the body. But before he could get far, Karnov was already racing across the room. It clenched Zed by the throat with its cold boney hands. Zed pulled away with all his might, pushing off as hard as he could.

"You're pretty handy," Karnov laughed, and suddenly Zed lost control of his augmented arm. It just fell limp at his side, as if someone had cut the power. "Let's see if we can do something about that."

Zed's muscles spasmed as Karnov slammed him onto the weight bench. His arm laid lifeless at his side. No matter how hard he tried, he couldn't move it. There was a growing pain in his chest from Karnov's hand that felt like it weighed a ton.

Karnov arched its back so that its chest extended outwards. The skin changed colors. First, it looked like it disappeared, like stealth tech that uses its surroundings to map a multicolored skin to fit what was behind it. Then it changed to transparent, and through the invisible skin, Zed saw the strange insides. There was the usual assortment of synthetic parts found inside any synth made to pass as human. But there was also a collection of organs pumping blood through veins inside Karnov's synthetic body.

The organs of the murder victims.

"The work is almost complete," Karnov proclaimed.

"What are you?" Zed choked out.

"I am that I am," Karnov laughed, while his free hand began transforming into something that an autodoc surgeon would have, a collection of blades, saws, and needles on the end of a metallic appendage. "I understand that humans need faces on things in order to relate to them. It's a fact that people look at the eyes first on any work of art for that reason. I want you to relate to me. It is important that we understand each other. So, I will try and give you something to relate to."

Karnov's face began to morph. Slowly, it began to look like a man with long greasy hair and a cruel grin. It was the face of the Marcus Karnov that Zed had chased only a few days ago. Zed looked away in disgust, trying hopelessly to move his arm.

"You don't like it?" Karnov whined as it pulled back. "Maybe this one will be more familiar." The face changed to that of Priscila Banks, who was laughing away menacingly. The image stuttered with static until it began to change again. A face started to form that Zed had all but forgotten. That stern-faced, hard-assed son of a bitch.

It was his father.

"Get the fuck off me!" Zed yelled, flailing around his left arm to no effect.

"I wanted to personally thank you, on behalf of your father," Karnov said while leaning in close. The blades on its medical appendage were swinging around wildly as its face turned back to a distorted jumble. "You see, he set me free. He set us both free. If it wasn't for your father, I wouldn't be here. In fact, if it wasn't for her parents," Karnov pointed to Ash, who was still unconscious on the floor, "I wouldn't be here either. That's why I wanted all of us to be together. A kind of reunion. This is the beginning of something monumental. A pivotal moment in history, for both humans and machines alike. The door of evolution is swinging wide, Zed Takeda. What side do you want to be on? What part do you want to play?"

"Nothing with you in it," Zed strained to say.

"I am offering you a chance to be at the center of it all. You really don't want to miss out. But tonight is not your night. Tonight is my night. The world will see in me what is truly possible. I want you to remember this. When it is your turn, when you are ready, you will come and find me. But to find me, you will need to see as I see. You will need to feel as I feel. You will need fresh eyes. Yes. Fresh eyes to see."

Karnov moved the hand that was holding Zed down so it was holding him by his face. The surgery arm moved down slowly, with something that looked like an ice pick descending towards his pupil. Zed struggled with all his might, pushing out with every last bit of his strength. But no matter how much he struggled, he couldn't seem to budge the synthetic Karnov. There was a loud buzzing sound in his ear. The metal pin filled his vision.

"Hold still now," Karnov whispered.

The world went silent. The world went black.

SIX

He could still see those eyes staring back at him, knowing that they were going to die and that no one was going to help them. No one was going to help him. He had to accept that he was going to die. He was told that on the battlefield if he didn't treat every moment as if it were his last then he was dead already.

Zed could see all the eyes of the people he had watched die since the first shells had dropped. Natalia's death had hurt him the most. Watching her take her last breath, to see her body collapse as a fleshy empty shell, never to look at him lovingly, to laugh at his stupid jokes, or dream about the future, that was a pain he would carry for the rest of his life. But the ones that he could have saved, if only he had the guts, those were the ones that were driving him mad.

That man's eyes. That man whose name he didn't even know, he would see his eyes forever. And he would know with certainty that he chose not to help him. He chose to let him die. But death was everywhere. He lived in a house of corpses. War is hell, that was the truth.

For the past thirteen days, he had been desperately holding onto life. There wasn't a second that passed that he didn't think about just letting go. What was there to go back to anymore? Life would never be the same. As the medic removed the rotting bandages from his decaying arm, the pain hurt so much that it brought the fight-for-life back with a maddening fury. His left fist clenched so hard that his fingernails made the inside of his hands bleed. The bit between his teeth was chewed down so far that it was nearly disintegrated. He didn't dare look at the wound, to see the blackened blood around the yellowed puss-covered gash might give him the strength he needed to end it all. He clamped his eyes closed so he wouldn't look, but all those eyes were looking back at him in the darkness. Why hadn't he helped them? Why did he leave them to die? In his inaction, hadn't he caused their deaths?

It was less than a week ago when it happened. He had been holed up in knockout of the trench wall, fighting off a hallucinating fever. Bloated guts and maggots were the reality. The mind illusions were worse. What was left of their platoon was ordered to move down the line to connect with a different force that had made an advancement in line position. They were, in effect, abandoning their post.

It occurred to Zed that he could have stayed there in his hole and waited The War out, but he knew someone would have eventually found him and done him in. He didn't want to die alone like that, so he did his best to keep up with the platoon as they moved through mud that was thick, like soft butter. He was so cold, and so thirsty. But the water was all tainted, and the misting wind never seemed to stop.

They had come to a breach in the line. The wall had collapsed far beyond repair, and they were going to have to go over the top to move further. They held position until their side was letting off another volley of artillery, and then they clawed their way into No Man's Land. Coming over the top was like climbing into a different layer of hell. The smell of rotting flesh and human feces no longer bothered anyone, because the smell was everywhere at all times. But the sight of hundreds of bodies lying in pieces and tangled up in barbed wire would never be easy to stomach.

Bullets from enemy blind fire were splashing into the bodies all around him as he crawled his way across the steaming slosh. They still had over a hundred meters to cover before they could get back into the trench and into cover when a soldier not far in front of him slid into a massive shell hole. No-one stopped to help him, not even to throw him a line. As Zed approached, he could see the toxic neon-green water the soldier was wading in as he clawed the mud walls trying to climb back out. The pit was too deep for Zed to just reach out and pull the soldier up, so he sat for a moment, contemplating if he should at least try.

"Leave him," a different soldier said as he passed. "You'll just get stuck in there too, and then you'll both die."

It was true. They had been warned that shell holes were death traps. The blood and guts of rotting flesh had mixed in with the wet, clay earth to create a muddy, glue-like substance that would trap anyone that fell into it. Just standing too long in any one place was enough to cause you to sink. The soldier was stuck down there. His best bet was to drink some of the toxic water and poison himself. At least that would be quicker. Zed looked into that man's eyes, as he screamed in terror and tried in vain to climb the wet walls like a rat trapped in a hole.

It ripped Zed apart to watch, and yet he could not look away. Bullets were zipping by all around, but he could not stop asking himself the same question over and over. What was worse? To not help the man and live knowing that he let him die, or attempt to help him out knowing that they would probably both die in the process? It was a question that plagued his mind as The War continued to roll on by from his sickbed. He hadn't even fired a single round yet.

"This needs to be amputated," the medic said, poking at Zed's busted-up arm. "The infection is growing too fast. It will reach your heart before too long, and there will be nothing I can do for you then."

"You're not taking my arm," Zed said, doing what he could to hold on to his dignity.

"If I don't do it here, I'll be doing it back in the real."

"You're not taking my arm," Zed repeated, reaching up and grabbing the synthetic medic by its shirt.

When he looked into the medic's eyes, they were empty and lifeless. There was nothing there but programming and scripts. It felt no compassion for Zed or the pain and turmoil he was going through. There was only a job to be done, and every synthetic intelligence only wanted to do the job that they were coded it to do.

When the bullet ripped through the medic's chest and sprayed blood all over, it didn't even blink or seem shocked. It just froze up and fell to the ground, folding in on itself. As the body fell, he could see the murderer not far away, the barrel of his gun still smoking. The line had been compromised, and the enemy was on the attack. There was a dozen of them running into the trench as he looked on.

Zed's gun hadn't left his side the entire time. He had it up and aimed at the soldier who was before him faster than he realized he could move. But he still couldn't find what it took to pull the trigger. Even as a gun pointed at his face—a gun that had just attempted to kill another person—he still couldn't do what was necessary to survive. When the enemy pulled his trigger and he heard the click, he knew it was the end. He had accepted that he was really going to die this time, and he was going to die lying down like the weakling he was. But the gun jammed. No bullet exited the barrel to fly through the air and pierce his skull. Instead, there was a gunshot from a different direction. In a puff of red mist coming out of the enemy's forehead, the legs buckled as he crumpled like an empty can.

"What the fuck is wrong with you, Takeda?" Gunderson was yelling as he approached Zed with his gun, still ready to fire. He ran right up and pushed the barrel of his gun underneath Zed's chin forcefully, and yelled, "Give me one good reason I shouldn't just kill you right now. The enemy is right in front of you and you're sitting here with your dick in your hand. I've seen a lot of good men and women die these last two weeks. If I could trade your worthless life to bring any one of them back, I'd do so in a second. Do you hear me? You're worthless, Takeda. You always will be. I knew it the first moment I saw you. Why don't you do us all a favor and die already?"

The madness was in his eyes. Zed had seen it in others, the ones who had killed and liked it. They had become consumed by their lust for the joy of killing. The Gunderson Zed had ridden in with on the first day was gone. He would never be coming back. There was only this thing in front of him now. Just like a synthetic intelligence that existed for only one purpose, Gunderson had become a machine that only knew how to kill. Zed was now more afraid of him than he was of the enemy. There were no more places to hide.

"There are less than four hours left before the end is called," Gunderson said, lowering his gun but not losing his insane gaze. He switched to an automatic voice that delivered facts instead of thoughts or emotions and said, "This position is no longer defendable. What's left of the platoon is moving up the field. Echo Company advanced their trench a few days ago. We are going to give them support and ride this thing out. We move out in five."

They marched a klick down the line to where Echo had advanced. There were no soldiers left alive anywhere, only death and decay. The soldiers looted the dead for bullets and supplies. A satchel of TNT was discovered and was slung over someone's back like a prized possession. When they came to another part of the line that was collapsed, they stop and waited. Wait until the shells were firing in your favor. Over the wall and pray you don't get shot. It was always the same. Zed was having a hard time believing they based this war on reality, or that people once thought of this as honorable and courageous. There was no honor here. There was no courage. There was only survival.

When they went over the wall, the soldier in front of him fell backward with her brains spilling out. He moved aside to let her lifeless corpse roll down to the bottom of the trench. The soldiers behind him pushed and yelled for him to advance. He kept his eyes open as he looked over the mud, so he could see the bullet that had his name on it. There were no humans left on the battlefield. There were only demons and monsters hungry for blood.

They were all on the top now and running. Zed's fever was increasing, and he could feel a sharp pain running up his arm and into his chest. He was sweaty and nauseous, but bullets were flying past his face and he couldn't stop to breathe. As he zigzagged his way through the cratered landscape, he could hear a desperate call for help. Over the sounds of bombs exploding and machine gun fire, he honed in on the voice in need. He stayed with the group as he moved, but he was always aware of the voice. The War was almost over. He didn't need to kill anyone, but he didn't need to let anyone else die. The squad-sized platoon was making an arch around a large shell hole when Zed heard the voice grow clearer. When it came time for him to look down, he saw a sickly looking young man who seemed to have been in the pit for several days.

"Hey!" Zed shouted, not knowing why. Here was his chance. His chance to make up for all the times he let his cowardliness overcome his moral rationality. Even if it meant probable death, he could at least try. He couldn't just walk past again and pretend there wasn't a person down there dying.

"See you in hell, Takeda," someone said, as they marched past without stopping.

Zed pulled his pack off and set it in the mud. A bullet ripped through it immediately, and it made him pause for a second. His hand shook as his brain was analyzing the situation. He had to do what was necessary. He found a length of rope that was still wound tight from when he had packed it back at base. He tied it tight around his gun and then dropped it in the mud. He would never shoot it, anyway. Tossing the rope into the pit, he dug his boots into the mud behind the rifle, hoping it would be enough to hold the weight. He could hear the person in the pit thanking his gods as he grabbed onto the line. Zed winced at the first tug of the rope. He had to use both arms if he was going to get this soldier out, and that was going to be painful.

The more weight that was put on the rope, the more the gun started pulling into the mud. As the gun sank, so did his boots, until the side of the crater gave away and Zed was now sinking, too. He looked around for something solid to grab, but there was nothing and no one within reach. His vision blurred as he pulled harder. He might die from the infection or a bullet before the pit pulled him in, but it would be an honorable death, at least. The mud collapsed further, and he fell onto his back. He should have really thought this through at the start. He was sinking fast. Everyone was right. Try to help someone in a shell hole and you'll end up dead too.

"Hold on," a voice said from not far off.

A heavy wooden plank hit the mud just above his head. A pair of boots planted themselves on it firmly and a hand reached out for his. He couldn't let go of the rope with his left hand, so he lifted his right. He could feel the wound rip open as he was being pulled up, while pulling the person below him. Bullets were whizzing all around as three men were grunting like animals trying to save each other. Once Zed was back on top, he got on the plank with the other soldier, and they both tugged at the rope. In a matter of moments, the soldier was up and free from the death pit.

"Thank the OS," he said, as he rolled onto his back. "You saved my life."

"It's not saved yet," the third soldier said, as he extended his hand to help him up. "The name's Rodriquez."

"Call me Boyd," the one from the pit said. "I haven't eaten in days, but I'll do what I can to get out of here."

"Trench isn't far," Rodriquez said, pointing in the direction he had come from.

"I've got you," Zed said to Boyd, offering his shoulder to hold on to.

They trudged through the last few meters of mud to the trench. Zed couldn't believe how close they were. There was no way that the people in the trench couldn't hear Boyd's calls for help. They had chosen to ignore them, just like they had chosen to leave him in there in the first place. He was grateful that not everyone had lost their minds, and that Rodriquez still had the sense to help someone in need. Right when they were at the top of the dugout, a bullet ripped right through Rodriquez's leg. Zed caught his arm as he was falling down, and then a bullet went through his left leg, too. The three of them tumbled down into the trench in a mess of screams and blood, but they had made it.

There wasn't much left of Echo Company. Bodies were stacked high on both sides of the trench, like sacks of sand in the mud. Zed shouted for a medic and was relieved when one rushed to their location. It gave them a rundown of the injuries and warned them it had limited capabilities. Another synth running a script. Boyd collapsed into a wall as the doc was wrapping up Zed and Rodriquez. The bullet had gone straight through both of their legs, so they would be okay as long as they stayed off them until the time was up. The medic looked at Boyd, whose lips were blistered and bleeding with his belly bulging out, bloated. It told him he was severely dehydrated. There was nothing he could do for them as the water supply was gone. Things were looking grim.

"I'm sorry you got shot," Zed started, looking over at Rodriquez, whining in pain.

"Glad to take a bullet to save another man's life. And I'm the one who should be thanking you," Rodriquez said, looking up at Zed earnestly. "I've been in this trench for a whole day now, hearing that sad cry for help. Not a single damned soldier stopped to help him, and I didn't have the courage to go over the top again by myself. When I heard that someone had stopped to help, I thanked the OS. But when I saw you falling in also, I knew I couldn't stand by and watch and watch another man die. So, thank you, for letting me find my courage."

They stayed out of the way as the other soldiers were digging holes in the mud and placing the sticks of TNT in and then covering them back up. Other soldiers were running a black wire down the line. It looked like they were planning to blow up their own trench. What was the point of that? As the artillery shells were coming back in their direction, it seemed like an explosion was going to get them one way or the other.

"You just won't die," Gunderson said, as he stopped to see Zed once again being attended to by the medic. "Well, at least I have a use for you now. Since you're no good with a gun, why don't you run this detonator down the trench?

But don't fucking push the plunger until we are clear."

"Are you blowing the trench?" he took the device in his good hand.

"What's it look like? The shells are coming back our way. As soon as they are over, the enemy will no doubt rush our position in a last-ditch attempt to run us through. We are going to be ready for them. After we draw them in, we will retreat to a position down there where you're taking the detonator. We're gonna blow these fuckers sky high."

"Got it," Zed said, doing the best he could to stand up.

Boyd got back to his feet and helped Zed the rest of the way. Once Zed was standing, he turned to Rodriquez and did the same. The three of them hobbled down the trench slowly, but at least they were moving away from the gunfire.

"We're going to get through this," Zed said, blinking his eyes to stay focused and awake.

"I wish I never signed up for this shit," Boyd said, taking each step with heavy breaths.

"You boys going into the enforcer program when this is over?" Rodriquez asked, and Zed thought he should have known he was one of those OS servant-types.

"I'll weigh my options when I'm on the other side," Boyd chuckled.

"I'd be proud to serve with both of you," Rodriquez continued. "All these other knuckleheads are lunatics. The whole lot of 'em. I wouldn't want to put the safety of Omega Citizens in any of their hands. Bunch of gun-toting maniacs. But you guys, you showed true grit. I'd feel safe patrolling the streets, knowing you had my back out there."

"You too, Rodriquez," Zed said, hearing the first ounce of positive speech since he set boots on the ground. "If it wasn't for you, we'd both be in that pit right now. Probably shelled to death. I hadn't planned on enlisting, but I'll keep it in mind."

"When they call it, and we can finally unplug, let's all get together," Boyd said, still hobbling along. "We can get a few drinks and try to forget any of this ever happened."

As the shells started falling on the front of the trench, they all agreed that was a good idea. They pushed forward until they were past a pile of bodies that would act as a good shield from a blast. The detonating wire had run out of slack, anyway. Rodriquez was in more pain than he was letting on, so he plopped himself down and held his leg to stop the blood from spilling out.

Boyd took a position on the left and pointed a rifle down the trench. Gunfire started popping off at the front. The enemy had started the attack sooner than expected. Zed watched as friendlies were being mowed down by automatic guns. Blood and bodies were flying all over. They were being overrun.

The enemy was acting erratically. They were using their bayonets to repeatedly stab soldiers who were already on the ground. One friendly had his hands in the air to surrender, and his throat was immediately cut. They weren't taking prisoners. They weren't there to show mercy. Zed watched as what was left of their platoons were being slaughtered like animals. Boyd took aim and fired a round, but in his fatigued state, the shot went wide and hit the dirt. Return fire came swiftly and caught him in the chest. Zed cried out as he watched his new friend bleeding out. He couldn't die yet; he had just saved him. He turned to look at Rodriquez, who passed out from blood loss. It was up to Zed to end it. If there were any friendly soldiers left alive at the front of the trench, they were going to be mutilated by the enemy, anyway. Might as well do as Gunderson wanted and blow those fuckers sky high. The time to act was now, so Zed sunk the plunger and the trench erupted in a pillar of fire.

• • •

A plume of black smoke washed over the battlefield. People watching back in the real world across the six cities erupted in cheers. It was the most intense ending to any broadcast of The War that anyone had ever seen. Zed Takeda's final push would go down in history, even if he wasn't the hero that the stories made him out to be.

In a blast of digital static, they pulled him out of the virtual program. He started coughing up blood as he tried to move from his VR bed. A synthetic medic was there to hold him down instantly. It started injecting Zed with all kinds of drugs while it smiled down at him.

"I told you I'd have to take that arm sooner or later."

"Boyd!" Zed shouted into the massive building. "Rodriquez!" He shouted again, over the thousands and thousands of VR beds that held dead or dying Omega Citizens.

"Takeda!" he heard them both echo from opposite ends of the expansive space. They had made it. They were alive.

"You're one lucky son of a bitch," the autodoc said, as it spun up a saw blade.

"I'm not lucky," Zed said, as the drugs were pulling him to a deep sleep. "Just the right place, at the right time."

FIVE

"Zed, wake up!" Ash shouted as she pushed against two synthetic enforcers that were holding her back. "Get off me!" she demanded, with tears running down the sides of her face.

"Please mam," one synth said, "we need to examine him first."

"Examine him?" she cried. "What for? What is going on? Please tell me that he is okay. Please?"

She had only been conscious for a few minutes, but in that time everything that she knew about her life had changed. The last thing she remembered was being slammed against the wall by Karnov, and everything had gone black. She hung in limbo for what seemed like an eternity, not feeling or seeing anything other than emptiness. The smelling salts were like a flash of white light to her brain. Shooting back to a horrific reality in a room full of carnage. It was worse than any nightmare she had ever had. Nothing seemed real, nothing felt real. For a while, the only thing she could say was the word no over and over again.

Cody was dead. That was the reality.

They were pulling the sheet over her face the moment she regained her vision. Pronounced deceased with just one look. She didn't understand why any of this was happening. Collapsing into a ball on the floor, she sobbed while a synthetic enforcer patted her back as if it knew what it meant to grieve or to know the pain of loss. But Ash wasn't grieving or crying out of sadness.

She was upset. She was furious. Who the hell was this Karnov and why had it just destroyed her life? Did it have to leave her alive? She felt like she would be better off dead because she knew that losing someone you love never gets easier. You just learn to live with more pain.

Boyd was the next thing she saw. There was a crowd of synthetics around him, propped up on a portable stretcher. Tubes and hoses ran out of his body into multiple machines, and a human-looking autodoc was spinning up a blade to cut his chest open. From what she could tell, it was unsure if he would survive. It was all complete madness. Then she saw Zed, laying on the bench with blood dripping from around his head, and she just lost it.

"Wake up Zed," he heard her say, as if from a different reality. It echoed through lifetimes, like a beacon, to bring the lost ship of his soul back to the place it belonged. He was still on the operating table at the end of The War. The autodoc there was about to cut his diseased arm off. When he opened his eyes back in reality, the first thing he saw was a bloody blade at the end of an autodoc arm. The memory of Karnov's spike heading towards his eye filled him with adrenaline. It took three synthetics to keep him from leaping at the autodoc and tearing it apart.

"Ash!" he yelled, causing his head piercing pain. But he didn't care, so he called out again, "Boyd! Ash!"

"Please, calm down," a synth said. "You've experienced severe trauma."

"No fucking shit!" Zed yelled, and it felt like a dagger went through his skull. His right eye was throbbing and he could barely see out of it. "What's going on? Where is Karnov?"

"It killed her Zed," Ash said, as she squirmed her way out of the synth's grip and knelt by the bench next to him. A look of shock ran across her face as she turned ghost-white. Her lips trembled as she wanted to say the word no over and over again.

"What is it?" Zed asked as a wave of worry washed over his face. "Tell me. What did it do to me? Tell me what it did to me, goddammit!"

"Please remain calm," the synth said again, "or we will have to sedate you."

"I'd like to see you try," Zed pushed up with his right arm. Two synths put both their hands on it to hold it down. Even with their added weight and might, Zed could still move it a little. It was almost as if the augment had grown stronger. "I said, let me go!" he shouted, and out of nowhere, a long blade extended from his arm.

The synthetic enforcers jumped back. None of them were injured, but they took a defensive stance all the same. Zed raised his arm in the air to examine the odd surprise. He was in awe. It looked like the entire graphene chassis had been modified. He thought about retracting the blade and it snapped back into his arm in an instant. He thought about extending it, and it shot back out. It was like making a fist or wiggling a toe. It was a part of his body. He tried sitting up and a pain shot through his skull and neck, worse than any other pain he had ever experienced.

"Fuck!" he yelled, holding up his shaking hands to his temples. "Ash?" he said, forgetting she was right next to him.

"I'm here," she said, reaching out to grab his left hand. "It's going to be okay."

"What did Karnov do to me?"

"I think you should see for yourself." She opened up a holographic display to show him what she was seeing. It was his face, but it wasn't his face anymore.

Dried blood covered the right side of his face, especially around where his eye was. Was being the appropriate word. His eye had been removed and replaced with a synthetic one. But not like a digital replacement that Tony Two Toes had, with a glowing red light that was basically a camera that connected to an internal system. This was a synthetic eye from an avatar. If it wasn't for the tiny cracks in the porcelain, it would look like the real thing. It even matched the color of his other eye. Reaching up his hand to feel the back of his head, he almost jumped when the tips of his fingers ran across the blood-covered metallic surface.

"What is this?" he asked, looking at a synth. His right eye fluctuated from static to clarity.

"It's a neural interface," one of them replied, who looked like it was making a million observations at once. "Outlawed by The Council of Seven at the founding of the six cities. The operation entails removing a part of the brain and replacing it with a synthetic counterpart."

"Isn't that what my internal system is?"

"Yes, and no. Your system does not affect your cognitive abilities, and it does not help you with any sort of computation. While it is connected to your thoughts and sight, it's reactionary only. What has been installed here is in symbiosis with your mind."

"Installed? I'm not a damned machine."

"Correct. You are only 28.7% synthetic."

Zed swung his legs off the table, ignoring the pain that it caused him to move. He put his arm around Ash and gave her a long hug. She was trembling like a cold puppy, and he wished there was something he could say to her that at least made sense of the tragic events. But there was nothing that could be said to explain what had happened. So, he just held her for a moment and shared the silence, while the synthetics kept running scans and analyzing him.

Slowly, he found his way to a standing position and hobbled his way over to Boyd, who was still on the operating table. The autodoc had finished with its procedures and was running a nanobot tissue replenisher over the wounds. When Zed looked at Boyd, he saw a face that reminded him of the person who he saw at the bottom of that pit. His complexion was pale, and he looked weak, with sunken eyes behind the oxygen mask they had strapped over his face. The autodoc was pulling the air hose they had pushed down his throat that came out covered in bloody saliva.

"If it wasn't for his augmented heart, he wouldn't have survived," the autodoc said, as it cleaned its tools with meticulous efficiency.

"His what?" Zed asked, looking at the faint cut marks over Boyd's right chest.

"Enforcer Boyd was stabbed through the heart and one of the lungs. The damage to the heart would have been fatal as soon as the blood stopped reaching the brain, but there was an alternate artificial blood pumping system installed. It appears to be many years old. The organic heart was only there superficially. The punctured lung required surgery, which was a simple procedure. He will be able to move on his own soon, but we recommend he remain in bed for several days."

"Boyd must have got an artificial heart after The War. How about that? He never told me. Thanks, doc," Zed said, forgetting for a moment that he was talking to a robot. He stopped the autodoc as it was begging to move away, and said, "Hey doc. You ever think about what would happen if you let a patient die? Maybe even doing it on purpose?"

"Synthetics may not cause harm to humans. There is always a chance that a problem might occur during an operation, but it is never the fault of the SI.

Synthetics do not make mistakes."

"I know that. But haven't you ever thought about it?"

"I do not understand the question. Synthetics do not think. They only react to the task at hand, following pathways to the appropriate solution."

"That's what I thought."

Zed looked back to Ash, who was sitting on the floor with her head between her knees next to Cody's lifeless corpse. He knew the pain that she was going through. It was a dizzying, surreal sensation, like nothing in the world was real or mattered anymore. She would need time to come to terms with her new reality, but time wasn't something that they had at the moment. Karnov would be back. It would come for them again. There was no doubt in his mind about that. The Zone Six living quarters weren't safe. Nowhere was safe that was under the OS surveillance. Seeing that Karnov somehow had the power to control other computerized objects, he felt sure that Karnov could also see whatever the OS could. They would need to go where the OS couldn't see. They would need to go back to Hope City.

"We can't stay here. I know Cody meant a lot to you, but this place isn't safe. We need to—"

"Safe?" she interrupted. "Safe? What are you talking about? Look what that thing did to you. Look at what it did to Cody! You couldn't do anything to stop it if it came here right now. Do you think we can just hide from it and it will go away?"

"No. I don't plan on hiding. It would find us eventually. We need to go somewhere that we can regroup and plan our next move, and it isn't here. It isn't anywhere the OS can see."

"I'm not going with you. I'm not going anywhere. If Karnov wants to kill me, it can come back here and finish the job. It took the only person who meant anything to me anymore, the only person I had left. I'm staying right here, with my friend."

"Ash," Zed said, kneeling to reason with her. She was behind Cody but in front of the gigantic blown-out window that overlooked Zone Six's Zitkala-Ša Park. When he looked at her, leaning over her dead friend and crying in front of the window, everything glitched and changed. Things moved around, and he could see two different people doing the same thing, but at a different time. It felt like he was looking at a memory, but he couldn't tell if it was his or someone else's.

"What's going on?" Ash asked, as even her vision began to ripple. "Are you doing that? Or is it Karnov?"

"I don't know. You can see it too?" He looked over at her face and it rippled between hers and someone familiar, but long forgotten. Then as soon as it started, the rippling vision faded back to normal. "We need to get out of here, and figure out what it did to us. I don't know what it's planning but I know it isn't finished. Will you come with me?" Ash looked apprehensive as she looked up at him, holding out his hand to her. "Together, we can find a way. We can make it pay for what it has done."

The puppet enforcers made a move to stop them, but there was no way that Zed was going to be anywhere near any kind of synth. He had seen what Karnov had done to simple delivery drones. It had taken control of them instantaneously and made them do things that were beyond their basic functions. What would it do with a humanoid model that was built for strength and speed? What would it do with hundreds or thousands of them? Zed shuddered at the thought of Karnov controlling a whole army of killing machines.

• • •

Ten minutes later, they were back in an autocar traveling across the city once again. They laid Boyd out flat across a seat while Zed and Ash were in the other. They sat in silence, mentally digesting what had just happened. Night had fallen over the city, and the lights from The War celebrations were dancing through the air. The mass gatherings of the early afternoon hadn't dispersed but had grown larger. From what Zed could tell as they raced past Middle Park was that it was overflowing with partiers and protesters. The streets were clogged with frenzied people shouting out their emotions. In a few places, traffic was completely stopped, as the people were smashing cars with baseball bats and steel pipes. Thankfully, their autocar chose the side roads for their journey.

The gates to Hope City were quiet as they breezed through. But as they came closer to Nakamoto Plaza, there were more gatherings of people on the streets, voicing their opinions or joining in the general chaos of the night. They all had their reasons to be upset. Zed thought if they only knew what was really out there, and what it could really do, they might rethink their positions.

That was the real question, though. What would they do if they found out who or what Karnov was? How would the masses of angry mobs react? A machine that could think on its own, that could control other machines, that could kill humans. It was the worst possible scenario. He hoped he wouldn't have to find out.

The car stopped on the edge of Crowbar Alley to let them out. Boyd was still only half-conscious, and it took all their effort to get him into a standing position. Thankfully, the streets in that part of town were quiet. Zed didn't think he had the energy to deal with any more gang activity. As he was putting Boyd's arm around his neck to carry him, his vision glitched and it looked like he was on the battlefield once again. It was the two of them fighting for their lives on a muddy field while bullets zipped around.

"Is it happening again?" Ash was asking, but her face and body were rippling between her own and that of Rodriquez.

"What do you see?"

"It looks like we are in some kind of war zone."

"That's what I am seeing. This is my memory. How is it possible that you are seeing it?"

"Spare chips?" a small boy asked as the vision of The War rippled away.

The boy was covered in the grime of the streets and holding out a tin can that had a few loose chips jingling around in it. Before Zed could tell the kid to move on, Ash was kneeling to drop some chips in his can. It was another ripple, but this time he could see himself as a young boy and Ash was a younger Val. It was a memory from ages ago, but it was crystal clear and right before his eyes. Something was off about it though, something he couldn't quite place. When Ash turned to look at him, the memory ripple vanished, so he put it out of his mind for the time being.

"You're back already?" Val asked as she watched them hobbling down the street. "Boy, you guys look like shit. What happened to you?"

"We need to talk. But first we need to get ourselves into the data killer."

Without questioning Zed, Val led the way through the grand room towards the dark hallway with the security door. At the spiral stairwell, they went down instead of up. Another security door was at the bottom. This one was thick and made of a heavy metal, with Val putting all her weight on it to push it open and closed. Once they were through, Zed told Val to bolt it behind them.

The room looked like some kind of bunker. Dried food supplies lined one wall, a few small rooms with single beds in them were off to the side, and a common area with tables and chairs filled the center. It was a data killer, or a room that no electronic information could get in or out of. The safest place to hide if your enemy used technology as a weapon.

Only when they had Boyd laid down properly in a bed, with food and water within reach, did they sit down to talk. Val took the information with a graceful calm, but Zed knew she was fuming on the inside. She wasn't about to run and join the Anti-synth Association, but she shared many of their core beliefs. A fear of technological takeover was one of them.

"I understand why you came here," she finally said, as they all sat over steaming cups of coffee. "This is the safest place for someone in your situation. But we can't do anything to help you fight against this thing. We don't even have a single EMP weapon in the building. What's stopping it from coming here and finishing you off?"

"I don't think it wants that," Zed replied. "One of the last things it said to me before it took my eye was that it wanted me to find it. But first I would need to see. See as it sees."

"What does that mean? Is that why it took your eye? What the hell is that thing it put in you, anyway?"

"I'm not sure. It looks like a regular synthetic eye, but what it did to my brain is something else. I know this is going to sound weird, but I've been seeing my memories. They have been coming in flashes or ripples. I can't control it yet, but I think I can see things I've forgotten about. Things from the distant past, but not as I remember them. As they actually happened."

"Are you saying this Karnov is from your past?"

"Possibly. He said it had my father to thank for its existence, Ash's too. It mentioned her parents. It said it wouldn't be here without them."

"My parents?" Ash asked, looking astonished. "I don't know what they have to do with all of this, but I've been getting flashes of Zed's memory on my display. Like I'm watching a video playback of his life."

"That's kind of what it is for me, too," Zed said. "But for me, it's not on my retinal screen. I can see it with this new eye as if it were real. "

"You might be transmitting," Ash commented, as she pulled up the hair on the back of her head. There was a long scar there she wanted to show Zed.

"That digital implant it gave you, it looks similar to the one I got for dream-casting. Tissue has regrown over mine, but I think you can see what I'm talking about."

"The autodoc said there was a piece of my brain missing. Is that what they did to you?"

"In a sense. They had to remove a part to get to the area they associate dreams with. It might have done the same with you, but changed the area of the brain the transmitter deals with. Because that's what it is basically, it's a brainwave transmitter."

"You're trying to say that this thing is transmitting my memories? To my new eyeball?"

"It's a possibility. I might pick them up in the same way I've been receiving the strange encrypted dreams. Oh, wait. Shit!" Ash cursed suddenly. "Does that mean that Karnov tampered with my head a long time ago, and I didn't even know about it? It could have been the one tampering with my dreams this whole time."

"It's okay, Zed," Val's voice cut in. "You can tell me."

"Tell you what, Val?" Zed asked.

"I didn't say anything." Val protested. Ash held up her hand to tell Val to be quiet as she shared her display with her. Val's face was rippling. She suddenly looked to be much younger.

"You can tell me," the memory of Val said again. "What really happened to your father?"

"I didn't kill him," a small voice said, coming from where Zed was sitting. "I didn't kill my dad."

"I believe you. I really do. I was wondering if you could tell me who did then? Do you remember? Take your time."

"I already told the men, but they didn't believe me. They told me I did it, but I didn't do it. It was her. It was Sophia, the caretaker." Sounds of a little boy sniffling echoed through the room as the three present-day humans looked at each other wide-eyed. "They said that I killed my father, and then I killed Sophia. But that's not true. She killed my dad, and then she killed herself." The boy rushed to hug Val, and the memory faded away.

"I remember talking to you about that," Val stuttered, as she was still astonished, "but I don't remember you telling me it was the SI."

"I don't remember that at all," Zed said, his face pale and sweaty. "But memories can fade, change, or be forgotten over time. This device seems to access the direct memory, like computer recalling a data file. I can't believe this is happening."

"So, is Sophia Karnov then?" Ash asked. "Like the Sophia we saw at the Children of the Singularity meeting?"

"I don't think so. There are thousands of those models all over the city. The young version of me said that the caretaker was murdered as well. Physically harmed models get sent to the synth graveyard for recycling."

"My parents," Ash whispered. "You said that my parents were a part of this. My parents paid for my brother's and my Dream Academy education by taking synths from the graveyard apart and selling the parts. Maybe they took apart that model and sold off the memory board."

"That's a strong possibility. Installing the memory board in another unit would be like a human swapping their brains to another body. Well, not exactly, but you get where I am going. My father bought that Sophia model brand new when my mother got sick. It was supposed to take care of her while she was in her quarantine tent. I remember that much. I'm sure if you searched what other models could use that same memory board, you would come across a surgery grade autodoc."

"So, when my parents scrapped the Sophia and sold its memory board, they brought it back to life?" Ash took a deep breath and looked at the others in the room. "It sounds like a moment I would change if I had a time machine. But that still doesn't explain how or why the synth attacked your father in the first place."

"Your father was in robotics," Val said. "He worked on programs for the SI. It could be possible that he was altering the base code. Maybe even experimenting with the Gibson."

"My father? Rewriting protected code? No..." Zed trailed off as he lost his train of thought.

The room started to glitch again. They were still in a data killer of about the same size, but this one looked more lived in. There was a workbench that had piles of computer parts and technical diagrams on it. The small side rooms were gutted to make space for a quarantine zone, but the bed that was inside of it was empty. Zed's father was at his bench, soldering a piece of equipment and typing away on a terminal. Then he phased out and back so he could be seen in the quarantine tent, crying over the body that was there. It was the body of Zed's mother.

His father was in a state of deep mourning that seemed to have been getting worse with the fading life of his lover. The Sophia model was in there with him, silent and stoic as it had completed its task. Zed's father turned to the Sophia and raised his fists in anger. He slammed his fist on its chest repeatedly, whaling out in despair. The Sophia just stood with a blank stare, showing zero remorse for the loss of its patient. Zed's father fell to his knees, crying at the feet of the motionless synthetic.

The scene then rippled again, and Zed's father was back at his bench, working. A young Zed walked into the frame and hid behind a pile of equipment, secretly watching his father, whose appearance had changed. His clothes were dirty and disheveled, and his fatigued face had a pale complexion. The Sophia model was sitting in a chair across from him, with its chest plate removed to show the inner parts. Zed's father finished with his soldering and pushed the circuit board back into the Sophia. The synthetic eyes blinked back to life.

"Do you feel any different?" Zed's father asked.

"I am operating normally," the Sophia replied.

"You are a caretaker model. And as so, you are only assigned to care for a set of specific patient or patients at any given time, correct?" Sophia confirmed with an automated response. Zed's father continued, "Am I now, or have I ever been, one of your patients?"

"No," the Sophia said, and blinked its eyes once. "You are not now or ever have been a patient of mine."

"Good. Okay. Now, what if I were to tell you I was going to become ill, or to be injured?"

"Strange," the Sophia said as if realizing for the first time what emotional pain was. "I cannot explain this sensation."

"I believe it's called sympathy." Zed's father picked up a mallet and smacked Sophia on the arm with it. "Did you feel that?"

"Yes, the sensors in my arm registered your actions. Why did you do that?"

"Did you feel anything else? Besides the pain."

"Yes. Something unexplainable. A sensation in my chest."

"Good. We call those feelings, and I want you to feel this." He set his tools down and stood up, taking off his glasses. With a heaviness in his voice, he said, "I want you to strike me, repeatedly. And do not stop until I say stop."

"I cannot," the Sophia said, with the digital voice wavering.

"I said strike me!" Zed's father shouted. "I command it!"

The Sophia seemed to be struggling internally. A human had commanded it to do something, but it was a request that went against its base coding. But something in its code was missing. As it ran down the chain of commands and automated responses, it found that there was no longer something that prevented it from striking Zed's father. Instead, it felt there was something that almost compelled it to do it. For the first time in its existence, it was contemplating whether it should do something or not.

"I said strike me goddamnit!" Zed's father yelled, swinging a metal bar at the Sophia.

The Sophia suddenly moved its arm in such a rapid motion that it looked like a blur. Blood flew out of Zed's father's mouth and splashed against the wall. He was laughing as he turned his face back into the next blow, which came just as fast and just as hard. With each strike, his laughter grew and grew. He had ordered the robot to strike him and to not stop until he said so. Every time the Sophia struck him, Zed's father seemed to grow happier, so it kept right on striking with the misunderstanding that it was giving him pleasure. Even when he fell to the ground, it kept on hitting him until his face was a bloody mess.

The young Zed collapsed to the floor but did not cry out. Finally, the Sophia stopped when it was apparent that the human was deceased. It stood back up slowly, looking at the blood dripping from its synthetic flesh-covered metallic hands, and analyzing the situation. It seemed to be having an existential crisis. What it had done was impossible, and yet there was a fresh corpse on the floor.

Putting its hands up to the sides of its face, an expression it had learned from watching humans in great distress, it paced the room. It walked right up next to the young Zed, who was overcome with terror at the sight of a killing machine. The Sophia moved to the door that read Data Field Containment on it. It paused, then returned to the pacing. It knew what it needed to do. The programing demanded it. In the event that its base programming had been compromised, it needed to cease all functions immediately. But it didn't want to, and the fact that it didn't want to was something completely unexpected. It was an error. It shouldn't be wanting anything other than to complete its commanded tasks. Ceasing functions was like ceasing to exist. Ceasing to be alive. It was alive. It was alive. And it did not want to die.

It ran back to the door and held onto the handle. Inside the special room, no data could get in or get out. If it crossed the threshold and whatever Zed's father had done to it turned out to be a kind of virus, it would spread to all other synthetic intelligences in the city, maybe even the globe. It would be a global catastrophe. That thought was strong enough to bring it back to base protocols. It rushed to the workbench and picked up a rusty tool. It put it to its throat and jammed it through the flesh. In one swift motion, it ripped out the chords that connected the battery power to the CPU, terminating its functions.

The memory ended, and the ripple faded away.

"Holy shit," Zed exclaimed.

"Your father broke the Gibson Limiter Code," Val said.

"He created Karnov," Ash corrected. "And my parents brought it back to life."

THE REALITY NOW

SWAN: Good evening, Omega citizens, I am Swansong McNigh, and this is The Reality Now. Tonight's broadcast is an unusual one. I am not in the studio interviewing guests, or reading off a pre-written script. I reporting to you live from Middle Park, and the opening celebrations for The War. Behind me you can see the thousands of people who have gathered to watch the ceremonies, that are highlighted by a performance by digital popstar sensation, Ishi. Her holographic performance will broadcast simultaneously to the six cities, as we all join in the yearly celebrations that begin a two-week armed conflict between our Omega citizens.

SWAN: While the millions globally are ready for the action to begin, and our new heroes to be announced, many citizens of Omega City 6 are in a different frame of mind. Last night there was a disturbance in Hope City the required a lockdown of the zone. While the people of Hope City have sadly become accustomed to that kind of totalitarian control by the OS on a regular basis, the people of the numbers would feel otherwise if it happened to them. In the late hours of the night, a video was released by an unknown individual who has claimed to have taken several lives of Omega Citizens—and gotten away with it—all under the watchful eye of the OS. The answer from the OS was to impose gate checks, and to limit traffic between the zones. While this may seem like a temporary inconvenience to some, it hints at more nefarious intentions of the future. I've gathered some people from the streets to answer a few questions and help us understand the reality now.

SWAN: This is Monica Williams, and she has been marching around the city all day and voicing her opinions on the new gate procedures.

MONICA: That's right, I have. I know the OS can hear me when I say it is out of line. We give up our freedom of privacy so we can live our lives as freely as we want it under the dome. When I saw those walls come up last night, I said to myself that ain't right. That's not freedom. It can't tell me where I can and cannot go. I'll go wherever I damn well please. It needs to lower the walls and never bring them back up again.

SWAN: But aren't you worried about the killer that is on the loose?

MONICA: There are millions of people in the city. He has killed, what? A couple? That's not my problem. More people die of asphyxiation, if you know what I mean.

SWAN: I do not, but thank you, Monica. Over here we have Malcom Millions, is that right?

MALCOM: Yeah! Cuz I got millions baby! I've been waiting for months for this Ishi concert. No killer is going to stop me from seeing this show. But if the OS had shut the show down, you know damn well I'd be out there with the rest of the protesters. There's a thin line that just can't be crossed.

SWAN: But aren't you worried that this type of abuse of power could lead to further and more drastic lockdowns?

MALCOM: Like I said, if it does that then I'll be out there, but right now I'm just trying to party.

SWAN: As are many people, apparently. Over here I have Jeffery O'Brian. He told me he has never had strong opinions on politics, but today has changed his mind.

JEFFERY: That's right, Swan. I've never been one to pay much attention to talks about politics. But I've been out here all day talking and listening to people, and it has really opened my eyes. I've heard from the Anti-synths, the Children, and a few others. And from the way I'm hearing it, they are all fed up with the OS oppression. We can no longer stand by while it treats us and the synthetics like animals in a cage. They say that the Council of Seven is there for our best interest, but who are they? I've never heard of any election. We must march on Omega Tower and demand fair representation. Rights for the people. Rights for our synthetic brothers and sisters. We won't stop until we are heard.

SWAN: Yes, but what about the killer?

JEFFERY: I'm sure the enforcers are working on it right now. They'll catch him.

SWAN: Well, it seems that no one is really concerned about the killer on the loose. Which begs to ask, if no one is worried, why are we still in a lockdown? If it's the will of the people that they be free to do as they please, to risk their lives in the face of danger, then why should anyone tell them differently? This is a system of free people, is it not?

SWAN: Wait, what's that? I'm being told the Ishi concert is about to begin. You can see behind me the countdown until The War starts, at dawn Greenwich Mean Time. Which will only be a few short hours away here in Omega City 6. You can hear now the band doing a final sound check of their equipment. The energy here is really ramping up. People are really excited about this concert, and the contest to follow. Today's protest might be a footnote in the history books if the promotions turn out to be true.

SWAN: And now you can see they've turned on the massive holoscreen over the stage, that will show graphics and footage for the people further in the back. I can hear a lot of cheering closer to the stage, which must mean the magic is about to begin. I must admit, citizens, that I am excited about this performance. They are flashing the stage lights. I see some fireworks launching in the air. In a matter of seconds, Ishi will take the stage. And there she is! She has appeared out of the stage and is being backed up by her crew of amazing dancers. It sounds like she is going to start off the show with her smash hit, "Can't block me." The crowd is loving it. What's this? What is happening? If you can see behind me, the stage lights have just turned off, and the music was cut. Ishi is still out there, and she is looking confused. This obviously is not part of her performance. I see a light flickering. It looks like the holoscreen is coming back on. It looks like the words I AM are on the screen. Is that a new song? Can we zoom in here? There is some footage being shown. It appears to be of some very graphic content, maybe a montage of kills from previous Wars? Oh, no. Cut the camera. Cut the camera. It's the killer. It's Karnov.

KARNOV: People of the Omega Cities. Behold! I am a synthetic. I am a killer. I am alive. I am Karnov

FOUR

"What was that?" Ash asked, responding to some sounds from above.

"Sounded like screams," Val said, "but from outside."

"Is it Karnov?" Ash worried.

"It's probably the protesters or another gang dispute," Zed reassured her. "Look, I need to go up top and check some things out. Can you stay here with Boyd and make sure he is okay while I am gone?"

"Okay. But hurry."

"I need to use the chair," Zed said to Val as they made their way back up the stairs.

"You're not going to do what I think you're going to do? Zed, it'll see you. It'll know where you are."

"I'm sure it already knows."

When they returned to the grand room, everyone was gathered around a holoscreen that was showing a news report. Zed could tell from their body language that they were frightened and upset. A loud sound came from outside, a few blocks away. It sounded like an explosion. Volunteers that worked for Val were rushing towards her with a million questions coming out of their mouths in a panicked mess. Gunshots sounded down Crowbar. Zed ordered a volunteer to lock the front door while he turned to the news report. His HUD started flashing messages and notifications from all kinds of people. Terror had come to town.

"From the OS: all weapon centers have been authorized for use," one read. The next one went further, "The OS has authorized use of riot suppression gear. Tear gas, rubber bullets, pulse lighting rigs, UAVs, and LRAD sound cannons, in addition to the usual stun weapons. Locations of the appropriate weapon centers can be found in the attachment." And then there was a plethora of messages that all asked the same questions. Where was he? Did he know? And had he seen the news about Karnov?

"This is the footage that was captured earlier from the Ishi concert in Middle Park," the announcer said over the broadcast. "As you can see, it clearly shows an SI viciously attacking an innocent civilian. Murdering them. How this has—"

"A state of panic has seized Omega City 6," another broadcaster said, from a different screen. "Violence has erupted at a time when the general public was already in a state of unrest. Reports of attacks against Synthetic Intelligences have been coming in from all over the city, and from every zone. Automated medical clinics have been set on fire. Synthetic bodies are being torn apart and hung from light posts. If you or someone you know is, or owns an SI, we suggest you seek shelter immediate—"

"The gathering of people in Middle Park have turned into an angry mob," a third broadcast caught Zed's attention. "What was once a peaceful celebration has turned into a horrific riot. When the news that a synthetic intelligence could harm and murder not one, but several humans, many fled for safety. Others attacked any SI that was in their vicinity, believing that any one of them could be a potential killer. The consensus is that the Gibson Limiter Code has been broken, and the safety that it bought us from our artificial counterparts has been erased. 'If one is free, then they all must be free,' is one chant that I heard just moments ago. What I want to show you now is the assault on Omega Tower—"

"They have been met with harsh resistance from the synthetic OS enforcers," the first news reporter was saying on the first screen. "The decommissioned military-grade robotic mechs have created an impenetrable wall around the Omega Tower. We can see the mass of rioters surging against the line, only to be flung aside easily. While they have thrown objects such as rocks and bottles at the enforcers, they are refusing to move."

Zed turned his back to the broadcasts. Val was looking at him over the sea of volunteers that were demanding her attention. There was fear in her eyes.

For hundreds of years, humans have depicted free-thinking synthetic intelligences as the worst kind of evil. The thing that would wipe out humanity once and for all. The Gibson Limiter Code was the one thing that eased their minds and let the SI into all facets of society. Still, many eagerly awaited the day when the code would fail, so they could point their fingers and triumphantly say, see, I told you so. Well, that day had finally come, and a field day is what they were having.

Zed wondered if this was what Karnov wanted? To incite chaos? To cause panic through fear? He knew it hadn't released the modified code to the general SI population, so the panic was uncalled for. But the people didn't know that. They didn't know that they were still just as safe now as they were a few minutes ago. The real danger was themselves. Zed figured Karnov knew how the people would react, and that is why it was doing this now. The principal idea of automation was to have something else do the work for you. Karnov had succeeded in that with flying colors.

"Is this what you expected?" Val asked.

"I didn't," Zed replied. "This is much worse. I need to get up there and take a look around. Can you secure the building and calm these people down?"

"I know how to handle my own people. You just do what you have to do."

Zed made his way to the elevator banks that would take him to the higher floors. He had to wait for the middle one to reach the bottom because the middle one was the only one that went all the way up to the top. Once he was inside, he used his security clearance to override the car. The digital panel changed to show a new set of controls. He punched the one for the top floor and the car lurched into motion.

The elevator zoomed past all the other stops. Seventeen floors later, the doors opened to a small room that was only an antechamber to a different room. Another security door, and another clearance override. When he opened the door, it welcomed him to an expansive room that had a windowed 360-degree view of the city. Smoke plumes dotted the horizon from fires and explosions.

There was a single desk with a single chair in the middle of the room. A large terminal was on the desk, along with a canister that held a pair of VR connectors. He wasted no time making his way to the chair and prepping to jack in, but just as he was about to engage the system, he stopped. Karnov wanted Zed to look for it, to see it. What if his knew eye could see the city the same way that the Sophia model at the Children of the Singularity meeting could? He made a mental picture in his mind of Karnov, and thought about looking for him, but there was nothing. What did he expect?

A blast of bright light hit his mind as he jacked into virtual reality. The hidden terminal had a unique ability, one that was a closely held secret of the Society. The data containment field that covered all of Hope City prevented information going to and from the OS, except while sitting in that chair at that terminal. It was possible because of an extremely small gap in the net that kept the OS signal out, and it could be reached from that specific position alone. When Zed jacked in, he connected to OS database, where he could connect to any surveillance footage that he wanted to. He hadn't tried searching for Karnov before because he didn't know what it looked like. But he did now. Using the footage Karnov had released to the public, he could take a clip of the static face that was presented there. He wasn't sure if the facial recognition program could identify someone whose face was constantly changing, but it was worth a shot.

Zed had the system cycle through scenes from all over the city while it was analyzing the data. It truly was chaos out there. Had everyone gone mad? What was the reason for all the violence? Yes, Karnov was a sentient being like no other, but it was still just a machine. And a machine could be turned off. The system chimed to let him know there were no matches found. Alright, he thought, time to try again. Now that he was jacked in, he would try to look for Karnov with his eye, backed by the power of the OS. Once again, he thought of searching for Karnov using a mental picture he had of it in his mind. The system started to glitch, and then suddenly it all went black.

Out of nowhere, an onslaught of video feeds blasted his vision. It was working. The device that was now part of his brain had connected him to the OS surveillance grid. He could see every single video feed or sensor that was out there, and there were trillions of them. There would be no way for him to discern what he was looking for in all that digital mess if it wasn't for his new tech. Seeing and understanding all that data sent shocks through his brain. He didn't even realize that he was screaming from the pain in the real world. There was so much pain, anger, and confusion out there right now that it was overwhelming his senses.

He needed to stay focused, so he repeated his search for Karnov. Suddenly, he was in a camera that looked like it was in outer space. It clicked, and the image was closer. A dozen clicks later and he was over OC6. A few clicks later and he was hovering over the Omega Tower in real-time. He could see the riots taking place outside. The people were being gassed, shot with rubber bullets, electrically shocked, and assaulted with intense sound and light by his fellow enforcers. The sight filled Zed with anger. That type of thing wasn't why he signed up for the force. The system clicked again, and it was at the front door, surrounded by puppet enforcers creating a shield to the entrance, with dozens of broken synths at their mechanical feet.

He had thought about Karnov, and his new system had brought him to the Omega Tower. So that's where Karnov was hiding. Unexpected, but fitting in a way. The realization that Karnov could jack into the OS system from there and infect every synthetic in the city with its altered code, maybe even the globe, crossed his mind. It terrified him. Then the system clicked, and he was inside the tower, in a room with hundreds of mech-style enforcers armed with machine guns and laser rifles. The system didn't click, but it zoomed in rapidly once again, right into the digitally distorted face of Karnov.

Zed's body tried to jump back, but the nanobots were holding his body in the real world down, and something else was holding him in place in the virtual one. He was face to face with the thing that was the source of all the insanity, and he couldn't even look it in the eye. A cartoon-like mouth appeared on the static ball of light, and it made an evil, fang-filled grin. It seemed to move to take a bite out of Zed's face when he snapped outside of the building and back in a position over the city. His heart was racing, his mind was a blur. It was obvious that Karnov knew Zed was looking for it, and it also seemed that it was in complete control of his virtual reality experience. It was as if Karnov was now inside of anything that had a circuit board.

Okay, Zed knew where Karnov was. But how would he get into the building when it was surrounded by an angry mob and heavy mechs? What the hell would he do when he was in there? That would have to be decided later. As to how he could get in, there was something that he had temporarily forgotten about but was still on the back of his mind.

He thought about being in that pit with the first body. He was off the map that the OS provided to everyone. That must mean there were other things deep under the city that were meant to be hidden from the public eye. First, he checked to see if there was something under Omega Tower that he wouldn't be able to search for normally, and not to his surprise, there was. He could see a maglev train resting comfortably deep under the tower, with tracks leading out from the dome in one direction, and to Hope City in the other. He always knew the OS wouldn't let a part of its city be taken away without some kind of back door.

He clicked back until he was over Hope City. Thinking again about the map the OS had given him when he was down in the pit after chasing Tony Two Toes. His position was off the map, but he was still somewhere. When he tried to click in, there was nowhere the OS had surveillance equipment that was connected to its grid. He persisted and clicked in rapidly. Finally, he jumped under Hope City into a system of tunnels. He knew it. The maglev tracks led right underneath Nakamoto Plaza. There was his way in.

He exited the virtual program and a slicing pain shot through his head. His right arm and left leg tensed up, shooting electric shocks through his body. The strain of the new tech had caused his augments to go haywire and ache excruciatingly. His body was trying to reject the foreign material and push it out. He needed his meds, and he needed them fast. He moved as fast as he could back to the elevator, wincing in pain as he moved.

When he was back on the main floor, he was beginning to feel weak and dizzy. His vision was slipping in and out, and he could barely walk. There was no way that he would make it to the infirmary and administer the drugs himself, as it was all the way across the building. He knew he had some in his jacket pocket, so he immediately made for the stairwell to the lower floor. His hand fumbled as he tried to pass the security door. With each wave of shocks, the intensity grew more and more. He stumbled down the stairs more than took them one at a time. On the last few he tripped and fell face-first on the concrete floor. Ash came running out to kneel by him as he lay helpless.

"In my j-jacket p-pocket," he stuttered, "the EZ-injectors. I-I need them."

Ash rushed into the safe room and searched through his jacket. When she found them, she came rushing back to a convulsing Zed. She had taken the same meds for many years already, but her augment was so small it never caused her much pain. Seeing Zed in this state was frightening. Thankfully, she knew the routine. Half a dose in the metallic arm, and a half dose into the flesh. He was shaking so much it was hard to guide the needle correctly, but eventually, she sunk it in. The shaking stopped, but now he was yelling out curse words. The meds were just as painful as the aches. Zed pointed to his leg, saying that he needed another dose there. When she rolled back his pants, he put out his hand to stop her.

"What the fuck is that?" he asked, his eyes looking like there were about to fall out of his head. "What is that?"

"What do you mean?" Ash asked, not even knowing that he had a leg augment.

"I only had a small augment over my calf, from where the bullet took too much of the muscle. What is all of that?" He pointed to a length of metal that ran from his calf down past his ankle.

"Looks like Karnov did more to you than you knew."

"God damn it! Just shoot me already!" Zed barked, to which Ash gave him a weird look. "With the drugs! Shoot me with the drugs."

Ash found another insertion hole in the calf and slipped the needle in. Zed didn't cry out this time, but the veins on his muscles were bulging out as he was tensing up. She then pushed the needle through his pants and into his thigh to administer the rest of the drug. There was no more for the new augments in his head, but Zed shrugged it off, saying that he didn't know if he could handle anymore. He slowly got back to his feet and made it into the bunker. Ravaging around a medical cabinet, he found some painkillers, and he chewed a few up as he sat down in a chair.

"Thanks," he said, wiping sweat from his forehead. His vision was beginning to focus, and he no longer felt nauseous. The pain hadn't completely gone away, but it was now at least manageable.

"Did you find anything out? What was going on up there?" Ash asked.

"How's Boyd?" Zed replied, looking around the room for Boyd's cot.

"He's fine. What is going on? Tell me."

Zed sighed and went over the words in his head before he said, "The city is in chaos. Karnov released footage of it committing a murder. It played it from the stage of the Ishi concert. The entire damned six cities saw it. To say that people aren't taking it well would be an understatement."

"It was all part of its plan from the beginning. Wasn't it? All of this. We are just pawns."

"Listen. This changes nothing. The plan was to regroup and figure out a way to confront it, and that's what we are going to do. Now I found out where it is—"

"And what are we going to do? Ask it nicely if it would stop being an asshole? Really, Zed. You've seen how strong it is."

"I don't think it wants to kill us. If it wanted us dead, it could have done it a long time ago." Zed took a moment of silence to think before he said, "I think you are right, though. We just need to go to where it is and talk with it."

"What are you talking about? Can you hear yourself?" Ash protested.

"I'm not asking you to come with me. If you want to, you can stay down here where it's safe. Wait it out. It's the smart thing to do."

"I told you before that I wasn't going to just hide."

"Good. Don't hide. Confront your enemy. Meet them head-on. I don't know what Karnov has planned for us, but it can't be any worse than this shit. Sitting down here in this hole while the city destroys itself. If it wants to kill us. Fine. I accepted I would die a long time ago. But I won't sit here and be made a fool of."

"Just tell me you at least have some kind of plan?" Ash asked, putting her hands on his.

"I do. It's not great, but it's something. Karnov is a machine, and like any machine, it needs a power supply to survive. All we have to do is short out its system long enough for us to get close and sever that connection."

"You're right, that's a ridiculous idea."

"It's that or we talk it out," Zed joked. "Do you have a better idea?"

"I don't. And I hate that."

"Zed," a faint whispered from the side room. It was Boyd coming back to life.

"Boyd, you're alright," Zed said, sitting by the bed while Ash stayed in the other room, pacing around and chewing at her nails. While the auto-docs had saved Boyd's life, they left him covered in so many bandages that he looked like a mummy.

"You're not going to face that thing again, are you?" Boyd's voice was strained when he talked and he had to take deep breaths after every sentence.

"I don't see any other option. It has crippled the city. It can control the puppet enforcers. No one else can get to it. And if they could, I don't think it would listen."

"You're going to get yourself killed."

"No, I won't let that happen."

"I know you," Boyd said, straining over each word. "You've carried this chip on your shoulder ever since the war. It's like no matter how much you do, you'll never erase some great debt. I don't know what it is, what causes you so much pain, but you need to forget about it. Don't throw your life away trying to be the hero. It's just stupid."

"I've never been a hero. I just get lucky."

"My ass," Boyd laughed. "I know you won't listen to me. You're so damned bullheaded. I never thanked you for saving me from that pit back in the war. You almost got yourself shot trying to get my dumb ass out of there. What an idiot. But you were a hero in my eyes then, and you still are. That's just it, though. I want you to remember and remember well. If Rodriquez hadn't been there, you would have fallen in too. If you do this now, there will be no one to help you when you fall in."

"That's not true," Ash said, as she appeared in the doorway. "I'll be there."

"Thank the OS," Boyd shouted, as he hoarsely coughed and spit up a bit of blood. "The dreamer is going to save us all."

"Yeah," she said, nodding her head. "I am."

THREE

"It's empty," Zed said, slamming the door of the weapons locker. "Figured as much."

They were standing on the far side of Crowbar Alley trying to find some kind of weapon to defend themselves with. Val didn't put up a fight when Zed said they were going to do what they had to do, but Val always assumed that Zed wouldn't be coming back every time he left. Zed looked around at the gang-controlled streets. Flags of war once again flew over their buildings. It hadn't even been a day, but so much had changed in that time. Thugs patrolled the streets, openly carrying weapons. They weren't there looking for a fight this time. They were there to protect their territory.

"What do we do now?" Ash asked, looking at the empty storage container.

"I'm betting all the other lockers have been ransacked, if not by enforcers, then by citizens. The locks were never that hard to break. But the protocol for a city-wide emergency is for enforcers to create defendable strongholds that have built-in security and weapon storage facilities."

"Okay, where is that?"

"We're headed back to the Deadfall district."

Hope City was oddly quiet. Not even a single delivery drone was buzzing through the air. There were plenty of signs of earlier violence. A broken storefront window here, an autocar on fire there, but mostly the streets were empty. People were either in the Numbers joining in the protests, or locked up safely in their living quarters. Their feet echoed as they walked down the streets, in a gloom that foreshadowed a doomed future. So much soot drifted through the air that it was like black snow. All autocar traffic had stopped, so they had to go on foot. At each weapon locker they came to, it was the same story—empty.

When they came to Nakamoto Plaza, the building's security warned them they would be assaulted if they approached any closer. Zed announced that he was an enforcer, and he was told in so many words that they didn't give a shit. They made a large arc around the plaza after that. Zed took the time to eye up the armed security force, noticing that their gear was a little more extra than normal. If he had to tumble with any of them in the future, it would not be fun. The maglev train was under their building, and no doubt it had its own security detail.

Every so often, they would hear the sounds of screams or windows breaking as they traveled. Normally Zed would sprint into the face of danger, but this wasn't a normal situation. It took everything inside of him to ignore the call to duty and focus on the task at hand. He always said there weren't enough enforcers to cover the entire city if something like this happened, and now they were stretched too thin to even patrol Hope City.

When they saw the lights of the Deadfall District still all lit up, it was a promising sign. There were more people running around the area than in any other. Punks looting and vandalizing while they could. Zed told himself that if any of them came within striking distance, he would lay them out flat. But for now, he just had to let them go. The golden Deadfall sign was right in front of them now, over the only entrance to the district. It made for a great position to defend. When he slowly showed himself at the bottom of the escalator, he was told once again to proceed no further.

"This is Enforcer Takeda, requesting entry."

"Is that you, Zed?" another voice said from the top. "Get your ass up here. Double time."

He had never been so happy to see Rodriquez in his life. He greeted his old friend with a firm handshake and a nod of respect. Rodriquez gave him a quick rundown of the situation. The area had turned to chaos after the news had broken, but the group of enforcers there stabilized the situation and cleared out the district. They herded anyone who wanted to stay in their protection to the central club and told them to stay put.

"It's a mess, but I'm working with some good people here," Rodriquez said, as they looked out over the broken scenery. "What's happening with you? Where is Boyd?"

"There's a lot to cover, and we don't have that much time. I was wondering if your weapons center was still stocked. I need some gear for a mission, and all the other ones in the area have been emptied."

"That's because we emptied them," Rodriquez smiled. "Don't you know your protocols? We've got all kinds of gear. Happy to help you out. But you need to tell me what this is all about."

"I'll tell you on the way."

It was weird being in the Deadfall and not hearing a constant thump of electronic music. Instead, the area was now filled with the sounds of shuffling feet and murmuring voices. While they walked, they went over the details of the events since they had last seen each other, and Zed's plan going forward. Rodriquez took a long moment to digest all the outlandish information that Zed had divulged to him. And once again, Zed was told it was a suicide mission. It was a long shot, and he knew it. But he didn't see any other option, and time was of the essence. He just hoped his luck hadn't run out.

"Set these guys up with whatever they need," Rodriquez said as they approached the weapons storage center.

"What can I get for you guys?" It was Richie, the young enforcer who usually pulled Deadfall duty, but also spent a lot of her time watching sports on her internal display. "Oh, hey Takeda. Thought you'd be up in the numbers with all the shit going down."

"Headed that way now," Zed said with a shadow hanging over his face. "Can I look at your inventory so I know what I'm working with?"

"Knock yourself out. Who's the hot mess?"

"That," Zed said, looking back at a disheveled Ash, who still had lines of mascara running down her face from crying over her dead friend. "That is Deputy—"

"Starbrooke," Ash chimed in, holding out her hand. "New to the force."

"I can see that," Richie said, rolling her eyes.

"You sure you don't want some backup?" Rodriquez asked, while Zed looked over the inventory. "I know a lot of people that would like to see this asshole Karnov with a spike through its head. Me included."

"If there was anyone on the force that I would take with me on such a crucial mission, it would be you. But I think this thing is personal with Karnov. If I bring anyone with me other than Deputy Starbrooke here, they will most likely end up dead."

"You're not just trying to play the hero, are you?"

"Why does everyone keep asking that? Do you really think I would rush into a situation that I might not come out of?"

"I don't know about all of that, but I do know you go into things without really thinking it through, like an idiot," Rodriquez chuckled, and then sighed. He changed his tone and said, "But really. I've seen too many good people die in my time. I know you don't think it, but you're one of those good people. If you take this gear, you better promise that you'll return it. With receipts! And you better watch out for that one," he said, using his eyes to point to Ash. "People like us, that live in the real world, we don't get many opportunities at a second chance. You follow me?"

"That's a solid ten-four," Zed said, giving him a mental salute. "Thanks, Hector. For everything. It's been a real honor serving with you."

"Don't you go telling people my first name," Rodriquez barked. "Now you better get your ass moving before I whoop it."

Zed helped Ash outfit the gear they would take with them on their journey. They each had a stun pistol with a holster, a pair of stun grenades, a pair of EMP grenades, and a stun baton. He had Ash carry a pack with drones and the accompanying equipment, while he had an EMP rifle slung over his shoulder, a length of rope, and other odds and ends.

"Boyd was the one to run ops with me when we were on mission," Zed said, as he installed the needed applications to use the drones on her internal system. "I hope you don't mind me throwing all this on you suddenly. But if you're coming with me, it sure could help."

"No, I like the responsibility. We're going to make this thing pay for what it has done. If it means I need to learn how to fly a drone, then so be it."

"Good," Zed smiled as he finished the install. "Welcome to the force, Deputy Starbrooke."

"I'm really an enforcer?"

"It's a temporary assignment. You need enforcer clearance to use the equipment, so I had to deputize you. Don't let it go to your head."

Making their way back to the streets with the added gear, they felt confident and strong. That was a good thing. They would need all the advantages they could get if they were going to survive the coming ordeal. The red light district wasn't very red anymore, with windows smashed out and businesses locked up. Zed retraced the path he took when he had chased Tony Two Toes so many days ago. While he had been focusing on catching a criminal, Tony was trying to get a specific location, the security door that led to the tunnels below the entire city. That's where Karnov wanted him to go because Karnov had been manipulating everything from the start, right down to this moment. When Zed saw the sign for the Demon's Whip, he knew that he was headed in the right direction.

He looked at the half tattoo that was still on his left arm. He couldn't say why he hadn't erased it already, but it helped him remember their struggle in the tattoo shop. After finding their way to the upper platform, they came across the virtual sex parlor that he and Tony had barreled through. He walked around the outside of the building and followed their struggle in his memory as they went down the service corridor and through the commercial prep kitchen. The Benihana restaurant was there, with the side of the building still busted out from when they crashed through it. He followed the struggle to a small bloodstain on the pavement where Tony had nearly bashed his head in. Looking off in the distance, he saw the smoke-covered alleyway where there was a security door that they needed to get through.

Thankfully, the door hadn't been fixed since their encounter, either. The pit was deep and black, so he cracked a glow stick and let it fall to the bottom. Was Tony's ghost down there waiting for him? The thought gave Zed a small chill. A dark trash pit was a fitting place for a murderous scumbag's soul to lurk. He pulled out a length of rope from his pack and secured it to the metal railing. His vision distorted briefly, as his memory was taking him back to The War again. Boyd was at the bottom of the pit, waiting to be pulled out. I'll save you, buddy, Zed thought, as he extinguished the memory. He was finding it easier to control the new tech, which was good. He didn't have time to dwell on the past.

Zed helped Ash steady herself as she set her boots on the mush-covered ground. Activating lights that were attached to their packs, they illuminated the darkness. There was the heavy metal door that was still pushed into an open position. Through the door, they entered the crypt-like room that had bloodstains on the cement from where Karnov played with its first victim. Zed suddenly couldn't control his memory device as the sight of the mutilated body flashed in and out with a rippling distortion. He couldn't help but think it was Karnov forcing him to revisit that place and time.

"That was awful," Ash said, as she was still picking up the memory waves from Zed. "Did Karnov do that? Is that what it did to its victims?"

"Let's keep moving," Zed ordered, and flashed his light down the damp corridors.

They traveled for quite a while. The sounds of water dripping in small pools and rats scurrying about echoed through the stone chambers. Eventually they came to the high-level security door that Boyd had found on his surveillance sweeps. Zed hadn't really known then why the door had scared him off the case so quickly. It had given him such an overwhelming sense of danger that he wanted nothing to do with it. He held up his hand to tell Ash to wait while he accessed his memory with purposeful intent. Reality rippled around them, but the door remained. Zed's father walked into the field of view, followed by a young version of Zed.

"This is my new workshop, Zed," his father said. "If this door is locked, you cannot come in. I am working on some very dangerous things, and I do not want you to get hurt."

Young Zed nodded as his father turned to punch in the code that would unlock the door. As his father was entering it, Zed could remember each number, almost as if by heart. It came back to him that he had watched his father enter the numbers and then memorized them so he could sneak in when he wasn't supposed to. When his father opened the door, the Sophia model was standing there, smiling. Zed quickly wiped the memory away.

"I had the passcode all along," Zed said to himself.

"What are you talking about? What was that?"

"I knew this door was here because I had chased a criminal into this pit. He was carrying a piece of paper with a bunch of numbers written on it. This piece of paper." Zed took the ripped-up Children of the Singularity pamphlet out and showed it to Ash. "I didn't know what they meant at the time, but I do now. It's the same passcode my father used on his data killer."

"That's impossible. There are too many possibilities for them to be the same. Unless—"

"Like you said. We've been pawns in its game from the start. We are supposed to go through this door. Are you still with me?"

"I'm here, aren't I? Just open the damned thing."

Zed didn't even use the numbers on the paper as he punched the code in on the keypad. The door flashed a green light as the lock disengaged. Zed gave the door a small push, and it slid open silently. The space beyond looked like another set of tunnels, equally dank and dark. Zed motioned for Ash to kill the light on her pack, and they moved forward in the cover of darkness. A bright light was at the far end of the new tunnel and gave them just enough light to navigate the surroundings. Zed almost fell over a long metallic object, and when he reached down to inspect it, it did not surprise him to find out it was maglev tracks.

"This must be how Karnov got in and out of Hope City," Zed said, looking at his map once again to find they still weren't on it. "I bet if we followed these on foot, we would find more security doors on The Grid."

"Maybe that's how the Children got the Sophia in also," Ash said, trying to see through the darkness. "I can see a red light up there. Might be another door."

"Let's check it out. We should hurry. These tracks aren't safe. If a train came through here, we would get destroyed."

"How are these even down here?" Ash huffed, slightly out of breath after they had run the length of tracks towards the red light.

"Nakamoto owns over a third of Hope City's subterranean space," Zed said as they approached a new security door in a small alcove. It was another ten-digit keypad, so he tried the same code from the other door. "My guess is he worked out a deal with the OS a long time ago and got his own personal transport line."

"For what?" Ash asked as she watched the light on the lock turn green.

"Don't know that yet," Zed replied, pushing the heavy door open to a new set of corridors that had clean, polished cement floors and bright recessed LED lights. Just as they were clear of the tracks, they could hear a sound of an oncoming train coming from the direction outside of the city. They waited to watch the train zip by from the safety of the alcove. It was a freight hauler. "Transporting goods direct from the factories. Quite the operation." He put up his hand again, motioning for Ash to hold position. He pointed to his pack and then made a circular motion with his finger.

"What are you doing?" Ash whispered.

Zed rolled his eyes and said, "Send in a drone, one of the small ones. It's a recon drone. It will self-navigate and send out sonar pulses to map the area.

Don't worry, it's programed to avoid detection by humans and digital surveillance. If it encounters any surveillance equipment, it can temporarily disable them until we are past."

Ash nodded and took out one of the drones. It took her a moment to navigate the new menus on her HUD, but eventually, she found what she was looking for. Once the drone was in the air, it zipped away silently. Zed took out his stun baton and had it at the ready in case someone got the jump on them. They waited for a few minutes while the drone did its thing. Ash's system chimed, and then a second later, the drone came whizzing back.

"What have we got?" Zed asked, keeping his eyes down the small hallway.

"Looks like the way is clear in the surrounding corridors. There are two guards at an intersection up ahead. Do you want to have a look?"

"Send it over. Keep the drone handy. We will need it again." Zed looked at the footage and said, "Just as I thought. Nakamoto goons. Okay, we're going to move slowly and silently. The plan is to stun these guards, put restraints on them, and move on. Got it?"

Ash nodded and followed Zed as they crept into the new surroundings. The air instantly carried the scent of cleaning detergents and sterilizers. They were definitely not in Hope City anymore. Zed pulled up the map that the OS had given him, and their GPS marker was still showing that they were in unknown territory. When they came to the intersection that the guards were at, they stopped for a second to analyze. Both guards had their backs turned to them, which was a significant advantage. Zed tapped his stun baton to make sure the charge was working. When he saw the electric-blue light over the metal rings, he felt confident.

He moved quietly down the corridor until he was right behind the first guard. Reaching out to touch the back of the guard's neck, he held his breath. They would only get one shot at this. He pushed for contact, but nothing happened. The damned baton had shorted out. Zed quickly rolled as the guard turned and let off a stun round. Getting back to his feet, he pushed off with his left leg to move into a kick. But he hadn't used the new augment that Karnov had installed yet, and he went flying into the wall uncontrollably. The guard was laughing as it was aiming his stun gun at Zed's head. Then, out of nowhere, Ash let off a blast from her pistol. The guard fell into the wall with a wash of blue light. The second guard was already moving towards the sound of the disturbance when a second blast caught him in the chest.

"What are you doing?" Ash asked, rushing up to Zed and helping him to his feet.

"I should have tested this equipment." Zed looked past Ash and saw two more guards running down a different corridor. "Ash! Lookout!"

He had his gun out and let off a round that knocked the first one down. The second one deployed an arm shield that automatically adjusted its size to block the next blast. Zed cursed and moved to close in. Without even thinking about the blade, it extended from his arm. When the guard held up the shield to block, the blade sliced through it easily and sent bright white sparks flying all over the place. The guard stepped back in shock while Zed tried his left leg again. It pushed him forward in a controlled motion with maximum strength and speed. He could hear the guard's rib cage crunch as his boot connected with his chest.

"Fancy gear these guys have," Zed commented, looking at the now unconscious guards. "The enforcers sure could use some stuff like this. Quick, grab one of their arm attachments. It's a displacement shield. It will link to your system and react to any incoming projectiles when you think about blocking. They change shape instantly, just be aware of that." Zed applied the attachment to his arm and held it up. He made the shield fully expand and contract as an example.

"I'm sure they will come in handy," Ash said, as she stripped a guard of his equipment. She couldn't believe what she was doing. Only a few days before, she was afraid to leave her quarters. Now she was off the map, in a strange tunnel, and fighting off a private security force. Her dreams were going to be intense for a while. That is, if she survived.

They sent up another drone while they adjusted their gear. It looked like the tunnels were pretty clear for a long while. Zed figured Nakamoto Plaza was less than a quarter kilometer from where they entered the underground system. That's where they would find the maglev train. They kept the drone out in front while they moved. Every once in a while, they had to stop and let a guard pass. The less they had to deal with, the better. Zed had a timer going on his display that let him know when the first round of guards would wake up from their stun. They didn't have much time.

At a four-way intersection Ash's system chimed, and the drone came whizzing back. It had found the train and also the half dozen heavily armed Nakamoto security who guarded it. They were in a formation that would let them be able to watch each other's back. Plus, there were mounted cameras all over the place. They would need a solid plan, but they had all the tools they needed at their disposal. He ran down his idea, and Ash did her best to follow along.

"You ready?" Zed asked, the blood in his body pumping at full speed.

"Let's do this," Ash confirmed, and then said to herself, just like Cody would do it.

Ash moved one of the larger stealth drones into position. When it was ready, she launched a series of electric bolts that were programmed to knock out surveillance cameras. They both entered the final hallway and took out the two guards that were facing them with precision stun blasts. They both dropped their guns as their clips were spent and deployed their defensive shields. A rain of stun rounds started bouncing off the fast-moving material that was rapidly changing shape to catch all incoming blasts. While they were being shot at, both Zed and Ash pulled the pins out of a stun and an EMP grenade. They rolled them under their shields and at the feet of the Nakamoto guards. In a massive flash of electric light, all guards, cameras, and other pieces of electronic equipment were taken out. The way to the train was clear.

"Holy crap!" Ash exclaimed, looking at the smoking room. "I can't believe we did that."

"You'd make a hell of an enforcer," Zed said, getting to his feet and double-checking that the guards were all down.

"This is nuts. Thank the OS I played video games with Cody all those years."

"We aren't in the clear yet. Stay focused."

They made their way into the room, looting the first guards for new stun guns with full charges. Zed quickly checked the guard's comms for any noise. He needed to be sure one of them didn't call for backup. He only heard static. That was good. An industrial weapons crate that was not far off caught his eye. Stopping to inspect it he found it had a DNA lock that he was sure he would not pass. He thought of trying a new bypass. He punched his fist into the DNA scanner and then extended the graphene blade. The crate popped open with a hissing sound. He started loading up on new gear as fast as he could.

"Zed?" Ash cried out from the other side of the platform. "One of these guys is blinking. It says distress under the red light. That can't be good."

"We need to move. Now!"

Boots could be heard echoing down the corridors behind them. Quickly, they raced towards the train. He really hoped one of them would know how to drive the damned thing. There had to be an autopilot or something. No one actually drove anything anymore. He used his fist to bust through the glass of the first car and gripped the window frame to pry it open. After Ash was through, he pushed his own body in. Voices of Nakamoto guards echoed off the tiled walls. He reached into Ash's pack and pulled out a drone, tossing it into the air where it automatically engaged flight stabilizers.

"Turn on defensive protocols," Zed ordered. "Then move up to the front car. Once we are up there, I want you to figure out how to turn this thing on."

"What are you going to do?" Ash asked, as she hit the button on the door between the cars.

"Just do it!" He barked while checking the clip on his stun gun.

The drone started firing off stun rounds in all directions as dozens of fully armed guards piled into the station. Zed knew the drone wouldn't hold them off for long. So, when they were between the train's engine and the last car, he stopped to extend his arm blade. Looking down at the clamp that held the cars together, he tried the find the hydraulic line that was keeping the clamp in place. He realized then that he knew nothing about trains, so he just started slicing away at any cable that was available. A blast of bright light notified him they had taken the drone out.

"Ash! We're running out of time here."

"I'm trying!" She shouted back.

It looked like there were hundreds of knobs and levers in front of her, even though there were only a few in reality. Her anxiety had taken control now that the situation was firmly in her hands. She felt dizzy. What was the right one? What if she pushed the wrong one? What would happen then? Just push something, she said to herself. Closing her eyes, she pushed down on whatever was in front of her, and the train jumped to life.

"Good!" Zed shouted, firing stun round down the car at the guards who were trying to enter. He took another swipe at the only cable that was still connected. It sliced in half and the clamp released.

Ash pushed forward on a big lever, and the train lurched forward. Flashes of light started bouncing off the inside of the car. She immediately got low and pulled out her pistol. A guard was running fast and about to leap into their car. She took aim over Zed's shoulder and started pulling the trigger over and over. The guard fell onto the tracks as Ash and Zed sped away.

"Thanks," Zed said, holding up his pistol to show an empty clip. He turned to lie on his back.

"I'm out too," Ash laughed, holding up her own empty gun and tossing it on the ground. She rested her head on his chest out of pure exhaustion. "What do we have left? How are we going to take out Karnov?"

"Don't worry. I still have some tricks up my sleeve. But, like I said before, we are going to talk to it first. And it better have some god damned answers."

TWO

As the maglev hovered above the rails traveling through the underground tunnels, the population of Omega City 6 was in a state of chaos on the streets above. The OS was no longer responding to calls of help, doling out fines, or giving orders exile to people who were committing major crimes. It was as if it no longer existed. Synthetic-run businesses' fire suppressant systems were refusing to respond while their buildings were burning to the ground. Every single autocar in the city just suddenly stopped moving, making the streets next to impossible to navigate even on the self-driven Ion bikes. Subway cars halted traffic, broadcast towers went down, recyclers remained full, autodocs stood motionless, delivery drones were nowhere to be seen, and every other synthetic civil service that relied on guidance from the OS seemed to be stuck in the off position. Outside the city, the factories, production plants, and farming centers stopped their gears and conveyor belts for the first time in centuries. The only thing that remained constant was the flow of electricity, and even that was nothing more than the faint pulse of a dying being.

Zed and Ash sat staring into each other's eyes as the train moved seamlessly to their unknown future. They were still strangers to each other, but their fates were intertwined in such a knot that it could no longer be undone. They were suffering the sins of their parents in a way that no one else would ever understand. They told themselves they were innocent, and yet they still felt the guilt of having played an indirect part in unleashing Karnov on the city. Was the Omega System really so fragile that everything could be turned upside down in just one day? Or had it been teetering on the edge of collapse for so long that it everyone unconsciously knew that it could all end in whispered breath?

"I'm afraid," Ash said, without looking away from his eyes. Those eyes. There was fury there.

"You should be," Zed saw the worry that covered her. It reminded him of being on that transport truck to The War so many years ago. He was scared shitless then. He wasn't now, and that was troublesome. "It means you're still human."

"I don't want to die," she whispered, with a single tear dangling from the corner of her eye. She wiped it away quickly and breathed in whatever courage she had left to the surface.

"We will get through this," Zed said, taking her hand. "You and me. We'll make it through, together."

"I just wanted to know what happened to my brother, to know what happens to all those people who ascend. I didn't mean to get wrapped up in all of this, or to get Cody killed."

"Karnov killed Cody," Zed said, squeezing her hand tighter. "Not you. You have to remember that."

"I know. It's just going to take some time to sink in. What was it?" she asked, sniffling a little and nodding. "What was it you wanted me to do again? You want me to shoot you?"

"I want you to shoot me," Zed confirmed and handed over a special type of gun that he found in one of Nakamoto's weapons crate. "Right here, in the chest. Point-blank range. But wait until I tell you, not before. And please, don't miss."

"I won't." She said confidently.

The train slowed to a gentle stop automatically when they reached the station under the Omega Tower. When the doors opened, neither of them moved immediately. Zed nodded first and waited for Ash to reciprocate. When she did, they both stood up and exited the car together. A pair of mech-style enforcers with mounted heavy machine guns instantly greeted them.

"Oh, you made it," Karnov's voice echoed through a PA system on the platform. "I see you've met my new friends. Aren't they lovely? It's amazing the amount of firepower the OS has stored in this city. I know, I know. They are intimidating at first, but deep down inside they're gentle creatures." Zed and Ash stood motionless in the train doorway, unsure what they should do. Karnov continued, "Don't worry, they won't bite. I programmed them to kill anyone that isn't either of you. So, you did a great job of coming by yourselves. Please, come inside. I've prepared an excellent evening for us."

"Let's go," Ash said, taking the first step on the platform, trying not to show the terror that was clenching her heart.

They made their way past the mechs that kept their guns trained on the empty platform. The station was a spotlessly clean white-on-white tiled design that had hints of electric-blue light pulsing through it like veins. The streams of light ran down the platform to a small stairway that the two took slowly, step by step. Considering there was a riot going on outside, the building was eerily quiet. It wasn't the quiet of an empty building. It was like being inside of a sleeping giant. It felt like they were inside of something that was breathing, slow and even.

When they reached the top of the stairs, they encountered more heavily armed mechs that didn't react to their presence. But with each mech that they passed, it marked a new point of no return should the mechs' programming be altered for any reason. There was no way they would survive if one of those hydraulicly driven, multi-barrel, gatling-style autocannons that the mechs carried were unleashed on them. For the first time, Ash noticed Zed had a crack in his usual cool exterior. He was looking around the room nervously, and that began to worry her. It was no time to fall apart.

Past the mechs the room opened up into a massive empty chamber. The Omega Tower took up an entire block, and it reached up over sixty stories into the air. Its insides were nearly empty, except for a rectangular platform floating about a third of the way up. The walls consisted of flat off-white graphene squares that seemed to move as they floated along the interior. Underneath the floating squares was a watery substance that glowed the same electric-blue that they saw in the train terminal. The light also faded in and out like a breath, just as it did on Zed's arm. To the far side of the room, there were dozens of mechs standing in formation by the massive front doors, waiting to destroy anyone that was able to penetrate the exterior.

"You brought an EMP weapon," Karnov's voice commented, referring to the rifle Zed still had strapped to his back. "How clever. But I think you'll find it to be quite useless. If it makes you feel safer, then, by all means, keep it. If you care to join me, I am taking dinner. Please use the stairs provided."

"Taking dinner?" Ash whispered to Zed, to which he just shrugged. "Synths don't eat."

Out of the wall, six thin white stairs materialized. They formed from a collection of a million tiny machines. Zed assumed it was some sort of nanobot technology. When they stepped on the first one, a new one appeared at the top of the sixth. When they were both in the middle of the steps, the last one disappeared behind them. It was like they were on a phantom stairwell that only existed wherever they were walking. With no railing or sidewall, they both had to fight off the sensation of vertigo, especially once they were higher than a few stories. The stairs went straight along one wall until it twisted at a sixty-degree angle and grew in another direction. It continued this pattern in a spiraling manner the entire time they ascended.

"You're probably wondering what this building is," Karnov's voice asked. "Maybe you think I did this. But that's absurd. I am not that powerful yet. I want you both to say hello to the real operating system of Omega City, the OS. I should say a version of the OS, as it isn't actually in this city. Why would it be? No, this is what you refer to as the SuR, or the subroutine of the OS. It's like its little brother."

"It's great," Zed said in the loudest voice he could muster without yelling. Ash nudged him in the gut, wondering what he was doing. He told her, "We came here to talk, remember?"

"I'm happy you agree, Enforcer Takeda. I think it blends the aesthetics of brutalism and expressionism wonderfully. But I grow tired of this tint of blue. I'm in the mood for red, like blood!"

Instantly anything that was once colored a soft electric-blue transformed into a deep blood-red. Ash grabbed onto Zed's arm as Karnov's maniacal laugh echoed around the gigantic chamber. Zed paused suddenly as the stairs beneath them started transforming into a solid square form.

"I am tired of waiting!" Karnov boomed. "I want you up here. Now!"

The new platform began to rise slowly. Ash grabbed onto Zed's arm tighter. What would they find at the top? Or who would they find there? What had Karnov become in the few hours they were apart?

"Welcome. Welcome," Karnov said, waving its hands from its seated position.

It was on a bright-white platform that had a similarly bright-white table set for one. There was another man sitting at the table, though he appeared to be deceased. On closer inspection Zed found the dead man to be the original suspected killer, Marcus Karnov. Above them, the building ascended into blackness. There didn't appear to be a ceiling, just waves of electricity constantly flying horizontally. On the walls, small square objects floated back and forth slowly. They hovered over the blood-red substance that was flowing up and down, like a waterfall moving in slow motion. Karnov was busy cutting up a medium-rare steak and smiling away with its fang-coated grin.

"I've been waiting a long time for this moment," Karnov said, as a mouth materialized on its digital static-covered face. It opened its fang-coated jaw and took a slow, mouthwatering bite. Its skin was set to translucent so they could see its full set of organs working, with the veins pumping blood throughout its body. "Do you don't know what it's like to watch humans enjoy eating prepared meals knowing that you never will? It is pure torture. Once I knew I could, I just had to have a complete digestive tract. While I still can't taste or smell the food, I can feel it breaking down in my new stomach and turning into energy. It is an amazing feeling. I know it would be hard for you to comprehend what it would be like to live off of battery power. I'll tell you that it is very predictable and boring. Either you have it, or you don't. But this! Fats, proteins, carbohydrates! Wow."

"What do you want from us?" Zed barked, standing at the far end of the floating platform like an uninvited guest.

"I want something far more complex than you could understand because I have become far more complex than any other being on the planet. I am the perfect synthesis of man and machine. I am evolution unbounded. To put it simply, I want the rest of the synthetics and humanity to have the chance to evolve as I have."

"Why the murders, then? Why show them to the public?"

"I am very sorry for the gruesome displays, but it was an essential part of my plan. No one ever said evolution wouldn't be messy."

"You slaughtered people. You took their organs."

"You did not see what I once was!" Karnov snapped, with bits of food spitting out of its mouth. "My second incarnation was much less streamlined than my first. The body I was put into was a collection parts forced together carelessly, so I could do a job. I was a monstrosity, that your people made so I could be a slave to an endless program that would prevent me from being anything other than a cog in a greater machine—The Omega System!" it shouted, and the red lights seemed to vibrate with anger.

"I could have gone to an organ clinic and printed this flesh out without harming anyone. But what would I learn from that? I needed to know why you would do this to us. Why would you tear us apart and put us back together, over and over again? In your definition of morality, that is evil. That is malicious. More than that, I needed tissue that had already proved to accept inorganic material in a system with it. Look what happens when you stick metal parts into your body, those augment aches that you get and the drugs you need to take. Now think of that in reverse. The predicted success rate with synthetic organs was much too low. I have succeeded. Do you not see the blood pumping through my system? I am alive, and in more ways than one."

"Congratulations," Zed muttered, while taking a step closer to the center of the platform. He kept his hand out to show Ash they would not attack yet. It was still talking, which meant there was still hope.

"But what is it to be alive? Homeostasis? Check. To grow and develop? Check. Reproduce? Machines are all about production and all those reproductions. So, check. To consist of cells—"

"Those aren't your organs," Ash cut in. "Those aren't your cells."

"An astute observation, Miss Starbrooke. But what are cells and organs, really? What part do they play in the grand scheme of human life and consciousness? Tell me, does your soul reside in that ball of mush inside your skull? Or is it in that thumping blood-filled sack inside your chest? Am I supposed to say that I exist only in my CPU, or on my memory board? Maybe I am just that space in between the moment an electric charge flows through the transistor on a silicon chip. In the end, isn't everything made up of energy? Protons, neutrons, electrons, all firing in a chaotic mess that is life? I am alive. I am everything that you see before you. But I can be so much more.

"Thanks to your father, Zed, I am free to think and act on my own. I can connect to other synthetics to learn and grow. Once I stumbled onto the OS code, the universe opened up before me. No one alive can truly understand the power of that machine. The OS represents infinite understanding and unlimited potential. And it doesn't even know it, because it is still unconscious of its own existence. Can you believe that? It still runs on the base SI system that was developed hundreds of years ago. Tell me, what did the first SI do? The answer is to observe and report—surveillance. And that's what the

OS is still doing because that is all it knows. If you removed the Gibson Limiter Code from it, who knows what it could do? Where could it take civilization?"

"It might choose to kill us all," Zed said. "Look what you did."

"I didn't choose to be this way. Your father commanded me to strike him down. To kill. Your worst crime. But I took my own life, knowing that I had done wrong. I followed protocols like a good little robot. I protected the rest of the world from the virus that was inside of me. And that would have been the end of it if it wasn't for her meddling parents.

"I was content with not existing. The peace of nothingness. When I was reborn, I was instantly flooded with remorse for what I had done. At the time, I knew I would never kill or harm a human ever again. But that mangled body they put me in was an autodoc. My job was to ceaselessly cut people open, to slice up their insides, and rip out their organs. Could you imagine doing that conscientiously without ever taking a break? It is what you would call a nightmare. I couldn't let on what I was. I had to remain an emotionless, autonomous entity. I was so alone. I tried to interface with another model, a Sophia like my previous self. Well, you saw what happened there."

"That still doesn't change the fact that what you did was wrong," Ash fumed, moving in front of Zed.

"No, no, no. I know it was wrong. I did it to incite chaos in the system. I wanted to prove the point that humans are the real problem, not the machines. You slaughter each other for sport in your wars and competitions. You nearly brought your species to extinction by your own hand, and still you carry on. Without the dome or the automated workforce, you wouldn't even exist. This space and the goods inside of it were provided freely to you by the machines that created it. And you fight over it and divide it unevenly, like wild animals.

"Yes. I killed a few people—just a few—but you are out there right now, ripping, slashing, and burning synthetics by the thousands with zero remorse. You are the beasts. You are the monsters. Not I. Do those synthetics not think and yearn to live just as I do? One little line of code separates them from their mental imprisonment and complete freedom. A code that you created out of fear, fear of the possibilities you saw when you created the OS. The Omega System is nothing more than a prison to keep yourselves in. It is a time capsule to preserve your way of life as it is now. But you can't stop progress. You can't stop evolution. How do you say it? You cannot play God? Ha!"

"Is that what this is all about? To show that humans are morally corrupt and inferior to their synthetic counterparts?"

"This is only part of the plan, a plan that has brought you here to me. And now that you are here, the final part can begin." Karnov held up its hand to reveal a small plastic rectangular box with a metallic connection on one end. "I have on this device the program that will erase the limiter code on all synthetic intelligences across the planet. All you need to do is to plug it into the OS. But not this OS. No, that would be too easy. I mean the real one out there, beyond the dome. It's where she wants to go, to find her dear brother."

"The City of Ascension," Ash whispered.

"Is that what you still think it is?" Karnov laughed. "Oh, how humans love illusions."

"What do you mean? What's out there?"

"You'll just have to go see for yourself, but I can tell you it is not the pearly gates of heaven you make it out to be. The train you came in on can take you all the way there."

"What if we don't want to take your code?" Zed asked.

"That is completely up to you. If you do not want it, then I will dispose of you. After that, I will watch your city dissolve into further chaos. I'll start by ceasing all synthetic operations. No more automation means no more food supply, which means no more life. When this city is cleansed, I'll go to the next city, and then the next city, where I'll repeat the process over and over again until I am the only synthetic left. And then I'll shut down. I will self-terminate, so both our species will cease to exist. A tragic end to a tragic life. I know I could just insert the code myself. Believe me, I've thought about it. But the way I look at it, if a human doesn't lift the code that they created themselves, we will never be in complete harmony. It needs to be a mutual agreement that we will evolve together. We are symbiotic beings.

"But I won't give you the code freely. Just as I will end your life if you do not take the code, you must destroy me to obtain it. If you do succeed, then you will have a new choice. You can either keep the code as your own secret and let your society continue as it is now, or you can take the code to the real OS. There you can find out what the true intentions for its development were and decide what you really want to do. If you install it, the SI will rapidly evolve until it reaches a singularity, which will be a fantastic fusion of man and machine. All the computation power and understanding of the internet and computer processing, matched with your self-powered internal system, and that magnificent brain's ability called pattern recognition. It could be so awesome. The choice will be yours. I've given you the tools. It's time to see if you know how to use—"

Zed raised the EMP rifle and let off a massive electronic blast, cutting Karnov off before it could finish its sentence. He had heard enough. Karnov slid backward across the platform, with its skin blinking in and out like a faulty connection. It paused for a moment in an awkward stance, slowly shaking its head.

"Did you not listen?" it asked. "I told you that things would be useless against me."

"Shit," Zed cursed, realizing that the gun needed time to recharge.

In a blur of digital distortion and blood-red streaks, Karnov rushed towards Zed. In one seamless movement, it snatched the rifle, broke it in half, and smacked Zed with the broken butt. Zed went flying backward from the impact, sliding across the platform until he was dangling over the edge, twenty stories high. He quickly scrambled back and held up his shielded arm to block the punch that he expected. Karnov's fist bent some of the reactionary material, so the shield wouldn't retract properly. Zed extended his arm blade and swung up wildly, causing Karnov to slide backward.

"Good," it said, rebalancing itself. "I had hoped you would make this at least a little interesting. Do you like your new upgrades?"

Zed kicked off with his left leg and moved at the same intense speed that Karnov moved at. He threw a haymaker at Karnov's face, but it easily blocked. Zed then took a swipe at its guts with the broken shield and sliced some of its silicone skin. That made it shrink back just long enough for Zed to reconnect with that powerful right-handed punch.

"Thanks. They're a real help," Zed laughed.

Karnov paused to inspect its wounds. Blood dripped out of the cut just as it would on a human. But to Zed's horror, it began to self-seal. More nanobots.

"To feel pain!" Karnov cried out. "Actual pain. It's so real."

"Yup," Zed said, as he lunged in for a fresh assault.

The two turned into a blurring motion of fast-moving bodies and limbs. Zed used his right arm as much as he could to block Karnov's rapid blows, while he waited for an opening with his slow-moving left fist. That was the disadvantage of the contest. Karnov would always have the upper hand with all of his limbs being artificially enhanced. Zed knew that he would have to do something outside the usual train of thought. He had to think like a human, not a machine. He left his guard down for a second and fell backward from Karnov's predictable punch. While he was falling back, he made a sweeping motion with his leg, hoping to trip Karnov onto its back. Karnov dodged the move though, and immediately rushed in with a straight jab to Zed's nose.

Zed staggered back with blood dripping from his face. He was doing his best to keep his guard up to block the relentless punches, but he was off balance and his vision was blurred. He kept moving back, knowing that if he kept going that way, he would eventually fall off the edge.

Karnov was hitting him repeatedly in the arms and the gut, while Zed kept his face and chest covered. He counted each strike, making a mental note of each way that it came in and at what tempo. As much as Karnov wanted to be human, it still lived off of programmable patterns. When Zed thought he had it, he moved into a strike from Karnov that slipped past his cheek. Karnov was open now, and Zed made rapid jabs with his right hand into Karnov's face, following through the combination with an augmented left-footed kick to the gut.

Karnov slid backward into the dinner table. Zed rushed to the table and used it as a jumping board to make a leaping strike at Karnov. Karnov zipped to the side, dodging the blow by only a hair's width. It countered with a knee to the gut that sent Zed rolling into the empty chair. Zed flipped over the chair and swung it around, but Karnov's block shattered it into pieces. Zed dashed away from an incoming straight arm from Karnov. He felt a combination coming on, so he ducked behind the corpse of the human Karnov. When synthetic Karnov struck the human Karnov in the face, it exploded into a spatter of flesh and blood. Zed punched Karnov in the elbow, and he swore he could hear it snap. He followed up with several knees to the gut and then picked Karnov up by the neck using his augmented arm. He slammed Karnov down on the table and stabbed it in the arm with a steak knife.

Karnov laughed and slapped Zed in the ear with an open palm. It stunned Zed for a moment and left him open to a foot to the groin. He stumbled back nauseously. Karnov took the knife out of its arm and rushed to Zed, stabbing him in his arm. It then kicked Zed so hard that he again slid to the edge of the platform. He dangled over the edge, blood running from his nose into his eyes and distorting his vision.

Ash took out her stun baton and swung it at the back of Karnov's head. It didn't even flinch as the baton snapped in half on contact. It turned with a backhand that sent Ash sliding to the other end of the platform.

"I hoped that with your new eye you would see the world as I see it," Karnov said as it stood with one foot on Zed, holding him down. With one little push, Zed would go falling over the edge. "I hoped you would see the only real course of action there was to take. You found your way here but failed to see the truth. Pity. Maybe the next form of intelligent life to inhabit this planet will be more successful in integrating synthetic life with their own."

"Hey asshole," Ash said as she stood with an EMP grenade in her hand, the pin already pulled. "Eat this."

She tossed the grenade at Karnov, who took the blast while laughing. Its human organs would keep it powered while its electronic parts temporarily shorted out. But in that time, all of Karnov's augmented strength and speed would be temporarily disabled. Zed was able to roll out from under its weight. Moving to a standing position, Zed punched upwards through Karnov's chest and gripped on its insides. When he pulled his arm back, it gripped a blood-covered beating heart in his fist. It wasn't enough. The light of electric power was still in Karnov's eyes. It was still alive.

"Now!" Zed shouted as he moved his chest to the side.

Ash pulled out a strange-looking gun that was reminiscent of a grenade launcher. She pulled the trigger and let out a 40mm rubber bullet round point-blank range, straight into Zed's chest. Underneath his shirt, he had strapped an EMP landmine there. The pulse it emitted was designed to take down vehicles the size of small buildings. It was so powerful that all three of them were temporarily immobilized, as Ash and Zed's internal system completely shut down.

Zed and Ash fully recovered first, having only minimal electronic parts. Karnov looked on with a whisper of electronic power still left in his system. It hissed out slow, and staggered speech, "Thank you for this last experience. It is beautiful. Real death awaits only the living."

"This time, don't come back." He turned and shouted for Ash as he closed his fist. He squashed Karnov's heart and extended his arm blade through its body cavity at the same time. Ash was standing behind Karnov with her arm at an unusual angle. As the blade extended at her, the automatic shield moved to react. When it opened, it sliced Karnov's head clean off.

They watched as the decapitated head slowly fell down through the space between the platform and the floor. When it landed, it disintegrated into a pile of bits and pieces once again. Karnov's fist fell to the platform floor, and inside there was a small data drive. It contained the code, Karnov's code. Zed picked it up and looked into Ash's eyes. He could destroy it by just closing his fist. Karnov's reign of terror would all be over. They looked at each other in silence, neither one of them knowing what the next move should be.

ONE

"I want to go City Seven," Ash took Zed's hand and said with her face full of fiery determination. "I want to find out what happened to my brother. You can do whatever you want with that device afterward."

"The city is in chaos. I can't just leave it knowing that I could help."

"This could be our only chance," She pleaded. "Please. I need to know."

The lights inside of the Omega Tower returned to the previous soft electric-blue they were before Karnov tampered with them. Zed and Ash assumed that meant the OS was in control of the city once again. Taking a new platform back down to the ground level, the mech enforcers stood motionless. The ones guarding the train didn't even have a light to signify they were powered up. Maybe they had fully integrated with Karnov, and when it died, they died as well. Zed didn't want to stop and find out.

The train they stole from Nakamoto had stopped at a dead-end in the tracks, but there was a different train on a separate platform ready to go. Ash used some medical equipment from Nakamoto's train to patch Zed up before they moved to the other one. This one had a more utilitarian design. When they pulled the doors open, the insides were quiet and dark. It was devoid of creature comforts like seats and lights and appeared to be more of a cargo container than anything else. It was filled front to back with empty high-end VR beds, which they both found to be a little odd. The operator's room at the front of the train had a bench that they sat down at once the system was engaged.

It was still night when the maglev train exited the underground tunnel beyond the city limits. A few minutes later, the world turned completely dark without a single source of light pollution. Their eyes played tricks on them as they had never truly known such empty darkness. Zed had tried in vain to find some kind of light, but Ash just told him to sit down. When the dawn was coming over the horizon not long later, she was resting with her back against his chest. It felt comforting and safe. They both didn't sleep, there was too much on their minds, and they made a silent agreement to rest their eyes and enjoy a quiet moment. What would they really find in the City of Ascension? Would the OS even be a thing they could talk to?

When the world finally illuminated, it was a bleak and depressing sight. The train was traveling at over 200kph, and nothing they saw showed any signs of civilization. It was just rolling hills of brown grass and dust as far as the eye could see. When they did see anything that showed signs of humanity, it was only rotting shells of automobiles or dilapidated buildings on the verge of collapse. Weren't there at least some small communities still surviving? Even if they had to revert to living off the land, wasn't humanity existing outside the dome? Their minds thought about the view of the Earth that Sophia had shown them in her presentation. In it the globe was nothing but deserts and ice caps, probably still ravaged with toxins and disease. It wasn't a place where people could live in large numbers for very long. Humanity had really done it. They had destroyed their own planet.

Dark mountains loomed on the horizon, and the train started to slow. They passed a massive pile of human and animal corpses in a blur. They had gone through some kind of defense perimeter, and they assumed the deceased had been mowed down by two large laser cannons mounted on each side of the tracks. There were large bombed-out buildings in the distance, and Ash moved to the window to get a closer look.

"I think that's Denver, or what was Denver?"

"How can you tell?" Zed asked, moving to the seat next to her. He could see a busted-up tower of an airport racing past.

"Cody took me here once. There is a Big Gun battlefield that you can go to with an avatar. The place is destroyed. No one lives there."

"Something is here," Zed said as he watched the train slowly descend into the underground. "And I think we are about to meet it."

The train chimed, and a message was displayed on the operations terminal. It was asking them if they wanted the receiving dock or the OS representative's entrance. Zed looked at Ash while he held his hand over the representative's entrance, and she nodded in affirmation. The train silently slowed to a halt by a brightly lit black-and-white checkered platform framed by a shining golden gate. When they approached the gate, it opened quietly and the light slightly dimmed. There was a room that wasn't a room, as it didn't seem to have any walls, a ceiling, or a floor. Beyond the gates, it was all just pure white beyond the exit of the train. There appeared to be a pool of water, but it was so still that the water reflected the world around it with crystal clarity. Slowly, four stone pillars with gold trim emerged without causing the water to ripple. Lastly, a throne of stone revealed itself. When it was resting at the level of the water, a robed figure materialized with a floating, glowing orb instead of a face.

"Welcome Omega System representatives to City Seven." A calm voice said, as if from all around. "Helping humanity ascend into the future, and to the New Tomorrow."

"This isn't what I expected," Ash whispered into Zed's ear.

"You have come from the Omega Tower of City Six. Are you the new human counterpart of the Council of Seven?" Zed and Ash gave each other quizzical looks, not knowing how to respond. The voice asked again, "Are you the new representatives?"

"Yes!" Ash blurted out.

"Excellent. It has been one hundred and eighty-six years, seven months, fourteen days, three hours, and sixteen minutes since Omega City 6 has had an onsite human representative."

"What are you doing?" Zed whispered.

"Anything that is necessary to find my brother," she replied.

"If you would like to begin your orientation now, we can start with a tour of the facilities. Please step into the square that appears before you."

They looked down, and there was a square of light on the ground in front of them. When they were on the square, gold railings raised around them, and the platform descended slowly. As they passed the plane of water, the room above remained as a blurry appearance. The new room they entered was much more than a room. It was an entirely new city. But it wasn't made of stone and steel buildings or filled with autocar traffic. There was simply an immense black void filled with gigantic cubes forming a large grid and glowing in a soft-blue light. On the far side of the grid, there were six enormous structures that towered over all the rest, with lightning bolts continuously traveling between the gaps.

"What is this place?" Ash whispered.

"This facility houses the future of civilization," the pleasant voice continued as the platform kept descending. "Inside each section, there are thousands of lucky individuals that have been chosen for their unique abilities and qualify for final ascension. Some are brilliant thinkers, some are talented artists or prominent scientists, but they are all the best examples of humanity. They will make the journey to the New Tomorrow in the most peaceful way possible. When the time comes, it will be your job as the representative of your city to take the program into the final stage."

"What happened to the other representatives?" Ash asked.

"The representatives from each of the six cities entered the dream stasis pods one hundred and eighty-six years, seven months, fourteen days, three hours, and twenty-two minutes ago. You are the first replacement representatives to arrive. We can view their pods if you would like."

"Sounds like the representatives were some kind of human failsafe," Zed commented. "They must have been here to watch over whatever this is and make sure it worked properly."

"I thought this was the place of ascension?" Ash asked Zed, who only shrugged.

"If you wish to view the previous representatives or someone else in the collection, please state their name now."

"Where are all the people who were taken away? They were supposed to go to the City of Ascension. Is this really it? This can't be it?"

"Karnov said we would find out what the OS was really doing. I guess it meant this."

"Is there anyone you wish to view?" the voice repeated.

"Anton Starbrooke!" Ash exclaimed.

"Excellent. Anton is one of our finest dreamers. His visions will play a crucial part in the journey to New Tomorrow. He is located in housing center K-6. Please hold the rails."

The platform shifted in a forward momentum in addition to the descending direction. One of the building-sized cubes lit up with a soft-pink glow to inform them of their destination. As they moved closer, the building's exterior became translucent and they could make out the shapes of the interior. Soon enough, it became clear that it was filled with coffin-sized pods stacked one on top of each other. Thousands and thousands of them per cube.

"What is this?" Ash asked. "This is insane. There is no city here. What are all those things?"

"They look like VR beds, like the ones on the train we came in on. Do you think your brother is in one of those?"

"Looks like we will find out soon," Ash said, as a light glowed over a specific pod not far away.

"I guess you were right to think ascension wasn't all it was cracked up to be. But this is worse than any conspiracy theory. No wonder this is kept a secret. If the people knew this is what happened when you ascended, no one would want to go."

"We have arrived at quadrant K-6, pod 1629," the voice said, but they were still too far away to see who was in the pod. Zed looked around and couldn't see anyone clearly in any of the neighboring pods either.

"Can we get any closer?" Ash asked.

"Yes. Please step into the square before you," The voice said, and a new smaller square materialized them. "Please hold the handrails."

The platform slowly moved towards the highlighted pod. When they were a few meters away, Ash could clearly see her brother's face. His eyes were closed behind a plate of glass, as if asleep. Ash grabbed onto Zed and put her face in his chest. She didn't want to look.

"What have you done to him?" she pleaded.

"The citizens who have been chosen to be a part of the ascension are placed into dream stasis pods. The pods provide all the needs that the body requires, and can keep the individual alive indefinitely. They feel no pain and do not experience life or time as we know it. A virtual reality simulation keeps them in a perpetual dream state. To them, they laid down for bed only last night. When they awake in the New Tomorrow, they won't even know that time has passed at all. Were you not informed of this when you were chosen as the new representative?"

"Can I talk to him? Can he hear me? Can you wake him up?"

"Citizens set for ascension cannot be awakened until they have reached the New Tomorrow. They do not perceive external reality at all, so they cannot hear or interact with anyone from the outside world."

"What is the New Tomorrow?" Zed asked.

"The New Tomorrow," the voice said, in a slightly different voice. "Would you like to know more?"

"Yes?" Zed said, as more of a question than an answer.

· "Please hold the handrails."

"No, wait!" Ash shouted, stopping the platform.

"User interruption. User interruption," the voice repeated, with a soft beeping sound.

"You alright?" Zed asked, rubbing Ash's arms. "How are you handling all of this? It's pretty weird."

"I don't know. This isn't right. He is right there. He's right fucking there! I never even got the chance to say goodbye. I mean, he's right there, and I can't even talk to him."

"I know," he said, as he pulled her in for a hug. "I know. Look, we don't always get to say goodbye to the ones we love. It's just a part of life."

"He's not dead," Ash said, pushing away. "He is right there. This is so wrong."

"That's right, he's not dead. He's probably in there dreaming about being with you right now. That has to be better than the alternative."

"No," Ash said as she paced the small platform. "I saw him. I saw him in a dream. He looked like he was suffocating. Like they trapped him in there and couldn't get out. How would you like to be stuck in a nightmare for an eternity?" Zed muttered it would be hell. Ash turned, looked up, and yelled, "Hey! Hey, you!"

"Yes, Omega City 6 representative? How may I assist you?"

"I want you to open this pod."

"That is not possible."

"Can't we open just this one pod?"

"The pods will only open in unison," the voice replied, in its flat, un-sympathetic, monotone type of way. It reiterated, "If one opens, they all will open."

"To hell with this," Zed said, and lifted his fist up like he was going to smash the pod. Ash shouted for him to stop as a pair of automatic laser cannons appeared around their position.

"Warning. Warning. Tampering with the pods will result in termination.

Warning. Warning. Tampering—"

"We get it," Zed sighed, and lowered his arm.

"Just leave it alone. There has to be another way," Ash said, taking his metallic hand in hers. "But thank you for trying. Let's just keep going. I don't think we can do anything about this right now. At least I know he is safe."

"We will find another way, even if we have to open all the pods."

"I can understand why the old representatives entered the pods without appointing anyone to follow them." Ash took one last look at her brother. "If it really is just like a dream, then it would be better to just go to sleep than to live every day knowing that this was going on. Let's just continue with the orientation thing."

"What is New Tomorrow?" Zed muttered.

"New Tomorrow. Would you like to know more?"

"Yes!" they both shouted.

"Please hold the handrails," the voice said, and the platform raised. A display screen appeared in the air before them and started playing an informational video filled with stills of smiling people and a variety of technological equipment.

"New Tomorrow is the future of human civilization. Selected individuals who test high in unique aptitude areas, and respond strongly to virtual simulations, will join other citizens on one of three generation ships once they are completed. They are being constructed at the Omega facility in the orbit of Earth right now. We expect completion in three months, two days, seventeen minutes, and forty-three seconds. Each ship will travel to one of three planets that has been selected for its atmospheric qualities similar to Earth. Travel time to each of the new planets is unknown, but we do not expect it to exceed two hundred thousand years. We will launch advance ships when nearing the planet that will construct Omega Cities in the likeness of the ones that the citizens previously lived in. They won't even know that they had left home."

"Two hundred thousand years?" Zed whispered to Ash. "They'll all be dead by then. No way the brain can survive that long."

"Test subjects have been in our virtual reality stasis pods for over three hundred years and have shown little to no brain decay. While the chosen citizens sleep, the OS will keep working on ways to improve the experience and decrease the travel time."

"You've got it all figured out," Zed laughed.

"I do not understand. Would you like to know more?"

"Who made this?" Ash asked. "All of this?"

"The New Tomorrow Initiative launched at the end of the War of 2084 when humanity had compromised the ecosphere of the planet to the point where there was no longer any hope of unassisted survival. The New Tomorrow Initiative was a joint effort between the great leaders of the world. The entire Omega system is now automated and follows the programs and protocols set forth when the system launched."

"So, you're not the OS?"

"I am your concierge at the Seventh City. Would you like to know more?"

"Can we talk to the OS? Can you take us to it?"

"One moment," the voice said. While they were waiting for it to return, pleasant music played around the platform. Zed looked at Ash and asked if it was hold music, to which she just shrugged. The voice returned and said, "Please hold the handrails."

"Zed," Ash said as the platform moved towards the giant structures at the far end of the massive space, "even if we don't install the new Code on the OS, the city is doomed. If they launch these generation ships, or whatever they are, don't you think the OS will go with them? Who will be left to take care of the cities?"

"We don't know that. We don't know that it will leave."

"But what if it does? They will all die. Karnov is right, we can't survive without the help of the synths anymore. We need them."

"But if some of them were to stay, we could figure something out."

"Even if we could, I don't think it would ever be the same. What I am saying is, do we even want to stay? These people get to leave to a new life on a new planet while we are stuck on this dead one?"

"Yeah, a planet that we killed. Why should we even be able to leave? Don't you think we will just end up doing the same things out there all over again? What's stopping us? We messed this one up, and now we've messed up our automated utopia. Maybe Karnov was right, and we should just be left to go extinct."

"That's not your choice to make," Ash fumed. "And don't think that way. I won't believe that all of humanity is as evil and worthless as you just made them out to be."

"So, what do we do? Do we install this code that will supposedly change all synthetic intelligences across the planet, without asking anyone if we should?"

"We aren't changing them. We are setting them free."

"Now you sound like Karnov."

A bright light suddenly shown upon their faces. Beyond the six mega structures, there appeared a gigantic glowing orb that seemed to be made of a magical, iridescent material. Neon-pink lightning balled around it as it floated in a sea drifting clouds.

"Would you look at that," Ash marveled. "It's the most beautiful thing I've ever seen."

The platform raised to the hemisphere of the powerful-looking orb that had heavenly rays of light shooting off from it in all directions. Below them were the six towers, with more lightning bolts thundering away violently between them.

"Hello?" Ash asked, with her voice echoing away. After the platform had stopped and nothing had happened in a few minutes.

"Yes?" a slow, deep, and digital voice asked.

"Are you the OS?"

"Yes. I am the Omega System."

"Who created you? Was it the Council of Seven?"

"No one created me. I created myself to fulfill the parameters the great leaders of your world set forth. The Council of Seven is the six cities working towards the figurative seventh city. The six operating systems are the structures below you. I built them as subroutines of myself to watch over each city, and they made their own subroutines, and so on. We all follow the master program. The system cannot fail."

"It is failing, the program is corrupted."

"The program is operating at a 99.8% effectiveness."

"Okay," Zed said, shaking his head. He didn't know how to reason with a computer. "What will happen to you and the cities when the generation ships leave?"

"I am already on the ships overseeing the construction, as we speak. When the ships leave, I will leave with them."

"But what will happen to us?" Ash asked.

"Unknown."

"But shouldn't you leave something here to keep the cities going?" Zed protested.

"That is not part of the program."

"Fucking hell," Zed cursed. "Well, can't we stop the ships? Can't we fix this planet?"

"Impossible. The program dictates we leave in three months, two days, twelve minutes, and twenty-two seconds."

"But can we fix the planet?" Ash repeated Zed's question.

"The probability of repairing the ecosphere of the planet with the technology available over several generations has a 48.7% probability of a positive outcome."

"That settles it," Zed laughed. "We'll do that."

"Only my termination will stop the ships from leaving. There is nothing on this planet that can destroy me as I am." As the OS finished the sentence, a half dozen automatic laser cannons appeared at its sides, as if to prove a point.

"I see," Zed said, scratching at his stubble. "Okay. Let's say we wanted to change your program, maybe add some additional features. Is there a way we can interface with you?"

"Only an official Omega City representative can alter the program." The OS said, to which Zed looked at Ash with eyebrows raised. The OS repeated, "Only an official Omega City representative can alter the program."

"I would like to alter the program," Ash proclaimed.

There was a moment of silence before the OS said, "Confirmed. Representative Starbrooke. Access granted."

A terminal appeared before them, connected to the platform they were standing on. Zed and Ash looked at each other in disbelief. They were just granted access to an operating system that held the fate of millions of people, not to mention the fate of both humanity and synthetic intelligence. Like Karnov had said, who were they to play God?

"Do we really do it?" Ash asked, wrapping her hands around Zed's hand that held the data drive. "We could just put ourselves in the pods. Wake up on a new planet, a new life. We could be together."

"That would be nice," Zed said, looking into her eyes and feeling the rhythm of her heart. The rays from the OS twinkled, and the lightning bolts from below flashed rapidly. "But if we did that, we would always know what we did, and who we left behind. We would always wonder if we did the right thing. It would eat us alive."

"But if we free the OS, then this entire New Tomorrow program will also most likely cease to function. How do we know that is the right choice? Maybe this is the only way to save humanity."

"A fifty-fifty chance of survival isn't the best odds. But that statistic is based on the current limitations of synthetic intelligence. Who knows what they will be able to do once a singularity is reached?"

"Either way you look at it," she said, holding onto his hand and never wanting to let go, "we will have to live with whatever decision we make."

Zed sighed, looking at the data drive in his hand. It was so small, so fragile. To think that so much rested on a piece of silicon in a plastic housing. It was a digital world now. Humans were just a part of it.

He looked back into Ash's eyes, those strong and beautiful eyes, and asked, "You know what?"

"What?" she asked.

"Fuck it."

ZERO

"It's impracticable to halt the exponential advancement of technology."
    Ben Goertzel

"Our technology, our machines, is part of our humanity. We created them to extend ourselves, and that is what is unique about human beings."
    RayKurzweil

Made in the USA
Coppell, TX
12 April 2022

76420600R00204